The Gilded Lord

Myths of Cadere Series
Book Two

Briar Grey

Dedicated to the memory of Kathleen H.

Original cover image by www.canva.com

Copyright © 2020 Briar Grey
All rights reserved. This book or any portion thereof may not be reproduced or used in any manner whatsoever without the express written permission of the author except for the use of brief quotations in a book review.

All characters are a work of fiction, and any similarity to any person living or dead is purely coincidental.

Please note: book contains strong language and potentially disturbing scenes.

The Gilded Lord

One

Ghosts lingered in the soft half-light, adrift upon a shimmering breeze; screams pierced the darkness and the spirits broke away, as the sorrowful howls thrust up through the shadows and twisted slowly into pitiful sobs.

Twilight was fading outside, its gentle grey gloom reaching across to unveil the stars that lingered above a broken temple; shadows crept through stained glass windows and brushed against threadbare tapestries in a room swathed in the perfume of death. Bones were scattered across its dusty wooden floorboards, their disjointed shards clinging to shreds of bloodied cloth and droplets of flesh, and a hearth upon the eastern wall cradled the fragments of a skull, weakened flames cradling the grimy remnants. A putrid undertone hung upon the air so heavy with the stench of decay that it seemed to choke the strands of light attempting to penetrate its squalid shroud. Small dark pools squatted upon the floor with tattered blankets and pillows strewn amongst them, the corners of fabric drinking up the rancid fluid.

A bed had been dragged towards the hearth, its feeble occupant a man whose face had long since turned away from the pitiful sights before him. A shabby robe was draped across his skeletal frame, his skin taut and smeared with oil and blood alike, and a silver chain around his neck pressed its small crystal against his throat; his torso was laced with welts and burns, and a barely healed scar ran from his clavicle to his ribs. Breath rattled in his lungs, whispering its primitive farewell, and as his body obediently rose and fell it shifted some of the greasy film that had settled upon him, clinging to him with a venomous bite.

The door to the room lurched open and a burst of golden light sent the shadows skittering away to far corners; the man recoiled at the intrusion, tightening his closed eyes and whimpering, unable to flee.

"Bryn?"

The word was soft, familiar, and full of pain; he tensed slightly, a quiet gasp breaking the sullen reticence.

A woman stepped over the threshold, her footsteps sending thin clouds of dust into the murky atmosphere; the torch in her hand pushed a warm halo across her face and dark cropped curls.

Her deep chestnut eyes studied the man before her, filling with tears. "Merfyd's bloody balls, why didn't the priests warn us he was this bad? Look at him, Aneira. Look at what they've done."

Another woman appeared in the doorway and shook her head sadly. "They cannot perform miracles Tarian, no matter what they would have us believe. We should have expected this."

"We should have *expected* them to find a cure, like they promised that they would. Just do the spell and let's go."

Aneira moved past her; the torchlight settled for a moment upon her freckled skin, catching in her flaxen hair and icy purple eyes; she spread out her hands, muttering a few words under her breath, and as sparks flew from her slender fingers a delicate frost gathered upon the man's wounds.

He winced, and whimpered again.

"It's done."

Tarian placed the torch into a nearby sconce and quickly gathered Bryn into her arms. "We need to get him out of here. Now."

Aneira left the light sputtering against the dirtied stone and followed her friend outside into the cold, dark corridor. Pallets lined the hallways, the rotting bodies upon them covered with thin soiled sheets, and gaunt mages still awash with feverish sweat clawed at the ancient stone walls, begging for the Lady of Death to finally turn her moonlit gaze towards them.

The High Priest waited in the shadows, concern etched upon his face; he waved to Aneira as she neared his hiding place. "Ah, Minister. I've been informed that you're taking Brynmor back to Mysta this evening."

She cleared her throat. "Is that a problem?"

"No, no, of course not! We are always happy to see our patients leave our care."

Tarian grunted. "That's not what I would call it."

"I regret that we cannot do more." Sorrow flickered across the man's features. "When the Gods saw fit to spare us, I truly thought that they meant it as a sign to take in those mages who had been affected by the blight. Oh I… I don't regret my decision; I just wish we had been able to save them, instead of becoming a house for the dying and the dead. I hope you do not judge us too harshly; the past few years have been quite a strain for us here at the temple."

"For *you?* Oh yes, how hard it must have been squatting here amongst your ancient relics with the Gods watching over you like favoured children. Nowhere in Sepelite has been spared this rotting blight! We walk through the countryside just to find it littered with the corpses of mages infected and putrefying, mothers dying in childbed whilst their little ones don't even draw breath, and those who were left behind succumbing to starvation."

He held up his hands. "I didn't mean to imply that –"

Her eyes blazed. "I was sent to the western coast last spring, did you know that? All of its towns and villages are nothing more than dust. What the famine didn't manage to destroy, the earthquakes did."

"Tarian." Aneira's voice was soft. "This is not the time." She turned to the High Priest. "We are eternally grateful for the care you have given Brynmor, and to all those afflicted by this pestilence, my lord."

He bowed his head and walked away, refusing to even glance back at them.

Tarian glared after him, and then shook her head. "Useless old fucker. I bet he never even tends to the sick, just sits in his antechambers with his hands down his –"

"Come on, this isn't going to do any good. Elgan and Saeth should be waiting for us by the cart."

The women walked through the maze of musty corridors, largely ignored by the other priests and their charges; their footsteps echoed through the shadows, but no more words were spoken between them.

The arched wooden doors were hanging open, a measly string of moonlight filtering in across the flagstones, and as they slipped through to carefully descend the fractured steps outside, the stench of Maeror's streets washed over them like a blackened tide. Aneira vomited.

"I'm pretty sure that's sacrilege."

"Somehow, I think the Gods have more important things to be concerned about." The mage wiped her mouth with the back of her hand as she looked out over what had once been a thriving city.

Most of the buildings had crumbled into dust following a cluster of violent tremors, although a few still stood against the reddened sky. The Temple of Brig stretched its marble walls up towards the starry heavens like old, cracked bones; its once grand entrance had deteriorated over time to resemble a gaping maw, occasionally opening up to fill with terrified, agonised screams. Fractured statues stood at either side, broken sentinels of an age passing into history, their sacred braziers forever doused.

The small town square, once famous for its marketplace of sprawling stalls and tents filled with exotic rarities, now sat a mere ruin of ghosts and stone. The nearby graveyard had swollen with the ranks of the dead, spilling out over its boundaries when mass burials had become necessary; eventually the priests had relented and cremation had become commonplace. Tales still slithered through the temple walls of ghoulish creatures that crept into the desecrated place to feast upon the remains of those who were not given to the flames.

Aneira sighed heavily as she took it all in. "It's getting harder to remember it as it once was. The large smithy with its song of metalwork, the taverns full of thirsty farmers and merchants, the travellers who lounged in front of the old inn."

"You're forgetting the brothel that used to stand next to the temple." Tarian grinned suddenly. "And yet you spent so much time there."

Aneira cleared her throat again. "Yes, well, I… ah… hmm."

"Minister?" A man stepped out of the shadows, orbs of soft yellow light bouncing around him. "How were things at the temple?"

"Ah, there you are Elgan. We should travel back to Mysta as soon as we can." She looked up at the scarlet miasma that had smothered the sky for over three years now. "This place is cursed."

"I am beginning to think that myself." He looked over at Tarian. "How is Bryn?"

"I'm a guard, not a physician. Where's Saeth? We need to leave."

"She thought it would be a good idea to make sure the way was clear, and will join us up ahead. Put Bryn on the cart and we'll get going."

Tarian lifted him gently onto a cushioned pile and covered him with a thick blanket; he flinched and turned away, fevered dreams coursing through his mind.

Thunder rolled over the horizon through a mist of bruised cloud, awaiting the next jagged spear of light; the celestial cradle crackled with spite as the air heaved and shuddered below.

Silhouetted figures advanced across the barren terrain, their movements slowed by gusts of wind that howled as they bit into exposed flesh and bone. A small caravan battling against the elements had little hope of success, but desperation clung to the men and women who pushed against the torment.

A creature stalked their wake, having already followed them for some time; it waited for weariness to set in, ignoring the shrieking gale and slashing rain, and thinking only of the hunger that clawed at its empty belly.

An old man started to lag behind the others, strength and hope both failing against the brutal onslaught.

The Saprus watched, its spiny teeth dripping with mossy saliva as its head twitched, sweat beading across the ridge of small horns that clipped in between its four wing-like eyes. It glanced around for signs of a rival predator, any natural reluctance to strike pushed back as its stomach gurgled; it wrinkled its elongated nose, the scent of meat too enticing to ignore.

The magic caught it off guard.

Bolts of ice threaded underneath its silvery skin, digging into its flesh; its body jerked as the spell sank deeper, taking hold of internal organs and freezing them slowly. Its gnarled hands clasped at its head as it fell to the ground, gasping for breath.

A woman stepped out from behind a quivering tree, a ball of flame hovering just above her palm. Her lilac eyes scanned the beast's terrified face, and a smile crept to her painted lips; fire engulfed the Saprus only a moment later.

The old man nodded at her gratefully and hobbled after his family. "Saeth?"

She looked up and grinned. "Aneira darling, you're too late, I've killed the bastard thing already." She picked up a bag and slung it across one shoulder. "How's Bryn? Did the priests actually manage to do anything useful this time?"

"It's not looking good."

"No surprise there. Maybe we can do something for him instead." She clapped her on the back. "After all, that infernal conviction of yours has to be good for something. Did anything follow you here? No? Now that's a shame, I *do* enjoy watching these fuckers burn."

They walked over to the cart and Saeth studied the dying man's face for a moment, her mirth vanishing. Tarian nodded at her and glanced away.

Saeth took hold of one of the handles and shook her head. "I still don't understand why we have to pull this bloody thing ourselves. What a sorry sight we must make, the Eminent Minister of Mysta and her friends dragging this old thing across the countryside instead of just using magic."

Aneira glared at her. "You know that could destabilise his condition even more."

"At this point I'm not sure it would make too much of a difference."

"You have seen to the deaths of many, most of them going too early to their graves. He doesn't need to join their ranks."

Saeth raised an eyebrow. "You want to have this conversation now?"

"No, not really." She sighed. "You know that I admire your ability to slaughter whoever is deemed necessary. I'm not sure what we would do without you."

"Don't slather me with kindness; I'm not one of your sycophants in need of constant praise. Killing is an art form, and I take great pride in my work. Those who have died by my hand did so in the knowledge that it was not an amateur who took their life. Tarian understands."

"Don't bring me into this."

Aneira clicked her tongue. "That's not… she was just a guard for the Conjury."

"Precisely! Think of all the nasty fuckers she cut down in the line of duty before those idiots succumbed to the blight and dispersed, leaving us to sink into hedonistic anarchy. At least, we *could* have done that, without your… timely intervention."

Elgan chuckled behind them, and Saeth blew him a kiss. Aneira scowled, turning back to the path before her.

Something slithered in the undergrowth nearby and then wriggled away, out of sight.

*

The journey back to Mysta was a quiet one; the small group kept mainly to shadowed paths, and nothing ventured to attack despite the hundreds of watchful eyes that tracked their movements through the gloom.

The city loomed out of the darkness like a curled fist, angry and broken; iron wrought gates swung open to allow the cart to pass through the hushed streets. Sentinels and guards bowed their heads at Aneira as she walked by.

Mysta's people busied themselves in some semblance of routine, quiet and sullen as though sorrow had embedded itself into the very roots of the place. Lanterns railed against the darkened hours, their small bursts of pale light a welcome relief along the winding walkways and crumbling balconies.

Ancora, once the palatial home to the Conjury, sat in silence. Tattered teal and gold banners adorned its outer walls, and its grand arched doorway was slightly ajar. The cart came to rest at the base of its stony steps, and Elgan cast a glance at Bryn before he walked away, disappearing swiftly down a darkened alleyway.

Tarian carefully took the feverish man back into her arms; he muttered as she moved, turning his head into her chest. She carried him gently into the place that had been his home for decades, heading up the sweeping staircase that clung to the westernmost wall, its marble banister cracked and covered in a thin layer of dust.

Aneira remained outside, her gaze locked upon the scarlet veil that hung across the sky like a bloodied shroud. She shivered.

A bell tolled from atop the nearby Temple of Merfyd, and a line of priests dressed in blue velvet ventured out to wander the streets, offering up blessings and prayers wherever necessary. Most of the mages who had survived the initial onslaught of the blight were weak, and their power had almost completely deteriorated; the rest had managed to find ways to adapt, seeking out new threads where the older ones had been severed or damaged. There were fewer sinking into the jaws of death now, but suspicion and paranoia were still rife in hidden corners where voices dripped with venom and accusations sprang forth with teeth bared. An ancient forest that prowled Mysta's borders was thought to hide the remains of evil deeds brought about by such poisoned words.

A woman with dark hair and bright purple eyes walked up to the Minister. "How did it go? Have they found a cure yet?"

"Your faith is a lesson to us all, Delia." She smiled kindly. "We brought him home, and you… you may want to say goodbye. I do not think he will see another dawn."

"Oh. I'm sure Tarian will want some company during… well, you know." She nodded sadly, and a yawn escaped her lips. "My apologies, Minister. I've barely been getting any sleep recently, and when I do I seem to dream of nothing but an ominous figure sailing towards us, only to crash against our shores in a ship made of blood and bone."

"We have all been granted the same vision. Does it worry you?"

"No, it's just… well… Sam keeps telling stories about King Dullahan of Luxnoctis, of his thirst for war and brutal cruelty, and he thinks the dreams are meant to be a warning."

"Sam should learn to curtail his wild imagination." Aneira smiled again, keeping the fear from her face. "We have not seen nor heard anything of the Monarch for hundreds of years, there is no reason for him to return now."

"Of course you're right." Delia blushed a little. "I'll go and find Tarian. My apologies, Minister."

Aneira watched her leave, feeling a pit of fear in her stomach; Mysta was only just beginning to recover following the magical cataclysm that had tried to tear Sepelite to pieces. If the Eternal Monarch was to launch an attack now, there would be little hope of defending themselves. She cast a quick glance around her before she climbed up the steps towards the shadows of Ancora.

An elderly man hovered near the entrance, his bony hands rubbing together as his faded amethyst eyes darted from Aneira to the cloaking gloom behind him; she smiled warmly at him.

"Your Eminence." His words whistled through his broken teeth. "I have information for you. No charge, no charge at all for the Daughter of Mysta. The murderous ones come on a wave of moonlit blue, to see with eyes unclouded and to touch with hands unsoiled. You're not dead and so the words can fly, because the spirits don't listen anymore, oh no."

"I… thank you, Alban, that was very informative. Have you been getting the dreams again too?"

"Yes, oh yes! The pictures tumble over and over until they merge into such webbed puddles! A menace from across the sea with so much knowledge, fear and hatred, and a tongue that whips scandal upon the icy breeze. How can we stop it, you ask? Oh no, Eminence, we cannot! There is no way to push back against the rising tide of the Monarch. They rush in, and out, in… and out, and all before them are lost and all behind them are drowned. So all that is left to decide is whether you wish to sink into a watery grave. Think not to stumble and stagger for footsteps all bloodied and rotten leave no prints to follow… there is death upon fingertips, and in the whispers of breath, and it peers out of sorrowful eyes like a hissing snake."

Aneira sighed heavily as she watched him scuttle away. Slumber was starting to pull at her mind, but there were still duties to attend to before she could allow herself to slip away into any kind of tortured dreamscape.

Softened cries came from a nearby room, and her heart sank.

Tarian sat in a shadowed corner with her head in her hands; her eyes were wet with tears and her breathing was coarse, and she bit down upon her lip until it bled. Torches flickered in iron sconces nearby, casting a gloomy trace over her dark, heavily scarred skin.

Delia knelt down in front of her and placed a hand gently upon her knee. She glanced over at Bryn's body, which was being tended to by a priest. Tarian clutched his silver pendant in her hand, its small crystal hanging down like a frozen tear.

"I'm sorry."

"If we had done something sooner we might… I could have…" Her words broke into sobs and she pushed the mage away. "It's over. It's all over."

The priests burned his body some time later, and scattered his ashes outside the boundary of the town.

*

Twilight was slowly creeping in like a ghost, hushed and pale and devoid of warmth.

Aneira stood on one of Ancora's balconies with her hands clasped behind her back, her face turned towards the grimy smear that ran across the celestial cradle; she had often wondered about it, this bloody portent of the blight that had ravaged her homeland.

Alban rattled around in the room behind her, muttering to himself about bloodshed and heartache, and how many could turn to the grave before shadows receded into light.

Her head throbbed and pain prickled behind her eyes; sleep had evaded her for most of the night, and she had seen instead the image of Bryn's ashen corpse dancing relentlessly through her mind.

She moved to lean against a marble post and gazed down at the streets below. Despair seemed to cling to the foundations of every building, and it worked its way up Mysta's spine with each new dawn even now. The Conjury had been the beating heart of this place, and after it had been ripped out the people had simply lost all hope. She curled her fists and snarled; she would see Mysta back to the shining beacon it had once been, and then all around it would have to heal too.

"Your Eminence? A boon from far flung shores has been given!"

"Leave the package on my desk and make sure that the courier is compensated before he leaves – out of my own purse, of course. He has travelled far to come to us in our time of need once again." She turned to look at Alban. "Offer him food and a warm bath too."

He bowed and set to his tasks.

The Minister fell back into melancholy thoughts. Minutes dripped by like poisoned honey until a clatter of hooves rang out in the distance; her trance broken, Aneira went back inside. She eyed the bundle sitting upon the carved wooden desk, hiding beneath its unassuming cream and gold cloth, and a smile finally crept back to her lips.

Tarian glanced up, her eyes swollen and red.

Elgan was leaning against the doorframe, sorrow sketched upon his features. "How are you feeling?"

She shrugged and looked away.

"Come now, you know that Bryn wouldn't have wanted you to wallow like this."

"His opinions and desires died alongside him." She got to her feet and walked over to the window, pressing her forehead against the cold glass. "We should have gone sooner; we might have been able to do something."

"Tarian…"

"Well those fucking priests weren't! Why haven't we been able to stop this fucking thing? How can we have all of this knowledge, all of this power, and still be so fucking helpless? What is the point of it all? Tell me!"

"I wish I had answers that could bring you comfort. At least he didn't die alone in that cold place; you brought him home, where he would have wished to be. Take some solace in that." He moved a little closer. "Are you going to write to Cadoc? I can do it for you, if you wish."

She sighed at the mention of her brother. "He and Garth would never forgive me if I let someone else tell them. I'll send a letter aboard the next ship bound for Caeli."

Silence fell between them like a thickened veil; Elgan traced his fingers along a thin scar that ran across the back of his hand, the metal of his rings cold against his olive skin. His lilac eyes glazed over as he vanished into old memories. Tarian watched him for a while, wondering if she should say something, but Saeth's footsteps rang out through the nearby hallway, and so she retreated back to the world beyond the pane.

Morning finally broke over the murky horizon, spilling its grim sallow light across the languid countryside. Silence draped around the Temple of Merfyd like a watchful lover as priests filed out down the steps; a few carried emaciated corpses, their taut skin covered in blisters and pustules, whilst others kept their heads bowed in silent prayer. Plumes of perfumed smoke arose from thuribles and censers, trying to mask the scent of rot and decay.

Aneira watched the parade without making a sound. Sorrow gripped her as she searched for familiar features within the gnarled faces of those heading for the pyre; her heart sank and she turned away.

A young man stood nearby, holding his hat in his hands; he bowed when she noticed him.

She forced a weak smile to her lips. "Is there something I can help you with?"

"Thank you Eminence, but I... I am just here for my sister. She was taken to the temple a few weeks ago, and they've asked me to attend this morning's ceremony. I thought there would be more people here."

Mysta still showed the scars of its recent skirmish with oblivion, and its survivors were often reluctant to brave its streets before the sun had climbed high.

She cast a glance around the largely empty alleyway and sighed. "Well I shall come with you, and we will both ask for the deliverance of your sister's soul to Lady Amara. What is your name?"

"It's Halwyn, Eminence. My sister was called Carys… she was only four years old. I… I don't know what to say to the Gods on her behalf." His voice cracked and he rubbed his eyes with the back of his hands. "I don't understand why they would take her like this. She never did anyone any harm but they struck her down anyway, just like they did to my mother last year."

They walked together for a time; Aneira's mind strayed back to the image of Bryn as he turned to ash, and she shuddered. The smell of burning flesh had clung to the southern border of Mysta for far too long; those who resided nearby had become accustomed to the stench, and seemed unaffected by the smoke that billowed almost constantly in an attempt to drown it out.

"Your Eminence!" Alban's voice cut through her thoughts. "Your Eminence, words of utmost urgency flow from my lips to your ears!" He cast a glance at Halwyn and wrinkled his nose.

Aneira gestured at him dismissively. "Wait for me in Ancora. I will return after I have attended the funeral."

"But…"

"I must pray for a young girl who has been taken to Amara's side to be with her mother."

Alban raised an eyebrow and turned away.

Halwyn smiled weakly at her. "Thank you, Eminence. I don't think that I could do this alone."

Flames devoured the pyres and snarled at the uncaring heavens. Aneira watched the bodies of mages being swallowed by the insatiable fire, and her prayers died upon her lips. It took all of her strength not to throw back her head and scream at the Gods; instead, she took Halwyn's hand into her own and squeezed it gently. He glanced at her, weariness etched upon his face.

"I hope that your sister finds peace in the sunlit lands and is welcomed into Amara's eternal embrace."

"May we both join her there one day."

"I must return to my duties and add the names of these people to the scrolls of the departed. Be well, Halwyn."

"And you, Eminence."

The walk back to Ancora was difficult; with each step Aneira wanted to howl and weep and bash her fists against her head. No matter how many stones were put back into place, nor how many books were picked out of the dust, no matter how many rituals were performed and prayers belted out in their glorious names, the Gods had forgotten Sepelite and left its people to wallow in the diseased mire.

Alban paced back and forth atop the stony steps; every few seconds he would stop and fidget with a bound scroll, the string fraying a little more with each touch. His eyes were slightly glazed, and his mind had dropped into the depths of some distant place. Aneira watched him for a while, intrigued by the occasional limp that seemed to reassert itself in his right leg every so often to give him a rather erratic gait.

He looked up when she finally approached, and only then did she see the perspiration upon his brow. His mouth was turned down in an ugly grimace, and he shook his head as he held out the scroll. She raised her eyebrows, but took it all the same.

"Not here, not here! There are too many eyes, always lurking out of cobwebbed corners and sinking back into unholy shadows. It is the way, always the way of things, darkness that swarms and bites and stings. Always the way, always the way."

"Something has you rattled. What's wrong?"

"Not here!" The words hissed through his teeth. "Inside, Daughter of Mysta, inside!"

Ethereal eyes followed their every move; hands unseen and unfelt reached out to grasp and came away empty. Crystallised tears fell into the pools of oblivion, rippling out across an eternity that was as hollow as it was dark.

Aneira shivered and glanced around; tranquillity usually seeped from the very walls of this place, but with Alban hovering at her side and this parchment in her hand she felt unnerved. Her heart throbbed against her ribs and pain prickled behind her eyes; she shook her head lightly and gritted her teeth.

Her study was warm, bathed in the golden ruby glow of early morning. Letters sprawled across her desk, some traitorous and others full of praise; a near empty ink pot squatted next to a worn quill and an empty chalice.

She sat down and sighed, looking at Alban. "Are you going to tell me what's going on?"

"The letter, read the letter! It's all there Eminence, everything you need to know and everything you did not wish to! Send help, send aid, send a chorus of demigods and demons to push back the unwilling tide!" He pulled at his hair. "Now is the time, Daughter of Mysta, to prove to the people that you are truly here to protect them! They look to you with eyes upturned and tears enough to fill the wretched sea. Do not see them fall into despair and mourning, until the only path before them is one of extinction! The void calls out to them, as it does to you, to us all, but you must be the shining lantern amidst the darkness! Show them the way and do not falter!"

She stared at him. "What are you talking about?"

"*Read the letter!* Eminence, it is as you feared it would be! We are to be invaded, struck down in our beds and cast aside like so much debris. For every man, woman and child that seeks your protection will come ten warriors to put them to the sword! Their blood will fill the alleyways and the ports, and their screams will sink every ship sent to bring them home! You cannot let us down, Daughter of Mysta! Read!"

She undid the string with shaking hands and let her eyes wander across the scrawled words. Her heart sank. "Bring Elgan to me."

Time crawled by in stunned silence.

Aneira reread the letter, its poisoned contents slithering into her mind and settling there with no hope of release. Tears welled in her eyes and she got to her feet, tapping the scroll against her palm.

Footsteps echoed in the hallway outside. She wiped her eyes and cleared her throat; Elgan entered the room moments later, Alban in close pursuit. The older man's gaze flickered between them and he shivered.

"Would you please tell me what's going on?" Elgan fixed Aneira with a look. "Why did he drag me from my studies with one of his rambling tirades?"

"Calm yourself old friend, it was at my bidding. I have received word from our scouts near the western coast; they have concerns that need to be investigated immediately. I cannot leave Mysta at the moment, so I need you to put together a group to follow up on it."

He frowned at her. "What the fuck are you talking about? I'm busy trying to figure out a way to stop this damned plague; I don't have time for whatever ridiculous nonsense this is."

"I'm sorry Elgan, but I need you to gather a team of warriors and mages alike and head out to Calyx before sunrise tomorrow."

"*Calyx?* That place was destroyed by a quake two years ago! You want me to travel for the better part of a month through Vulnere just to look at a ruin?"

"Take whatever supplies you need, but leave before sunrise. This is important, Elgan. Don't let me down. I will see you as soon as you return."

*

Banners waved in the whispering wind like silver snakes in the iridescent moonlight. The ocean curled around the hull of the large wooden ship, its bow breaking gently through the glittering water as it sailed eastward.

A figure stood upon the deck, hands clasped behind their back; atop their head a thin crown mirrored the stars that lingered in the glassy heavens above. There were others who moved around like pacing shadows, shards of fading hope fluttering in the darkness, and all were silent, as though a single word might shatter the illusion of calm that had draped itself around them. Crisp, clean air full of promise waited ahead, with clear and boundless skies.

The figure turned, glancing back for a moment, and then moved slowly away. The world seemed to shimmer around them, and the emptiness they left in their wake was overwhelming.

Tarian opened her eyes to the thick red miasma that clung to the celestial cradle. Pain throbbed through her head and sorrow crept back into her heart; this same vision had haunted her every night since leaving Ancora, and each time she awoke feeling a little more disheartened at the grotesque scenery around her.

"Are you all right darling?"

"Just another dream."

"Ha! Be glad you don't have to cope with the ones that we do. You were lucky to be born without magic – it's nothing but headaches and nightmares."

"You can shoot *fire* from your fingertips."

"And you can cleave a man in two with a sword. Magic is a tool my dear, nothing more and nothing less, no matter how much we pretend otherwise. I would just as soon sever a head as I would incinerate it." Saeth held out a wooden cup full of steaming liquid. "I keep telling you that this will help shake off the dreams. Don't you trust me?"

Tarian looked at the green concoction warily; the tea was bitter and slimy, and as it slid down her throat she wrinkled her nose in disgust, fighting back the urge to vomit.

Saeth laughed. "The benefits are worth the taste, I promise."

The scouting party had spent six days working their way towards the Vulnere forest, which stretched out across Sepelite's western coastline like a festering axe wound. It spidered out in long tendrils to both the north and south, hiding all manner of creatures in its lurking shadows. Once it had covered the belly of the countryside, but towns and cities had arisen over the centuries and the woodland had been pushed back, devoured by farmland.

A few curious beasts had prowled around during the second night and then the third, growling and snarling, but nothing had attacked. Even so, fires had burned throughout the darkened hours to keep them at bay.

Elgan finally returned to the makeshift camp they had thrown up amongst the shadows of the abandoned settlement Antur. The moon was high in its cradle, shining smoky light down onto the festering ruins that stuck out of the ground like shards of bone.

Saeth grinned at him. "Isn't this place supposed to be haunted? Did you find any spooky ghouls during your walk, my love?"

He rolled his eyes as he kissed her gently. "You should be sleeping. We have a long day of travel ahead."

"Tell me something I don't know." She shivered and gazed out into the darkness. "Did you hear that?"

"Have you managed to scare yourself with stories again? There's nothing there, and even if there was it wouldn't be anything more than some hungry beast weighing up its chances. Ask some of the warriors to go and take a look if you're concerned, or throw out a quick fireball and scare it away."

"No…" She sat up straight. "It's more than that. It's the same feeling I had the other night, like something is watching us that shouldn't be. An evil presence hiding just out of sight. Oh don't look at me like that darling, there's someone out there, I'm sure of it."

He shook his head. "Maybe you should cut back on the tea."

She got to her feet and kicked him gently. "Fine, if you're so convinced that it's safe then I'll go and have a look myself."

Tarian watched the woman leave and then raised her eyebrows at Elgan. "Was that wise?"

"It's probably just another Saprus, she can handle anything that –"

The wind whistled suddenly through the darkness, bringing with it the corroded scent of death; an abrupt heaviness settled upon the air as though the stars pressed down upon the small band with grim intent. Energy bristled around the campfire, frenzied and furious, pulling at the flames until they winked out.

Saeth came flying back, her eyes wide. "Wake them all! Rouse yourselves! I can't face it alone! Get up before we're all dead! Go!"

Tarian's hand went to her sword; she got slowly to her feet and backed away, each careful breath burning in her lungs. Her mind crowded with a strange fear, something she had not felt on the cusp of battle for many years, and her heart hammered against her chest. She glanced around at the whirl of magic as she moved until she stumbled against a lump of mossy stone and her thoughts snapped back to Saeth.

A bolt of lightning raced past her, narrowly missing her ear; it arced out into the gloom and pierced the ground a few feet ahead. Flames exploded out of the earth and scattered clods of dirt, spiralling up and out as they sought flesh to boil and bone to burn; the air crackled with sorcery as huge stakes of ice burst in the sky and rained down in jagged splinters.

Tarian tried to steady herself as nausea gripped her stomach and sweat beaded her brow; she turned then, and saw Delia only a few paces away, holding out her shaking hand. She moved towards her.

Elgan screamed with effort; blood stained his neck as it dribbled from his ears and nose alike; his lilac eyes shone as another barrage cascaded from his fingertips. His spells were being met with fierce resistance: a lone figure in the shadows had thrown up an arcane barrier that deflected all attempts to penetrate it. Saeth was by his side, swearing loudly with every movement she made; they were lighting up the darkness and blasting out elemental force as though it was effortless, but in truth his body felt like it was aflame.

Lethargy pulled at his mind; he gritted his teeth and pushed it away. He could not fall, not now; sleep would have to come, and soon, but not just yet. A growl arose in his throat and a thunderbolt flew from his hands, shattering against a lump of nearby rock.

"It's no use!" Saeth's words were barely audible over the cacophony. "We need to flee!"

The figure was advancing; their energy speared through all of the wards the mages had set up to protect the warriors, who were now in formation and ready to engage. They would be annihilated within minutes.

"Go! I'll cover you!"

"I'll not leave you to face that alone!"

"Saeth, just go! Rally the others and run!"

"But…"

He ignored her pleading looks and sent out another coil of magic; it fizzled out before it hit the ground. His stomach knotted and long buried dreams resurfaced in his thoughts. For a moment he envisioned his own body, broken and lifeless, being torn apart by carrion birds as starving rodents gnawed upon his bones. He raised his arms and flames shot through the gloom, rippling out in every direction, weaker than before. He shuddered with the effort, and his mind roared. He turned on his heel, and fled.

Tarian looked at Delia as they moved; her face tingled and her legs shook beneath her as she ran. A jagged rock caught hold of her shin and sliced through the fabric of her clothes to carve a deep ruby trail across her flesh. Sweat trickled down her back and her lungs burned; her mouth went dry, and her head throbbed with pain. She staggered, her vision blurring, and slumped to the ground.

"Tarian!" Delia skidded to a halt and dropped down at her side. "Can you hear me? Tarian! Fuck… you're bleeding. Why are you bleeding?"

"Get her to her feet!" Saeth bolted past. "This is no time to rest! Move, move, move!"

"Leave me and get yourself to safety." Her whispered words floated between them for a moment.

"No, come on! Only one creature can command that kind of energy and you do not want to meet him on the battlefield alone!"

A hand gripped Delia's arm and pulled her to her feet; she stared at Elgan as he tore her away.

Minutes fell into one another as the group dispersed across the countryside, men and women disappearing into the horizon and losing themselves in the darkness that resided within.

Saeth fell to the floor, exhausted. Blood oozed from her nostrils as she gasped for breath. Sleep overwhelmed her, and plunged her into frenzied dreams.

Elgan and Delia collapsed beside her moments later, their magic spent.

Red faced and furious, the woman glared at her friend. "How could you?"

"If he had caught us we would all be dead – or worse. I'm sorry we had to leave her behind, but it was the only way."

They sat in silence for a while, until Elgan slid into slumber.

Angry tears rolled down Delia's face, mingling with sweat and dirt; she wiped it away with the back of her hand, and looked up at the ruddy heavens. "Don't take her yet, I beg you! She is good, and kind, and she doesn't deserve to die like this!"

"Worry not, little mage." A man stood a few feet away with Tarian's body in his arms.

Delia watched him for a moment, relief and confusion flooding her veins, and she burst into tears.

He placed the guard gently down at the mage's side, and smiled warmly. "She'll be all right, don't you worry. Amara doesn't seem to want her yet, but I think she'll need some rest and a bit of patching up." He traced an old scar that ran across his bald head as he looked out into the distance. "I'd better get going, there are things that I need to do. You'll make sure she gets back safe and sound?"

"Of course. Thank you!"

The sun broke over the horizon, spilling light out across the jagged landscape.

*

Saeth awoke from her fitful sleep with a gasp, the nightmares retreating to hide in dusty corners; Elgan still slumbered nearby, groaning softly and turning away.

She sighed and rubbed her face. "Aneira's going to have my bloody hide."

"And why is that?"

"You had better be sitting beside me alive and awake Tarian, or I'm hearing your groggy voice from beyond the grave and I always swore that I would not inherit that ability." She dropped her hands and turned around. "Well fuck me, I'm not insane. Not yet, anyway."

"One of the warriors brought her back." Delia handed her some freshly brewed tea. "He must have been behind us. I've tried to heal her as best I can, but she's exhausted."

"Where did you even find the ingredients for this? Never mind, I don't actually want to know. We'll take her home and treat her, don't worry. Perhaps our valiant swordsman could carry her back there?"

"He left almost immediately, and anyway I'm not sure you can call him a swordsman." Delia took hold of a strip of cloth and dabbed Tarian's forehead. "He had a greataxe on his back."

"I think you must be misremembering, my dear. There were no axes in Ancora to equip anyone with."

"No, I'm sure that I saw it as he walked away." She frowned. "But I suppose I was tired, and there was so much going on... maybe you're right."

"Don't worry about it darling. Drink some of that tea yourself, and make sure our lucky friend here has some too. Oh... she's gone back to sleep. Well then, more of the shitty tasting beverage for us!"

The air was warm and thick as the sun clambered higher into the sky, its rays pushing through the scarlet cloud and leaking down to kiss the earth below.

"So the Eternal Monarch has finally touched Sepelite's shores." Delia's words hung like bloodied serpents poised to strike. "I never thought that I would see the day."

"If that truly was Dullahan then it seems my dear grandmother's tales need to be altered. She always swore he had refused to take the field for centuries, and there was certainly nothing in her stories about him stalking mages without revealing his mortal form. This is… disconcerting." Saeth shuddered and looked away. "We should return to Ancora before we do anything else."

Banners waved in the wind, dark blue and silver shining in the scorched moonlight. A red mist skirted across the ground like a wisp of ghostly breath stretching out through the earth.

Spiders crawled in the shadowed undergrowth, their webs trailing across the boughs of the hushed woodland in a glittering crescendo of threaded ether; a castle loomed upon the horizon, its stonework half hidden behind a veil of cloud. Music drifted upon the air, soft and gentle and macabre.

Tarian stood, alone and unafraid, near the edge of the trees. Her arms were outstretched and her head was tilted back, a cold breeze wrapping itself around her bare skin. Someone watched her from afar – she could feel their ghoulish presence inching closer as the seconds ticked by, their skeletal hands reaching out to take hold of her.

A whisper snaked upon the wind: her name, in bashful tones, as though it was both a promise and a curse entwined.

Tarian awoke, her eyelids fluttering against the intrusive sunlight.

Delia sat beside her, cup in hand. "Ah good, you're awake again. We need to set off soon, and Saeth wants you to have something to eat and drink before we do. I had my bag with me when we fled, and

I've managed to save you a few strips of dried meat, and some nuts and berries, and this tea is fresh. Well, almost."

"Brig's breath, not that stuff again. Don't we have anything else?" She lifted a hand to her brow. "My head is trying to kill me, I swear."

"The herbs will help you to relax a little, and maybe even divert your dreams down a different path." Delia held up a hand. "I'm not prying, but you called out in your sleep… several times."

Tarian downed the tea and nibbled at the meat, her eyes darting around at the people who had managed to gather here. The warriors were all gone and only a few mages remained, vulnerable and fragile. There was little point in carrying on towards Calyx without the protection of steel and sword, and even the journey back to Mysta would take them over several leagues of barren grassland bordered by treacherous boulders and shrubbery that could hide all manner of small beasts.

A loud, powerful screech shook the heavens, shattering Tarian's thoughts; she paused, her body suddenly numb. A shadow passed over her as the sound came again, and her heart began to hammer against her ribs. A single feather the size of her forearm dropped to the ground, sleek and garnet red.

"Sceleratis!" Elgan's voice shot through the air. "Everybody scatter!"

A winged beast circled above them, its yellow flecked eyes following their movements as it let out yet another fierce cry. Its raptorial feet, amber in hue and adorned with bloodied talons, reached out to grab its intended prey, as it serpentine tail whipped through the air.

"By the Gods, how did that thing sneak up on us?" Tarian looked at Delia and frowned.

"It's so… beautiful…"

The Sceleratis dived towards them, narrowly missing one of the mages; it shrieked in frustration and began its ascent.

"It's a creature of Dullahan, it must be!" Elgan shook his head. "We can't fight that thing alone! We need to get out here! Tarian, Saeth, one of you take hold of Delia and *run!*"

The entranced sorceress held her hands out towards the sky; she wanted to see it again, needed to bask in its glory, but Saeth was at her side, pushing her away. Tears filled her lilac eyes and she whimpered. "No… just let me…"

"I can't move her! Tarian, help me!" Saeth sent a ball of flame spiralling up towards the beast as it passed overhead; the spell missed and dispersed into the ether.

The Sceleratis turned its head towards her.

"Shit shit shit!" She let go of Delia and ran.

Talons scraped along the ground as the creature sailed past, a gust of air in its wake knocking Tarian to the floor. Elgan fired a thunderbolt that brushed against the tip of its tail, but it ignored the obvious distraction and landed near its quarry. It screeched, and Saeth fell to her knees.

"Shit shit shit! Fuck off!" She turned and flung out a dagger of ice that caught it across its feathered face.

It bore down on her, arcing its large back and spreading out its wings, hunger in its eyes; it opened its beak once more and the shrill call echoed out across the arid landscape.

The woman stared in fear, unable to move as it advanced, reaching down to snap her body in two.

A sword cut across its leg, biting into the skin and sparse flesh beneath. The Sceleratis balked, turning to see Tarian, defiant and snarling, stab at it once more. She spat at the beast and made to flee, blood still dripping from her blade.

Elgan raced back to Saeth's side and dragged her to her feet, pulling her away.

Delia was already running towards a distant group of rocks, fear upon every ragged breath. She slid behind one of the nearest boulders, her lungs aflame. Her legs screamed in pain and her vision swam before her in a blaze of white and blue. She leaned against the stone, its cool surface solid against her sweaty flesh; dizziness washed over her, turning quickly into drowsiness. She rubbed her face and rolled her shoulders in an attempt to stave away slumber; a cluster of trees lined the eastern side of the grassland, a simple barrier that led to the farms beyond, and she needed to reach it as soon as she could.

The Sceleratis shrieked again, but it was quieter, more distant this time. She peeked out from her shelter and sighed. It had travelled some way now, still in pursuit of Tarian. Her stomach knotted; she could go after them, cast a few spells to catch the beast's attention, but she knew there wasn't any chance she could reach them before her friend had perished. She would simply be running to her own death.

Turning away, she got back to her feet and fled.

Scraps of flesh and bone littered the ground; blood pooled before sinking into the ravaged earth. The smoky air crackled with magic, remnants hissing and spidering towards the bleeding celestial crown.

Banners struck out through the haze, their bright colours dampened by the unnatural mist that clung to the air. Silhouetted figures stood amidst the carnage, their eyes fixed upon the crumpled figure at their feet.

"What would you us do with her, Your Grace?"

"She still draws breath. Bring her to me."

*

Shadows spread out, long and comforting.

The air was stagnant but filled with life, insects humming and fluttering to and fro in the dense undergrowth; vines curled around thick trunks and boughs, small explosions of colour scattered across their threads as they blossomed; rodents scampered in the darkness, birds nested overhead, and spiders hung in large, delicate webs that stretched between branches.

Saeth lounged against a mossy rock, her eyes closed against the quiet gloom that clung ceaselessly to the atmosphere. Her knees were scraped and bruised, there was a fracture in her foot and two more in her ribs, but she was alive. Curative magic was already working at repairing her injuries.

An earthy scent brushed against her skin and sank into her dark curls with their streaks of silver; she took a deep breath and a weak smile traced across her lips. Memories of her home lifted into her mind: Carus, far to the north, drenched in woodland thick and mystical and full of men and beast alike.

"I see that something has amused you even here."

"Darling." She opened one eye to look at Elgan. "There's no need for a lecture. I was lost in thoughts of ancient places whilst my healing was underway, that's all."

He paced up and down, hands clasped behind his back. His leather armour was scuffed and dirty, his brow furrowed in concentration; he glanced at her again but said nothing more. His mind curled around thoughts of Dullahan and Luxnoctis, and how Sepelite would surely suffer under the Monarch's hand.

"It's all just myths and fireside tales my dear, nothing more. No one here has ever actually seen the bastard other than in foggy visions and dreams. The books that tell of his exploits are so decrepit they should have crumbled into dust long ago and been left to rot in the ashes of some hearth."

"You seemed pretty convinced when you were running for your life."

She shrugged and looked away. "We need to go back to Ancora and report all of this to Aneira. She wanted the position of Eminent fucking Minister, she should be the one dealing with this, not us. I'm getting too old for this my love, can we not just leave for Caeli when we are done?"

"I thought better of you than that. Brig's balls, how do these things survive out here?" Elgan swatted at an insect that danced in front of his face.

"They're carnivorous."

"*What?*"

"They feed on our flesh whilst we sleep. Some of the others, those small pink ones, gorge themselves on our blood."

Elgan paled and turned away; Saeth chuckled and closed her eye. The buzzing around her grew louder, interrupting her attempts to drift back into dreams of sweet smelling flowers and golden sunshine.

Sighing, she looked down at her foot. "I think I should be all right to move again in a few minutes. Is there any sign of Delia or the others? I'm not certain we can wait much longer."

"No... it seems unlikely that anyone else would have managed to get away. You know what Sceleratis are like." Elgan shuddered. "We will have to be careful, and try to avoid any settlements if we can. If Dullahan is making his way across Sepelite he will likely target what is left of the populated areas first."

"Perhaps you could have pointed this out before we fled without any of our supplies."

"It's been a while since we had to rough it like this, but we've done it before and we can do it again." He held out his hand and helped her up. "Aneira's not going to be happy."

"Well then maybe next time she can wander across the blasted countryside into the nest of a giant monster, and we'll stay in Mysta tending to the mundane needs of its small populous."

The wind whistled around them, teasing at her greying hair. She frowned and uncurled her fist; a small flame danced upon her palm for a moment before winking out.

"Come then. Ancora awaits."

*

Delia sat down upon the floor, a tired grin on her face.

The man across from her rolled his eyes. "There's no need to look so smug."

"Sure there is! We travel all that way with you spouting tales about the terrifying Eternal Monarch and how you would gladly walk up to him without fear, and then you run away screaming with shit in your smallclothes! I don't think you can keep calling yourself Sam the Fearless now."

He grunted and looked away. "It's not funny. He would have slaughtered us all; he still might! The sooner we get home the better. We'll be protected within Mysta's walls."

"I hope the others manage to make it back safely." Delia's heart was heavy with worry. "I should have gone after Tarian."

"Oh sure, run after a bloody Sceleratis with nothing but a few weak spells. That definitely would have gone in your favour."

She rubbed her face. "I'll brew us some tea. Are you hungry?"

Sam put a finger to his lips, a slight frown crossing his brow. Delia followed his gaze to a small bedraggled creature approaching them at speed.

"By the Gods, what is that thing?"

"We should leave. Now."

It staggered into the makeshift camp a few minutes later. Its head and legs throbbed with pain, and a trickle of viscous fluid seeped down its left arm. The strips of its greasy hair, long and unbound, were tangled with clumps of dirt and blue flesh. The two beasts who had abandoned this place were watching; it could feel their eyes boring into its skull.

"Back, back… no way back." The words were little more than a rasping growl. "They call me Sprig, I don't know why. Find my… own way. Take the trinkets and leave me and lead me to uncovered graves. Blood, bone, and meaty flesh, all cracked and consumed and yet still to rise again."

It plunged its gnarled fingers into the embers of the fire they had left, searching the remnants for a scorching kiss, something to dull the pain. Emptiness rose up to conquer its hollow heart, and it screamed.

Vengeance glittered in its pale eyes.

Delia cast a glance at Sam, her eyebrows raised; worry racked his face, but he said nothing. An ill wind wrapped around them, pushing out across the barren landscape; a small winged feline sat atop a nearby rock, watching them with its amber eyes.

"Quicken your pace. I've never wanted to die out here in the wilderness. At least the beds in Ancora are warm and soft."

The Jittern tilted its head and yawned at Delia; she raised an eyebrow and turned away.

Two

The sun rose slowly, treacherously, through the humid miasma; speckled light pushed back the swarm of shadows that had snagged upon the arid ground during the night. Jagged rocks pointed up towards the smothered heavens, accusatory and ancient; there was little life left in this part of the world, although a few spiders scaled the craggy faces and small slugs pitted their silver trails alongside the beaten webs.

A figure moved through the sunken silhouette, bare feet brushing against dry and brittle shrubs as small clouds of dust spiralled in their wake. There was no music here, no ancient melody borne upon a chill whisper of wind; the land did not pulsate with a magical hum. It was quiet and eerily beautiful, and still so close to death.

Hands outstretched, head leaning back and eyes closed, the figure took a deep breath; pallid light washed across a serene face, tracing the lines and scars that had sunk into the warm, olive skin. A pale blue glow surged from upturned palms, slowly cascading down towards the parched earth, and a weak smile flickered across tight lips.

A cold breeze whispered suddenly across the landscape, brushing past dormancy as it resonated with the slightest hint of a choral echo; the heavy vapour that had blinded the skies shifted for a moment, and small holes began to tear in the scarlet shroud. Archaic ghosts rose from unmarked graves to gaze at the scene, and from their beaten thrones the Gods looked down with passing interest. Vitality sparked.

Footsteps broke through the trembling quiet, and the serenity vanished.

"Your Grace? The woman is awake and is asking to see you."

"I will be along shortly. Make sure that she is offered food and something to drink, and see that her injuries are tended to."

"Of course, Majesty."

Tarian's head throbbed, and she scowled at the man who dabbed her face with a damp cloth. The Sceleratis had left a gash across her temple and wounds in both of her arms. Most of her armour was in tatters, now useless and discarded to one side; her linen underclothes and mail chausses were splattered with blood from a deep cut to her stomach. Poultices covered each wound, and she had been given a sweetened herbal wine to dull the pain.

"You're a lucky one." The man started to wrap a clean bandage around her head. "To fight such a beast and only come away with these small tokens? That's near a miracle, I'd say. The name's Rafael, by the way, although you'll not hear people refer to me as such very often. '*Oi you*' seems to suffice most of the time."

"You're a healer?"

"Hmm. *Physician* if you don't mind, seeing as how I don't have any magic in my veins. Hold still now, if I bind this too tightly it'll cause more damage than good."

"I suppose I won't be any use to your damned Monarch if I'm in too much pain. What does he want with me?"

Rafael raised his bushy eyebrows. "Who?"

"The King, of course. Who else would I be talking about?"

"I think you'll be needing a conversation with one of the commanders about that. It's my place to get you patched up, nothing more."

Fear struck at her then, and she glanced away; she had heard tales of Dullahan's violence, how he was a ruthless tyrant who indulged in perverse pleasures and had no compassion left in his antiquated heart.

"Did someone mention me?" Another man strode towards them, carrying a small tray of bread, fruit and ale. He was tall, slender, and clean shaven, which served to show an old scar running across his jawline. Streaks of grey had started to creep into his short black hair. Gold rings glittered upon his long, dark fingers, and his icy purple eyes settled upon her face as he placed the food down.

"The lady here wishes to know what the King wants with her."

"I see." He nodded slowly. "May I ask your name, madam?"

"Tarian."

"And you wish to see the King?" He tapped his chin thoughtfully and sighed. "I suppose we should have anticipated this. The essence of this place is so drained that it's no wonder… hmm. Tell me Tarian, are your mages well?"

"Why?" She glared at him. "Are you concerned that they won't be able to play a part in your pathetic war?"

"My concern comes from the fact that I have seen little to suggest Sepelite is sustaining its magic. Our own mages suffered greatly, so I imagine yours fared no better."

"Why did you attack us with a Sceleratis and bring me here? Is it because you think we're so weakened by the plague that we can't put up a fight? You're wrong; we will not go meekly across the sea to play your twisted little games!"

Rafael stood up and dusted his hands on his trousers; he looked at the mage and shrugged. "Should I fetch the boss?"

"No, I'll go. You stay with our guest and ensure she doesn't murder anyone before I get back." He bowed at Tarian and took his leave.

A cool breeze snaked through the scene, dancing lightly across Tarian's arms and neck; she shivered and looked up at the physician. "I will slaughter you all if you try to take me anywhere against my will."

"You're in no state to go anywhere, lass. Calm yourself, the danger that you imagine is not anywhere nearby. Have something to eat."

"I'll not touch that poison."

"Suit yourself." Rafael tore off a chunk of bread. "No doubt the boss wanted you fed and watered, but I'm not going to force it down your throat. You want this? No? More for me then, it's not often we get to eat roasted monster flesh." He laughed when she recoiled, splattering himself with gobs of meat. "Didn't realise you were so high and mighty as to not take advantage of an opportunity when it presents itself. Imagine the faces of your friends if you told them you ate the Sceleratis that tried to devour you."

"What do you know of my friends?"

He rolled his eyes and wiped his greasy mouth with his sleeve. "I assume you have some, although Gods know why if you're like this all of the time. Do you accuse them of trying to poison you too? Is that why you were trying to fight that fucker by yourself? No one waiting in the wings to help out because you chased them all away with your accusations?"

"What is this, first level torture?" She got to her feet and shook her head. "I hadn't realised that Luxnoctis subjected its captives to inane bumbling idiots to try and break them."

"Really Rafael, that food was meant for Tarian." The mage had quietly returned, and was now standing with his hands on his hips. "As it is you'll need to come with me; you've been granted an audience. You might want to wear this." He held out a gambeson.

"And what happens to me if I refuse?"

The man sighed loudly and pinched the bridge of his nose. "I don't have time for this. Just follow me."

The camp seemed fairly large, if a little disorganised; tents had been haphazardly pitched, and men and women were gathered around fire pits to eat, drink, and tell stories. Masked banners stood off to the sides, piles of weapons and armour at their bases. This was not a group who expected to attack, or be attacked, any time soon.

Near the western edge was a round pavilion, its patterned canvas drawn back to show lanterns glowing within. Two guards had been posted outside, and they stood to attention when Tarian's guide drew near. He turned to her and gestured towards the tent; she eyed him warily, and entered. He followed.

The air was warm, tinged with the scent of lavender; a wooden chest sat off to one side near a pile of blankets and cushions. Tarian looked at it all in turn, confused.

"I hear you've been asking to speak to me."

The voice behind her made her jump; her heart began to throb against her ribs, and sweat beaded her forehead. She turned slowly.

A woman stood before her, bathed in the early morning sunlight; her expression was serious, but not altogether unkind. Her bright blue eyes were ringed by deep lines, and there were scars running down her neck; a crown of flowers crafted from white gold sat amongst her greying hair; a braided leather bracelet clung to her left wrist.

Tarian stared at her. "I asked to see the King. I will not be toyed with, do you hear me? I am not a piece to be used in his twisted game!"

"I am glad to hear it." A smile crossed the woman's lips. "Although it would seem that we have much to discuss, Tarian of Sepelite. I admire your courage and enthusiasm, and admit I am a little intrigued by the fact you seem disappointed in me." She watched her carefully before continuing. "You have no desire to face Erebus, and yet you desperately wish to know your fate."

"I don't know who the fuck that is and I don't care; just tell me where Dullahan is."

"I imagine your relief will be great when you hear that he is dead."

A snarl of laughter crept from Tarian's lips. "Do you honestly expect me to believe that an immortal king is dead? You must think me truly naive."

"I do not."

"I've had enough of this. He has me saved from that monster only to be dragged to this cesspit of a camp, where I'm meant to listen to these ridiculous lies?" Her eyes darted to the mage who now stood beside the strange woman. "Who *are* you?"

"My name is Bowen." He splayed his hands and bowed his head. "I am the former leader of the Ferus unit of Caedes Aurum, an elite group that was in the service of King Dullahan, known to some as Erebus. And before you stands Queen Mylah, Empress of Land, Sea, and Sky, Eternal Monarch of Cadere, and Mistress of all Magics."

"No, that's impossible. Dullahan is…" Her words trailed away.

"Slain."

The air around Tarian grew heavy, seeming almost to hum. Her eyelids fluttered and she staggered; darkness washed over her, and she fell.

Mylah caught her in a swift movement, and looked down at the woman's face. "Take her someplace soft and quiet Bowen, and stay with her. Answer any questions she has without hesitation, she must learn to trust us. We need to know what the fuck is going on."

"Yes ma'am."

Moonlight poured down onto the shadowed balcony, washing over the marble with its eerie luminescence. Stars glinted high above, specks of silvery dirt amongst the darkening cosmic cerement.

Vines crept around pillars to both the left and the right, nightly blooms showering the scene with a mild musk. A golden glow poured out from the open doors, gateways leading back into a world of vibrant music and dancing, of scandalous pairings and sacred bindings meant to stop ancient wars. A shadow slid out across the floor.

She turned her head slightly as the intruder approached. Ternate footsteps echoed down through the ages and she winced.

"You dropped this." *The deep tones of his voice sent a shiver down her spine.* "I thought you would like it returned."

She didn't move, but looked back out across the landscape, at its rolling hills and distant mountains, all shrouded in darkness. Torches and beacons twinkled here and there, marking out villages and settlements.

He was beside her now, and in an outstretched hand held a necklace made of ribbon and jet. Blood dripped between his feathered fingers.

"The ambassador is waiting somewhat impatiently for your appearance."

He withdrew for a moment, sighing quietly, as she ignored the proffered jewellery. "We always knew this day would come, Amica. Please don't be angry with me, I could never give you away like this with an unburdened heart."

"But you will give me away." *Her words were soft, and sad.* "You will."

The music swelled behind them and there was a chorus of chattering voices and applause.

"They will not wait for much longer."

"Let them wait forever." *She squared her shoulders and, with one quick motion, leapt over the balcony. The wind rose up to catch her, playing with her hair and pulling at her skirts as she sailed down towards the darkness.*

Tarian awoke lying upon a pile of blankets and pillows inside a dimly lit tent. Incense filled the air, the heady smoke twisting through the gloom like a grey snake.

"Take it easy. How are you feeling?"

"Like someone hit me with a club." Her head throbbed as she struggled to sit up. "You're still here then? I thought I might have dreamt all of this."

"I am indeed no wisp of imagination – at least not that I know of." Bowen's smile did nothing to put her at ease. "Are you hungry? Thirsty?"

"You don't truly expect me to believe that Dullahan is dead and that woman…" Her words trailed off.

Bowen cocked his head to one side, before following her gaze to a banner that stood just inside the tent; upon its fabric of dark blue and silver was the sigil of a crescent moon pierced by an ornate dagger.

"I've seen that before."

"How curious; I will have to mention that to Her Grace. I didn't think anyone in Sepelite would know of her crest."

"I saw it in a nightmare; several of them, in fact."

"So you dream as though you were a mage, but you are not."

She shot him a look. "What do you know of who I am?"

"Your eyes do not carry the mark of the arcane, and your scars suggest a pattern similar to that of… of some old friends of mine." He waved his hand dismissively. "But enough of that for now. Her Grace instructed me to answer any questions that you might have."

"Who are you?"

"I told you, my name is Bowen and –"

"But if what you said before is true then an immortal king is dead."

"Yes."

"Perhaps you're not familiar with the word *immortal* in Luxnoctis. Does it have a different meaning over there? Immortals don't die just because some woman slits their throat and puts a crown in her hair."

"The Eternal Monarchs have a… complicated lifespan." Bowen sighed. "From what I am told, once they have taken on the role they should only ever be vulnerable to their successor. Dullahan held on for a long time, too long as it turns out. His death was necessary to strengthen magic, but without another Monarch in his place it could have rotted away completely. By finding ways to avoid his own death, he tainted the world around him, and magic started to suffer; without Mylah, it would have eventually killed us all."

"Is that what caused the cataclysm?"

"Cataclysm…? Oh, the Sundering. Yes."

"So it affected all of Cadere." Tarian rubbed her chin and then caught Bowen's bewildered look. "What?"

"You have no idea how many times I've had to repeat *Cay-dah* to people back home in an attempt to get them to say it correctly. Her Grace could have snapped her fingers and given everyone the knowledge, but she refused to do so. Apparently they had suffered enough change and deserved to absorb that information at their own pace. I doubt she would have thought that if she had been the one to try and instruct them all."

"You would love it in certain areas of Caeli then; they've been known to pronounce it in all manner of ways. May I have some of that wine? So Dullahan *was* immortal but also not – under the correct circumstances – and when he died he caused some kind of explosive magical reaction?"

"Not exactly; his continued existence was the problem, not his demise. Would you like some pastries, or fruit perhaps? We have meat and elven style biscuits too, if you wish to try some."

Tarian downed the goblet of honeyed wine and took a plate of sweetmeats and berries.

Bowen lapsed into silence whilst she ate, his chin resting upon his steepled fingers. She watched him for a few moments, wondering at the faraway look that had glazed over his pale lilac eyes; there was pain in him, buried deep and locked away. She could sense it as though it was a starving wolf pacing back and forth, waiting for a moment to strike.

"Bowen." Rafael's voice snapped them both from their thoughts.

"Yes, what is it?"

"The boss wants to see you, says it's urgent. Good to see you looking better, lass."

"I can't leave Tarian alone."

"Well I'd offer to stay but she'll likely accuse me of trying to murder her. I see *your* offer of food wasn't tainted by some murky motive."

"Maybe she could smell your breath and assumed the worst." Bowen looked back to Tarian. "Would you like to accompany me? You may stay here with Rafael if you prefer."

"Oh may she now? I've got better things to do than sit around looking after someone who thinks I'm out to kill them in a cowardly manner. I'm a physician, I know more efficient ways to push someone into Amara's ample bosom than bloody poison." He turned on his heel to leave.

Bowen rolled his eyes. "I guess you had better come with me, then."

"Who's Amara?"

"Oh she's… she's the Goddess of Death. Do you not –"

She laughed and shook her head. "Only fucking with you. We have temples here too. Come on then, let's go see this queen of yours."

A heavy mist hung over the landscape like a static sigh; a miasma of half dead magic had infused with rotting phantoms who were snagged in pockets of foul, festering spells, and whilst it clung to the atmosphere of Sepelite it would slowly drain the life from everything it could.

Mylah stood with her eyes closed and her hands outstretched; she inhaled deeply, slowly, taking in the scent of the withering vale and reaching out with her mind to search for the decaying threads that curled around each other in the bowels of the earth.

A pale blue glow emanated from her hands once again, building upon her palms until it overflowed and trickled between her fingers towards the arid expanse.

She could hear the cries of the dead spiralling out from their uneasy resting place, caught and caged and without hope. Power swelled within her as her thoughts turned to them; a cool breeze rose up from the magic in her grasp and exploded out across the dusty terrain, sending clouds of ashen dirt skywards.

All around her the voices grew louder, more desperate; she parted her lips and whispered archaic words long thought lost. Thunder growled in the empty heavens and the world around her shook; the queen never moved.

The cages opened and their captives were finally free; souls burst out of their ethereal cells and spun up into the atmosphere, climbing higher and higher until they sank into Amara's shadowy embrace.

Mylah lowered her arms and opened her eyes; the heavens no longer bled, and life spurted up from the ground – grass, flowers, insects.

She sighed and inclined her head slightly. "You approach me very quietly these days, old friend."

"Forgive me Your Grace, I did not want to interrupt again. Rafael said you wished to talk with me."

"I think perhaps we had better let our guest speak first, Bowen." She turned to face them.

"How…" Tarian stared at the blossoming scenery in awe. "How could you possibly do this?"

Mylah frowned at Bowen. "I told you to answer her questions."

"I did."

"This is impossible." Tarian looked up at the clearing sky. "This is *impossible*. It's been so long since… that mist…"

"The healing will only travel so far before it begins to deteriorate; I must continue journeying across the rest of Sepelite, and then move on to Caeli."

"Brig's breath, is that why you're here? We thought you were an invasion force sent to drag us back to Luxnoctis, or else to conquer and plunder. This changes everything! If we head back to Mysta and speak to the Minister I'm sure she'll understand. How are you able to do this? I've never seen magic do anything like it. Can you cure the blight too? You can't be… I mean, the King isn't able to… but if you're not then… oh fuck me. You were telling the truth, weren't you?"

Mylah started to head back towards the camp, the skirt of her indigo gown sweeping across the rejuvenating ground as she moved; she walked in silence, her gaze trained somewhere upon the horizon. Tarian and Bowen trailed behind her, giving the guard time to watch her homeland heal; the air around them had lightened, no longer carrying the staining tinge of decay, and the firmament was now unbound and glorious, with no hint of the rusted smear that had smothered the stars.

The sun would rise once more over the bones of Sepelite, and see it born anew.

Bowen didn't say a word; he had seen Mylah give breath back to a suffocating world, but the deaths of his friends and peers still hung heavily around his neck. He would often see their faces in his dreams and awaken thinking he could hear their laughter.

"Did she do this to Luxnoctis?"

"Yes." He withdrew from his melancholy thoughts. "It took some time. The damage was… great. That place is divided in more ways than one; its four realms are each drenched in magic, and for years had been governed by different bodies. Dullahan had them slaughtered, suggesting that they were his corrupted rivals when in truth they were nothing but pieces in his game. I shudder when I think what would have happened if he had retained his throne."

"So…" Tarian glanced at Mylah. "If she's here, who is looking after it all?"

Bowen smiled ruefully. "Berne is currently in charge of keeping everything on track I believe, when he manages not to wander off elsewhere and interfere in trivial matters. He's… an old friend, and now an adviser to the queen. It was believed safe for us to make this journey once people had taken positions of power in all of the regions, under a treaty of peace. Waging war would be an idiotic thing to do – the land *is* recovering from the suffering caused by its former sovereign, but slowly. There are precious few resources to be wasted on further conflict, and this peace was long awaited in Luxnoctis, so I doubt anyone is foolish enough to disturb it. That aside, I have faith in those who have taken it upon themselves to oversee the restoration efforts; there is a gentler, less fearful attitude amongst the populous now. Duke Roth even recently remarried."

"I have no idea who that is, or why it's significant."

"Apologies." Bowen smiled. "I forgot that you're so new."

A soft breeze wrapped itself around Tarian's legs and then slid away; she inhaled deeply and closed her eyes. "Surely you will have to traverse all of our territory, north and south, east and west, to see her work done? If the spell only travels so far…"

"We sent scouts ahead with Locus crystals. They resonate and amplify certain magic, and when placed correctly allow the spell to ripple out in their direction."

"You already had people here?" Tarian looked at him and shook her head. "What else don't we know about you? Do you breathe fire?"

"Not to my knowledge."

"Does she mean to leave soon?"

"Her Grace has had some troubling dreams of late, and wishes to continue on towards Caeli once Sepelite has been healed. We will pack up our camp and head to a new spot as soon as we return."

"You will not come with me to Mysta? The people there would love to hear of Dullahan's downfall, and if they could see how this woman means to give them back their world…"

"Are these not things that you could tell them? If those in power do not believe you, then surely your friends will? Hope travels faster and brighter than you might imagine."

Tarian hesitated for a few moments. "My friends and I were separated by the Sceleratis. I had thought to find them before heading home."

"Perhaps we shall travel together then, for a time."

*

Scattered light broke through the trees, settling upon territory ravaged and weary; magic murmured through the stillness, creeping through the desolate wastes and whispering tales of belated hope.

Life swelled within the bowels of the earth, and as death started to withdraw its long, skeletal hand, a new melody sprang from the beleaguered core. Ancient songs were finally put to rest, their chants faded, twisted, and timeworn; relief spilled out from celestial graves.

Thin trails of smoke rose from the embers of small campfires, with men and women sleeping nearby, lost in realms of light and dark alike.

Mylah stood in the shadows, watching those under her command as they slumbered; she cast her eyes towards the heavenly cradle and then turned away. The world around her seemed a hollow shell of what it had been before; she unclenched her fists and allowed the spell to tumble out into the ether. Magic spread out before her, rippling across the ground and sinking into the soil, drawing out the breath that clenched around the roots of trees and sending it spiralling into the sky.

Voices called to her from beyond the horizon; pleading, sorrowful cries intoned her name and cursed her absence. She sighed quietly, and tried to push them from her thoughts; there was still work to be done here. The sounds faded, lurking around the edges of her mind like a vengeful spectre.

She steadied herself against a gnarled trunk and rested her head against its peeling bark; the tremble of sorcery beat within, and though she longed for quiet it soon became a cacophony thrumming throughout the tree.

A spider crept past her face, trailing its way into some hidden crack away from prying eyes. Magic cascaded from Mylah's hands once more, spreading out across the vast swathes of land and swallowing it whole. Her head throbbed, and as dizziness washed over her mind she sank to the ground and closed her eyes.

Seconds dripped into minutes, hours; the queen remained curled up against the solid stretch of wood and allowed her thoughts to wander across bright continents and dark oceans as though she were a bird borne upon a westerly wind.

The sun had clambered high when she finally opened her eyes. Noise from the nearby camp echoed towards her and she frowned, turning her face back to the tree trunk for a moment. Her hands pushed through newly sprouted grass, and a gentle breeze brushed against her cheek.

After a few moments she sighed heavily. "What is it?"

"Your Grace." Bowen bowed low. "The scouting party has returned from Mysta, and we have also had word from Berne."

"Do I need to return to Luxnoctis already?"

"No ma'am, it was simply an enquiry as to how we are faring at present. He has managed to enlist the help of a mage or two to conduct work with portals, and was eager to show us his success."

She seemed to consider his words for a moment, and then gradually got to her feet. She dusted herself down, and looked at Bowen's outstretched hand with yet another sigh; she took the crown from him and planted it firmly upon her head. "Did you give him a reply?"

"The portal was not stable Your Grace, and it collapsed before I had a chance to answer. I did tell him not to use novices for that kind of spell, they tire far too easily."

Mylah rolled her shoulders and started back towards the camp without another word.

A tall, slender man was awaiting the Monarch's return. Dressed in dark leather armour, he held a scuffed helmet in one hand whilst the other was wrapped around the hilt of his dagger. Sunlight glinted in his mop of brunette hair, and his dark eyes darted to and fro. A large scar ran the length of his neck, biting up into his stubbled jawline and sliding away behind his left ear; day old bruises had formed beneath his right eye, and mottled his pallid cheekbone with soiled kisses.

He bowed low as Mylah approached. She gestured for him to follow her into the tent and then sent Bowen away with instructions to seek out Tarian.

She opened a large wooden chest, producing a carafe of wine and two goblets. The man licked his lips nervously; he took the drink she offered with a trembling hand.

"Did you find anything of interest?"

Sweat prickled his brow. "It… there is not much there, Your Grace. The terrain here is… is unknown to us and everything seems so… that is… it…"

"Go on."

"We could neither confirm nor deny what the woman said." He gulped the wine suddenly and set the goblet down, moving his hand back to the metal hilt of his weapon. "There were no signs of anything unusual… we heard a noise… er… a noise, ma'am and there was a creature. I took out my dagger, this one here, let me show you…" He drew it from its sheath and looked down at it. "My name is William Daymond and I… I seek retribution for the true King of Luxnoctis!" His hand thrust out in a swift movement, the blade a blur of light and steel.

The dagger did not pierce her skin, but instead snapped in two; he stared at it, mouth agape, before falling to his knees.

She cleared her throat, and flicked her wrist. A portal tore open beside them, ringed in blue flame; the air around it shimmered and crackled, and the man's eyes grew wide.

"Berne?"

"Your Grace?" A faint, and somewhat bemused, voice drifted from the other side.

"It seems you were correct." She took hold of Daymond's arm and pulled him up to the spell. "Take care of it for me. Oh, and stop fucking with Bowen, would you?"

"As you wish, boss."

Mylah hurled the whimpering man into the portal. A faint smell of burnt flesh lingered in the air for a few moments before the spell dissipated and the gateway vanished.

Tarian roared with laughter; she shook her head and slapped the man who sat beside her on the back.

He grinned and rubbed his nose. "It's all true, I swear!"

A group of scouts had recently returned from Mysta; they had not ventured into the city itself, but had silently wandered the perimeter and taken note of the funeral rites that were being conducted. The conversation had quickly moved to other topics; ale and anecdotes flowed with ease, and as such tales of war crept in, cracked here and there with bawdy jokes and outlandish embellishments.

"I thought we were all well and truly fucked that day." One of the women took a swig from her tankard. "There was no chance we were coming out of it alive. It didn't matter – we were there for our last stand, to show the bastard that he hadn't broken us. I knew some of those who were defending his keep, people I had been friends with for years, and I killed them all the same. He had declared us traitors fit only for execution, and they went along with it." She shook her head. "We followed her into battle, prepared to depart this life beside her. And then she only goes and kills the cunt. The bloody immortal, invulnerable, *invincible* king falls to her blade. She saved all our hides that day."

Others in the group murmured their agreement and raised their dripping tankards.

Tarian glanced around at them. "You respect her a great deal."

"Perhaps you didn't hear me." The woman grinned. "I was about to be nothing more than a memory caught upon the winter wind: Nelia Hale, famed scout and former blacksmith's apprentice, suddenly as insignificant as dust. My cousin was part of her squad when it was decimated out in the desert by Venandi – they're these hulking beasts that will rip a man to pieces in seconds – but she survived. The Gods obviously saw fit to save her, and I'm bloody glad that they did. There were some who grumbled, said she'd sacrificed her men in order to survive, but I never believed it. Without her we would all be dead… or worse."

"I'm afraid I must steal your guest away for a short time." Bowen's voice made them jump as he stepped into view. "Nelia, Her Grace would like your report on Mysta whenever you are ready."

The woman nodded; Tarian got to her feet, somewhat unsteadily, and saluted at her new friends. They raised their drinks once more and watched her stumble away, clinging to the mage's arm for support. The conversation quietened down and a cool wind blew in from the west.

Tarian's mind swirled for a few seconds, and she thought she could hear a voice calling softly upon the wind. The moment passed, and she looked at Bowen. "So what is it now? Am I to be interrogated and put to death for asking about your beloved queen?"

"Not unless you feel it's necessary." He grinned, and then cleared his throat. "No, I'm taking you to get some armour fitted. These lands are dangerous, and I would prefer it if you were as prepared as possible in case we run into anything."

She had almost forgotten the Sceleratis attack, and the reminder was an unwelcome one; the world was so quiet, calm and still, that it all seemed like a fading nightmare. High above, the sky reigned in pale blue tinged with wisps of ivory cloud; blossom had sprouted on nearby trees, and grass burst out of the ground like tiny emerald swords.

"The Conjury would have shit themselves at the amount of power she commands. And then they would have tried to worm their way into her favour in an attempt to obtain control."

"It wouldn't have been anything she hasn't encountered before." Bowen glanced away to intone a quiet spell, the air around him shivering momentarily.

Tarian took the opportunity to look around; latrine pits had been dug about half a mile away, and the smell drifted by them in faint waves. She wrinkled her nose.

A blacksmith had set up an anvil and a few tables nearby, and she worked tirelessly at her trade. A pavilion pitched to one side of the smithy emanated the stench of blood and burnt flesh.

"Come, the armourer is not far. He'll have you outfitted in no time."

They wound their way towards a small open tent; the ground was laden with trunks, chests, and small tools. A man watched their approach, his hands on his hips and a disgruntled look upon his aging face.

"Don't tell me." His voice cracked the air like a whip. "You brought me another mage who wants a chainmail coif so she can feel like a proper… wait, no, this one's eyes aren't purple. So what'll it be this time? Leather? Chainmail? Plate? Some unholy combination of all three? Because if it is, *you* can be the one to tell Manon. Last time she threw a hammer at my head for suggesting that, and I doubt I'd get away without my arse on the anvil if I tried again. Where did you get this gambeson? It looks like the lass can barely move, let alone fight. Amara's tits, this is going to take a while."

Tarian wandered away quietly some time later, leaving Bowen in the heat of an argument with the armourer. Her new gear fit well, and was of better quality than that she had been given back in Ancora. The blacksmith had even come over to give her a new sword, and a shield with Mylah's crest painted on the front.

She looked out towards the horizon. Red mist still loitered there, a bloody smear upon the sky to remind her of all that she had lost.

Bryn's face whirled through her thoughts and she gasped; for a moment she could hear his voice calling out to her, but his words were snagged upon some unseen boundary, full of pain and longing.

She could smell rot and decay as though festering bodies had been piled at her feet; her eyes stung and welled with tears. She stumbled blindly; the walls of the temple suddenly burst out of the ground and towered around her, the murmurs of a priest's chant echoing everywhere.

Fear flooded her veins and she couldn't breathe; her chest felt heavy and tight, and a snarling clamour roared through her skull. Her head swam and her vision blurred completely; she reached out but could feel nothing, not even the muggy breath of air. She was moving, but she knew not where she was headed; there were voices around her, screeching and shrieking, and the smell of a stagnant pond suddenly cut through that of the cadavers. She could hear chattering laughter, mocking and jeering as a pale hand reached out to grab hold of her shoulder and push her into a gaping pit; she screamed as she fell to her knees.

"Really now, I don't think that's necessary." Mylah's voice ripped her from the illusion.

The images fell to dust, and reality reasserted itself. She had staggered into the Queen's tent, and they were alone.

Tarian panted for a few moments, her lungs aflame and her nostrils filled with the scent of her own blood; as her sight cleared, she got to her feet.

The other woman stood with her back to her, stripped to the waist and bent over a bowl filled with hot water. A small towel was draped around her shoulders.

Tarian watched her, confused. "Couldn't you just do that with magic?" The words tumbled out before she could stop them.

Mylah cast a glance over her shoulder. "I spent a long time in forests and deserts, sweating beneath leather armour." She wrung her hair out into the bowl. "There were many things that I missed being able to do, and this was one of them."

Tarian wiped a trickle of scarlet from her nose and, in the moments of awkward silence that followed, wondered what to say. "Why is it that you call Dullahan by another name?"

"Dullahan was a monster, Erebus was just a man. I grew up in Amissa, where he was always known by both names, and he had them all slaughtered for it. I remember him as Erebus for them, for what they sacrificed in order to keep his secrets, and for myself, for all that he took from me."

"Oh." A few seconds ticked by. "Shouldn't there be guards posted outside?"

Mylah chuckled. "I haven't known someone this inquisitive in quite some time. There were, but one of them was clearly hungry and the other couldn't stop yawning, so I sent them both to take care of their immediate needs. There was little point in them standing out there just making noise. So... is there any particular reason you came here, or did you simply mean to question my bathing methods?"

The lilt of a newborn song drifted into a slight change.
Icy sparks infiltrated the breeze, its suddenly chilled breath sweeping over the countryside and rattling all within its grasp.

"I didn't mean to... that is I..." Tarian shivered and looked around the tent until something caught her eye. "What's that?"

Mylah followed her gaze to a jagged red stone sitting upon a nearby table; she was silent for a few moments before she shrugged back into the bodice of her dress and laced it tightly. She moved over to take the rock in her hand; a dark glow spread out across her palm. "It's a Solis crystal. They can draw an exorbitant amount of power from a mage in order to create a portal for mortals to cross without causing harm to anyone but the caster." She offered it to Tarian. "If you have magic in your veins, the stone will alight when you touch it."

Tarian took hold of the crystal, and it immediately dulled. "Magic was never my forte." She examined it closely. "How does it work?"

"It connects to another, called an Occasus. Bowen has been experimenting with them, but I wanted to see it again… just for a little while." Mylah sighed. "Would you mind taking that one back to him for me? Here," she bent down and rummaged in a large wooden chest, finally pulling out a black leather belt, "take this."

Tarian raised an eyebrow, but buckled it around her waist and slipped the Solis crystal into one of the small pouches that were tied to it.

A hint of whispered laughter clung to the air, twisting down towards unsuspecting minds and infiltrating unguarded thoughts.

Tarian's vision spun for a moment. She shook her head and looked up at the strange queen. "Your men admire you greatly."

"I earned their respect a long time ago."

The westerly wind rose again, spinning up clouds of ashen dust and dispersing them over the sweeping swathes of land. Ghosts wailed into the abyss there, as grasping hands clawed at the edges of the void and pulled at clods of bloodied dirt.

"No. It is more than simple respect. They see something in you that they cannot find elsewhere; you are their hero." Tarian watched her carefully. "You do not even care, do you?"

"Stay your tongue, girl." Mylah shot her a look. "You know not what fragile ground you walk upon."

Tarian snorted at the response; her head buzzed with a sudden shrill noise, as though hundreds of insects were trapped inside her skull. The skin around her eyes started to burn, and she could smell blood once more.

Mylah's gaze narrowed.

"You are their idol."

"Stop this."

"Don't you see?" Her voice was almost a hiss. "They *need* you to be more than you are! A mere queen will not suffice, nor empress, nor mistress. You know how they look upon you with eyes of adulation and hearts of empty joy."

"Enough."

"Listen to me!" Her mind raced with thoughts not her own; confusion descended like a fog and as her tongue lashed out with poisoned words, she could do nothing to stop it. "Listen to me!"

"Enough!"

"They reach for you through the darkness, but you ignore them! You turn your hollow head away from those who need you, who desire you, with the greatest strength imaginable! You, who are their leader, their great hero, their *Chosen One*."

"What did you say?" Mylah's words were like ice.

A second of silence followed, pierced then by cackling laughter. "You heard me, old woman! You… the *almighty Chosen One of the Gods*."

Mylah had advanced upon Tarian. Her eyes were cold, hard, and they bore down like those of a wrathful divine; her body had tensed, and there was a snarl upon her lips. "*Enough*. Be gone from my sight."

"Does the Chosen One not wish to –"

Mylah roared.

Her hand slammed into Tarian's throat and she lifted her up until her legs dangled above the ground; her eyes blazed an icy blue, and as she threw the woman clear across the tent, a magical shock wave exploded from within.

Tarian burst through the linen wall and over the ground outside; the buzzing in her head intensified to a shrieking cacophony. She could hear someone screaming, though it was distant and drowning within other sounds; her vision had turned completely white and blinded her to whatever was going on around her.

Her body smashed against something hard and came to a sudden stop, cracking one of her ribs in the process. The air rushed from her lungs, and vomit rose in her throat; her hands touched her face and came away wet.

Her lips were suddenly numb, and panic swirled in her veins; something brushed against the inside of her mouth. Her jaw dropped, and a cluster of red and white spiderlings burst out, scuttling over her teeth and tongue and chin. Maggots squirmed inside her ears; she could feel them writhing against her skin, hungry and callous, trying to find a way to penetrate down into her brain.

Clawed hands were upon her then, pulling at her skin and flesh and bone, tearing it all away and pushing in something else, something unholy and unbalanced; she arched her back and tried to call out but all of her words were lost, caught in a crystalline web that traced down her throat towards her burning stomach. She was to be lost, forsaken and abandoned to a darker realm where fiends of shadow would surely rip her to shreds.

"Tarian!"

The sound echoed like a thunderbolt.

"Tarian!"

It came again and again, until the darkness receded; scales slid from her eyes and a blinding light washed over her. She slumped against the ground.

Rafael slipped once or twice as he ran over to where the woman lay, pushed up against a splintered workbench. He took her unconscious body into his arms with a slight grunt; his grey eyes darted over the thick trails of blood and sweat that streaked down her cheeks. One of her wrists looked to be broken, and there was heavy bruising to one side of her face that was creeping down onto her neck.

Concern twisted his thin lips into a grimace as he slowly made his way back through the camp, ignoring the frenzied movements of the soldiers and scouts until he reached the medical tent. Once inside, he lay Tarian down upon an empty cot; two mages scurried over, their hands already aglow with magic.

"What's going on? What happened to her?"

"I think she got hit by the shock wave… ain't certain though."

"Where did it come from sir? Are we under attack?"

"Just bloody fix her, that's what you're here for. Damn mages always trying to stick their fingers in where they don't belong."

The sky clouded and an eerie murkiness descended; Rafael looked up as a low growl engulfed the campsite. He reached over and unknotted the ties that held open the canvas, shutting away the wounded from the angered world.

Stars glistened in the heavens, oddly arranged and closer than they had ever been before. A warm breeze carried a strange scent upon it, like the winter blooms of Rotroot, only sweeter.

The ground beneath her feet was shadowed, soft, and still; the gentle glow of night flowers permeated the surrounding gloom, small bursts of cerulean and amethyst amidst a swathe of velveteen black.

Chanting voices drifted in from someplace nearby; haunting female vocals filled her mind, lulling it into a newborn haze. She closed her eyes and tried to listen; the words were unknown to her, but their sorrow crept into her thoughts until tears fell freely down her face.

A whisper came to her then, wrapping around her morbid thoughts and caressing them gently before whirling away, as a gentle touch brushed against her cold hands.

"You come to us, Little One, but in a time before we sought you. Why are you here?"

"I don't know…" *The statement fell away, quiet and edged with sadness.* "I don't know."

"'Tis guidance she seeks." *Another voice crept in, harsher than the first.* "There is naught but shadow before her, and we have not the answers she desires. All that we have would tear her down. Send her away."

"Nay, she is our own. See how her spirit glistens; see the light she brings within her. We could take her now, allow her to rest. Peace is what she truly craves, for her life has been so wrapped in chaos."

"It cannot be, Little One. I had not thought to meet with you yet, your cascade is not for us. Go back, and look out unto the world you were given. There are burdens to be shared, and those to be carried alone. Seek not this place again. Go!"

Tarian jolted awake.

It was dark, and the air was warm; the faint scent of blood and burnt flesh hung over her, sinking down into her hair and skin. Her head throbbed and part of her neck was numb; Bryn's pendant clung to her chest like a venomous claw. She struggled to sit up as she adjusted to the gloom; two mages slumbered nearby, and it was quiet except for the occasional murmur of wind outside.

She slowly got to her feet, grimacing as pain shot across her brow; lightning sparked before her eyes for a moment, her body trembled and her thoughts shivered, but she was alive.

Some of her new armour was piled near the back of the tent, including the belt, although the helmet and weaponry were missing. She pulled on what she could and stood for a few moments, tired and confused, before heading out.

Night had fallen, and the encampment was largely quiet. Stars peppered the sky, whilst on the ground a few fires had softened into smouldering embers. Tarian waited for a few moments, expecting someone to catch hold of her arm or escort her quickly back into the hazy medical tent, but no one came.

She moved slowly, wandering through the quietened camp until she found a sword and shield lying near a broken workbench; they were heavy in her grasp, but Bowen had been right about one thing – this world was perilous, and she had no desire to travel across it unarmed.

She slipped away into the darkness.

Dawn leaked over the horizon, a milky crimson hue bleeding out into the world to wash over the stifling murk. The walls of Mysta seemed to soak up the opaline twilight and cast out long tendril shadows in return.

Aneira stood upon her balcony, her eyes scanning the distant horizon as fear and confusion racked her heart. Her stomach knotted and magic burgeoned at her fingertips; she finally turned to face Elgan, who stood with his hands clasped behind his back, and she sighed.

"I'm so sorry, Eminence. There was nothing we could do for her. She gave her life so that we could retreat from the Sceleratis."

"I felt death tremble through the air as though it were a spider's thread, but I thought…" She motioned for him to follow her back inside. "It attacked without warning? A creature of that size?"

"I believe… I believe that King Dullahan of Luxnoctis has breached our shores."

Aneira sat down at her desk with another heavy sigh, and steepled her fingers beneath her chin. "I see."

"Forgive me Eminence, but you do not seem surprised."

She was silent for a while, her thoughts swirling around long held theories until the man before her cleared his throat. She leaned back in her chair. "I have had my suspicions for some time, Elgan. I thought that if I shared them with you, you might think me mad, or else simply mock me."

"The Eternal Monarch is nothing to laugh at; I would have understood. But this is not the time for that argument. Dullahan is closing in on us. He could pounce at any given moment; we need to fortify the town immediately. Close the gates, equip every man, woman and child who can hold a weapon."

"It will not be enough." Sorrow flooded Aneira. "Everything I have done here to try and help those who were torn down is all for naught. I need to speak to you of something, and you must listen to me before you dismiss it."

"Go on."

"I have been scouring the libraries of this place since I first took over. There are texts and scrolls older than you can imagine, hidden away in dark corners and bound not only in leather and iron, but in enchantments so strong they could have come from the Gods themselves. Elgan, we need to be rid of the Monarch, and I believe that I have found a way. We need to find the Anghenfil."

He stared at her. "What? Next you'll be telling me that you believe in fire breathing Eordracan. Aneira, these are just children's stories meant for nothing more than telling at a winter fireside."

"No." She rubbed her face and looked at him, her eyes cold. "It's more than just that. There are tales of cataclysms throughout the ages, just like the one that tried to tear us apart. It's the Monarchs, Elgan, they're the ones at fault and without them there would be no more suffering! We would all finally be safe, forever. Our children and grandchildren could live free of the fear of tyranny, and we could go to our eternal rest knowing that we had rid the world of the corruption that threatens it. I have found many accounts of a creature known as the Gilded Lord, or the Venerated King of Hallowed Ember and Carrion in older texts, who stood in direct opposition to the Eternal Monarchs. They *are* vulnerable under the right circumstances, if we just –"

"Eminence?" Alban appeared in the doorway, his eyes bright.

"What is it now?"

"There is someone here to see you."

A woman pushed past him, lantern light catching upon her armour; she smiled weakly at the pair before her.

"It can't be…"

"I thought you said she was lost to that beast?"

"No one could have survived that! Is this some trick of the King?"

"She's as real as the moon in the night's cradle." Alban nodded enthusiastically. "As real as the bones lying deep within the earth. And much does she have within untwisted thoughts, many tales to tell!"

Three

Bells tolled through the mist, a deep lowing call that echoed across the edges of the shadowed woodland and out to the rocky terrain beyond.

Spiralling columns reached up towards the pale sky, releasing small cascades of dust whenever the wind bit into their chalky flesh; waxy light skimmed over the surface of a lake, gently teasing its way along only to pull away and disappear into the trees. Mylah sat on the edge, one foot dipped into the milky water; her eyes were closed against the dawn, her thoughts lost in some other world; she did not stir as another's breath brushed against her neck.

"You cannot keep returning here, Mortifera. You are hallowed spectre, haunting this place which no longer belongs to your kin, and such presence disturbs greatly my brethren." The words were a guttural whisper, slowly and cautiously formed. "Seek you not this place for solace, for we have nothing left to hold out as an offering."

"Be at peace Vatis, I have not come to negotiate further. I will keep to the accord we agreed upon, I have no wish to see your people at war." She opened her eyes and looked at the creature before her.

It glanced away, its amber eyes flickering over the quiet scene and back again; a soft breeze pushed against its violet skin and through the crown of silvery feathers atop its bony head. Almost skeletal, the creature moved in a jarring fashion, its elongated limbs bending and cracking in a strange manner as it backed away slightly, showing its jagged yellow fangs.

A few seconds dripped by in silence.

"Why are you here, Mortifera? Seek you not the solace of youth long lost to ashen flame, I can understand, but why sit you here at this place of yearning? What causes a slip away from distant soil so in need of aid?"

"I already told you that I have no desire to change the terms of our agreement; you are welcome to this land."

"Did not words speak of this? Ugly tongue of mortal kin is full of deception and loss; what was spoken was not right? Meaning fell into chasm, perhaps? Sorrow lights your way, to my mind, and not the warm serenity you thought to find out in the wilderness beyond."

"Forgive me." She sighed deeply. "I misunderstood. My mind was elsewhere, that is all, and I suppose that is the answer to your question. I just came here to think."

"Think?" The creature narrowed its eyes at her. "Think you not elsewhere? No, no… something occurred, to my mind, something that was not meant to stray into carefully chosen path."

"I… I was confronted by a woman that I had not thought to meet, who spoke of things I was not prepared to hear."

"Mortifera cradles the pieces of her heart evermore. There will yet be pain, and so can ghouls grasp at her easily to pull her apart. Speak of it, lighten heart and burden."

A small snake slithered across the dusty ground, breaking free of its dusty shelter and winding away towards an unknown crevice.

Shadows stretched out across the expanse as beasts crawled and clambered their way over the rugged terrain, grasping for an embrace loving, cold, and dead.

Mylah turned to look at the Vatis. "You say I inflict fear, but your people are gathering around us even now."

"To hear the spoken word of Mortifera is neither blessing nor curse, but intoned in shrivelled prose sing the Gods themselves."

"I am not the mouthpiece for divinity, nor do I ever wish to be." She pinched the bridge of her nose and exhaled softly. "There are spirits enough willing to speak through others, if you desire to listen; I have no more lessons for you to learn. I only wished to be alone, but it seems that isn't possible, even out here."

An audience had grown around them: a mass of talons and fangs and twitching eyes, all breath bated and withheld; expectant souls were reaching out once more only to come away wanting.

Mylah felt something brush against her foot, and so she gazed down into the lake; a dark shape moved within the cloudy water, its long fingers gently tracing along her blue stained skin.

"Mortifera is troubled by something other than the stones she placed upon barren hill?" The Vatis blinked its four eyes slowly. "Whispers of winter claw at troubled thoughts and the Shade creeps still in haunting dreams, but it is not these things that fling Mortifera to such troubled shores."

"No... it is not. I told you there was a woman who said things I was unprepared for, but that was not everything. In truth, I don't think that the words she spoke were her own, they were too tailored to my own heartache for someone so new, but I... reacted."

"Ah." The creature nodded. "Mortifera is magic kin, honoured Valiskar."

"Anger flared in me like fire and I... I don't know if she still draws breath."

An uneasy silence descended upon the creatures who had gathered to listen; Mylah turned away to look at the horizon.

The Vatis watched her carefully. "Favoured lands beguile, but contain no answers to such challenge. While away time like thread not yet spun, seek pallid light and golden waves, but think not to understand ghoulish confrontation until sword in hand, eye to eye. Think back to things unfolded, and furled as banner across dimmer skies, and see stepping stones that give way to moments anew."

Bowen looked up from his book and sighed; Rafael stood before him again, with the same concerned look upon his face that he had worn the previous five times. The physician fidgeted uncomfortably.

"What is it now?"

"I need to speak to the boss about chasing down the Sepelite woman. It's my fault she ran off like she did, I shouldn't have left her alone like that. I need to make up for my mistake; what if she's lying in a ditch somewhere, bleeding out?"

"Her Grace has not yet returned."

Rafael scratched his head and looked away; worry pitted his face and knotted his stomach, invaded his dreams and thoughts alike. He had searched the camp twice over for any sign of Tarian and found none; parties that had been dispatched to scout just beyond the perimeter had come back empty handed. There was little point in retreating towards the western coastline: the queen would want to advance eastwards, and anyone who lingered would be left behind.

Bowen rubbed his brow and awaited the inevitable question.

"What if she gets hurt again, sir? It's not right, not right at all."

"There is nothing more we can do at the moment. Go back to your duties and try to put this from your mind. Tarian knows this place far better than we do; I'm sure that she will not put herself at unnecessary risk."

Rain lashed against the outside of the tavern as thunder rumbled overhead. A fire crackled in the hearth, occasionally spitting out sparks and smoke like an angry god. The air was thick with the smell of warm stew and fresh bread; spiders scuttled along dribbling window panes and disappeared into cracks along the warped frames.

Berne sat at a table, his eyes fixated on the storm beyond the glass. His fingers were curled around a mug of untouched ale, his mind elsewhere.

A gust of wind coursed around his ankles as someone opened the door; the woman behind the bar grumbled about shutting the damn thing and then disappeared into the kitchens.

He looked up when a hooded figure sat down across from him, soaking wet. "Evening Fletching."

"Berne." Mylah drew back the hood and shook the raindrops from her hair.

He pushed the mug towards her. "Looks like you need this more than I do. What's going on, boss? Don't tell me that you missed me so much you had to run back and help me wallow in this shit hole? Or was Bowen getting on your tits with all that bowing and scraping?"

She smiled weakly as she raised the drink to her lips, but said nothing.

Berne watched her for a few moments, and then got up from the table. "Looks like you need a good meal, too. I'll tell Old Jen to draw up two bowls of whatever it is she's got in the pot."

She watched him stride over to the bar and holler his request into the kitchen only to be greeted by an obscene gesture and a flurry of profanity. He winked at the woman before he sat back down at the table.

"Gods Berne, it's all going to shit."

"Hmm, sounds like we're going to need another round of ale. I thought things were going well in Sepelite? Your spells were working, from what I saw. Is it the guardswoman? Did she not make it?"

"I don't know." Mylah rubbed her brow and glanced up at him. "Something happened that I... I'm not proud of."

"Something other than you taking Bowen in my place, you mean?" He grinned. "Must be bad. Has he asked to be named Seneschal yet, by the way? No? Ah... maybe don't mention that I brought it up, then."

"I attacked her, Berne."

He raised his eyebrows. "As in verbally ranted, or left her as a pile of gooey mess on the ground?"

"She said some things and I... I don't know what happened. I think she might be dead."

"You could tap into Bowen's mind and find out."

"You know I don't like doing that."

"I'm not surprised. Gods only know what kind of boring thoughts that man has. I sometimes wonder if he's ever had even an inkling of deviance. That aside, if it's bothering you this much, then you need to find out what happened, both to her and to you. Her survival meant enough that you had me carry her back to her useless fucking friends, so surely it's worth having a quick conversation with the

Lord of Mundane Sexual Positions. That is… I'm assuming he is, I've never actually asked anyone. I can't wait to tell him that you whipped up a portal just to have me carry an unconscious woman across a field."

"Don't you dare. He actually lectured me the other day about frivolous use of magic, said it was setting a bad example for the novices."

"Ha! He grew some balls!"

"Right up until the end of his sentence, when his eyes grew wide and his mouth dropped, and he apologised profusely."

"So close, Bowen, so close."

She sighed and was quiet for a few moments. "I should go. Thank you, Berne."

"Aye, see you Fletching. Guess I'll eat two bowls of stew, then." He clapped his hands together. "Today is a good day."

Bowen turned as the air around him quivered and smoked. "Ah, Your Grace. Are you ready to move on?"

*

Light rippled through the thin curtains and washed over the cracked stony floor; shadows danced in the hushed fireplace, wisps of magic and song that stretched out with longing fingers. The room was quiet, calm, with only a whisper of breath and the echoing of distant footsteps to send a shiver through the balance; a lone candle flickered defiantly as it neared its waxy end, trying to illuminate the pile of dusty scorched tomes and scrolls that lay scattered across the wooden desk.

Aneira sat with her chin resting upon her hands and stared at the pages before her. Thoughts dashed to another time, another place, in a frenzy of frightened words and images. Her heart throbbed in her chest and sweat trickled down her spine as Tarian's revelations reared once more. Darkness was upon them, and it meant to tear down everything they had worked so hard to rebuild. Mysta would fall back into ashen destruction: fires would rage in the streets, corpses would litter the ground, disease would creep up through the foundations and wind its way into the hearts of those who had already survived so much.

"Your Eminence?" Alban appeared in the open doorway, papers in hand.

She looked up and gestured for him to enter; pain prickled behind her eyes and she sighed, turning away from the poisonous words before her.

"Scribbled prose from the scouts to confirm *some* of the tale spun by swords and tongues alike, Eminence, and those provided by the courier ring ever true. There is indeed a small force moving in from the west with the head of a blue scaled beast who roars into the heavens and shatters the bonds of the Gods. They also say that... Eminence... it seems I would make a liar of myself, but ghosts and men whisper alike. They say that the sky has cleared behind her and that she who creates the magic to do so would tear down the ruby veil and see us washed of all sin."

"She cannot *create* magic." Aneira glared at him. "She manipulates it in a way that we have not been able to do. Was there any sign of a glamour enchantment?"

Alban shook his head and the room darkened a little. Aneira sat back in her chair and looked at the ceiling for a few moments, her mind elsewhere. The man fidgeted, his fingers twitching.

"Could it be possible that what Tarian says is true?" Aneira's words were soft, barely more than a whisper. "An Eternal Monarch taken down by a simple blade? There are tales of the others in the libraries here, of Luctus, Adain, Eira, and Terrwyn... and there are still more I have yet to decipher... but all came to a grand and gloried end."

"A good story is one that enraptures its audience, and sometimes a little exaggeration can dance amongst the history."

"Hmm." She waved her hand dismissively and looked back at Alban. "What is that?"

"An updated death toll, Eminence." He held out a folded piece of paper. "The priests will soon see to the rest of those who have gone beyond your grasp."

"Very well." Aneira rubbed her face wearily. "I will make sure to be there, although I must consult with Elgan and Tarian again before I do anything else."

A cold wind whistled through the window, fluttering its veil and scattering the pages upon the desk. The candle finally winked out.

A storm gathered in the west.

Curses borne upon an orchestral wind arose from graves long since lost to the ravages of time; voices drew forth from the bowels of the earth, guttural and sanctified, a howling crescendo of hallowed verse. Melodic decay drifted towards the celestial cradle, scented with the rotten breath of a thousand caged souls screaming for release; holy exodus crept out of the ground with long, gnarled fingers and began to spin its fragile web.

Eyes that had been shut away from the horrors of the mortal world creaked open. Magic that had once been buried and abandoned suddenly awoke.

Flames sparked in the firmament.

Aneira strode through the gloomy hallways with renewed vigour; her stomach knotted and pain seeped into her limbs, but she knew the way forward now. Shadows leapt back as she approached, crawling away into hidden fractures in the walls. Alban scuttled some way behind, his breath rasping upon the chilled air as he struggled to keep up; the walls of Ancora seemed to bend to her will, protecting their newfound saviour.

Bells were tolling somewhere to the east, calling out with their sad lulling cry. Aneira's heart sank as she thought of the bodies needing to be paraded through the streets before their souls could ascend into Amara's loving embrace. She pushed the images away and steeled herself; those who had suffered at the hands of the Monarchs would be mourned, but her priority had to be saving those still living from following in their footsteps.

Warm light poured out of an open doorway, warding away the gloom; the room beyond was eerily quiet. Elgan sat in an old chair with a book idling in his lap, his eyes glazed over and his mind elsewhere. He snapped back to reality when Aneira entered.

She watched him for a few moments and then cleared her throat. "It's time."

"Eminence…" His voice was tinged with sorrow.

"I believe that what Tarian told us was the truth. We need to rally Mysta's defences before that witch breaches our walls and slaughters everyone inside. If Dullahan is truly dead, and she was the one who killed him, we have to be prepared for the kind of power she may command."

"Aneira." Elgan looked at her then. "Tarian also said that she might be an ally, here to help us disperse the pestilence and heal Sepelite's many wounds."

"Or she could be here to conquer us, and re-forge the spells that Dullahan wrapped around our ancestors to bind them to his will. The Monarchs are not our friends – they are not even truly human. We mean nothing to them. She already hurt Tarian, after sending spies here who have told her Gods only know what! I will not put my people at risk just to have a potential alliance with a foreign queen. They are worth so much more than that, Elgan. I will not betray them and see them suffer again."

"How do you propose we stop her?" He rose to his feet and the book clattered to the floor. "If she is as powerful as Dullahan was said to have been, then we have little hope of being able to do anything."

"I have a plan, but I need your support."

Tarian lingered outside, shadows wrapping around her as she listened to the ongoing discussion. Elgan would mutter agreement every so often, but Aneira barely seemed to notice; there was a fire within her that Tarian didn't recognise, a holy vengeance that had surged from some hidden depth.

She rubbed her forehead and looked away. A tattered cloth of teal and gold lay across a dusty table, covered in broken glass and tarnished candlesticks, and further down the corridor were rooms empty of everything except their ghosts.

She sighed and closed her eyes; Aneira was still talking, and it was obvious that nothing could sway her from the path she had chosen. Mysta meant more to her than her own safety, but the magic that this new Queen commanded was stronger than she was willing to understand, and Tarian feared the forces that seemed to be at work. She could clearly recall the panic that had filled her, leading her in her stumbling blindness to that tent, and then the words that had gripped her mind and hissed out through her mouth like venomous snakes. The memory was a bitter one, tinged with fear and vulnerability; Aneira and Elgan had insisted that it had simply been a trick played upon her by the foreign spell-caster to justify her violent response.

"What have we here?" Alban's voice crackled through the air. "Seek you redemption in this place, or must you loiter like a lost spirit?"

Tarian glanced at him. "Fuck off old man."

"Swords without shields should beware their sharpened edges. Metal rusts in ways magic does not." He shuffled past her, heading towards the brightly lit room just beyond. "Brothers running amok along Caeli's crumbling shores turn not a thought to beleaguered sisters, and care not if she should slip into oblivion's foul curse."

She rolled her eyes and snorted. "Idiot."

Her head throbbed with sudden pain and she staggered to one side; slumber pulled at her mind so she made for one of the empty rooms.

Alban scowled and finally slipped into Aneira's chamber. "Eminence!"

She turned and frowned slightly. "What is it?"

"Watered down words seek to turn you from the light, Daughter of Mysta. Listen not to rotten songs played upon broken bark!"

"Is it physically impossible for him to speak without riddles?" Elgan raised an eyebrow, and then looked back to Aneira. "Saeth and I will see you at the funeral procession." He left without another word.

"All is ready, Eminence. Crowds will gather within the hour. Time slips by as surely as the tide, and the fruit ripens upon the trees." Alban grinned and steepled his fingers. "Great things await, for the Gods themselves smile upon those who protect the weak. Your gifts have already been enough to see recognition rain down from divine cradles, and surely with this last push we will see celestial reverence elevate you beyond all comprehension."

"I sometimes think you are beyond comprehension, my friend. Come, walk with me; we still have much to discuss."

The journey to the southern border was a gloomy one; Alban rattled away, seemingly more excited with every new idea that sprang from his mind. Aneira listened for a while before she drifted away into her own thoughts. Fear crept around the edges like a prowling beast, sending shivers through her whenever she pictured the crowned tyrant advancing upon her town.

A murmuring chant filled the air as they approached the funeral pyres. Elgan waited alone, his head bowed; potent incense swirled around the base of a shrine to the Goddess of Death, her marble statue reaching out with one hand and pointing up towards the heavens with the other. A priest stood nearby with a basket of flowers.

Aneira took one and laid it at Amara's stony feet. "Take these souls into your arms, Hallowed Lady, and grant them the rest they could not find upon our mortal shores."

"Guide them into the peace of the sunlit valleys." Elgan smiled weakly at her and inclined his head. "I wasn't sure if you were going to make it, Eminence; so many people seem to require your attention, after all."

"I am hoping that this is the last one of these ceremonies we will have to endure. After that so called queen has been chased from our realm, perhaps she will take her blight with her and leave us be." Aneira's eyes shone for a moment. "We will be safe and well again; children can be born without fear of what is to become of them, the Conjury can finally reform, and Mysta will become a shining example for the rest of Sepelite. Our suffering is nearing its end, and once we are free of the icy grip of the Monarchs, we will never have to worry that these troubled times will come again."

Fire devoured the wooden pyres and lashed up towards the sky.

*

The air was warm, thick, and muggy, and it hung around the gathered crowd like a stained shroud, stinking of death and decay. Heat slithered down through the bloody miasma, and sweat beaded upon the brows of those who lingered outside Ancora, their voices low and fearful. The Eminent Minister stood upon the steps, her head bowed as she spoke to a hooded man beside her. Other figures filed out of the building and into the throng, carrying plates of fresh bread and tankards of honeyed wine.

Sunlight cut through the clouds and struck Aneira's face, sinking into her ash blonde hair and washing over her pale skin. She stood upright to finally face those who had amassed before her. Her arms rose slightly, and silence befell her captive audience.

A moment or two hovered in uneasy silence.

"Good people of Mysta." Her voice was strong and unwavering, ringing out like a death knell. "We raise a toast today to those we have sent into the loving embrace of Lady Amara, kith and kin we hope to see again one fair dawn when the time comes for us to lay down our own burdens. We honour they who have gone before, who will light the way and welcome us home, and I hope that by sharing in our grief together we may lessen each other's pain."

Saeth wound her way silently through the crowd, listening to the speech as she took hold of a tankard and downed the liquor. There were quiet murmurs amongst the onlookers, nods of approval and tears wiped away upon the backs of hands.

"I know that your hearts are heavy with sorrow, as is my own, and though I do not wish to add to that, I fear I must share some grave news with you. A brief time ago we learnt that an invader has landed upon our shores. The Monarch has sailed from Luxnoctis, but it is not King Dullahan that heads the army that even now advances upon our fair town. He lies dead these past three years, slain by the very woman who hopes to conquer us, to tear down our walls and set our homes aflame. She calls herself Queen Mylah, Empress of Cadere and Mistress of all Magics."

Confusion and panic swept through the crowd like wildfire; Saeth's eyes darted from face to face as a frown furrowed her own brow.

Aneira held up a hand and nodded. "I understand your concerns my friends, believe me. Even I doubted that such a thing could be true, but we now know that she is the cause of all of our suffering. Dullahan died at the time of the cataclysm that saw so many of our brethren struck down, and she came to power just as the magical blight swept over our lands and our skies began to bleed. She thinks us all to be fools and knaves who would bow and scrape to her every whim, who will believe her lies about coming under a banner of peace, simply to slaughter us in our beds. But we are not the weak and pitiful prey that she thinks us to be! My people… I promise you now that I will make no treaties with such a vile creature, no matter the sweetened lies that may spill from her pursed lips. I will never betray you, and I only ask that you do the same! Protect yourselves, and each other, and do not give in to the shadows that she will surely bring forth!"

"How can you know all of this, Eminence?"

"This can't be right! Sepelite hasn't seen hide nor hair of a Monarch in hundreds of years!"

"Why would they come to us now? We don't have anything they want!"

"Let her speak!" A man pushed to the front of the crowd. "Her Eminence is a good woman, she wouldn't deceive us. We can trust her."

"Thank you, Halwyn." Aneira smiled warmly. "I know that this is a lot for you to take in. I did not believe the letters I was sent from our allies along the western border, so a scouting party was sent out to Calyx some time ago. They never reached their destination, as they were attacked by a Sceleratis. A Sceleratis that we have discovered was sent by this hateful queen to instil fear in the hearts of our courageous mages and warriors alike. But before it had time to wreak the havoc it was meant to, one woman's bravery turned the tide. Tarian, a former guard for the Conjury and my own trusted friend, thought to sacrifice herself to save her comrades, and in doing so gave them enough time to retreat. She later awoke in the invader's camp, badly injured, and it was here that she learnt how they have had spies sweeping across Sepelite for some time. They have been watching us, my friends, but we have proven too clever for their feeble schemes, and so she was taken directly to the Queen. When she didn't tell her what she wanted to know, she was violently attacked, barely escaping with her life."

Saeth raised an eyebrow and shook her head before disappearing into the shadows. The man who stood beside Aneira watched her move; he whispered something to the minister as Saeth disappeared back inside Ancora.

Storm clouds gathered upon the horizon, and shadows loomed in from the west.

Aneira looked out across the crowd, her face full of sorrow. "It has been demonstrated before Tarian's very eyes that the invader has the power to disperse the miasma that haunts our sky, and to bring life forth from even the most barren ground. Her minions were sent on secret quests to plant crystals all across Sepelite that supposedly amplify her *healing* magic, but it is my belief, and that of my esteemed colleagues, that these actually helped her to spread the pestilence three years ago. I am so sorry that we could not find the cause before many of our loved ones were lost. It was a cruel and twisted game for her to play, but even I can see the logic in it. She weakens us, infects and takes away our magic, only to appear as a saviour some time later to a nation so grateful to be restored that it cannot see past the mask to the true demon beneath."

The sky darkened.

Saeth leant against the doorframe and sighed loudly.

Tarian looked up from her book. "Ignite those torches, would you? I can't see a fucking thing in this dim light."

"Did you not want to listen to our dear minister's little speech, darling? You seem to have quite the prominent part in it."

Rain drummed softly against the window.

"I don't care for all that endless noise." Tarian shifted uncomfortably and rubbed the back of her neck, her fingers darting to Bryn's necklace. "But maybe I should head outside. People might have questions that only I can answer. I don't want them to be afraid."

"She will do what she can to protect them." Saeth slid further into the room and held out her hand. A small flame sparked to life upon her open palm. "We all will. Come, let us go back to her captive audience."

Thunder rumbled overhead and magic crackled through the air, twisting the rain into a lashing crimson onslaught. An icy wind whipped through the crowded streets before lightning snaked through the rusted clouds down to the world below, skittering across Mysta's stony walls and scattering the men and women who had sought refuge in their shadow.

"Flee from this scene, Eminence!" Alban tugged at Aneira's sleeve. "There is no natural breath to this storm!"

The ground shuddered and fractured, slowly turning black; silver flames burst out of the cracks and swamped the streets with sulphurous smoke. Screams ricocheted from within the fetid haze. Ancora began to creak and groan, its great bulk straining as bolts of energy battered against it like closed fists. A tattered banner of teal and gold was ripped away and thrown down to where the Eminent Minister stood, staring at the sudden destruction around her.

A woman with dark hair and fierce lilac eyes ran past, bellowing an archaic incantation.

Aneira watched her go by, a slight frown creasing her forehead. "Delia? What are you...?" Her thoughts snapped and she gasped, magic burgeoning in her veins. "By the Gods, they'll die out here without our help! Alban, get as many inside Ancora as you can."

"But Eminence, I don't..."

She ran down the steps and thrust out her right hand, sending out a shock wave that pushed back against the shrieking wind. Rusty water coursed down her face as she moved through the confusion, shouting for people to retreat to the safety of the building behind her.

Lightning cracked to her left, piercing the crowd that swayed there; howls of pain shot up into the clamour as flesh burned and skin blistered. Thunder roared once more and the earth answered with a terrifying quake; Mysta trembled and shook, casting down its shrine to the Goddess of Death, her statue shattering upon the ground. An unholy chant seemed to rise then upon the wind; mournful and accursed it slithered through the ruinous town and crawled into the minds of all who heard it, tearing and gnawing until sanity began to slip.

Tarian bolted past the Minister, dragging two young children by the hand; she hurled them towards the steps and into Alban's poised grasp. She turned on her heel and dived back into the fray, fighting through the frightened throng; people were scrambling through the smoky streets, trying desperately to find shelter. Dust and debris flew through the murky air as masonry trembled, fractured, and began to fall; one of the outer walls was lurching back and forth, large cracks snaking up from its foundations. Geysers of magic shot out of the ground, flames of blue and silver spreading out in blistering lines that incinerated all who stood before them. Thunder growled again, and the heavy clouds blocked out the sun, casting Mysta in shadow.

"Fall back! Get to Ancora!" Aneira's words were almost lost in the cacophony of screams and feral magic. "Fall back!"

Tarian moved past her once more, a line of men and women stumbling behind her; a few grandparents were clinging to crying children with ash smeared faces. Blood mingled with the rain to leave copper trails across their skin.

Alban ushered more civilians inside; his eyes darted to and fro, searching the crowd for any sign of the Eminent Minister.

Plumes of magic shot up as she fought against the onslaught that threatened her city; buildings were crumbling all around them, crushing those who had thought to wait out the unnatural storm inside. Horses were screaming from the stables to the west as fire engulfed them; people fell in the streets only to be trampled as panic coursed through their kinsmen.

Lightning struck at the outer wall, lashing at the cracks until it finally gave in; a thunderous note plunged through the air as the stonework shuddered one last time and collapsed in a cascade of rock and grit that shot out across the ground. A large, clawed hand reached through the newly formed crevice.

Delia darted through the gloom, shooting out bolts of ice in an attempt to quell some of the flames that had surrounded a nearby house. Its inhabitants rushed out of the smouldering doorway and nodded at the mage.

"Tell them to shore up the sides of Ancora. I'll be there as soon as I can to help reinforce it." She cast another round of magic but it fell beneath a fork of jagged lightning.

"Ah… poor little magus. You should not have tarried here so long." A rasping voice cracked through the air behind her. "Your life for theirs, I suppose? Is that truly a fair trade? There were five, maybe six, in that dwelling and yet I see only one of you."

Something grabbed hold of her waist, its gnarled talons sinking easily through her flesh; she gasped and struggled to turn around, but the creature merely laughed and tightened its grip.

Saeth ran through the heaving mass of bodies and smoke, sweat dripping down the back of her neck as magic burgeoned in her veins and she threw out another curl of fire.

Beasts with silvery skin and wing-like eyes were clambering through the collapsed wall, their arrival heralded by a fanfare of terrified screams; a carpet of broken bones and severed limbs spilled out into the dark wilderness beyond Mysta's crumbling barricade.

Lightning skittered down to the ground once again, and she slipped upon the drenched cobblestones, her spell shooting wide and crashing into the side of a nearby building. Aneira was at her side within moments, pulling her back to her feet and shouting above the discord.

Monsters were pouring into the town; spidering hands worked at widening the breach until ice formed like thick tendrils, pinning them in place, and soon growls of frustration rippled out. The smoke cleared a little to show the Eminent Minister standing before the intrusion, arms thrust out to the side and blazing with pale green light. She snarled and hissed, and the layer of ice spread across the gap, enveloping the beasts in its way.

A large Saprus greeted her intrusion with an embittered laugh; with a swift motion, it threw something out towards the woman.

A headless body landed at her feet. Aneira refused to look down, but her scowl deepened and she raised her hands. Emerald flames shot up in a ring around the creature.

"You have trespassed upon our ground, unholy fiend. Tell me why, and I may grant you a death more merciful than the one you deserve."

"The magus speaks without having anything to say." It grinned at her. "She of the Many Names summoned us here, and so it is her bidding that we do. Blinded are these others by lies and wanting, and never will they see the crown for what it truly is. She of the Many Names is who gave us our escort, and our entrance, and she will be the one who raises us beyond the understanding of these pitiful onlookers."

The fire burned hot and bright, and it engulfed the monster until it was no more than ash; other spells exploded out of the earth and caught hold of flesh and fur and dragged them all into death's chilled embrace.

Saeth stared at the carnage. "Why the fuck could that thing speak? And what the fuck did it mean? Who was it talking about?"

"The invader." Aneira looked over her. "What was it Tarian said she called herself? Queen, Empress, Mistress, Monarch?"

"But… why? Why would she do this?"

Thunder rumbled overhead.

"She broke Dullahan's tyrannical rule only to take up her own. Come, we must return to Ancora and see out the rest of this storm."

Ancient whispers crept out of fissures ripped and newly torn, and snaked up onto older winds; curses once thought broken and dead found breath. The Gods turned their faces away.

"Do you feel that?" Saeth stopped and glanced around. "There's something wrong… but I can't tell what it is."

A tremor passed beneath their feet, sending shivers through the debris that littered the ground. Lightning flashed across the bruised clouds, and the rain stopped; the wind silenced its howling cry and fell away. The magic that had whipped through the streets and clawed at the walls dissipated, and the world was calm, grey, and still.

"I don't like this."

A drumbeat sounded far below them in the bowels of Cadere. It rose slowly, moment by moment, until the ground began to quiver and jolt.

Aneira's eyes widened. "Run!"

The ground cracked open in front of the two women and threw them apart. A fracture tore through the streets and Mysta trembled in a flurry of stone and dust. Buildings rattled as inside they became a maelstrom of shattered glass and pottery; a high pitched whistle escaped out of the tear, followed closely by a bellowing roar. The quake strengthened. No longer able to withstand the onslaught, the houses collapsed and buried their inhabitants under a blanket of stone.

Aneira struggled to get to her feet. Blood trickled down the side of her face, leaving smeared trails in the ashen dirt. The world around her was a swaying blurred mass; tears formed in her eyes as her ears rang and vomit rose in her throat.

The stench of death, blood and bile clung to the air; all around her were the sounds of the dying, whispered names and curdling cries, and still the ground shuddered beneath her. She took a few deep breaths, willed her vision to clear, and started to move.

Ancora rose out of the dust like a shining beacon; a few mages stood upon the steps whilst others knelt, exhausted, their spells weaving into its brickwork and protecting those who hid inside.

The Minister staggered onward, her own magic spluttering back to life; pain coursed through her head and her heart throbbed against her ribs. She stopped for a moment, holding her left side and letting the gore there sink between her fingers; silence crept in for a second or two, and her stomach knotted.

The drumbeat came again.

"No…" Her eyes widened. "No, please Gods, no…"

Cracks appeared nearby, tearing at the ground until rubble and bone alike fell into the darkened chasm below; fractures formed and ran along the floor, treacherous and mutinous and unstoppable, fractal scars upon the earth that split as they reached the steps of Ancora. Confusion crept into the minds of the mages who loitered there, and their magic dimmed for a moment. The great building suddenly groaned, its walls seeming to buckle; the sorcerers immediately cast new wards, their spells spiralling out into the firmament, and the creaking stopped.

The drumbeat came again.

Aneira cried out.

Ancora tipped slowly to one side. The magic intensified under a chorus of shouts and screams, and the stonework juddered to a halt. Sweat dripped down the brow of every mage, as their hands trembled and their knuckles whitened.

The drumbeat came again.

An unholy cry heaved up from the foundations, and Ancora plunged to the ground with a sorrowful roar. Stony debris shot out in all directions; the steps caved inwards and disappeared into some deeper, shadowed realm. Teal and gold banners drifted through the air to rest upon the ruined ground.

Finally satisfied, the shaking stopped and the world came to a quieter rest.

The Minister stared, her mouth agape. She took a few steps forward before falling to her knees; tears sprang from her eyes as she mouthed a silent prayer.

Amara had taken many this day. She could smell their deaths tainting the air and the ground of Mysta, and knew then that it would never be cleansed. Ghosts would cling to this place and wail until the sun crashed into the sea and Sepelite was lost forevermore. Her beloved town was no more than dust.

"Aneira!" The word cut through her melancholy thoughts. "Aneira, thank Merfyd!"

She looked up to see Elgan standing before her, his face a mess of dirt and ash. There were ruby smears beneath his nose and chin, and part of his left ear was missing; his clavicle had been slashed and his upper arms gored. He held out his hands and helped her to her feet.

"Where did you…?"

"There was another breach in the outer walls. Have you seen Saeth?"

"She was…" Aneira closed her eyes. "We were coming back and the… the ground split… I don't know where she went."

"I need to find her. Will you come with me? I don't think we should be alone, this place is unstable and –"

"Do you see now what she is capable of, Elgan? The invader from Luxnoctis has brought ruin upon us all." She looked at him, her eyes full of tears. "Where's Tarian, do you know?"

He shook his head.

"I will go and look for her. Meet me back here when you've found Saeth."

Elgan tried to protest but she just ignored him and wandered away, her steps jarred and unsteady. He sighed and rubbed his face.

The dust was beginning to settle, revealing the carnage that the storm had left behind. Everything was in ruins, the ashes still falling like snow to cover up the broken bodies that stuck out as unholy markers. Flesh, blood, and bone splattered the fractured floor; embers smouldered here and there, the remnants of unnatural fire, and melting ice dripped down the empty ruins of stone. Nothing was left standing save for parts of the outer walls, and even those were heavily damaged.

He picked his way through the mess, calling out his beloved's name and cursing himself for letting her run out into the fray without him. "Saeth! Come on you old bag, where are you hiding? This isn't funny." His words echoed into nothing. "Saeth?"

Pools of viscous blue liquid and splatters of meat testified to the demise of some of the monsters; scorch marks showed where defiant magical fire had beaten back the ruddy rain.

Elgan followed the trail, his heart pounding and his hands shaking. "Saeth?"

The head of a Saprus lay beside a collapsed building, its unseeing eyes staring up towards the celestial cradle. Its severed hands were a few feet away, and its guts had spilled out onto the ground in between to be picked clean by the scavengers that would eventually return to the scene.

A woman's body was nearby. Curly dark hair, streaked with grey, had spread out behind her head and lightly covered her broken neck. Her lilac eyes were partly open and turned towards the sodden ground. A drying trickle of red hugged the side of her mouth.

Elgan knelt down at her side and took her limp hand in his, kissing it gently. Tears welled in his eyes as he brushed his fingertips against her cheek.

A circle of other monsters, some blue skinned, others covered in dark orange scales, surrounded her. They were all in various stages of evisceration or decapitation, their bodies ravaged by now silent magic.

"Oh my love. Forgive me. I should have been by your side; perhaps together we could have…" He looked away. "You were right; we should have just gone to Caeli and left all of this mess behind us. We could have sailed across the Bay of Embers in the moonlight to see the Nereides dance in their watery caverns; eaten under the ruins at the Stars of Delyth, and slept through that ridiculous Necromancy Carnival just so we could wander through the Burning Relic Depths without any interruptions. Now see what I have done? In my folly, I kept us here in this accursed place…"

A slight breeze slithered by, brushing across his brow. There were whispers upon the wind, but he was too distracted to hear them, and instead gathered Saeth in his arms.

The softened sighs drifted away to darker shores.

"I'll not leave you here to rot amongst these unworthy creatures."

Footsteps echoed behind him and breath racked with sorrow rattled out into the calm atmosphere.

"Did you find Tarian?" He turned to look at Aneira.

She was quiet for a few moments, her hand curled tightly around something small and hard that she slipped into her pocket. "I found her body."

"At least she will have company."

"Do you see now the consequences of the invader and the terrible power she wields? Consorting with these… these beasts, and manipulating the essence of our land to provoke a storm of magic, and for what?"

"We should tend to the fallen, Minister, and see to the survivors."

"There are none."

He stared at her, dread creeping up through his body and taking hold of his heart. "What?"

"There are no survivors, Elgan. We are the only ones left alive. She has seen to the execution of every man, woman, and child that lived within Mysta's walls. There is nothing here but ruin." She dropped to her knees and wept.

"What are we to do?"

"We must find the Anghenfil and try to restore the Gilded Lord. He is our last hope against this tyrant, for if we do not stop her now she will go on to murder everyone and destroy everything Cadere has ever known."

He looked down at the corpse in his arms. "I must see to her burial, but there is nothing left for me here anymore. Let us find your Anghenfil, and tear down this creature who would see us all slain."

Four

Moonlight slipped down through the sanguine miasma and dispersed over the quietened landscape, glinting for a moment upon rain slicked rocks before sinking into the sodden earth. A haze of muttered conversation lingered upon the air as figures moved through the darkness, their torches orbs of twinkling gold against the shadows. Soft blue light would occasionally cascade to the ground and spread out like mist, leaving a carpet of flora in its wake; the rusty smear that adorned the heavens dispersed with a sigh, and so stars glittered against the velveteen black. A gentle breeze brushed through the undergrowth before spiralling away into the west.

A woman crept silently across the landscape and rejoined the group, throwing back her hood as she made her way up the line.

"Nelia, you return to us at last. Did your assignment go as planned?"

"Yes, Your Grace." She bowed swiftly. "Exactly as you predicted."

"The others will return to us within the hour."

"I understand, ma'am."

A copse of trees gave the travellers pause, and they soon melted into the blossom covered sanctuary with relief. Jitterns lounged upon the lower branches, watching the men and women curl up on the mossy ground and fall into stable slumber.

Mylah walked along the perimeter idly, her mind reaching out to memories of distant, happier times. A weak smile passed over her lips as her fingers played with the leather braid at her wrist.

Earthy scents rose up from the quilted ground; insects thrummed through the warm air and faded away into the twilight. Dawn danced upon the horizon, teasing the edges with lighter shades and whispers of amber. There were old bones buried here, deep beneath the soft blanket of soil, and their song drifted upon the early morning brume saturated in magic and loss. The queen listened to the ethereal poetry as she moved, long grasses reaching up to kiss her fingertips.

Birds chattered as the sunlight swelled; a small Jittern leapt down in front of Mylah and looked up at her with a curious mewl before stalking off into the undergrowth. She watched it go and then glanced around; no one had followed her. The world was, for the moment, calm and quiet.

She hesitated for a few seconds, and then brought her closed fist up to her mouth; she blew upon it gently as she uncurled her fingers. Pale blue magic drifted out and began to dance upon the air, slowly twisting and stretching; within a few moments, a woman and child stood before the queen, their sapphire spectral forms glittering like the night sky. Without thinking, she raised her hand to touch the woman's face, and the spell vanished. She was alone.

The world shivered gently.

"Your Grace?"

Mylah quickly wiped her eyes and turned towards the unexpected interruption. Bowen was striding towards her, concern etched upon his tired face; Nelia followed at an ever quickening pace.

"Your Grace, I fear something terrible has happened. There was some kind of magical interference on an incredible scale and, well…" Bowen held out his hand to reveal a broken Locus crystal.

"No doubt you're talking about the enchanted storm. I felt both its birth and its death." She glanced at Hale, their eyes locking for several seconds, before she looked back to the concerned mage with a practiced smile. "I take it you wish to investigate before we replace that."

He bowed his head. "Ma'am, I believe that Tarian was heading in the direction that such a storm would have hit. She spoke about travelling back to the town of Mysta before she left us, and according to the map our scouts drew up…"

"I see. We will go at once, of course. Bowen, there was something I wanted to discuss with you." She lightly touched his shoulder blade to guide him back towards the camp. "Your work has been much appreciated, and I was thinking of bestowing a title upon you. Something like Seneschal, perhaps?"

A cold wind blew in from the east and the trees whispered as the trio passed beneath their viridian refuge. Golden light dripped from the heavens as life sprang up from the soothed earth.

The makeshift camp was quiet, most of its inhabitants still lost in porcelain dreamscapes aside from the few men and women who sat around in hushed conversation. The physician paced up and down, shaking his head.

"Is something amiss, Rafael?" Bowen's concern deepened.

"They'll not wake. I thought to run through a few scenarios with the idiots you assigned to me, but they'll not wake. None of them will. Eh, where are those fuckers going?" He scowled at a couple of the scouts who had clustered around Nelia and were quickly moving away to the north.

"What's going on here?" Mylah stepped in between the man and his quarry.

"The mages are being lazy Your Grace, and won't rouse from wherever their dreams have taken them."

"I suspect it's a little more complicated than that."

"Doubt it." The man sniffed loudly and looked away. "Bloody good for nothing sorcery, interrupting everyone's day with its glittering foolishness. How am I supposed to teach when the novices are asleep? It can't be good for them anyway, might be gripped in some nightmarish realm with no hope of release."

Unease crept into Bowen's mind as he watched for Mylah's reaction, and saw none.

"The Seneschal and I need to travel some way to investigate a magical anomaly. Are you willing to come with us, or do you feel that you're needed here?"

"As Your Grace commands." His eyes flickered to Bowen. "Seneschal, eh?"

"We will leave the warriors here to watch over this place until we return. Give them some instructions to keep them busy whilst we're gone. You may both join me when you're ready to leave."

The Queen walked about half a mile eastward before stopping. She sent out another cascade of curative magic, and watched as it spread out across the land, chasing away the scarlet shadows and teasing life forth from the barren ground.

Her mind drifted once more to other places, to meadows and mountain passes, to burning battlefields and quiet starlit nights around a busy campfire. She saw the faces of Crowned Caritas Fourth who had fallen to Venandi back in the Corignis desert, those who had trusted her to command them well and keep them safe, those she had failed.

She heard footsteps approaching, and broke free of her melancholy thoughts. She flicked her wrist and a portal burst into life before her; the air shimmered and crackled, a faint smell of burning flesh upon it, and without a word to each other, the three of them stepped through.

Magic hung on the stilled breath of Mysta, coarse and heavy and decayed; Bowen wrinkled his nose and stifled a shudder as it settled upon his skin, tingling.

"All this was done by a storm?" Rafael whistled through his teeth. "Bloody magic."

Mylah looked around at the ruination before her. "Consequences befall even those who know not what part they played. But this... it was not meant to be like this. It was never meant to be like this."

"Your Grace?"

She moved a few steps towards the crumbling walls, taking notice of the carcasses entombed in ice; the men followed her slowly, each lost in their own thoughts.

The ground was cracked, scorched, and stained; puddles of dark red mirrored the heavenly scourge, as trails of the tainted water slithered down fractured pathways. Corpses littered the floor, covered in ash and dust alike; broken bones and severed limbs were scattered like discarded keepsakes amongst piles of rubble and stone.

"There are many ghosts here, and they howl at your presence." Bowen looked at his queen.

"I am not the divine entity that they wanted to come for them. But I can release them to her... I can give them that, at least."

"Is that wise, Your Grace? This place has been ravaged by magic, and to add more now could disrupt –"

"I know what I'm doing, Seneschal. Take the physician and look for survivors."

Rafael shook his head. "Survivors? In this mess? I don't see how there could be. Can't you two just… I don't know, wiggle your fingers and sense the living or something?"

"That's not how it works."

"There is too much anger and death here for even the most powerful mage to see beyond it to any delicate threads of life. Come, we have our orders."

They walked silently for a time through the chaos, their footsteps sending up clouds of soot. There was a nauseating smell that seemed to permeate this place, and it left a thin greasy film upon anything that it touched. Rafael held his hand over his mouth and shuddered.

"Are you all right?"

"I've seen many battlefields in my time, and patched up many soldiers. Some of them survived, some of them didn't. You get used to that, you accept that. But this…" The man looked around in despair. "What can you do with this? Children crushed in their homes, old men and women split apart, the ground opening up like it's bloody Lupusora. This is wrong, and there's nothing I can do to fix it; I can't help any of these poor buggers. At least the boss can send them away from here."

Bowen held up his hand to silence the man. The ground fell away into a shadowed chasm not far from where they stood; long strips of dirty tattered cloth were strewn around the floor. The echoes of magical detritus were thicker here, and the air seemed to hum. Light splintered over to the left, leaving shadows to swallow a number of rocks that were suspended in mid-air.

"Bloody magic, it's not enough that it kills everyone, so it has to… wait… what's that? Merfyd's balls!"

"What are you doing? That ground isn't stable, you shouldn't run!"

Rafael paid no heed, and lurched over to the anomaly; he crouched down, swearing profusely under his breath. "By the Gods, she's alive! Get over here, damn it! She's alive!"

"What are you talking about?" Bowen stepped cautiously over a headless torso and a mass of sinew that had been lured from its resting place by the physician's footsteps.

"I saw her breath moving some of this damned ash. She's alive! Him too, I think." Rafael pushed a slew of grime away from a woman's face and clicked his tongue. "Not sure why she would be afraid of poison, it seems not even a fallen city can see to the end of this one."

The scarlet smear upon the heavens dispersed above them, but the darkness did not shift from the earthly wreckage.

"Can we move them? The magic in this place is volatile, and those rocks could come down at any moment."

"She's unconscious, has sustained a lot of superficial injuries, and there's a bone poking through her leg there. Given the wounds she had previously there could be infections too. She does seem to be running a fever, and from the state of all of this," he gestured at the wreckage, "I'd say she probably has some more significant damage that we can't yet see. Moving her is incredibly risky. As for him," Rafael looked over to the man who lay in the dirt looking up at him with a wide grin, "I don't know."

A gnarled, partially burnt hand shot up and grabbed hold of Bowen's wrist. "I stood in the presence of the utmost glory, the unashamed and audacious nobility. Glories I have known, and though my blood paints this abandoned canvas, I go to my death knowing that I served the Daughter of Mysta and never did I falter." The man's eyes glazed over as dark liquid oozed from his mouth, and his hand dropped back into the dirt.

"He ain't getting back up."

"All right, well, we should take Tarian back to Queen Mylah where she'll be safe, and then we can look for other survivors."

"In that case, place your scarf over her face. It looks clean enough, and we need to protect her from the debris in this bloody place. Last thing she needs is more dirt getting in the wounds."

"Are you sure? That seems –"

"Just shut up and do it." Rafael gathered the woman carefully in his arms and winced; her ribs were slick with gore. "This may be a bad idea."

"We don't have any choice. If we leave her here she'll slip into Amara's realm, and there'll be no way back for her. This place drank enough blood, it doesn't need hers too."

They made their way slowly through the mounds of rubble and flesh. It was quiet and calm, although a growing sense of unease crept into Bowen's mind as they meandered through the smothered chaos. Nothing called out to them now, neither living nor dead, and it seemed as though they were walking through some ungodly nightmare. The abyss had swallowed almost an entire town, and it had no need of further satiation.

As they neared the place where they expected to find Mylah, Rafael paused, a frown deepening the lines of his forehead. Bowen looked first at him and then at the queen; he swore quietly.

"What is that?"

A creature lounged before them, relatively short and squat in stature; its acid green skin seemed to shine as though wet, and yet an aura of emerald and sapphire light surrounded its limbless body. One of its bulbous eyes was missing, long jagged scars marking the long healed wound, the other surrounded by inflamed and discoloured skin; the sclera was dark green, almost black, and was sliced down the centre by a thin yellow slit. Its large mouth was constantly open, and surrounded by a thin bony ridge in place of lips; brittle fang-like hairs hung down from the upper ridge, blue and grey in colour.

"It's known as a Morsus. Don't ask it any questions, or we won't be able to get away, and try not to be offended by anything that it says. It would seem that humans and elves are viewed as significantly inferior in the eyes of the monsters."

Mylah turned to the men and nodded at the woman crumpled in Rafael's arms. "You found someone?"

"Yes, Your Grace. There were two survivors, but one perished before we could get to him. We believe we can save this woman though, if we get her back to camp."

"Ah, these mortals and their pitiful primitive medicine." The words of the Morsus were thick, almost gurgled, and spoken slowly. "Why even bother? One less to pollute the world is hardly detrimental. Instead of wasting such time, you should spend it explaining the deaths of so many of the Everlasting in this place; Saprus, Vatis, Vorax and Oculi were all slaughtered here by your disgusting, disreputable kin. If not for the presence of the Mortifera, I would see to it that you were sacrificed in their honour. May the Gods of the Fallen Gloom see to their eternal glory."

Bowen and Rafael exchanged a quick glance, but said nothing. Mylah was quiet, studying the injured woman; eventually she sighed and flicked her wrist, and a portal opened up beside her. "Take her, but Bowen?"

"Yes Your Grace?"

"Ice up her leg. We don't want any infection taking hold."

He stared at her for a few moments. "Yes ma'am."

The magic died behind them as they stepped back into the small woodland. Some of the mages were asleep, but others loitered around the makeshift campsite with a few of the warriors.

"You three, by that log! No, I don't care what your names are, set up a table and bring me my kit. And someone get rags and clean water!" Rafael turned to Bowen and lowered his voice. "That thing – the Morsus – how did it speak?"

"Probably best not to think about it."

"Does it have another mouth? Somewhere inside that gaping maw?"

"Like I said, probably best not to think about it."

The physician barked a few more orders and sent warriors and mages alike scurrying as he laid the woman's body gently upon the table. He pursed his lips as he looked over her wounds, and sighed deeply. Cuts and bruises seemed to cover her skin, and her left leg was broken in three places; one of her hands and four of its fingers were fractured, and her right shoulder was dislocated. Burn marks ran down her neck, the skin scorched and blistered, especially around her clavicle; a barely healed gash at her temple had reopened.

Most of the injuries were covered in dirt or ash, and infection had already begun to set in.

"We'll do what we can." Rafael flicked his gaze up to meet Bowen's. "Couldn't the boss lift her rule just this once?"

"She never has done before, but I will ask her when she returns."

"If Tarian's still alive by then." He grunted and shook his head again. "What was she doing talking to that thing anyway? And what the fuck is an Everlasting?"

"Monsters have a relatively complex and varied outlook on the afterlife, but it mainly revolves around their spirits gaining entry to some sort of paradise. They believe that humans and elves are lesser creatures, soulless and devoid of worth, and that we have no gods who could guide us after death. We are therefore mortal and they, in a sense, are not."

"So it's just some bullshit they tell themselves to feel superior? Hand me that cloth, would you? I assume Mortifera is just their word for mortal queen?"

"It is either a name or a title that they have seen fit to give to Her Grace. They don't see her as human, possibly because of the Vessel attack that nearly took her life."

"She sure does have a lot of those these days. I'm not sure how we're meant to keep track."

"A lot of what?"

"Names."

Moons loitered in an amaranthine sky free of stars, and strange flowers blossomed on a bed of black grass. No winds blew, but the silhouetted trees swayed from side to side and whispered excitedly with a rustling of canopies and vines. Mountains rose in the distance, great jagged beasts that pierced the horizon and faded away into shadow.

"She wanders, yet her soul lingers in another realm." The words were calm and softly spoken. "Why is she here?"

"It is nothing of importance. Leave her to meander through the meadows, she can do no harm. There is no power within her that can hurt us. We should turn thoughts instead to the other, she who came before when a fever severed the ties to her own world. Fools believe in her leadership, and fools will die because of it."

"We could grant this one magic before she returns to her own realm."

"No. That would see peril bloom like a poisoned springtide we could not control. Just let her tread upon the soft turf, oblivious to the dangers around her. Bring us the chalice and see to it that the other is overseen. Her pain blinds all other guidance, and only ruin and tragedy can follow."

*

Bowen looked over the makeshift canopy that had been thrown together and his heart sank a little. It would provide some shelter from the elements, but that seemed inconsequential now; Tarian's fever had tightened its grip, and she was slipping away. Some of her cuts had been bound with magic, others with thread, and her broken bones had been reset, but there was damage they could not undo. Her heart quivered in her chest like a wounded bird and her skin was turning grey, as breath rattled quietly in her lungs, barely passing over her lips.

"Perhaps it would have been kinder to leave the lass to her fate."

"It's not like you to say such things." Bowen raised an eyebrow. "She might still recover. I've seen it happen before when all skilled hands thought it was a lost cause."

"Aye, and I bet she could too if the boss…" Rafael's words trailed away and he shrugged. "Never mind. That kind of thinking leads down a path I don't want to follow. I need to go and see to those mages that are still asleep; watch over her, and call me if there's any change, good or bad."

A wind blew in from the west, cold and crisp; Bowen looked down at the woman as soft footsteps echoed behind him. "Your Grace."

"How is she?" Mylah moved to his side.

"It is unlikely that she will survive for longer than an hour or two now. We have done what we can, but it will not be enough. I know that I should not ask this of you ma'am, but if you would just…"

"You overstep your bounds, Seneschal. You of all people should understand why I cannot help in these matters. If I treat one injury then I would have no grounds to turn away another, and another, until eventually I would have no role other than that better suited to a physician. Besides, I cannot heal every scrape and blister that causes temporary discomfort when it may very well lead someone to becoming a stronger soldier or a more cautious sorcerer."

"Yes, Your Grace. Forgive me."

Her shoulders sagged a little. "Where would it end? Choosing who may live and who must die… I will not be responsible for that, not again." She looked at him. "Would you see if Nelia has returned yet? I wish to speak to her."

Bowen bowed and left quickly.

Mylah watched him go and then turned her gaze to the woman before her. "It appears that the Gods wished for our paths to cross once more Tarian of Sepelite, and yet that seems to pose a great risk to you. Perhaps one day we may meet when you are not covered in your own blood." Her voice was soft, and tinged with sorrow. "Although I doubt it, somehow. There is always blood, or bone, or broken heart. An unending cycle of cuts and bruises until we each fall into Amara's realm, and under the light of some distant moon we seek redemption in her cold embrace. Still," she reached down and lightly touched her fevered brow, "you do not belong to the Lady of Death just yet."

Pale blue light flowed down from Mylah's hand and settled upon Tarian's skin for a moment before it sank gently into her flesh.

A shadow briefly passed over the sun, and then it was gone. The queen sighed quietly and stepped away, her hands clasped behind her back.

Rafael moved through the trees, muttering to himself as his thoughts wandered from place to place. Dark memories trailed through his mind in these quiet moments; faces of those long since dead hovered at the edges, reaching out with haunting whispers and pleas for mercy.

He shook his head and bid the ghosts to fade once more. Time was wearing on, and there was much yet to be done.

The scent of Mysta lingered upon his skin and in his hair, and it made his stomach turn. Chaos and death had followed them across Sepelite since their arrival, and he was beginning to suspect that the scouting reports had failed to mention a lot of details, or else they had not been fully briefed before their departure from Deamorte.

He pushed the idea away with a snarl; he was a veteran experienced in battle and later in medical care, excelling in a field that was dominated by mages. He had seen countless villages and towns razed, pillaged, and burnt; there was no reason for this one to affect him so. And yet, as the minutes slipped by, he couldn't rid himself of a growing sense of unease.

A few more of the mages had awoken, and a buzz of conversation wove through the makeshift camp; the physician glanced around until his gaze settled upon a familiar figure leaning against a distant tree, lost in thought.

"Useless bloody…" Rafael sighed loudly and turned to go back. "Can't trust these damned sorcerers with even the simplest of tasks. Watch the lass, don't fuck off and leave her vulnerable, call me if something goes wrong, how does that translate to go and brood by an infernal fucking tree?"

Soft rainclouds gathered in the east, blanketing the world from divine gaze. Archaic whispers threaded through the woodland, dancing through the undergrowth and teasing the minds of those who still loitered in its shadows.

The physician stopped in his tracks, his bushy eyebrows raised and his mouth agape; a cool breeze slithered around his legs. "Well I'll be damned. You! Go and fetch Bowen, tell him to get his idle arse over here!"

"Yes sir." The nearby scout ran off at speed.

"Brig's balls! Brig's bloody balls, how did…" Rafael approached the table, scratching his head. "How are you feeling, lass?"

Bowen came crashing through the trees a few moments later.

"And just what the fuck were you doing?" Rafael scowled at him. "I told you to stay here with her."

"Is she all right? What happened?"

"You've got eyes, don't you? Take a look."

Tarian was awake, her fever broken and her injuries mostly healed; she watched them both with a slightly bemused look.

"But I thought she…"

"Aye well, clearly we were wrong about that. Stubbornness is a marvellous trait in a person when it comes to survival, and this one seems to have it in abundance."

Tarian began to sit up. "Would one of you like to tell me what's going on?"

Rafael and Bowen exchanged a glance, until the physician finally shrugged and rubbed his nose. "Don't move around so much, you need to take it easy. A few of these injuries are going to take time to heal properly, and if you're not careful you might reopen some of them."

"I should go and fetch Her Grace."

"You didn't tell me the boss was back."

Tarian swung her legs over the edge of the table with a grimace and pushed herself off; she landed on the soft ground with a grunt. Rafael rolled his eyes in disapproval.

"I should speak with your queen, if she is here."

"You ain't getting rid of us that easily; we'll go with you just in case. I can't have guts falling out all over camp, it would ruin my reputation."

"Very well. Take me to her."

Bowen wrung his hands as he moved to one side of her; his stomach knotted and his mouth went dry as he thought of barging in on Mylah unannounced with a woman he had declared almost dead not even an hour ago. The queen had never questioned his competence, but she would surely overlook any personal bias if he started to display such a lack of it.

The pain was ebbing away from Tarian's body with every second that scuttled by, and her strength was returning. She frowned as she looked at the men and women moving around the trees. "This camp seems much smaller than the one you took me to previously. Is this a simple scouting party? Your blacksmith and armourer cannot possibly be here, and –"

"They were needed elsewhere."

Nobody turned to watch the trio pass by; warriors and mages consulted with each other as the scouts drifted away beyond the wooded boundaries. Bowen gritted his teeth as they skirted around the embers of a dying fire and Mylah came into view. She had her back to them, and the air around her rippled with a portal to Luxnoctis. Berne stood before her, his arms crossed and his brow furrowed. As they walked closer, the portal shimmered and another figure came into view behind him; a man was shackled to the soiled wall, his head lolling forward to show that clumps of hair had fallen out in an odd pattern across his skull. A large cut ran the length of his neck, jutting up into his marred jawline and away to what would have once been an ear. His naked torso was heavily lacerated and bruised, and was all that now remained of his body. His flesh and skin hung down in thick strips, and his broken spine dangled listlessly; one of his arms was no longer attached, lying instead upon the sodden floor, whilst the other had been gored and fractured.

"Did he yield any further information?"

"Not much; it was a little difficult to hear him at times. His skin ripped as the larvae writhed within, and he had a tendency to howl, but we did get the names of a few co-conspirators."

"Deal with them."

"Yes ma'am."

The portal winked out, and the queen rolled her shoulders before turning to face the people behind her. Tarian stared, her eyes awash with horror, whilst Rafael and Bowen shifted uncomfortably.

"I see you have recovered."

"What… what was that? What did you do to that man?"

Mylah gestured for the physician to leave. "What was necessary."

"Necessary? You think that torture is *necessary?*"

"He was a traitor."

"He couldn't even hurt you!"

"But he could have harmed someone else. Do you really think that you know my reasons and methods better than I do, Tarian of Sepelite? What right have you to question what it is that I do here?" She turned to Bowen. "I hope you have a good explanation for this."

"Your Grace, I apologise for the interruption. I haven't been able to locate Scout Hale as of yet, and since Tarian had recovered from her injuries and wished to speak with you, I thought perhaps she could provide some insight into what we encountered in the town of Mysta."

"I have no need of such information; that is why I did not ask you to seek it out."

"Don't talk to him like that." Tarian took a step forward. "You might call yourself the Empress of Cadere, but what have you actually done for anyone here? You must have known how dire our situation was, and yet you did nothing! You could have driven off the magical blight, healed the sick and saved so many lives, but you chose to sit over in Luxnoctis and do nothing!"

"You think I should have left a land badly damaged by decades of war to fend for itself? For another we didn't even know existed until recently? Luxnoctis had seen its magic deteriorate and decay until it created ghouls that hunted anything with life in its veins; crops failed and livestock wasted away into nothing, leaving people to starve and wither in their beds. You may have nothing and no one to think about other than yourself, but we do not all have that luxury."

Rage seethed within Tarian; sweat prickled the back of her neck and she bunched her hands into fists. Memories of Bryn swam before her and she stumbled; Mylah grabbed hold of her without thinking, but she pulled away and snarled. "You are as much of a tyrant as Dullahan could ever have claimed to be! We have suffered so much here, and yet what have you sacrificed?"

Mylah narrowed her eyes. "What have I *sacrificed?* More than you could know… more than I hope you ever do." She turned to leave.

"Don't you walk away from me! Your sycophantic disciples may believe your lies, but I can see that you don't understand what it means to be in pain, to have those you care about taken from you, and know that whilst someone had the power to stop it they never considered it to be worth their time."

The queen was still for a moment.

Bowen's heart hammered against his ribs as her eyes flickered to him and then back to Tarian.

"Everybody I ever loved is dead because of me." Mylah's words hissed with anger. "My family were burnt alive as I sailed away on a ship filled with my countrymen who were then murdered when it docked. My six year old daughter and her great-grandmother were slaughtered in their home, and my beloved threw herself from a tower because she could not stand the pain that brought her. My friends and comrades were eaten alive, executed, torn apart, and massacred in battle just so I could reach the King and slit his throat. Fanatical followers of his have hounded me ever since and they have seen to the deaths of many who were undeserving of such a fate. I have been the reason for hundreds going early to their graves, and though their faces will forever haunt my dreams, I shall never have the chance to walk in Amara's realm beside them." She started to move away once more, and her voice calmed. "No doubt you'll be leaving us again shortly. Bowen, see to it that she has suitable weapons and clothing for whatever journey she chooses to make. Oh, and when you are done, bring me the Solis crystal she gave back to you."

Silence reigned for a few minutes.

Tarian finally looked at the mage and sighed. "That was not what I intended."

"Her Grace has been… troubled of late. We were informed a few nights ago that a good friend of ours is gravely ill. He suffered many wounds at the battle that finally saw Dullahan slain, and never truly recovered. Now, what's this about a crystal I'm supposed to have in my possession?"

"Ah, fuck. I was meant to bring it to you but then that… incident occurred, and I forgot all about it. I did wear the belt with the pouch that she gave me just in case I ran into you again, but I must have lost them both."

"During the storm, no doubt?"

"Maybe, although…" She frowned. "No, surely not."

Bowen raised his eyebrows and tilted his head slightly. "What is it?"

"I wasn't far from Ancora when it fell…" She shuddered. "I had been trying to get back there, but I was injured and there was just so much chaos. Something had pinned me down before a flare of magic destroyed it, and I just lay there, watching the building collapse. A friend of mine came to find me, she kept calling out my name, but I was so tired… there was darkness all around, and I just wanted to close my eyes and rest. I could hear her voice, she was muttering about '*She of the Many Names*' and wailed that I had left her behind, betrayed her, and she would have to go on alone. She thought I was dead."

"Take your time; this can't be easy to talk about."

"No, but… what if she took the crystal? I know I had it when the storm began, and I can't imagine that the monsters that attacked us would have had the intelligence to know what it was."

Bowen tapped his chin. "It's possible. I will speak to Her Grace about this, and see what she thinks. Are you sure that she was talking about a woman of many names?"

"Yes." Tarian rubbed the back of her neck. "Although I don't know why. If your queen is so powerful, can't she just… I don't know, tap into Aneira's thoughts and see if she did take it, and if so find out where she's headed so we can get it back?"

"That would be extremely dangerous. Her Grace wields incredible magic, but mind-reading is a delicate art that takes many years to perfect. It would not just be a person's thoughts she would have access to, but their memories, dreams, and even their bodily functions. The slightest disturbance to the caster can result in a frozen heart or a melted brain for the recipient. It is also possible to lose yourself in the mind of another, and that can be quite a terrifying place to wander endlessly."

Mylah sat upon a fallen trunk, her fingers dancing absentmindedly along the moss that had curled around its flaky bark. She watched the Morsus approach in its slow, methodical way, and her thoughts drifted away to a different place; she could almost hear Kitten's voice calling out to her, and her hand went to the leather braid at her wrist.

The wind pulled at her hair, and she snapped back to reality. The creature had almost reached her position, so she got to her feet and waited.

"Mortifera, we have yet to finish our discussion, but still deception falls between us."

"I told you that I would speak to the others on your behalf when the time came."

"It is not that of which I have doubts." The creature finally came to rest before her, and its aura briefly shimmered red. "The mortal that was taken from the battlefield has recovered, instead of being delivered for honoured sacrifice."

"I never said you could have her body." Mylah raised her eyebrows and shook her head. "You think to trick me into feeling shame, Morsus. Is your hunger truly so great that you think it wise to manipulate our agreement?"

It said nothing for a few moments, but its eye swivelled to and fro as thoughts raced through its mind. A hacking cough finally broke its silence, splattering the floor in front of it with yellow slime.

"Your Grace?"

Mylah turned, and the Morsus growled; Bowen and Tarian stood before them, unable to tear their gaze from the squat creature.

"Is something wrong?"

"We, ah, wished to speak with you privately, ma'am."

"Such insolence!" The Morsus glowed red once more. "Pathetic mortals with ceaseless claims and wants and needs! This realm is nightmarish enough without having to associate with such filth! Be gone from our sight, pitiful beasts."

Mylah held up her hand and nodded at Bowen. "I will be along shortly, go back and wait for me. Has Hale returned yet?"

"Not to my knowledge, Your Grace."

An awkward silence descended upon the pair as they walked away; clouds gathered overhead and cast a quiet gloom across the landscape.

"What the fuck is that thing she's talking to?"

"It's a Morsus. Perhaps I should start teaching classification of monsters, seeing as no one ever seems to know more than the basics."

"But what is it doing here?"

Bowen shrugged. "You could always ask after we've informed the queen that your friend has stolen her Solis crystal."

"Sure, why not? Piss her off twice, I can't see that ending badly at all." Tarian stretched out her arms and looked up at the sky. "There's something you should probably know about Aneira."

"Oh?"

"She was… concerned, to say the least, about Mylah's arrival, and I fear I contributed greatly to that. But you have to understand, we had been under a great strain for years; the blight wiped out so many of our mages and the Conjury fell apart. Our sky seemed to bleed above us as though the Gods themselves had been slaughtered, and the ground beneath our feet became barren. There were shared dreams of an invasion from the west, and when Alban…"

Bowen waited patiently, watching her eyes swell with tears.

She shook her head. "Did you happen to see him? After Aneira's voice faded away, I heard him calling desperately for her. He came to my side and wept, saying she had gone to a place he could not follow, for he was too old to make the journey, and that if I had died elsewhere she would not have been blinded to his presence by my corpse. Then there came this strange rumbling noise, and he cursed rather loudly." She wiped the tears away with the back of her hand. "I think he cast some magic, but I didn't hear anything more of him after that. The light had almost completely faded, but everything around me was warm and there was this soft music from somewhere in the darkness. All I wanted to do was sleep."

"When we found you…" Bowen pinched the bridge of his nose and sighed. "When we found you there was an elderly man nearby, but he passed into Amara's realm within seconds of our arrival. There were several rocks above you both, being held at bay by a spell. He saved your life."

"Don't praise him too highly, he clearly thought I was already dead. Besides, Alban was never fond of me; he had desired my mother's affection long before she married my father. My brothers used to joke that he must have cursed me whilst I was still in her womb so I wouldn't carry any magic. His spell preventing my being crushed to death would have been nothing more than coincidence and luck combined." Realisation crept in like a long shadow and it wrapped slowly around Tarian; she was quiet for a while as sorrow burrowed into her heart.

Not wanting to press her, Bowen walked with his hands clasped behind his back and his head slightly bowed. The trees around them rustled as they passed, humming ancient secrets that no one seemed able to hear.

"People used to say this place was cursed, or haunted. Maybe both." Tarian's words were almost a whisper. "I wonder if that is what they will say of Mysta in time. My home is a pile of rubble and ash, and… all those people. Gods, I took so many of them into Ancora, we thought it would be safe. The mages were supposed to protect it, protect them, but… you found no other survivors?"

Bowen shook his head.

"Then it's all gone. They're all gone. What am I going to do now?"

*

The shadows had grown long when Mylah finally appeared, her face drawn and her eyes tired. She carried a small wooden cup filled with bitter tea, steam rising up from it like tiny white tendrils.

Bowen had fallen asleep against an old log, his head resting upon faded scorch marks from some long forgotten thunderstorm. Tarian sat next to him, one hand clasped around Bryn's pendant at her neck; she looked up as the Monarch slowly approached.

The queen ran her free hand through her greying hair. "Are you hungry?"

"One of your mages came by some time ago with dried fruit and some ale."

"All right. Do you mind if I join you? I want to apologise for, ah, for –"

"Throwing me across your campsite and nearly breaking my neck?"

Mylah grimaced slightly. "I never should have allowed myself to lose control like that, I'm sorry."

"Your friend is not with you?"

"My friend?"

"The Morsus. Bowen told me that you made some kind of treaty with them, but I truly wonder how you can stand to be around such beasts."

"We have hunted each other for centuries and left countless fields awash with blood. Atrocities have been committed on both sides; it seemed like it was time to try and make peace."

"But we ate the Sceleratis that attacked my scouting party, and that Morsus seems to think that humans are nothing more than soulless cattle."

"Yes, well. I never said it was perfect."

Bowen snorted in his sleep and turned his head away from the women; a small smile swept across Mylah's lips as she watched him.

"You care about him."

"We have known each other for a long time. After Eris..." She glanced away. "After everything that happened, he put all else aside to help me. I don't know how I would have made it through those first few months without both him and Berne by my side."

Tarian rubbed the back of her neck and shot a quick glance at the slumbering mage; he was snoring softly. Silence lingered between the women for a while; ancient ghosts danced upon the breeze and disappeared into the ether.

"How do you cope with knowing that you'll never see them again?" The words slipped out before she could stop them.

Mylah was quiet for some time, before she brought her closed fist up to her lips; she blew upon her uncurling fingers and birthed the magic that would conjure the forms of her loved ones.

Tarian stared in amazement at the glimmering figures of a woman and child standing before her, but when she looked over to Mylah she saw only sadness in the Monarch's eyes.

"Every time I summon these shadows, they're a little less accurate. Just... tiny details, worn down and lost as time passes by – a freckle missing here, a wrinkle smoothed out there. And one day I won't be able to remember them at all. They were everything to me, but as the years flow ever onward, I will forget their faces and even now... even now their voices fade from my mind. The markers I left by their graves will wear down and turn to dust, and my memories of them will do the same."

"What were they like?"

Minutes stretched out between them, the question heavy upon the air; the crystalline pendant around Tarian's neck glittered in the late sunlight.

"Eris was beautiful." There was pain in Mylah's voice now, and a desperate longing that fell into cracking sorrow. "The first time we met she seemed to me to be a goddess that just appeared out of nowhere, this grinning fool with red hair and dark eyes. She was passionate and driven, full of good humour, and as stubborn as an old man. Even Erebus couldn't make her back down when she railed against injustice and bias; she would get infuriated when she felt unable to stop him. There were times when I thought that her iron will was about to break and she might try to head-butt the tyranny right out of his skull. And she was powerful; I've never seen anyone fight like she could."

"Was she a mage?"

"She was not born with magic, but there was something arcane and terrifying granted to her later on that she could tap into. It was never something she felt truly comfortable with, and so she would mostly use daggers the way that her grandmother taught her. She could go through an entire battle without taking a scratch, and yet still managed to get bruised during training, or when she fell off a log, or…" Mylah's words trailed away as the figures before them shimmered and dispersed into wisps of pale blue mist; she shivered and sighed. "Kitten was a godling child. She was bright, and sweet, and she had a love of learning that only seemed to grow over time. I did not get to see her as much as I wish I had; no matter how many times I planned to visit, there was always another battle or campaign, or some pointless scouting mission."

The sun was sinking behind the horizon, and darkness began to rise up through the weary sky; a few stars peeped out as the Gods gathered to listen.

Mylah finished her tea and stared into the empty cup. "What about you? Do you have family that you would like us to take you to?"

"My brothers are in Caeli. I have nowhere to go now that…"

Bowen awoke with a loud grunt which startled both of the women; he looked at them in surprise, and then wiped his mouth with the back of his hand. "Your Grace."

"Seneschal. Sleep well?"

"Not really, this place is full of disturbing dreamscapes." He yawned as he sat up, cracking his knuckles. "I never thought I would miss the bland images that Corignis could serve up on a nightly basis if you just let your mind wander before you went to bed. Even Deamorte had a habit of… Your Grace, you're not wearing your crown. It wouldn't be right if that was stolen too."

Mylah raised an eyebrow at him. "Has something else been taken?"

Realisation dawned immediately and the mage scratched his jaw, his fingertips lingering upon the old scar that ran across it.

Tarian came to his aid. "I did not have the chance to return the Solis crystal to him, and I believe that a friend of mine may have possession of it… a friend of mine who had taken over the governing of Mysta, and is now convinced that you bring nothing but destruction and ruin to Sepelite."

"I see. Do you have any idea why they might have wanted the crystal, or where they could have gone?"

"There was something I overheard when I first returned to Ancora." She hesitated, and rubbed the back of her neck. "I don't know if anything ever came of it, but Aneira spoke of trying to find the Anghenfil and someone called the Gilded Lord. She was interrupted before she said anything about where they might be headed."

Mylah's face drained of colour and she got to her feet.

"Is something wrong, Your Grace?" Bowen frowned.

"I need to find Nelia, *now*. See to it that the campsite is packed up quickly, we must move before dawn."

"Of course, but –"

She looked back over her shoulder. "Thank you for your assistance, Tarian. You are more than welcome to accompany us whilst we try to find your friend."

Inky darkness swept over the skyline and swallowed the heavens whole; Tarian watched as the queen moved swiftly away and Bowen hurried after her.

Heaviness settled in the woman's heart and her throat tightened; the heavens were burdened with death rattles and broken whimpers. Her thoughts turned to the tiny flames barely lit and yet now extinguished beneath Ancora's hefty bulk, and sorrow flooded her veins. In those few moments, it seemed as though all the world had turned to shadow, and never again would it see the breath of sunlight.

Her chest heaved suddenly and great sobs spilled out into the oncoming night. Bryn's face swam before her eyes, gaunt and grey and free; her hand darted to the pendant that sat nestled against her skin, and for a brief moment a breeze passed softly over her cheek.

Noises rattled through the dusk as Mylah's retinue set to their tasks; Tarian glanced over and listened to the murmurs of people more accustomed to scattering to the wind than she, and after a moment she wiped away the tears that ran down her face. She got to her feet and dusted herself down, and moved out into the relentless darkness.

*

Heady smoke drifted up towards the celestial cradle, a whisper of aromatic herbs curling through the misty curtain of rain. A small Jittern watched from afar as a group of hooded men and women trudged through the gloom, their fiery torches pushing back the encroaching shadows. Magic and mist swirled at their feet, masking their weary footsteps and spinning out in ghostly tendrils to disperse into the ether.

The woods gave way to a small clearing of scorched earth and silent undergrowth; priests robed in red and white encircled a raging bonfire, incantations and incense alike drifting against the sodden darkness; a few solitary mages wove spells from the shadows to keep the flames dancing despite the weather.

A priestess moved towards the pyre, her hands held skyward; water ran down her olive skin as she turned her face up to the bleeding heavens. She brought her arms back to her sides and then turned to those who had gathered around her, and a smile crept to her lips.

Seconds ticked by in relative silence.

"Today marks a new beginning for us all. As we step into the light of the moon's rebirth I, Ava, Priestess of Merfyd, give the blood of the strong to the Gods as a holy sacrifice. No greater honour could we bestow upon this faithful and –"

"Stop!"

The crowd turned to see another woman crash through the trees, her black curly hair sticking to her pallid skin and her dark eyes seething with rage. Some of the priests shifted to one side to allow an armoured man to block her path and his arm was suddenly around her waist, holding her back.

"Get the fuck off me, Rhydian!"

"Steel yourself Seren or I will have the mages sedate you." He tightened his grip as she struggled against him. "Gods forsake you woman, relent! You know this has to happen."

The priestess turned back to those who had gathered around the pyre, and took an ornate dagger from the belt around her waist; moonlight slithered down the blade, kissing and curling around the sanctified metal. She took up a quiet chant as yet more hooded men appeared from the trees, leading a dappled warhorse between them; the great beast snorted and pulled against the reins, its eyes swivelling as the smell of the smoke gave way to the sight of the roaring flames.

"I swear to all that is holy if you do not unhand me I will see you dead!"

"It will all be over soon, you're overreacting. This is how things have to be, you know this. Stop acting like a child."

A gentle, melodic spell echoed out from the mages and the horse suddenly calmed; it walked towards the pyre without hesitation. Ava shot a glance at them before plunging the dagger into the animal's chest.

Seren's heartbroken scream echoed through the darkened woodland; she strained against Rhydian's grip but could only watch in horror as the blade was brought out of the horse's flesh to be drawn across its throat.

Ava, showered now in dark metallic scarlet, raised her arms once more towards the moon. "Oh Glorious Ones who look down upon us from Sylvad's golden shores, see now the offering, strong and fierce, that we so gladly make to you. May you bestow your blessings upon us, and guide us from the ferocious shadow that has loomed over our land for too many days and nights."

Seren, suddenly released from her restraints, glared at the detestable congregation gathered in the clearing; fire burned within her belly and vengeance within her mind. She turned from them in disgust and melted back into the shadows.

Ava sighed sadly and looked to Rhydian. "Go after her. Make her understand."

He nodded and disappeared into the trees.

"They will pay." Seren's whispers hissed within the gloom. "They will *all* pay. I will see their huts and hovels and temples turned into ash! The sky will be so thick with smoke that no deity will be able to hear their pitiful prayers. I will see this world given to the flames and I will rejoice!"

"You should not speak such monstrous words Seren, lest the Gods hear and turn them into prophecy."

She turned to watch as Rhydian stumbled around in the uneasy dark, his overly armoured bulk suddenly an encumbrance.

Copper tinted moonlight streamed through the thicket; insects hummed lazily in the undergrowth as rodents scurried underfoot.

"How could you let them do this to me? To him?"

"He was a fine creature who carried Father through many battles, and you after him; I understand why this must be hard for you, but his death could not have been more worthy. When they came to me for permission, I was –"

"His life was not yours to take, wretch!" She spat at his feet.

"Sister, you –"

"Do not call me that! I will never forgive the womb that carried us for spitting out a vile and cowardly subordinate such as you."

"Rhydian!" Ava's voice rang out behind them. "Rhydian, come and see! The Gods have heard our prayers and sent us our salvation!"

The man turned on his heel and left; Seren narrowed her eyes and crept after him, curiosity overshadowing all else.

The priests and mages all stood quietly, their heads bowed; the fire had already died, leaving only a trail of smoke and a smell that turned her stomach. There were more people in the clearing, all weapons and uniforms, and magic crackled in the air around them.

Ava pointed upwards, a wild grin upon her lips. Seren followed her gaze to the night sky, free of its rusted taint, and her eyes widened.

Her brother dropped to one knee before a woman who was watching him intently; moonlight danced upon the crown she wore in her greying hair.

"Sir Rhydian of the Holy Order at Delyth at your service, my lady. For many years I have aided faithfully those in Sepelite whose needs were greater than my own, but I wish now to pledge myself to you, Divine One, to seek honour in your most glorious name. I am yours to command."

"You are far from home."

Seren knew it was not the response her brother would have expected, and a wry smile flickered briefly across her lips. She shook her head, wiped the last few tears away with her hand, and returned to the forest.

Shadows reached out with long, spindling fingers, their cold and comforting touch sweeping across the woman's neck and shoulders before drifting away to paths unknown. Grief hovered at the corners of her mind, an unwelcome thrum upon the threads between memory and nightmare; the wraith of her father stepped out of the gloomy web, tall and broad and bedecked in tarnished armour. His matted flaxen hair stuck to his face, the once kind features mutilated by gore and gaping wounds; the skin around his empty eye sockets was charred and chunks of it were missing along his jawline, exposing a grisly maggot infested burrow.

   Seren shook her head and the ghost vanished. She turned her thoughts instead to the woman who had come at the behest of the corrupted priests and their unholy sacrifice, who had cleansed the sky of the blood that had clung to it for years, who had stepped onto a path with no return; her heart hammered against her ribs and dizziness washed over her. Her lungs were suddenly aflame, all breath burning the back of her throat and scorching her lips; she stumbled to one side and fell against a gnarled trunk. Her father's voice screeched out from somewhere nearby, and there were footsteps behind her; panic flooded her veins and her stomach knotted. She could smell the burning corpse of her horse, the stench of his skin and flesh and hair settling upon her like a soiled shroud; carrion birds cried out in the darkened canopies above as some of them took to the skies and spiralled away. Someone was behind her, following her every movement; she could feel warm, fetid breath upon the air and sweat beaded her brow. She pushed away from the tree and staggered forwards as the world around her slid and curled into something unnatural and coarse; ghouls peered out at her from every darkened crevice, leering and lurching with their waxy, gored faces. Her head throbbed with pain that leaked down behind her eyes; scarlet liquor slithered from her nose across her lips, dripping down into the howling undergrowth. Tainted light crashed through the trees and dragged across her, burning and scratching any exposed skin; she gritted her teeth as a taste metallic and unwelcome swarmed her mouth and lingered upon her tongue. She could feel them crawling up her legs: clawed insects with scuttling purpose and poisoned fangs, looking for vulnerable flesh to sink into. Her chest tightened and her limbs were suddenly weak; she could feel the strength flowing out of her into the ether, snatched and torn by phantoms archaic and frenzied, their ravenous hunger inflamed by the scent of her blood.

"Seren?"

Everything went still. She looked up, her breathing rapid and her vision blurred; the forest around her was quiet, and calm. A gentle hand touched upon her shoulder.

"Seren, are you all right?"

The familiar voice wrapped around her thoughts and ushered them away from the brink of destruction. The world righted itself, and the cruel apparitions vanished. A woman stood before her, warm light from the lantern she held washing over them both; she was dressed in a beige robe patterned with gold, strands of light grey hair tumbling down from a loose bun beneath the hood of her cloak. Her dark blue eyes searched Seren's face as she lifted her free hand up to her tear stained cheek and cupped it softly; wrinkles and scars creased her pale skin in places as a weak smile crossed her ruby lips.

Seren stared at her for a moment before she sobbed and fell into her embrace.

"Hush my little one, hush. What has pained you so?"

For a while there came no reply; Seren allowed her fears to seep away into the night as she buried her face into the woman's robe, the scent of sandalwood and honey wine awakening thoughts of home.

After a few minutes, she pulled away and wiped her weary face. "What are you doing here, Scole? I thought you were in Cragen."

"My duties brought me to Sepelite, but I am about to return to Caeli. There is a bay not too many miles from here with a ship waiting to take me back to Delyth, perhaps you would like to join me? I have a carriage here, so we wouldn't have to walk all the way to the shore. And you have been so sorely missed at the temple."

Seren snorted and glanced away. "I doubt the Gods wish to have me tarnishing their sacred ground."

"Your heart has been burdened again. What happened?"

"Rhydian gave them Torge as a sacrifice." Her voice wavered.

"Oh my dear, I am sorry."

"Ava drew his blood and sent him to the flames." She looked up at the sky. "And apparently summoned a queen with the power to clear the heavens."

"That would be Mylah of Amissa, the new Eternal Monarch." Scole took her hand and squeezed it gently. "I am sorry about Torge; I know how much he meant to both you and your father. But Ava would not have performed the sacrifice unless she thought it was necessary. It is not always easy to walk the path that the Gods set out before us, even if we understand why. You are aware that I too must follow the same rules and rituals as Ava when it is required."

"The High Priestess slitting the throats of a few sheep and goats on a festival day is not the same as murdering Torge in the middle of this forsaken forest."

Scole was quiet for a moment. "Come back to Caeli with me, Seren. You don't have to return to the temple if you don't want to, we could visit Cragen or journey up to the –"

"No." Seren shook her head and took a step back. "I can't, not yet. There are things that I need to take care of here."

Scole's eyes darkened. "You are not going after Rhydian or Ava, I hope?"

"Do you think so little of me these days? I have more important matters than petty vengeance."

"My apologies, dear one, I only meant… well, no matter. I will ensure that Torge is given the proper rites to honour his passing once I get back. You are always welcome at the temple, and I promise I won't try to make you join the priesthood again." She embraced Seren warmly and kissed her lightly on the cheek. "Not unless you wished to, of course. Will you write to me, at least?"

"When I can find the time." Seren inclined her head and fought back a surge of sorrow. "Safe journey home, Priestess."

A few minutes after Seren disappeared into the shadows, Rhydian stepped into the torchlight and knelt down before Scole. She laid her hand upon his shock of flaxen hair and smiled softly.

"I am here to escort you back to your carriage, High Priestess."

"Very well. I am anxious to get back to Caeli." She sighed and motioned for him to stand. "Take care of your sister, Rhydian. Her heart is heavy with grief and guilt and I worry for her. Try to give her solace and comfort, not your anger, when next you meet."

"She shouldn't allow her heart to govern her so readily. Torge has gone to the Gods, and his sacrifice brought us a kind of boon that I could never have anticipated. Truly we have been blessed."

They walked in silence for a while, occasionally glancing towards the sky as the rusted miasma released its grip and dispersed.

"Be careful with Queen Mylah, my dear." Scole looked up at him and then out into the darkness around them. "She is heartache made flesh."

"We all have burdens to carry, High Priestess, but I thank you for your concern. May I come and visit you when my duties so allow?"

"Of course, dear boy. I would like that."

*

Magic crackled through the air as a shock wave raced out across the bitter earth and pulled forth life from the once barren soil.

Prayers and joyous murmurs echoed through the throng of priests and mages, their eyes flickering between the Monarch and the clear sky.

Tarian sat upon a felled log some way from the others. Pain hummed through her head and she was tired; she rubbed the back of her neck and sighed. Mylah's spells seemed a little brighter than they had done before, like icy blue fire that singed the atmosphere and lingered within her vision.

Bowen walked over and held out a small wooden cup. "Are you all right?"

"Just another headache, nothing serious. Will we be staying here long?" She drank the tea and shifted uncomfortably. "I'd rather go on ahead alone if so."

"Her Grace used to get a lot of headaches, I shall ask her if there's anything she recommends for them. You could speak to Rafael of course, but sometimes I think if he's not stitching body parts back together he doesn't think it worthy of his time."

Tarian shivered and looked up as an armoured man approached, bowing before her; the murmurs in her mind faded.

"Is something troubling you? Perhaps I can be of some help? Sir Rhydian of the Holy Order at Delyth, at your –"

"Come and find me when she's ready to leave." She handed the empty cup back to Bowen, got to her feet and walked away, disappearing into the swiftly retreating shadows.

"Did I say something to offend?" Rhydian turned to the mage and sighed. "I seem to be doing that a lot lately."

Sunlight splintered across the horizon, a pale saffron spear to chase away the lurking twilight. Whispers hung upon the shivering air for a moment, crawling away to darker tides as morning clambered over the dreamy ruins; thoughts and voices slithered into unsuspecting minds, hissing and gnawing as they took root. Faded blue light hovered at the frayed edges of dreams long thought lost; ancient spells creaked into life once more, their ghoulish tendrils reaching out across the aeons to scrape along the woodland floor.

Tarian let her thoughts drift as she wandered through the trees; the crystal pendant grew heavy, the silver chain seeming to bite into her neck, and for a moment she thought she could hear Bryn's voice weaving through the glorious incandescence. She shivered and pushed onward.

Mist blanketed the ground, coiling around the woman's legs as she moved; old, decrepit melodies hung in the air for a while, their rhythms beating upon the wings of insects and birds alike. Veiled eyes kept hold of her, watching with interest as she roamed through their viridian kingdom, an unintentional intruder with a hundred shadows upon her heart. Words, soft and low, prowled through the waning half-light, hiding from the gilt tempest that clambered over the horizon and stretched out across the slumbering land. Remorse and shame lingered upon them, reaching out to brush against Tarian's throat and threatening to pull her down into the abyss alongside them.

Her hand strayed to the hilt of her sword, her fingers resting lightly upon the metal, and comfort curled around her heart; Ancora's ghosts released her from their grip and faded back into the realm of the dead.

A small bundle dropped down from a nearby branch; Tarian looked over to see an adult Jittern staring back at her, its head cocked to one side. She smiled and bent down, but it simply padded away into the mist.

"What is it doing?" A shrill voice broke the relative calm. "What is it doing? Silly human, silly, silly human! Who are you?"

Tarian looked down at a short creature that had crept silently to her side; standing at around two feet tall, its pale blue skin and patches of mossy green fur marked it as an Oculi. Thin strands of greasy white hair clung to its head, and its pale sunken eyes were rimmed with scabs of scarlet and grey. It snarled at her and wrung its hands, dancing suddenly from foot to foot and shaking its head. She watched it curiously.

"Beasts, oh wicked beasts! Coming here to my home, wicked! Who are you?"

She raised an eyebrow. "My name is Tarian."

"No, no, you lie! The scent of the Undead One is near! You bring destruction, just as she! Just as she! They call me Wren, I don't know why. They call me Wren and in wicked dreams I see them! Their faces all bashed in and splintered. Silly human creatures, full of spite. Spite and bile. They call me Wren. It's not my name."

"Did you want something?"

"Did I…?" It glared at her. "It comes into my home and asks! The Undead One… where is she? Titles and blood and bone! We would see it all burn, and then the corpses would sing no more. Their songs haunt the gloaming, so that torment and anguish is all we know! Silly… silly them. Silly us. They call me Wren. I don't know why. Where is the Undead One?"

Pain tightened around Tarian's head and her shoulders tensed. She rolled her eyes and walked away.

Wren's grimace widened, and it hissed. "How dare it! How dare it walk away! Silly, stupid human creature! It walks with the Undead One and bears her sigil, here in this sacred place! Winters pass and the corpses still sing!" It bared its teeth and started after her. "I will show it! It will pay penance and it will show its remorse, or else see its flesh rent from bone! They call me Wren. They call me Wren! We will feast upon the skin and gorge upon the meat, silly, stupid human creature! We will taste of its song, we will silence its lies! The Undead One will despair, for we will take its beast to slaughter! We will –"

Liquid spurted onto the ground as the tip of Tarian's sword jutted out from the Oculi's neck. Its eyes bulged and its mouth moved soundlessly, the last few words caught upon its jagged, oily tongue.

The weapon was withdrawn and with another swift motion it took the creature's head from its shoulders, before the body was booted away to twitch in the undergrowth.

Tarian rolled her shoulders and looked around for something to clean her blade; the world around her was still for a moment, before a low murmuring began to swell. She stood upright and lifted her shield slightly, her sword readied once more. Shadows were moving through the trees, surrounding her on all sides; she steadied her breathing and narrowed her eyes.

They swept into view like a snarling tidal wave, their feet pounding against the treacherous earth as their chattering voices flew up towards the cold and unforgiving heavens. Their eyes swivelled as they hissed and howled at her, occasionally reaching out towards Wren's corpse before snapping back to face its attacker. The scent of blood and flesh was upon the air, serving only to soak the senses of those freshly come to the scene and rile their anger further.

Vengeance was in their eyes, and war their souls.

Tarian took a step backwards, and for a moment nobody else moved; her gaze flickered from beast to beast, looking for the telltale signs she had been trained to see. The Oculi were almost motionless as they returned her stare, until a bird cried out from its sanctuary in a nearby canopy and the trance was broken.

A grotesque snarl ricocheted through the forest as the first creature launched its attack. Teeth bared and eyes wild, it hurtled towards Tarian at speed, leaping up towards her face; she spun on her heel and caught it with her shield midair. The Oculi landed with a graceless thud and squealed as its stomach was swiftly impaled by the sword still slick with the blood of its kin.

An unholy chorus echoed through the onlookers and they descended upon the human who had dared to defile their home. Two of them sprang up to claw at her face and were met with a mighty blow from the shield that cracked their jawbones and sent pain thundering through their skulls; the gory blade sang as it sliced through their necks and ripped out tendrils of flesh and viscera.

Tarian cried out as one managed to bite into her leg before she kicked it away, cursing the abhorrent creature under her breath. Sweat beaded her forehead and trickled down her back, as her heart drummed against her ribs; they were coming towards her in a wave, their turbulent cacophony shaking the dawn. The crystal pendant settled heavily against her chest and she roared, her voice drowning out theirs as she plunged the sword into their assault, hacking steadily at heads and arms and torsos.

Severed limbs littered the bloodied ground, lolling in pools of mush; the stench of bile and death arose and clung to the fetid air with its debauched grip.

A claw dragged across Tarian's cheek and split the skin; she tossed her head sharply and the perpetrator fell away. Blood seeped down her face as she crushed the creature's throat beneath her boot. She spun again and hit out at another that loitered nearby, its pathetic squeak almost lost beneath the sound of her own laughter. She stopped then and turned to those who were left, lifted her weapons to catch the early sunlight, and roared once more. They stared at her, humiliated and afraid.

"Come and die by my hands! Come! We shall see if your corpses do truly sing!"

The Oculi fled back into the trees.

Tarian lowered her arms, panting with sudden exhaustion as the exhilaration of battle wore away. She waited for a few moments to see if they would launch a second attack, but nothing came and the world was quiet once more; she knelt down and wiped her sword on some leaves before sheathing it. Her shoulders ached and there was a prickly heat creeping up through her leg; pain had clamped around her jaw and was spreading quickly to the rest of her head. For a brief moment she closed her eyes, pushing away the anger that had gripped her, and focusing instead on breathing slowly.

Once her heartbeat had calmed a little, she opened her eyes, and her cry echoed through the trees. The dirty streets of Mysta stretched out before her, shadows skittering across the rotting bodies that were strewn across the ground; pods of hair and flesh squatted in gooey puddles that rippled as a warm breeze passed over them, carrying with it the stench of fetid meat.

Tears slid down Tarian's cheeks and vomit rose in her throat; she stared at the scorched earth, desperately trying not to glance towards the mountain of rubble that had once been the almighty Ancora. Human remains were visible there, poking out of the treacherous ruins like scolding beacons to draw the eye and sever the soul.

Noises sounded from the west, and panic flooded her veins; something was moving about in the desolation, scavenging for food. Soon she could hear the slick, wet crunch that suggested an unholy gluttony satisfied only by devouring the dead.

She got slowly and unsteadily to her feet, the world before her sheathed by sudden fog; voices called out, screaming and pleading for mercy. Pain throbbed behind her eyes as she tried to move, her arms stretching out before her to become lost in the haze; something slithered across her feet and wrapped briefly around her ankle. She stumbled, squinting through the unyielding mist until her gaze was returned; amber eyes flecked with red peered out of the gloom as bony limbs stretched out towards her, beckoning with gnarled fingers that were tipped with bloodied claws.

Fear exploded in her mind.

"Flee, my little one. Get out of here!"

"Bryn?"

"Get out, get out, get out before the beast consumes you too!"

Her heart pounded against her ribs and her breath caught in her throat, but in a moment of betrayal and hesitation her body would not stir. She whimpered as the creature lurched forward, its head twitching to one side. She felt for her sword, but the sheath was empty and her shield had vanished; she was forsaken.

Laughter penetrated the distance between them, a disturbing clutch of guttural shrieks; she could not escape now, the monster had closed in on her and it knew it. She watched as its uncurled its soiled fingers and made to touch her face.

A hand clamped down on her shoulder. Mysta fell away into nothing, and Tarian stared at the empty woodland bathed in the peaceful golden glow of dawn.

"Are you all right?"

She turned slowly to face Queen Mylah, whose dulcet tones belied the savagery behind her eyes as she studied the remnants of Oculi scattered across the ground. Confusion and doubt crept into Tarian's mind and she shivered as the woman moved away, taking in the extent of the devastation with a heavy sigh.

Others were nearby, their voices carrying clearly across the calm atmosphere; Bowen was watching with concern, his eyes tracking the gash upon her face.

"Make sure you have a healer take a look at your injuries." Mylah flicked her wrist and incinerated the dismembered bodies. "Please tell the Seneschal that there is something I need to take care of, and I will join you again later."

Tarian watched her leave without saying a word. Her thoughts were sluggish and slow, as though her mind was reluctant to engage with reality.

"You're hurt." Bowen's voice slipped through to her and rattled the cage. "Will you let us help?"

Tears welled in her dark eyes as she turned to him; her heart ached and her stomach knotted, and as grief finally consumed her, she fell into his embrace.

Ancient melodies thrummed upon a westerly wind, spiralling up into an uncaring firmament and then away across the vast expanse beyond. Spectral whispers that clawed at closing minds and hushed thoughts exploded into a new crystalline cacophony, dragging along gnarled tendrils of guilt and remorse.

Time wandered on.

The Gilded Lord

*

Rafael paced back and forth, his hands clasped behind his back and his eyes closed in frustrated contemplation. Bowen glanced from him to the quiet woman wrapped in a soft blanket; Tarian sipped the Rotroot tea gingerly, her thoughts drifting away to distant dark places.

The scouts had moved on hours ago with Nelia at their head, vowing to return when necessary with a clearer idea of what lay ahead. The majority of the mages and warriors had accompanied them, leaving only a small retinue behind to guard those who were left. Mylah had not yet returned, although the day was stretching on towards noon, and people were beginning to get agitated.

"Where does she go?" Tarian's words were soft, but she did not look up at either of the men when she spoke.

Bowen sighed. "Many places, from what I can gather. Her magic is…"

"A bloody nuisance at times. Oh don't look at me like that; it would be a damned sight simpler if we knew where she was, but she just scurries off to who knows where, doing Gods know what. Striking up treaties with bloody monsters and conferring with ancient beasts that would be better off on a roasting spit than a council. And what's the point, I ask you, in having an agreement that the bastards don't even keep to amongst their own kin?"

Tarian finally looked to Bowen, who pinched the bridge of his nose and frowned.

"The Oculi refused to have anything to do with Her Grace or the accord between the Mortals and Everlasting, and as such they have forfeited the protection of the other races. Any faction or individual who attacks those protected by the agreement are considered to be an enemy without reprieve, and they are free to be hunted down by either side. Mylah gave the Everlasting the island of Amissa as a protected homeland, and they in turn have sworn to fight for her should the need ever arise."

"Aye, she could have an army of beasts at her command and yet here we poor saps are, trudging through the muck and the cold. Oh, you *could* be relaxing at home in front of a fire with a bowl of hot stew and a comfortable bed waiting, but how about instead you trail through a bunch of guts and gristle for no fucking reason?"

"Is something wrong, Rafael? You seem marginally grumpier than usual."

"Wrong? What could possibly be wrong? Other than being old and tired, and now I get to be followed around by the same bastard beasts that tore my cousin to shreds all those years past?"

"Perhaps you should thank Tarian then, for exacting a little vengeance in your stead?"

"Bah." The physician spat on the ground and continued pacing.

Footsteps approached from the west. The trio looked up to see Rhydian grinning at them; Rafael muttered under his breath and turned back to his own thoughts.

"Has there been any word yet on Her Divine Grace? Only I was hoping to speak to her about matters of great importance before too long."

"Then speak." Mylah's voice startled them all.

"I really wish you wouldn't do that, boss."

"I get to hear so much more of what people actually think when they don't know I'm listening, Rafael." A wry smile twitched across her lips. "You wish to speak to me, Sir Rhydian?"

He bowed low. "Yes Your Divine Grace, if it is not too much trouble."

"And are these to be your words, or those of a priest? You should learn to be wary of the cassock, for it often hides stains and deceptions greater than you could even begin to imagine."

A look of confusion passed over Rhydian's face and he frowned at her. "I… speak with no voice but my own, Your Divine Grace, I assure you. Although I see no reason for my lady the High Priestess Scole to be scorned in such a manner; I have always known her to provide the wisest counsel and never utter anything that she knew to be false."

Mylah waved her hand dismissively. "Get on with it."

"Forgive me but I am… disturbed by your attitude towards she who was like a mother to me, especially when there is no discernible reason for it."

"Priests lie – and I have heard enough of those lately. Get on with your speech."

"I… I mean no disrespect Gracious One, but it is unheard of to speak to a member of the Holy Order about our honoured leaders in such a way. If you cannot see the blessed path that she walks upon, I fear we may struggle to come to an understanding."

Tarian got to her feet and glared at the uncomfortable man. "Grow the fuck up; you're not licking the floors of the temple now. Either say your piece or shut your mouth, your rambling is giving me a headache."

Mylah stifled a laugh and raised her eyebrows at him. "Well?"

*

Seren paced back and forth by the campfire, her hands clasped firmly behind her back as she watched shadows dancing around the lonely wilderness. The ghosts of those long since gone flickered around the edges of the flames, teasing her as they hovered between the realm of the living and the realm of the dead.

"Go back to Amara and leave me be." She pinched the bridge of her nose. "And take your damned spectres with you."

"We are not ghouls conjured from some shadowed place, I assure you." A woman with flaxen hair stepped into the light cast out by the small fire. Magic sparked at her fingertips. "We are flesh and blood, just like you."

Seren snorted. "Don't bother with all that *kindred pilgrim spirits* bullshit. I don't care if you think that we are wandering upon the same path, or heading for the same rotten end, or that the Gods have brought us together for a reason. We were not all born with the ability to shoot lightning from our bodies, but I can and will peel the skin from your skulls and feed it to whichever beast approaches me next."

"Delightful." The spell winked out. "Are you part of the priesthood, perhaps?"

Seren made to move away, her lips curling in anger.

"Wait! Before you go, could you tell us if you have seen anything unusual come this way? Groups of people in armour marked with a foreign sigil, perhaps, or a woman with –"

"If you're looking for Mylah of Amissa then I suggest you be on your way and leave me the fuck alone."

"You do not approve of her?"

"Sacrifices were made that should not have been." Seren spat on the ground. "Now get out of my way before I feed your bloated carcasses to a wandering Saprus."

"Hold a moment." The woman glanced at her companion. "Would you happen to know anything about the Gilded Lord?"

Five

Sunlight streamed in through the small windows, drifting across dusty flagstones and away into the corners of the quiet room. A fire crackled in the hearth and candles flickered in sconces upon the walls; rattling breaths crept up into the stilled atmosphere, tiny traitorous clouds that whispered of a gentle, fading longing.

A bed smothered in blankets and soft cushions sat in the pale splendour, an old sword propped up against its wooden frame. Hushed noises echoed from outside: birdsong lifted from murmuring canopies upon a cool breeze, insects hovering around the late blooming flowers in the wild garden, people moving softly in another room.

Mylah sat silently, Tusk's hand clasped in her own. She watched as his chest rose and fell, the seconds between each breath growing steadily longer. Tears fell down her cheeks and she bit her bottom lip to keep it from trembling.

His words had trailed away some hours ago, and for a time now his eyes had remained closed; the moments seemed to drop into one another until they were finally stopped by one last drawn out sigh.

She kissed his hand softly. "Goodbye old friend."

After a few minutes, the queen stood and left the room, nodding at the attendants who were waiting to wash and prepare the body.

Bowen was nearby, pacing up and down, his thoughts clearly caught somewhere between misfortune and grief. She watched him for a short while before clearing her throat.

"Oh, Your Grace, has… has he…?"

She nodded. "He has gone to the Lady of Death, seemingly at peace and without pain; I think I was able to do that much at least."

"I…" Sorrow bit through the tension and he glanced away. "I will miss him."

"Does something else trouble you, Seneschal?"

Bowen hesitated as he wiped his eyes. "A messenger arrived from Metumontis whilst you were… earlier, a messenger arrived earlier. It seems that my family's temple has been ransacked, my lady."

She fought back a surge of anger. "Was anyone hurt?"

He nodded. "My father suffered a few broken bones, as did some of the other priests, but nothing fatal."

"At least that is something. I am so tired of all this death, Bowen. It seems to follow us around like a macabre child."

"Indeed Your Grace, but I am afraid we were not as fortunate as it may seem. Relics that were in my father's safekeeping have been stolen, including a tome on the Venerated King of Hallowed Ember and Carrion."

The Monarch struggled to keep her composure; she pinched the bridge of her nose and closed her eyes.

Bowen watched her quietly. "I'm sorry."

"What good are the bloody priests if they cannot even do their most basic task?" Her voice bellowed suddenly down the corridor. "They squat upon golden thrones in those desecrated halls, growing fat on wine and flesh and doing nothing that the Gods ask of them! Nothing! They dare to preach about morals and values and sanctity when they cannot even guard a book! A book! How fucking hard can that be?"

The ground began to tremble beneath their feet; dust showered down from the archaic stone walls and settled in the space between them. Magic crackled through the air in tiny arcs of blue light.

"Your Grace, I don't think anyone could read it, the ancient script is…"

Thunder rumbled overhead and the sky darkened; the candles in the sconces blew out.

"They claim to be a moral compass for the citizens of Cadere whilst they squander the powers bestowed upon them until nothing is left but pools of putrid deceit! How can they be entrusted with the souls of the living when they cannot even look after a fucking book? Answer me!"

Bowen stepped back a little and raised his hands; he glanced from her to the shuddering walls whilst he searched for something to say.

The drums of war echoed upon the distant horizon; militaristic phantoms rose from long forgotten verse and spiralled into a bloodied sky, their gnarled reach stretching out across the beleaguered landscape.

Anger swirled through Mylah as a storm, unimpeded by clemency.

Archaic songs splintered out into the hazy atmosphere; whispers of death and destruction were carried by ethereal hands until they plunged into dark, icy depths. Betrayal and intrigue cascaded across the centuries, timeworn and woven with decrepit thread; ashes and dust blew upon westerly winds until all was smothered but the grave markers of the sovereigns who had gone before.

Mylah screamed.

The wall beside her blew out in an explosion of ancient masonry that hurled across the courtyard; sparks and smoke filled the air in its wake.

Bowen stared at the destruction and gulped.

The queen looked down at her hands; she tried to steady her breathing before turning to the mage before her. He was searching the scene beyond the layers of dust to see if anyone had been hurt; a portal opened up beside him and he glanced back at her.

"We should investigate ourselves."

"But Your Grace, I –"

"That's an order, Seneschal. Move."

Drab skies loomed over the Temple of Katarina, a mixture of cloud and ash that threatened to smother the sky until all below it was awash with grey. Mounds of debris were being piled against a crumbling stone wall that opened up into a small grove of trees and wildflowers. Remnants of magic hung upon the heady atmosphere, hissing as they sank back down towards the earth, and thin trails of smoke crawled up towards the heavens, their fiery cores hidden beneath piles of broken wood.

Marble statues of the temple's patron goddess lined the walkway leading to the entrance of the grand structure. She was depicted as a benevolent figure in a hooded robe, holding a book in one hand and a thurible in the other.

People were scattered around the grounds in small groups, and a low murmur of indistinct conversation clung to the place like a soiled shroud. A few injured priests were lying on patches of grass, their eyes closed in quiet contemplation.

Mylah and Bowen walked through the subdued scene without a word; the mage scanned the faces of those who lingered in the gloomy daylight for his father, but to no avail.

"Good day." A man leaning against a carved pillar bowed his head. "And most humble greetings to you, Your Imperial Majesty, Empress of Cadere and Mistress of all Magics. You honour us with your presence."

Mylah said nothing, but furrowed her brow as she studied the man before her. He grinned as he ran a hand through his mop of thick silvery-white hair, his purple eyes darting from queen to mage; he wore a leather jerkin over a pale shirt, and dark woollen trousers. A small dagger hung at his hip, and golden rings glinted against his olive skin.

Bowen frowned. "You're not a priest."

"Ah, as observant as ever." A familiar voice echoed from within the shadowed doorway. "Good to see all that walking around distant lands hasn't dulled your senses."

"What are you doing here?"

Berne strolled out into the dim light. "I'd come up to negotiate trade with some of the villages nearby when I heard about the attack. Thought I'd come and see the damage, and offer any help that I could. I've sent messages down to Roth already. Merfyd here came with me from the tavern."

"Merfyd? Your family is religious, then?"

"Something like that." The man smiled at Bowen. "I wanted to see what kind of damage someone thought it necessary to inflict upon a temple dedicated to knowledge."

"Berne, I need to speak with you and Bowen. Now."

"I shall make myself scarce." Merfyd sank into a low bow. "I will be in the kitchens if anyone should have need of me. I believe that there are rations stored there which can be handed out to the needy without the priests catching on."

Mylah watched him leave and then turned to her friend. "Tusk passed away."

"Ah shit. Was he in a lot of pain?"

"No, I don't think so. It was… peaceful."

"Our numbers seem to dwindle more with each season that passes. Before long Caedes will be nothing more than a memory scratched into a tome somewhere."

Mylah glanced away. "So do you know what happened?"

"Not really. I've tried to get the priests to talk, but they all seem to piss their cassocks and run and hide when I press for answers. Something tells me they know more than they're letting on, but damned if I know what. I could try other means of persuasion if you like, boss."

The Monarch rubbed her forehead and sighed; frustration and sorrow were clawing at her mind, and all she wanted to do was lie down in the darkness to sleep. Her advisers watched her carefully and waited for her to speak.

"Bowen, perhaps you could find out some information from your father?"

"Of course, Your Grace."

The vast hall that made up the Inner Sanctum had once been a proud and beautiful place, decorated with intricate murals and carvings depicting the goddess Katarina in the realm of Sylvadeorum; the grand altar, adorned with dark green velvet and silks, had been flanked by water fountains inlaid with gold and opal and surrounded by offerings of flower wreaths, incense, and iridescent feathers.

Everything now lay in ruins.

A man sat amongst the rubble, his head veiled by a starched hood as he wept quietly. He didn't look up as Bowen approached, but mumbled a quick blessing and gestured for him to leave.

"High Priest Henrik?"

The man stirred. "Oh. It's you. Come about the book, I presume? Or are you just here to pick over the remains of your family's once great legacy?"

Bowen looked around at the mess and shook his head. "What happened here?"

His father snorted and got shakily to his feet, his dark eyes following those of his son. "Bandits, marauders, brigands, what difference does it make? We're ruined now. Everything we worked so hard to achieve has been snatched away, and we will rot here in our disgrace. The Goddess must truly have turned her eyes from us to allow this to come to pass. Our relics stolen, our sacred ground defiled, our reputation burnt to cinders. See now the carcass of our lineage, hanging by gilt thread and strips of dirty flesh."

"That book never should have been here. What were you thinking?"

"Knowledge is not denied to the followers of this path. You know that – or you should do, at least. Your mother spent long enough trying to teach you."

"Enough with the melodrama; just tell me who took it."

A door opened behind them and a torrent of pale light fell in from outside; the men looked up at a young priest who bowed his head.

"Forgive the intrusion, Henrik. It is time for the Tolling of the Other World, and we were unsure if we should go ahead."

"I'll be along shortly." He waved his hand dismissively and turned back to the mage. "What, did you find something else to disapprove of?"

"He didn't address you as High Priest."

Henrik shrugged. "What is the point in being such when your temple lies in ashes at your feet? I should have known that this day would come. Why would a child of mine have been born with magic in his veins if I had not somehow offended the benign goddess who saw fit to give me seven others without it?"

Bowen sighed and squared his shoulders. "Please just put the dramatics aside. The temple is hardly in ruins and your injuries seem to be less about broken bones and more about wounded pride. Tell me who took the relics, I need to know."

The older man shook his head and his shoulders sagged; he pushed the hood back from his face and ran his hands over his grey hair. Small scars bit into his dark skin, remnants from another life.

Silence descended over the pair for a while; the priest wandered around the Inner Sanctum sadly, taking in the scope of the destruction and picking up ragged shreds of fabric only to discard them again, whilst the mage closed his eyes and drifted into his own thoughts. Henrik soon made for the door and disappeared into the courtyard outside.

Mylah joined Bowen a few minutes later, and he glanced at her with an apologetic smile. She tilted her head, studying his expression without saying a word, and then looked up at the statue of Katarina that dominated the wall behind the desecrated altar.

He followed her gaze. "I don't think that he actually knows who caused all of this. His life's work has been torn to pieces and it has clouded his judgement, but I believe that if he knew he would have said so."

The queen rolled her shoulders and nodded.

"I don't think it's necessary for Berne to, ah, question the priests further."

"Do you actively try to ruin my fun, or is it just something that happens naturally?"

Bowen frowned. "When did you learn to sneak up on me like this?"

"The boss has been giving me lessons." Berne winked at Mylah. "Still, I've got nothing on her. Must be a benefit of being an immortal drenched in magic. You know Bowen, I always wondered why you left a life of pious luxury to sit in a desert and fire spells at whatever monster ambled past, but looking at this shit hole I'm beginning to understand."

"Focus, gentlemen."

Soft melodies crept up from the cavernous crypts below the sanctified stone. Archaic prayers danced upon fetid breath tinged with rosewater and severed tongues that crumbled into ashen harmonies.

Footsteps walked upon ground once soaked and sodden with scarlet, now long dried and forgotten; names buried for year after cobwebbed year sparked into life, terrifying and ghoulish and rotten.

Mylah steadied herself as dizziness washed over her once more. She frowned and looked at the men standing before her.

They waited.

Pain thrummed through her head. "So we know that an idiotic woman from Mysta is trying to locate the Gilded Lord, and a short time later a tome on that very subject goes missing from the temple it was supposedly secluded within. A temple controlled by the family of the man looking after her friend, no less."

Bowen stared at her. "Your Grace, I do not think that Tarian could be involved in this… this desecration. She has been trying to help us; it would make no sense for her to do such a thing. And surely you do not think that I…?"

Mylah snarled. "That you what? Would be foolish enough to see a pretty face and lose your self-righteous control? A whispered word upon a pillow can be as deadly as a poisoned blade, Seneschal."

Confusion snaked into his pale purple eyes. "Neither Tarian nor I would betray you, Your Grace. We are just trying to do our duty."

"Duty? What would either of you know of such a thing? Do you think that I cannot hear you conspiring together when you think me lost in nightmarish slumber? Do you think your traitorous whispers drift away upon the wind and fall upon no ears other than your own?"

"I…"

Magic crackled in the air around her, bolts of indigo that erupted across the defiled sanctuary and slithered away into the ether.

"Please Your Grace, let me explain."

"Enough!" Lightning shot down from the ceiling. "You stand before me nothing more than a liar and a coward! Twisting words with your vile tongue and seeking to bring me to my knees before you. I know what you are!"

Bowen glanced at Berne, his eyes wide. Sweat beaded his forehead and trickled down the back of his neck; his heart began to hammer against his ribs and his own magic flared instinctively. A pattern of ice formed beneath Mylah's feet.

She roared.

Flames shot up out of the ground, large plumes of sapphire and ivory that engulfed the room as the floor fractured and the walls trembled. Shadows scrambled to retreat before the blinding light as it exploded in short bursts, illuminating every corner and hiding place. Debris crashed to the earth and smashed into tiny pieces.

Mylah threw out her hands and bared her teeth; her mind raced as she fixed her gaze on the mage's head.

The statue of Katarina slumped forwards and shattered upon the ruined altar.

Bowen sank to his knees and screamed. Blood streamed from his nose and ears. The world rumbled and hissed as magic rocked back and forth through the electrified atmosphere, and a cacophony of ancient voices shrieked from the frayed edges of reality.

Everything went still.

Berne held Mylah tightly to his chest, his hand on the back of her head; trickles of scarlet ran down from his ears and nostrils.

She shuddered beneath his grasp, her breathing rapid and shallow; after a few moments, she slid into darkness and her body went limp in his arms.

Bowen gasped, the pain slowly draining from his body and his strength returning. He wiped his nose with the back of his hand and got unsteadily to his feet.

"How long has she been like this?"

The Seneschal looked from Berne to the unconscious woman in his grasp, but said nothing.

"Fucking… fuck. Are you going to be all right? I can get one of the priests to come and look at you if necessary."

The mage shook his head slowly and tried to calm his breathing. He moved a few steps away, his thoughts spiralling from one conclusion to another.

"I need to speak to Roth." Berne lifted Mylah and looked down at her with a heavy sigh. "We're in trouble, Bowen."

"I don't know what to do. I don't know how to help her. I don't know to stop her. Eris would have done; she could have dealt with all of this."

"Well maybe Tusk will put in a good word and the Lady of Death will see fit to send Winterborn back to us." Berne tried to smile. "But something tells me it isn't going to be that easy."

"Luck does not seem to favour us."

"Oh I don't know. We're not dead."

"Exactly."

*

Sunlight broke through the gloom outside, sending weak pale streams down to the wide eyed priests. They muttered and glanced at the temple, afraid of the noises that had resounded from deep within.

Henrik lay upon the grass, his eyes and mouth closed; a shadow soon fell across him and he sighed. "What is it now? I've already told you everything that you need to know and I have to contemplate on where to go from here. My time is precious, and better spent in the service of the Goddess than on the whim of some queen. See how Katarina forsakes us now? She shakes the very foundations of the temple we built in her honour, and sends mage after bloody mage into my presence."

"Father, please, I need to know what it is about that book that you're not telling me. This is a grave matter, not something for –"

"Dramatics?" Henrik scoffed and opened his eyes. "Do you understand the signs and portents that are all around us? Or have your titles and sorcery blinded you to such trivial things?"

"Why would you think Katarina is angered by magic?" Merfyd frowned as he strolled past. "You claim she is the patron of knowledge and understanding, and yet you think she looks down on mages? That sounds more like human prejudice than divine reckoning."

Henrik scowled as he watched the man disappear into the building. "That heretic should be driven out of these lands before he starts spouting filth that corrupts the initiates. All he has done is wander around these sacred grounds and tell us learned men that we do not know our own deity! What blasphemy to name him after one and yet allow him to be so… so…"

"Hmm. So about that book?"

"I already told you what I know."

Bowen pinched the bridge of his nose and then shook his head. "Very well. I suppose I'll just have to go to High Priestess Scole in Caeli and ask her for help instead."

Henrik sat bolt upright. "Go to another temple to discuss this matter? You wouldn't dishonour me in such a way!" His lips curled back into a snarl. "We always managed to keep ourselves out of Dullahan's business until you went galloping off to join his damnable crusade, and now you want to involve us in this lunacy with your new queen. Would you see us all turn to dust? Get out of here, and take her with you. You're not welcome upon this sacred ground."

Bowen made his way slowly back to Berne, empty handed and forlorn; his head ached and slumber seemed to be ever pulling at his mind. Magic crackled in the air around him, settling upon his skin like tiny daggers.

He reached the High Priest's antechamber and hesitated, his hand resting upon the heavy wooden door; fear prickled within and he swallowed, hard.

Berne turned around when he entered the room; Mylah was lying upon a makeshift bed of satin cloth and pillows, lost in thought as she stared at a large stained glass window. Bowen cleared his throat and she snapped back to reality.

She looked up at him with sorrow. "I am so sorry." Her voice was hoarse. "I... I don't know what happened."

"Your Grace." He bowed his head, thinking of what to say. "I'm afraid that my father has not been able to provide any more details about the book. It might serve us well to seek out Sir Rhydian and the High Priestess Scole on the matter instead."

Berne glanced at the queen and then started to pace up and down; he ran a hand along the scar atop his head and sighed heavily. Light scattered across the floor in front of him, a flurry of different colours leading away into the shadows.

Bowen watched him for a moment. "If we travel to Caeli within the next few days, I believe we can secure an audience with Scole. It is said amongst certain circles that the Temple of Elfriede has a vast library containing much knowledge considered to be lost to us."

"I don't think that's wise." Berne rubbed his chin. "Only a few months ago you were contending the frequent use of portals. As I recall, you were quite vocal about the potential negative effects that it might cause."

"But surely this is important enough to negate that? It would be a controlled spell, and we could shore up the magic to prevent any dangerous leakage."

Mylah sighed quietly. "Just tell him."

"Are you sure, boss? The more people who know…"

She waved at him dismissively and then put her head in her hands.

"Tell me what?" Bowen looked from the queen back to his old friend.

"There are things about Cadere that, in Luxnoctis at least, have been forgotten over the centuries. We are –"

A knock sounded at the door, which was swiftly opened and Merfyd strolled through; he bowed at the surprised trio.

"What is it, man? We were in the middle of something important."

"I'm sorry to interrupt." He looked at Mylah. "Your Imperial Highness. I have come to offer my services as a guide and confidante."

"Oh?"

"You are travelling east, correct? Heading towards Furatus and the Grave of the World?"

They stared at him.

"What makes you think that?"

"The tome that was stolen has set all your thoughts to ash, and fear ripples out through the ether as though it were a stone in a lake. Her Grace's magic is wild and uncontrolled, and her grief is a beacon to those who would use it against her. I can help with that… and I have wanted to see Mynydd for many years."

"Mynydd?"

"It's the ancient name for Furatus." Bowen glared at Berne. "Do I need to teach you history now, too?"

Mylah arose from her cushioned bed. "You know what lies in Mynydd?"

"I do, Your Grace. At least, I know what I have been told about it."

"Aye well." Berne raised an eyebrow. "It seems you're full of surprises. I assume you also know that cautions must be taken if a party is to head out to the east."

He nodded. "Of course. The things that lie in that place are best left to the dead; I would not see them rise again. But, my lady, I suspect that your advisers wish to discuss the notion of trusting someone only recently encountered in a tavern, who claims to be able to control magic."

Mylah smiled despite herself. "No doubt."

"In that case, I shall take my leave and await you outside. I might be able to find that High Priest and discuss some of the finer points of the divine hierarchy before we need to move on."

Bowen frowned at him as he left and then turned back to the others with a heavy sigh. "Are we really going to trust him? We have had issues in the past with strangers claiming to be something other than what they truly were."

"He's a good man and useful in a fight. Ah…" Berne rubbed the back of his neck. "There may have been a brawl or two in the tavern. He's skilled with magic, and his fists too. I can't see anything bad in him, and I would feel better knowing you have an extra ally on the journey."

"You're going south again?"

"I'm afraid I must. Although travelling with you and bashing in some skulls would be a welcome relief, there are too many things that I need to take care of here. Luxnoctis is recovering, but we still have a long way to go."

"I understand, and I am grateful for your help old friend." Mylah looked back to the stained glass. "So the path before us has been cleaved in two; either we pursue Aneira directly and try to cut her off before she finds what she is looking for, or we go to Caeli and attempt to garner information from the High Priestess."

Bowen frowned again. "Surely this is not a difficult choice? She is one mage with far less power at her disposal than we have at ours. We could easily catch up with her even if she has reached Furatus."

A wind arose in the west, cold and bitter and imbued with the cries of the damned. Shadowed clouds gathered upon the horizon and splintered as lightning forked down into the inky waves of the ocean.

Mylah tapped her fingers against the wall and closed her eyes; pain throbbed in her head once more and she fought back the urge to suddenly return to Amissa alone. The air was thick with tension and anticipation, and from outside she could hear the whispered murmurs of the priests as they conspired against her.

A day would come when their beloved temple was nothing more than the dust beneath her feet and all of their bones would be laid bare upon the ground, waiting to be bleached by the sun, and yet she would go on. Their duties could see them flayed apart and buried in ashen barrels beneath a sacred tree, and yet she would go on. Their goddess could forsake them and let them fall away in the spiralling abyss as their screams pierced the darkness, and yet she would go on. She was eternal.

"Your Grace?"

She shook her head and the thoughts dispersed. A look of concern was etched upon the Seneschal's face, and she could see the distrust in his pale purple eyes; the magic that flowed through his veins called out to her with its haunting melody, mocking everything that she had ever been.

Berne cleared his throat. "The boss cannot cross the threshold of Furatus."

"Oh. Is there a barrier of some kind? We should be able to deal with anything like that, surely? There are hundreds, if not thousands, of tomes in Luxnoctis alone, I'm sure at least one of them would provide the correct rituals necessary to... no? You're looking at me in that way I loathe, Berne."

"And what way is that?"

"When you know something that I don't."

Mylah held up a hand. "It is not so simple, Seneschal. What Merfyd referred to as the Grave of the World is not a place, but rather a creature. The Anghenfil of Mynydd, Guardian of Cadere. Surely you have heard of it?"

"In tales told to me by my grandfather as a child, yes. But nothing more serious than that. Everyone knows the story of the evil Anghenfil and its terrible bloodstained jaws designed to devour any living being that dares enter its putrid lair. There was a verse about it, if I recall correctly...

The sanctuary is broken
By the ringing of the bells
Their ghosts drift, earthbound
And drenched in dusk
In the ashes they dance
A whirl of green and grey

These moonlit spectres
Bloodied and betrayed
By the footsteps at the fireside
The sanctuary is broken
By the ringing of the bells."

"Our world is full of stories." She answered sadly. "All of which have been twisted and warped over time. Demigods and godling children, heroes and villains and ghosts, Monarchs and monsters. Elisus told me a tale before his death, and I think he sincerely believed it to be the truth, but what I have learnt since coming to this desolate throne would speak of something different, something… darker."

A woman caught Mylah's attention. She stood in the corner of the room, her eyes closed and her shaven head tilted slightly to one side as she listened to all that was said; her muscular arms were folded across her chest, the bare skin covered in intricate scars.

Bowen scratched his head and shivered. "I don't understand."

The woman opened her hollow eyes and looked at Mylah.

"The Anghenfil is no beast, but it is to be feared. It has existed since the birth of our world, it anchors the magic alongside the Monarch, and without it there would be a tidal wave of blood and bones the likes of which you could not even fathom."

"And you cannot go near it because…?"

"It can only be slain with the blood of a Monarch. The Gilded Lord knew this, and that in its presence we are vulnerable. Three Monarchs were butchered by him before he was stopped, although thanks to their magic and the vast army at their disposal, he never managed to reach the final chamber of its lair."

Bowen stared at her. "But… but Monarchs can't be killed by mortals. This has got to be wrong, surely? You said yourself that stories get twisted. You are invincible, to be killed only by your successor. This can't be right."

"If I travel to Mynydd and Aneira manages to bleed me, she could slay the Anghenfil and betray us all. If she gains the knowledge of the Gilded King, or Gods forbid restores him to power, she could instead take my life, so long as I stood within that place. It would be catastrophic, Bowen. We have to stop her."

Thunder rumbled in the distance, passing over watery graves and long bloated corpses whose rotten entrails still fed the hungering beasts that lurked beneath the waves.

Bowen paced up and down, his hands clasped firmly behind his back. "If what you are saying is true, then we cannot have you anywhere near that place. You should stay as far away from it as possible, and let us handle it instead."

"Sepelite still needs my help to heal; I must travel to its eastern shores eventually."

"No!" He cleared his throat. "I mean… it would be unwise, Your Grace, to do so whilst this woman is seeking your destruction."

"Many have tried to walk down that path already."

"But none with the ability to actually do it."

"He's right, boss. And besides, Sepelite isn't going anywhere – what difference will a few more weeks or months make, when compared to the possibility of you being dead and *never* being able to complete the process?"

She sighed heavily and rolled her shoulders. "I sent Nelia out with more Locus crystals some time ago… at least that will help, I suppose. I am sorry that we didn't tell you this sooner, Seneschal. It is just… the more people who know, the higher the risk of this being spread out across Cadere and the possibility of more adventurous vigilantes attempting something that they do not understand."

"How many aside from us do know, if I may ask?"

"The Veiled Council, and possibly those in the higher ranks of the clergy. Nelia has some idea, but we thought it better to shield her from the more… dangerous details. The Council has been known to eliminate individuals based upon the amount of knowledge they possess."

"And you decided to tell me. I don't know if I should be honoured or insulted."

"Don't worry." Berne grinned. "You would be a low priority target, I'm sure. That's why the monsters in Corignis never focused on you first – not enough meat to make it worth their while."

Mylah glanced back at the woman; her mouth had fallen open, allowing a cascade of viscous gore and writhing maggots to spill out towards the floor.

Pain danced behind the queen's eyes and she rubbed her face. "I suppose you will want us to fetch Tarian and Rhydian before we head over to Caeli."

"I think it would be wise, Your Grace. High Priestess Scole is more likely to listen to us if we already have an ally of hers with us."

Berne grunted. "A willing hostage."

"An *ally* of hers with us, and I see no logical reason to leave Tarian behind. She is the only source of information we have on Aneira, and she has proven herself to be quite capable in battle." He glanced at the other man. "She took on a swarm of Oculi by herself in the middle of a forest, before you ask the inevitable question."

"Ha! Sounds like we could have used her a few years back. Well, I had better take my leave of you both. Roth will be wanting to hear about trade, and I should let Rhea and Yvette know about Tusk. Take care of Merfyd, and let me know if there's anything else I can do to help. Fight well, boss."

"Bleed little, Berne." She smiled weakly at him and then turned back to Bowen. "Perhaps you could speak to your father again before we leave? We should extend some offer of reparation for… everything."

"As you wish, Your Grace." He bowed his head and walked away, muttering to himself and shaking his head.

She looked back to the corner of the room; the woman held a severed head in her hands, and tears were running down her dirt smeared cheeks. Sorrow clawed at Mylah's heart.

"Neta…" The word was rasping and drawn out. "Neta, wait for me… I'm coming."

"I'm sorry." Mylah slowly reached out towards the apparition. "Mama, I'm so sorry."

The spectre screamed as it vanished, and the queen stood alone and full of grief; she hung her head and said a quiet prayer to the Goddess of Death, imploring her to keep her phantoms at bay. She took a deep breath, steeled herself, and left the room once more.

*

Light broke across the jarring landscape, crawling over the inky ocean and up into the slumbering harbour as shadows seeped away to the underworld once more.

The silent heavens reigned above, stars glittering in the vast expanse; a chilled wind blew in from the murky waters and snaked its way towards a nearby town still draped in the mantle of darkness.

Buildings of marble and stone rose up from the ground like the beacons of titans from ages past, congregating together around a large courtyard adorned with grand pillars and statues thickly bedecked with flowering vines. Archways sheltered alleyways, and smaller side streets vanished alongside towering structures. Lit braziers sat upon steps leading up to a colossal structure: the temple, whose entrance was decorated with hundreds of perfumed flowers and flanked by banners of red and gold embroidered with the words *Elfriede the Beloved*, was surrounded by people waiting to petition the High Priestess. A low murmur carried upon the cool wind, a mixture of prayer and gossip that helped to while away the hours that dripped into one another before the bells rang to signal the incense infused arrival of Scole or her attendants.

Tolling sounded from deep within the marble building and silence descended upon the gathered crowd; the large arched doors creaked open several minutes later, and a man stepped out into the cold air. He pulled back the hood of his rich scarlet robe to reveal a thin golden circlet amongst his crop of black hair; his dark brown eyes scanned those who waited before him as he tapped his thin lips with long, beringed fingers. A few moments passed, and he gestured at those who were to follow him back inside.

A procession of other acolytes filtered out carrying trays of mulled wine and pastries to hand out to those who had not been chosen.

Aneira listened quietly to the elderly man who stood beside her near the back of the crowd; her eyes flickered every now and then to the temple attendants handing out the drinks and her sorrow swelled a little more. She pushed away thoughts of Mysta and its similar rituals, and tried to concentrate instead on the man's words. He spoke of his long dead wife, and his children who had all moved away in the decade past, but her attention drifted all the same.

"Did you know he's dead?"

She frowned. "Who?"

"The King across the sea." The man spat on the floor. "Cruel beast, that one was. My mother used to speak of him when I was young, in hushed whispers when my brothers and sisters were asleep."

A woman standing nearby nodded. "And now there are murmurs of a queen who took his place. I hear she's a bit blue."

"Well wouldn't you be?" The man barked a laugh. "To inherit that accursed title must bring about unfathomable grief."

"No, I meant literally."

Aneira glanced at them both. "You disapprove of the Monarchs?"

They exchanged looks and the woman moved away.

"Are you going to execute me?" The man cleared his throat. "Are you one of her agents here to dispose of us for speaking our minds, the way the old one used to before he turned his foul attention to his own lands?"

"Not at all. I simply escorted someone here who needs to talk to the High Priestess."

"I'm old enough to know that there's more to you than you like people to see, lass. There's a pain that runs deep, and if you're not careful it will engulf everything that you are." He sighed and ran a hand through his thin white hair. "This world has been heavy with grief for longer than you or I have graced it. As for the Monarch… it doesn't seem right to me that one person should have all of that power. Mages are bad enough and all they seem to do is fuck up the occasional spell. One of the useless bloody idiots set fire to my house once. But these kings and queens… they're worse. Look at what Dullahan did to our ancestors, and then to his own people only a few years ago. Waging war for millennia, and to what end? Countless dead, injured, or missing, and then he tried to sow seeds of chaos between us and the elves just to amuse himself. Now someone else comes in his place and what evidence do we have, really, that she isn't as bad?"

"Or worse." Aneira muttered the reply under her breath, but he caught it nonetheless.

"Exactly!" His eyes shone. "Ah, here's the wine. About time! One of these days that Mercer is going to let me inside, I just know it. And I shall give Scole a piece of my mind. But until then, we might as well feast upon their bounty, eh?" Without waiting for a response, he turned and vanished into the crowd.

Aneira declined the drink that was offered to her, and receded into the strained thoughts that seemed to endlessly haunt her mind; whenever she closed her eyes she could see the ruins of her beloved city dancing before her, strewn with jagged pieces of flesh and the remnants of chaotic magic. She sighed quietly and the images dispersed; as the wind blew in from the sea and pale light washed over the city, she pulled her cloak tighter around her shoulders and walked away.

Mercer tapped lightly on an intricately carved door; Scole's voice answered after a brief pause, and he pushed it open, turning to glance at the people behind him without a word.

She stood before a grand shrine, her head lowered in prayer and her arms spread wide; candles bathed the scene in golden light and incense filled the warm air. Berries and dried flowers were spread along the dark red altar cloth, and offerings of small gems and shards of reflective glass covered the base of a wooden statue of the Goddess.

A bell chimed in the distance, and Scole lowered her arms. She moved slowly to face the newcomers, and a smile crossed her painted lips.

"Petitioners to see you, my lady." Mercer bowed and then gestured to the others to do the same. "Should I take them through to your chambers?"

"We can speak here."

"Of course. There is a small matter I must attend to in the library, High Priestess."

"Go, go." She waved her hand and smiled once more. "I will join you later."

He nodded and left, shutting the door quietly behind him. Long shadows danced in the hallways as he wandered through the temple, the sounds of chanting prayers and murmuring incantations echoing from veiled doorways. Arched windows ran the length of the building, and so soft sunlight was starting to brush across the flagstones as he reached the library.

It was the largest room in the temple bar the Inner Sanctum, and one of the only ones where all of the candles were encased in lanterns. Thick velvet curtains had been hung to obscure the natural light, in order to protect the thousands of tomes that slumbered within the ornate freestanding bookcases and upon ebony shelves that rose from the floor to the ceiling along each wall. A spiralling staircase led to a secluded upper level where one or two people shuffled around silently, tending to the precious ancient scripts and scrolls that had been in the temple's safekeeping for centuries. Dark columns stood proudly in every corner and whenever someone walked past with a lantern shadows would dance within their elaborate designs; wooden desks were scattered throughout the room, a scholar or a priest bent over each one to scratch an inky quill over a piece of parchment. It commanded the sort of quiet that the rest of the temple could not, although a low hum still drifted in from the courtyard outside.

Mercer took a moment to close his eyes and inhale deeply; he was most at peace here, away from the endless duties and obligations that came with his position.

"What's wrong, Mercy? Too many nights spent in the tavern and the torture chamber rather than in bed?"

He sighed quietly and looked over at a woman sitting at one of the tables, her face partially shadowed by the hood of her cloak. She smirked at him.

"I thought you were in Sepelite."

"I was and I'll be heading back there soon, so there's no need for you to worry. You can skulk around these dusty hallways without interruption, sniffing the pages of the older books and rubbing the scrolls all over your naked body."

Mercer rolled his eyes and sat down nearby, scratching his chin. A stack of papers awaiting the temple's seal squatted nearby, and he eyed them wearily; a headache was already creeping in behind his eyes.

Soft footsteps echoed from behind, accompanied by the sound of cloth brushing against the floor. Mercer stood up and bowed his head.

"Ah, here you are." Scole smiled warmly. "The petitions have been dealt with, so when you are done with this I will need your help making the records of them all."

"Of course, my lady." He rubbed his brow. "Of course. There's someone sitting over there who I think will want your attention."

Scole glanced across the room and her eyes widened. "Seren?"

The woman at the table grinned and sat back.

The High Priestess crossed the room in a few strides and flung her arms around her. "Oh my darling girl! I feared that you would never come back! How did you get to us so quickly? Some of the ships have been struggling to get into port and –"

"I didn't take a ship, and I'm not back, not exactly. I met a mage a short time after I left you, and she offered to bring me here if I could help her find out some information."

"Oh I… I see." Scole kissed the top of her head and stood back. "Mages and their obsession with crystals will never cease to amaze me. They think they know the true potential of an item only to bastardise it with ridiculous magic. Still, I am overjoyed to see you, my dear."

Seren frowned; Aneira had not, to her knowledge, used any crystals to bring them to the shores of Caeli, but she shrugged off the remark and said nothing. She returned instead to the book in front of her.

Scole rolled her shoulders and took a moment to breathe; her wrists were aching and she could feel a familiar twinge of pain in her back. After a few moments indulged in such thoughts, she looked back at Seren and raised an eyebrow when the woman snorted. "Do you find something disdainful in the words, my dear?"

"*And when the Knight falls, a Queen shall rise.* If everything that this passage says is true, then it would make that abhorrent queen the Hand of Love."

"And that surprises you?" There was an element of concern in Scole's voice.

"How could such a creature be given that title? She is a tyrant and a dictator given only to violence and sorrow. There is nothing loving about her."

Mercer looked at them both, his eyes wide; he had not thought to check which of the books it was that Seren had decided to study. His heart began to pace a little quicker and sweat formed upon the back of his neck.

The High Priestess titled her head slightly. "I thought I had taught you better than *that*, Seren. Love is not simple compassion and understanding: it is the fire that burns between souls in the darkest nights, the blade awash with so much blood that others may find easy slumber, the clenched fist that breaks bones to keep kith and kin safe from danger. Love comes to us in many forms: corrupt, pure, meek, and roaring. It empowers and it destroys, and never are we left unchanged; she carries a great burden, just as you do."

"Hmm." She shook her head at her, before she turned a few pages and squinted. "And then, amidst the darkness, the Hand –"

"Seren!" Scole reached out and touched her shoulder. "I am tired of prophecies and ancient tales. Let us take a walk around the garden and see if any of my plants are in bloom yet. The apothecary is running low on certain poisons and I said I would take some to her as soon as I could."

"Very well." She sighed heavily and picked up a small leather satchel as she stood up. "I would like that."

"I will just gather some of my things, and then I shall join you outside." Scole watched her leave before she turned to Mercer and lowered her voice. "Burn that book."

The herb garden was bathed in warm sunlight, the streaks of gold dancing across viridians and emeralds and settling amongst soft petals and jagged thorns. A statue of Elfriede rose out of a flowerbed in the middle of the courtyard, a silver bowl full of water clutched in her outstretched hands; small birds flittered to and fro between the goddess and the hedgerow that ran along the western side of the grounds.

A hooded priestess sat quietly upon a wooden bench in the shade of an ancient tree, a small book open upon her lap.

Seren watched her for a short time whilst she paced quietly back and forth, her fingers brushing absentmindedly against the long grass that had grown up amongst the flowers. Music drifted upon the air from somewhere in the temple, soft and lulling and comforting. Her thoughts turned to darker places and grief threatened to overwhelm her yet again; she took a deep breath and steeled herself.

A door opened and the priestess finally looked up from her book; a smile flickered across her lips before she bowed her head once more.

Scole made her way over to Seren, strands of light grey hair teased free by a cool breeze that wrapped around her shoulders and fell away to the east; she reached up to cup the younger woman's face with her hands, and her expression softened. She studied her carefully, concern flickering across her dark blue eyes; after a moment, she took a step back and opened her arms. Seren fell sobbing into her embrace.

"There now, my young one." Scole began to gently stroke her hair. "There now."

"It isn't right." Seren's voice cracked with sorrow. "It isn't right."

"Be still my love, the Gods want not your tears."

"No, just the blood of those I hold dear." She broke away from her grasp and wiped her face with the back of her hands. "This is so fucked up, Scole. How can you stand there and say otherwise?"

"I understand that are you hurting child, but there is always a reason behind that which has been laid out before us, even if we do not yet know what it might be. I trust in the divine judgement of our creators, and that they mean to see us to a better end."

Seren snorted and shook her head. "More temple rhetoric I see. Repeating that ridiculous fucking drivel isn't going to make me overlook everything; you seem to have forgotten that I grew up within these walls, and I have heard it all."

"How could I possibly forget? You and Rhydian being brought to us was one of the happiest days of my life, I remember it like it was yesterday." Scole reached out to take her hand. "I know it wasn't always easy, and for that I am truly sorry, but I am glad that the Gods saw fit to lead your path here and entwine it with mine."

"You are glad that my mother was murdered at the marketplace and my father ran away to play at war?"

"That's not... that's not what I meant."

"Just forget it. How many times must we have this conversation? Should we turn it to how Rhydian was the easier child to look after, how he recited his prayers like they were lullabies, and how proud you were when he took up the mantle of a sanctified knight? Or should I now point out how I grew up to resemble my mother and so remind you that no matter what you did, no matter how hard you tried, that was a woman you could never be?"

"Seren." Her words were gentle. "I love you and there is nothing you can say that will change that."

"Enough." She ran her hand over head, her fingers brushing against her dark curls, and glanced over to the other priestess. "I see you and Meredith are still enjoying each other's company."

"I don't think you came all this way just to talk to me about that."

"No. I have what I came for and I should go... there are people relying on me." She kissed Scole lightly on the cheek. "Take care of yourself, High Priestess."

"Wait! Are you coming back? There are things I need to talk to you about and –"

Seren walked quickly away with her head bowed; her heart throbbed against her chest and for a moment she thought that it might burst. Long buried memories clawed at her mind, conjuring images and voices she had no wish to entertain. She clutched the leather satchel tightly in one hand and disappeared back into the maze of corridors, keeping her head down and her pace swift.

The crowd outside had mostly dispersed, leaving behind only a few stragglers clinging to the hope that the High Priestess might yet grant them an audience. Seren pulled up her hood and shivered as she vanished into the mists that had rolled in from over the sea.

Mercer wrung his hands as he listened to the scholar's garbled tale; the words were laced with worry and the man's eyes darted to and fro as though some great demon might jump out at him at any moment. The truth, Mercer knew, was far worse.

Ancient texts had gone missing from the library: at least one scroll and one of the older tomes, both from a section that should have been off limits to all but the most trusted of clerks and students. He couldn't explain who might have taken them, no one had asked permission to study those two particular items for several years now, and the High Priestess had not informed them of anyone who would be coming to take them. Punishment would need to be doled out, the scholar sweated a little when he acknowledged that fact, but the foremost priority would have to be finding the thief.

Mercer finally nodded and the man, relieved at his seemingly understanding response, visibly relaxed.

A few seconds ticked by as he considered what to do next; the scholar cleared his throat.

"Don't discuss this with anyone else before I have had chance to speak to the High Priestess." Mercer patted the man on the shoulder. "Go down to the kitchens, get a jug of ale and something to eat, and then head over to my study. We will talk about things in more detail when I return."

"At once, sir."

He watched him hurry away and shook his head; it had been a long time since any scandal had crept through the temple, and Scole was not going to be pleased at this hint of a shadow.

Bells were tolling again in the distance; Mercer rolled his shoulders and rubbed his face. Slumber was pulling at his mind, and the desire to slip into darkened dreams skulked around his thoughts like a hungry wolf.

A door at the end of the corridor was flung open and a flurry of novices hurtled out, flying past him as though Death herself meant to hunt them down.

Mercer saw a familiar face and reached out to grab the woman's arm. "Ada! What's the meaning of this? Where are you all going?"

"Do you not hear the bells, sir? Delyth is under attack! We've all been ordered to the cellars in case they breach the walls!"

"What?" He stared at her. "Who's attacking?"

Ada wrestled her arm free and ran after her friends without another word; Mercer watched her go with a frown. He spun around, steadied his thoughts, and made his way quickly to the Great Hall, all the while suppressing the dread that had begun to rise through him and was already knotting his stomach.

The banquet tables had been pushed back against the walls and a group of people stood in a circle in the middle of the room, their heads bowed in prayer; Scole was in the centre, her arms outstretched and her eyes closed.

Distant screams echoed from outside; Mercer steeled himself and waited.

The High Priestess snapped around to face him, her expression calm. "Ah, there you are. I hear you have something to tell me?"

He tried to keep the concern from his face. "A few items of note have gone missing from the library, my lady."

"Do you know who is responsible for such an act?"

"Not yet, High Priestess, but I was just on my way to question the man who was meant to oversee such matters when I heard about this… attack."

Scole raised her eyebrows. "Yes, well, don't concern yourself about that at the moment. Go and see to your duties, and trust in the Goddess to keep us safe."

"Of course, my lady." He bowed his head and turned to leave.

"Make sure you get some answers, Mercer. We cannot have people thinking that they can sin against the temple in this manner and go unpunished."

He looked back over his shoulder and met her gaze with a nod. She gestured at him to finally go.

A flash of blue light shot through the room and the ground beneath them trembled in fear; Mercer swore as he was thrown against the door and cracked his shoulder. Clouds of dust fell from the domed ceiling and panic spread through the small congregation. Another tremor rocked the walls until some of the sconces fell and shattered upon the floor. Magic crackled through the air, sending bolts of lightning spidering across the floor; the priests broke formation and ran from the room. Scole shielded her eyes and cursed loudly as another pillar of light burst out of the ground in front of her.

"My lady!" Mercer held onto the wooden doorframe with one hand and reached out to her with the other. "We must flee from this place!"

"No!" She waved him away. "Elfriede will protect me. Go and see to your duties!"

"I won't leave you here to die!"

"That's an order, Mercer. Get out!"

Another quake rumbled through the floor and he was hurled back across the threshold. He threw his hands up to protect his face as masonry crashed to the ground and shot a plume of debris out in every direction.

A few seconds passed before he dared to open his eyes; dirt and dust swirled around in the air and sparks of magic chased after unseen shadows. The entrance to the Great Hall was nowhere to be seen; a wall of broken stone stood in its place.

Mercer's heart throbbed; he scrambled to his feet and tried to find his voice, but the words would not come. Sweat beaded his brow, ran down the back of his neck and swarmed his armpits. He staggered forwards a few paces and placed his hands upon the barricade.

The Gods looked down from their sorrowful cradle as the seconds ticked by in silence.

"Priestess?" The noise was little more than a whimper.

Nothing sounded from within the Great Hall; Mercer rested his forehead against the stone and closed his eyes as tears rolled down his cheeks.

"Excuse me?"

He lifted his head to look at the woman who had spoken. She was dressed in armour he didn't recognise, and there was a concerned grimace upon her face.

"Are you a healer? We have need of your skills if so."

He glared at her. "Do I look like a healer?"

"Fucked if I know." She shrugged. "But in case you hadn't noticed, there's a bit of an ongoing problem outside and I was commanded to come in here to find anyone who could help. If that isn't you, could you point me in the direction of someone else?"

He shook his head and she rolled her eyes, jogging past him with a daggered look.

Mercer stood quietly for a few moments, his palm still pressed against the cold wall, before he sighed quietly. "I'm sorry my lady."

The ground trembled again, although less ferociously this time, and he staggered to one side. He wrung his hands for a second or two, and then bolted in the direction of the temple's main entrance.

The sky was dark, shrouded by thick clouds of black and green; lightning arced across the town and disappeared out across the ocean. Seabirds screeched as they plummeted from air to water, only to be clamped suddenly in the jaws of monstrous creatures that arose from the depths.

Howling screams echoed across the darkened expanse as Delyth's people succumbed to both ice and fire. Spells ricocheted off building and beast alike, burning skin and stone, and eventually snaked their way into the ground, now sodden with blood.

Mercer stood atop the temple steps and stared at the chaos before him; horrific creatures with skin sloughing from their bones loped around the place, their great talons impaling men and women before they tore them into pieces and devoured the severed flesh.

A terrifying screech came from above; Mercer lifted his gaze and staggered backwards. A Sceleratis circled the temple, its yellow flecked eyes locked onto his.

Suddenly entranced by the eerie beauty of the beast, the man found himself unable to move; he watched it descend as though it were a messenger of the Gods themselves, its raptorial feet stretching out to take him away to the heavens.

A huge bolt of flame caught it across the eyes and it bellowed, thrown off course; its great bulk crashed against a towering statue of some ancient hero, the marble sword piercing one of its eyes.

Mercer shuddered and snapped back to reality; he tried to decide on a course of action, but his own skills were not well suited to the battlefield. People were dying in the streets below and were already dead in the building behind him, and he felt completely lost.

Another horrifying cry sounded from nearby; he looked over to see a woman pulling her weapon free of the Sceleratis, chunks of its brain stuck upon the blade. She was decked in the same armour as the one who had asked for his help only a few minutes earlier, and a quick glance back at the blood soaked scene told him that there were many similarly dressed. Pain threaded through his veins; he knew all of the banners of Sepelite and Caeli, but this was not the army of a friend come to their rescue.

Tarian dropped back down to the ground and wiped her sword on the beast's neck feathers. Her blood sang with the excitement of battle and she spun around to cleave the head from another unholy creature as it sprang at her from the shadows. She strode through clumps of flesh and bone towards a man currently on his knees, and pulled a squalling monster from his back. She stamped on its head, sending out a flurry of gore, and then helped him to his feet.

"It seems I have to thank you once more." He dusted himself off and grinned at her.

"Who did you say you were?"

"Cael of the Necromancers Guild."

Tarian laughed as she raised her shield to deflect another attack. "You don't look like a necromancer."

He flicked his wrist and sent a cascade of indigo lightning shooting out towards the east. "What's that supposed to mean?"

"The ones that I've met before have all been skinny and pale."

Cael inhaled sharply and raised a slick eyebrow. "Is this one of those *casters looking like their magic* jokes? If it's not, then I should tell you that there are precious few rules in the guild, and none at all about appearance."

"Fuck off do you have a guild."

"Well of course we do!" Magic spiralled out to hit a monster across the brow. "How else would we keep a record of who is raising who? Think of the chaos if we all went about lifting spirits whenever and wherever we liked. And besides, having a guild makes us respectable. You know you're dealing with a certified necromancer when you come to us, not some charlatan who learnt how to raise the dead from some grotty old book they found in a cave."

Tarian sliced off another head. "Is that a common problem here?"

"Not anymore." He picked a chunk of sinew from his beard and flicked it away. "The guild has been in place for several centuries, and we welcome all who wish to learn."

Magic exploded overhead and showered them in tiny shards of ice; Cael frowned and brushed the pieces from his mop of dark hair. The silver rings he wore caught the sunlight, the metal suddenly bright against his olive skin, and he looked up to see the clouds breaking above them.

Tarian breathed a sigh of relief. "It's nearly over. We should get that injury of yours seen to before too long. I doubt even your guild approves of festering wounds."

He looked down at the gash on his arm and sighed. "I just had this robe washed, and now look at it. All torn and soiled."

"If only there was a way to fix that." She snapped a neck and threw away the corpse. "I suppose you'll just have to be ragged and dirty forevermore."

Lightning pierced the ground in front of them and they turned to see Bowen approach, broken staff in hand.

He held it out gingerly. "I believe this belongs to you."

Cael took the wooden weapon with a slight grunt. "Luck just rains down upon me today. Perhaps my shoes should split too, or all my jewellery could fall into the mud."

"Oh I don't think there's any need for that. Bowen, this is Cael."

"Of the Necromancers Guild." The man added swiftly. "And who might you be? Other than carrier of my poor ceremonial staff, that is."

"I am the Seneschal to the Eternal Monarch." Bowen squared his shoulders. "Former leader of the Ferus unit of Caedes Aurum, Elite Mage of the Moonlit Depths, Scholar of Venomous Beasts of Luxnoctis and the Greater Realms of Cadere, and Sanctified Son of the Temple of Katarina in Metumontis."

Cael raised an eyebrow. "I… see."

Tarian nudged him gently. "Someone over by your own temple seems to be trying to get your attention."

His icy purple eyes followed her gaze and he sighed once more. "Of course he's here."

"A friend of yours?"

"Ha! Hardly. That's an attendant of the High Priestess, goes by the name of Mercer. I say *an* attendant, he's more like Head Ghoul, and practically runs the underworld of the place for her, feasting on its necrotic belly. That's a favourite joke of the guild for you there." A grin flickered across his lips. "He's a nasty, if necessary, piece of work. Still, if you want to get to Lady Scole without an appointment – or a good reason – he's the man to make it happen, although it can come at quite a cost. For all that, he does allow our novices to work closely with him, which means the Necromancer's Guild and the Temple of Elfriede have been on good terms for years now."

"...Right. Well, let's go and see what he wants." Tarian glanced around at the destruction that lay at their feet. "Probably an explanation for all of this."

The clouds had dispersed completely by the time the trio reached the temple. Bodies of humans and monsters alike were scattered across the ground like shattered glass, but most of the buildings had remained largely intact. Indigo smoke trailed from fractures in the floor, the magic that spiralled from them almost spent.

Tarian sheathed her sword as they ascended the steps, clouds of dust drifting out with every movement. Mercer wrung his hands as he watched them approach; tears had washed away small streaks of the dirt and ash that covered his face.

Bowen thumped his chest in salute and bowed his head. "Greetings, Mercer of the Temple of Elfriede. We are envoys from Queen Mylah, Empress of –"

"She's trapped!" The desperate words blurted out, strained with sorrow. "She's trapped and I can't… I can't get to her!"

Cael looked at Bowen, his eyes wide. "If he means Scole then we need to deal with this."

"Please… please I can't get to her… she's trapped and I…"

They pushed past him, the necromancer leading the way through the rattled building; Mercer followed them inside.

Pieces of fallen stone blocked the path here and there, and one or two doorways had caved in, but the walls had held for the most part. Banners and tapestries trailed across the floor, and sconces lay in shattered pieces.

"Was she in the Inner Sanctum?"

"No… no, the Great Hall. She's trapped…"

Cael turned a corner and inhaled sharply; pain prickled along his arm and he shivered.

Tarian looked at him with concern. "Bowen can take a look at that wound for you. If you ask him nicely, he might even fix you up before you bleed all over the rest of your robe."

"That's not important now."

They walked briskly down the corridor, stepping over debris until they came to the wall of collapsed masonry.

Cael studied it and shook his head. "Somehow I doubt my spells are going to be of use." He bunched his hands into fists and threw out a spiral of indigo magic. It scattered across the barrier, but nothing happened.

"I don't think she could have survived this." Tarian glanced at Mercer. "I'm sorry."

He whimpered and dropped to his knees; Cael patted him on the shoulder.

Bowen closed his eyes and muttered an incantation, raising his arms slowly; magic spiralled around the base of the stones as sweat trickled down the man's neck. The barricade shifted suddenly, the broken slabs straining against the magic; his words became an echoing shout as he poured more and more energy into them, and the wall shattered. Pieces of rock shot out down the hallway, narrowly missing the caster. The spell finished, he slumped to the floor unconscious.

"I don't want to see!" Mercer's voice wailed out like a wounded animal. "I can't see her like that. My poor lady... I should have stayed... I should have..."

"What are you talking about now, man?" A woman appeared through the haze of dust and magic. "I told you to trust in the Goddess."

His eyes opened and he stared at her. "My... my lady? You survived?"

"It certainly seems that way." Scole brushed some of the ash from her robes and rolled her shoulders. "Now, is someone going to tell me what's going on here?"

Tarian stepped forward and bowed her head. "High Priestess."

"Ah, it's you. I should have known the followers of Queen Mylah would be caught up in this mess somehow. No doubt you have important matters to discuss with me, but I would appreciate it if they could wait until I have been able to help those affected by this twist of misfortune. In fact, it would probably benefit you to aid me in this task, and put to rest any suspicions about your coming here at the exact moment an attack took place on our fair city."

Tarian frowned. "Surely you don't think that we had anything to do with this?"

"Did I say that, my dear? I am not accusing you of anything; I am simply stating what the general populace are likely to believe. They will be scared, and angry, and looking for someone to blame. If the temple managed to sustain this amount of damage, then I dread to think what happened to those who were not within its sanctified walls. There may be many in need of burial, and others in need of funeral rites but without a body to grieve over. People will cry out for justice, or vengeance, or both. If you are seen as saviours, surely that is preferable to villains?"

Mercer finally got to his feet and wiped his face; he was trembling, and closed his eyes against fear and humiliation both.

Scole looked at him with pity. "Did you manage to question the scholar?"

He shook his head.

"You had better go and see if he still lives, then. We will head outside to assess the damage; come and find me when you are done." She looked down at Bowen. "Your mage appears to have overexerted himself."

"Probably from reciting all of his fancy titles." Cael grinned. "It's a good job he was here though. He's the one that managed to shift all of that rock."

Scole tilted her head to one side. "He managed to work a spell against the hallowed stone of a temple? Impressive. Perhaps he has those titles for a good reason, Necromancer."

Tarian gently kicked Bowen's leg and he slowly opened one bloodshot eye. His head throbbed with pain and he groaned as she hoisted him to his feet.

"I have some herbs somewhere that will help him wake up." Scole searched in her pockets and finally produced a small pouch. "They would be better infused in tea, but I don't suppose we have time for that now."

Tarian took them and gave them to the mage, who wrinkled his nose at the taste and fought against the urge to spit them back out. He brightened after a few moments however, and after taking a few deep breaths managed to stand without her help.

The journey through the temple was quicker with the High Priestess leading them, although every so often she would stop to examine a broken statue or push back a fallen banner. Concern would whisk across her face now and then, disappearing after a moment to be replaced with calm determination.

The chaos that had settled over Delyth had now dripped away into mourning. People loitered in the streets, dazed and lost in distant thoughts; wailing cries lifted up on a chill breeze that coursed over the docks and brought a shivering timbre alongside the warm coagulation of blood and body alike.

Remnants of magic skittered through the air and skulked away over the horizon. Most of Delyth had resisted the attack to some extent; those who lived outside the immediate vicinity were unharmed and aid was already starting to trickle in as people crept from their homes with blankets, food and water, and words of solace.

Scole looked around at the devastation with a heavy heart; tears welled in her dark blue eyes and her lips trembled.

"My lady!" A woman ascended the steps, the hood of her red and gold robes thrown back so the sunlight caught in her crop of dark hair.

Scole opened her arms and breathed a sigh of relief as the woman fell into her embrace; she kissed the top of her head and stepped back to gently cup her face. "You are unhurt?"

Meredith nodded.

"Well of course you are. You are meant for the Valley of the Winterborn, the Goddess would not see you from that path just yet."

She kissed Scole quickly and smiled. "Yes my lady."

"We have help from Luxnoctis, my darling one; would you point them in the direction that they will be the most beneficial?"

Meredith's eyes widened. "Luxnoctis?"

"Is that a problem?" Bowen stepped forward.

Scole waved away his concern. "Don't be so defensive, mage. Our ancestors cut off nearly all direct contact with both your homeland and Amissa nearly three thousand years ago. Your arrival is somewhat unprecedented."

The Seneschal shook his head. "You left us to be fodder for Dullahan's sick games."

"We did what was necessary to protect ourselves, nothing more." Scole's face flickered with remorse. "I have often wished that it could have been different, but with him focusing on your lands instead of ours we managed to disappear from his thoughts. I am sorry, for what it's worth, and although it is not the same, we suffered too. Friends and family members were abandoned, relics and knowledge was lost, even our own languages were forsaken for the common tongue in case the King returned. The seeds of fear that he sowed had deep roots. I hope your queen proves to be a better ruler than that monster."

Tarian rubbed the back of her neck. "So, what can we do to help?"

"I did send a scout of ours into the temple during the battle to find healers." Bowen glanced around at the mess. "I haven't seen her since."

"Ah, she found me." Meredith smiled warmly at him. "We set up a small camp just outside one of the guild buildings over to the northern side of the city. She's a skilled tracker, and we managed to locate many who needed help quite quickly."

"Nelia is one of our best."

"Indeed. Well, perhaps Meredith can take you over there if you wish to help with healing magic. Necromancer, I will need to speak to your guild master should he still draw breath. When you've delivered that message, get that bloody arm seen to."

Cael nodded and walked quickly away, disappearing down a darkened alleyway nearby; Tarian watched him go and then shivered.

"And as for you, my dear, I think you would be better suited to helping me. Come, we'll head out towards the docks."

Bowen kicked a decapitated Saprus head out of the way as he walked beside Meredith; it rolled down some bloodstained steps with a squelch and she eyed it warily.

"Did I hear correctly that you're destined for the Winterborn Valley?"

"It is the Valley of the Winterborn, but yes." She smiled at him again. "I have been called by the Gods for such an honour."

He was quiet for a moment. "A friend of mine once carried that title."

"Lady Eris, no doubt. We mourned her passing at the temple, although we never met. Anyone who partakes in the ritual is considered a brother or sister to us all. I know you think that we forgot you in Luxnoctis, but our mages and seers kept a close eye on all that was happening over there. Although I suspect that Sepelite cannot boast the same diligence."

"Winterborn was a good woman."

"Ah… her ritual was successful, was it not?"

"She had a daughter."

"Then her title was '*of the Winterborn.*' Had she not become pregnant, then she would have been Eris Winterborn."

He shrugged. "Does it matter?"

"Perhaps not everywhere. But here in Caeli you will find that people guard those titles fiercely; they are both sought after, and considered a worthy replacement for family names. For what it is worth, I am sorry that she and her child both passed away."

They turned a corner and the small medical camp came instantly into view; wards had been set up by a few mages who had come to offer help, and a large fire burned amidst piles of discarded bandages and strongly perfumed incense. A couple of bodies had already been washed and laid out upon wreathes of herbs and flowers; priests stood nearby, chanting solemn hymns.

Mages and healers darted in between rows of makeshift beds and canopies, administering salves, balms, and suturing wounds. Spells wove around gashes and gaping wounds, and strips of clean cloth were bound across cleansed skin.

Nelia waved to Bowen. "I'm glad to see you; we need all the help we can get."

Tarian sat down upon a patch of scorched earth and ran a hand over her head; images of Mysta swam before her eyes as dizziness washed over her once more.

Scole placed a hand on her shoulder. "Steady now, take a few deep breaths."

"Why did you ask me to come with you instead of helping out over there with the others?"

"There's no point in pushing yourself beyond what is healthy, my dear. I know that you are more than capable of pretending that everything is fine, but forcing yourself to do so is going to do more harm than good. I would rather have you sitting here with me, calming your mind, than running yourself ragged out there. We can let other people deal with it all for a moment or two."

Tarian's hand darted to the crystal pendant around her neck. Sorrow welled within her and she tried to push it away, concentrating instead on the sound of the waves as they broke against the docks.

"Can I get anything for you? Something to eat maybe, or some wine?"

"No... thank you." She looked around at the people who lingered in the distance. "Forgive me for saying so High Priestess, but it seems that Caeli did not suffer as Sepelite did following the Sundering."

"An odd time to bring up such a point, child, but you are right. The temple offers succour to all those who seek it."

Tarian nodded without giving the answer much thought.

"Your queen is not with you, I take it?"

"No, she stayed in Sepelite."

"Then this cannot be her doing. Don't look at me like that, I didn't mean to suggest that it was, but if the thought occurred to me then it almost certainly occurred to others – and that might help us understand why this attack took place."

She shifted uncomfortably under the older woman's gaze.

"Something similar happened to your hometown, did it not? Monsters, magic, ruination, and then the forces of the mystical Queen coming to your aid?"

"Not in so timely a fashion." Tarian rubbed her brow. "Mysta is utterly lost, and nearly all of its people lie in the dirt."

Scole nodded. "Someone has to be behind it all, and I would suggest that the person who did this," she gestured around her, "also ordered the destruction of Mysta. A strange and disparaging thought, unfortunately. Not all of the monsters who walk this land are so easily identified as those who named Mylah the Mortifera."

"How do you know about that?"

Scole raised her eyebrows. "I know many things, child."

"She wants your help."

"I'm sure she does, but I am not inclined to give it. Delyth is going to take time to heal, and I should be here to oversee that; my influence over the other provinces will wane considerably if I set that aside in order to ask them to support a foreign power."

"Would it change your mind to know that we have Sir Rhydian working alongside us?"

Scole smiled ruefully. "Not in the least, although I am glad to know that he did not abandon his duties. I am only surprised that you didn't bring him with you as a bargaining tool."

"We thought about it." Tarian laughed despite herself. "But he insisted on staying at Mylah's side to protect her. I'm not entirely sure what good he will be to an immortal, but there you go."

Footsteps echoed in the distance; Scole looked over and raised her eyebrows. Mercer was approaching at speed, his expression calm and his robes clean.

He bowed his head as he reached them. "My lady, I have done as you asked."

"And how did it go? Did he survive?"

"No, the scholar was crushed beneath a fallen cabinet."

"That's an ugly way to go." Tarian shuddered.

Scole raised a hand. "I shall add his name to my prayers for the fallen later tonight. At least it is fortunate that you were not with him."

"I do have some good news, my lady. After I discovered that he would no longer be of use to our investigation, I headed down to the cellars and found that all of the novices survived the attack unharmed, if a little rattled by the experience. I sent them to help the healers."

"Well that is something to be grateful for." Scole nodded slowly. "I am afraid we are going to be busy over the coming months, Mercer."

"Yes, High Priestess."

"What were you investigating?" Tarian looked at them both with unbridled curiosity. "Perhaps there is a way we can help each other."

"Some things were stolen from our library my dear, it is nothing to concern yourself with."

Tarian grunted and shook her head. "I always thought temples were supposed to be secure, but that's two that have been raided recently. Didn't you know? Someone took a couple of relics from the Temple of Katarina in Metumontis a short while ago."

The High Priestess watched her for a few moments before she smiled sweetly. "Is that so? You wouldn't happen to know what they were, I suppose?"

"Ancient books or scrolls, I think. Bowen will know more, his father is the High Priest."

Scole got to her feet and rolled her shoulders. "I should go and see if the healers require my help, and if not I will speak to him about all of that. Mercer, make sure our new friend here is all right before you go anywhere."

"Yes my lady."

She took Tarian's hand and squeezed it gently. "All will be well, child. Even the most terrifying nightmares fade in time."

*

A strange perfume drifted upon the air as Rhydian made his way through the dense woodland; thick vines that wrapped around the trunks of ancient trees had flowered with pearly blossom, hiding all manner of carnivorous arachnids who awaited the unwitting insects that were lured in to devour the sweetened nectar.

Mylah and Merfyd were some way behind, discussing archaic magic that he had no interest in contemplating; there were beasts lurking here in the undergrowth and between the trees that watched his every step, and he was determined not to be distracted by idle conversation.

The day was drifting slowly into eventide, and a wave of warm golden light washed over the canopies and filtered down to the forest floor. Rhydian felt a tingle upon the back of his neck and his energy began to filter away; with a low snarl he slapped away something small that had tried to latch on to the top of his spine.

He spat to one side and shivered slightly. "Bloody spiders."

The trees up ahead seemed to deteriorate into a snare of gnarled limbs, each one covered in thick webbing and doused in shadow. The wind stirred between them, reaching out to whisper at him and whirl away to darker depths.

Rhydian placed a hand on the hilt of his sword and continued onward. He had never feared the dark, but he did not particularly wish to meet whatever foul creature it was that could spin webs of that size and thickness.

Something moved up ahead; a loud hiss came from one of the canopies and the leaves rustled violently, but nothing dropped into view.

The man drew his weapon and furrowed his brow; the queen would be safe enough of course, but honour was at stake. He slowed his steps and risked a glance behind: Mylah and Merfyd had noticed his change of pace and were trying to gain ground before anything appeared. He turned back to the path ahead and shrieked; hundreds of monstrous arachnids had blocked the way. Their bodies were thick with navy blue hairs and their long legs spread out across the ground as their beady eyes flickered from him to Mylah and back again.

Rhydian raised his sword, but as the Monarch reached his side the beasts dispersed. He waited for a few moments, his breathing heavy, before lowering the weapon.

"Not everything is a threat to us." She patted him on the arm. "No matter how ugly they may appear to be."

Rhydian flushed a dark red and sheathed the sword once more; Mylah moved on ahead, so he cleared his throat and went to walk after her. After only a few steps into the darkened copse, a magical barrier hit him in the chest and flung him back. Merfyd was beside him in moments, helping him to his feet.

The queen looked back at them with a frown. "What's wrong?"

"I… I don't know. Could it have been an old spell or something? A ward, maybe?" Rhydian tried once again to get to her side and was thrown clear.

Merfyd's eyes widened and he shook his head. "Oh no."

"What is it?"

"That's neither a ward nor magic leftover from some potent bygone mage – this spell cannot be more than a week old at most." He shuddered. "And yet the power that emanates from it is like nothing I have ever encountered during my travels."

Mylah walked back to them and frowned. "What are you talking about? There's nothing in the way, stop messing about. Rhydian, get up and let us move on."

"Your Grace, he isn't playing the fool. There is something here that seems to have been designed specifically to let you go on ahead – but only if you go alone."

"Aneira." Mylah pinched the bridge of her nose and sighed heavily. "Tarian said she was a powerful mage, but I had no idea she could do something like this."

Merfyd tried to walk beyond the barrier and was stopped at the same point; concern etched its way across his face.

The Monarch flicked her wrist and a spiral of blue magic spread out in front of her, illuminating a large swirling spell wall that stretched out until it disappeared over the horizon. She stared at it and listened with a shiver to the murmuring of voices that emanated from its core.

"I don't think that you should try to dismantle this, Your Grace." Merfyd let his gaze wander along its serpentine ridge. "Something of this nature could cause catastrophic damage when released, and with the knowledge they might possess it could have the potential to wound even you."

"Why didn't you get flung through the air?" Rhydian couldn't keep the annoyance from his voice. "Why am I the only one who has to get bruised? Besides, why would anyone want Her Divine Grace to be... oh, right."

"So now what do we do? We can't let you go on ahead alone, that's clearly what she wants. You've got to hand it to her, it's a gutsy plan to try and lure the most powerful magical being in existence into a trap."

"It's not a risk if you believe you can kill them."

A rumbling howl echoed through the forest ahead of them, and Rhydian shuddered.

Merfyd took Mylah's hand and pulled her away from the magic. "We need to leave, ma'am. Now."

Six

Ribbons of smoke rose into the sky, meandering through the inky twilight; braziers had been lit throughout the wooded hillsides and their charcoal infused with a rich and heady incense, although a faint smell of death still lingered upon the air, drifting through the quiet shadows. Small lanterns hung amongst the trees, and though most were doused, a defiant few still beat back the oncoming darkness with halos of bright silver.

Gentle rain misted down from the sky, settling in the hair of the weary travellers who moved quietly through the bracken. Aneira glanced heavenward, a slight smile brushing across her face as the stars glimmered briefly before hiding once again behind soft indigo clouds. Seren placed a hand on Elgan's shoulder and raised a finger to her lips; he frowned, but signalled to Aneira to stop all the same. A frigid wind whistled suddenly through the warm darkness, wrapping around their shoulders before pulling away towards the west.

Something stirred a few feet away. Aneira's head snapped to one side and she narrowed her eyes; silhouettes were rustling behind thickened trunks and in the shady undergrowth, emanating a putrid stench. Magic ignited at the woman's fingertips, and she signalled at the others to spread out.

Elgan raised his arms slowly, summoning bolts of dark red energy that sparked and shimmered against the shadows. He caught a glimpse of Seren as she unsheathed the short sword hung at her hip.

One moment fell into the next, the only sound the patter of the rain against the verdant floor.

"They call me Sprig. I don't know why!" A small creature burst out of the trees and leapt towards Seren, its fangs bared.

She cried out as the Oculi caught hold of her arm and dragged its claws through the thin leather doublet she wore; blood rose up from the deep gashes, pooling in the serrated wounds and slowly spilling out across her skin. She took hold of the monster by its neck and wrenched it away, throwing the squalling creature hard against a jagged boulder. Another sprang forth, and another, until a crowd of the snarling beasts had filtered out from every direction; they threw themselves at the humans, teeth and talons bared.

Aneira thrust her hand in a wide arc, creating icy white flames that exploded from the ground and engulfed the attackers; they screamed and wailed as their bodies burst and boiled, the fur and flesh quickly turning into ash.

"Ah, these mortals and their primitive powers." Thick, gurgling words slithered out of the murk. "So angry at the world that devours them! See how they struggle against fate and beat their tiny little fists at the skies." A short, squat creature slid out of the darkness, its moist green body squelching along the ground, an aura of garnet and jade light flickering around its skin. It rolled its bulbous eyes at the surprised onlookers.

"What the fuck is that?"

"Ask not questions of the Everlasting, churlish one. I already have one of your disgusting kind in my possession; you may join it."

Aneira snarled; flames erupted beside the Morsus, vanishing before they could scorch its flesh.

"Deplorable fiend!" A hacking cough speckled the ground in front of it with slime. "I will see to it that your heads are consumed whilst your bodies still live!"

Lightning raced through the air and struck the creature's left eye, penetrating the gooey mass and striking outwards. A ring of fire flared once again, this time lashing and burning the creature's skin until it popped and blistered. Panic welled within and it tried to get away, only to be beaten back by another barrage of magic. Lightning hit the remaining eye, melting it into a gooey mess, and the Morsus began to tremble, its aura dulling to tarnished grey.

Aneira clenched her hands into fists, and the monster exploded. Thick chunks of sludge splattered the surroundings as a foul stench rose into the air.

The world was still for a moment. Elgan stared at his hands and a grin crept across his face, but when he looked over at Seren his delight vanished.

She was doubled over and struggling to breathe, as injuries to her hands, arms and face welled with blood. In a moment Aneira was at her side, quickly closing her eyes and mumbling under her breath; amethyst light passed over them both and her wounds began to close.

A twig snapped nearby. Elgan looked back to where the Morsus had emerged, expecting another attack, only to see an elderly elven woman staggering out towards him.

"Merfyd's balls!" He ran over to help steady her. "Are you all right?"

She looked at him, confused; her silvery hair was unkempt and stuck in places to her dirt strewn face. There were small gashes along her bare arms, and one of her fingertips was missing; several bite marks along her left wrist and shin were oozing pus.

"Can you hear me? What happened to you?"

"Please…" The woman pulled away. "Please don't hurt me. I-I didn't mean to do anything wrong and I'm going back home now, I promise. I didn't… I need to go, please let me go."

"You've been hurt and need help. We're not going to –"

"No! No, please, just let me go. I-I'll be good, I won't tell anyone you're here, I just… I just need to get back. Please!"

Seren looked at her and frowned. "We don't mean you any harm, we were just passing through."

"I… I don't have any coin on me but I was collecting herbs, you can have those. Oh, but I dropped them when… when…"

Aneira walked over and took her hand; the woman eyed her warily for a moment before her shoulders sagged and she watched as magic flared over her ashen skin. After a few moments, some of the injuries began to repair themselves.

The woman cried out softly and looked up at her. "You're a mage?"

"I am, and so is my friend here. We are not bandits meaning to attack you; we were just travelling east when we were ambushed by a few monsters."

"*Two* with magic? Could you help us?" There was a sudden desperation in her voice. "Please, my village is not far from here. I can give you food and shelter for the night in return."

"We would be glad to. I think some of these cuts might be infected, and I would like to look at them properly."

Seren glanced at Elgan; he pretended not to notice her concern, focusing instead on trying to work out if they were about to be ambushed a second time.

The world around them was calm as they wandered westward, shadows swallowing up any beast whose inquisitive nature may have been seen as a threat.

A small village eventually rose up out of the mist, its palisade laced with hanging lanterns to chase back the gloom; runes, small carvings and protection enchantments also adorned the wooden stakes. Thin trails of smoke drifted up from a few of the slightly larger buildings, and bleating calls sounded from a large pen nearby. An aura of magic clung to the place, shielding it from the dangers of the surrounding woodland.

The soft veil of rain eased somewhat, and the scent of death masked by heady perfume grew stronger. Several pyres had been built a short distance away, surrounded by bodies that had been prepared with oils, shrouds and flower garlands.

"Wynne!" A young man carrying an ebony bow ran out of the gates. "What happened to you? What have these *gelynion* done to you?"

"Be at peace, Emyr. They were the ones who dealt with the beast that sought to harm me."

He narrowed his eyes at her and shrugged. "If you say so, *tegau*. Did you manage to gather the herbs we need? Catrin fares no better, and Dyl is close to death."

"I did, but I dropped them when I was attacked. All is not lost though, these two humans have magic. They can help us!"

He spat on the ground and turned away.

Aneira shot a glance at Elgan. "We are more than happy to provide any –"

"I care not what you are happy for, *gelyn!* If you truly wish to help us then be on your way; your kind is not welcome here."

"Emyr is young and foolish at times, but please don't think he represents us all. Our people need your help."

"You shame us Wynne. We require nothing from the *gelynion* and they should be gone from this place!"

Seren bared her teeth. "Well in that case, we'll be on our way and you can stay here and rot in your little village of death."

"Wait! Please don't leave us like this! My girl is gravely ill and there are others who will not last much longer without medical aid." Wynne turned to glare at Emyr. "Silence your bitterness before you lead us all into oblivion."

Aneira stepped forward. "We are not going to abandon you in your time of need. If your friend here is unsure about our intentions, he is welcome to accompany us."

He snarled. "Why should I trust anything you say?"

"I cannot force you to do so, but I have no quarrel with you or any of your kin. My name is Aneira Morgan; I was the Eminent Minister for the city of Mysta in the west. This is Elgan Williams, an old friend of mine and former magical adviser to the Conjury, and Seren from the city of Delyth in Caeli."

"Delyth? You will know of the priestess Scole then?"

"Unfortunately."

"The smell of death hangs upon that old crow."

Seren grunted. "I've noticed."

Emyr seemed to consider everything for a moment and then shook his head sadly, turning away and disappearing through the gates.

Wynne breathed a sigh of relief and glanced at Aneira with a small smile. "We are free to enter. For a moment I thought he might call upon the power of the wards that protect this place… although even those are beginning to fail us now."

She led them through the subdued village, their progress watched from windows and cracked doorways; pale light spilled out into the gloom before curtains were quickly drawn and doors were shut.

A few sentries glanced their way as they slowly patrolled the perimeter, occasionally muttering both prayer and profanity into the encroaching darkness.

Wynne passed by a stone well and then turned down a quiet alley; a weak magical barrier resisted the intruders for a moment before it relented. No lanterns had been hung here to chase back the shadows, and the stench of decaying flesh flooded the air; rancid puddles, fed by drips from a nearby overhang, squatted upon the ground amidst piles of foul smelling amber.

The houses were dark, quiet and lifeless; bolts of ragged cloth hung over open windows, and most of the doors had been nailed shut, save for one or two that hung from their hinges. The woman stopped in front of one of these, sorrow creeping across her face for a moment before she glanced behind her.

A moment or two passed in silence, heavy and full of grief.

"You'll find Dyl in there. Please don't be offended if he is reluctant to accept your aid; the *gelynion* have not been kind to us in recent months."

Seren frowned at Aneira. "Is this really worth our time? I thought you said finding the Grave was to be our priority at all costs."

"What is the point of magic if it cannot save those most in need?" The Minister sighed softly. "The blight has hit your people hard, Wynne."

"We asked one of the local lords for help last winter when our stores were running out. He sent a group of armed men in response, and when we allowed them passage inside the gate they ransacked everything."

"I… I am sorry to hear that."

"He's dead now. It seems that the plague did not care for his riches. We were able to retrieve some of what was taken – but much was lost to us that could not be so easily replaced. Anyway, you're here now, and Dyl and Catrin shouldn't have to wait because of my ramblings." A weak smile flickered across her lips. "Please go on inside."

The air within was warm and musty, and heavily layered with dust. A few pieces of furniture were scattered about the murky rooms, although most had been taken to be broken down into firewood long ago. Two large mirrors were hung upon opposing walls in the long hallway, their cracked exteriors shielded by timeworn velvet. Stubs of tallow candles lay discarded in several corners, half hidden by mounds of dirt and ash.

"Well this place is just fucking delightful."

Wynne cast an apologetic look at Seren. "I know it looks bad, but it was never meant to be like this. Those who were affected the worst were sent here; it was originally meant to serve as a kind of quarantine, as well as giving our healers somewhere private to work. But they succumbed to the same sickness, and these houses were soon believed to be as tainted as their inhabitants."

"No one tried to help you?"

She shook her head. "No. Many of the nearby towns and villages were full of mages, and they all lie in rot now. But the red skies have abated and seem to have taken the disease with them. Catrin and Dyl were the last to be affected, thank the Gods… although Lady Amara hung her cloak over us so heavily that I doubt we will ever fully recover. We may head south once it is safe to travel, and seek out a new home away from the ghosts of this one."

Elgan left the women and moved carefully up the stairs, the wooden boards creaking under his weight. An old chandelier drooped precariously from the bowed ceiling, its broken prongs reaching out desperately towards the floor.

The path split before him to lead to three rooms, the first of which was filled with rubble where the roof had collapsed some time ago; another was completely barren of everything but a few dead rodents. He headed to the third, gingerly pushing the door until it snagged and refused to move any further. He frowned, muttering a few words under his breath, and the slab of wood disintegrated.

The body of a man lay upon the dirty floor; his blue tinged skin was covered in blisters and sores, and his once lilac eyes, now bloodshot and open, stared into an empty corner.

Elgan covered his nose with his sleeve and moved in to take a closer look; a pool of bile had gathered under the man's head, streaks of foam still clinging to his chin; maggots writhed in open wounds along the back of his neck, and a few of his fingertips had been gnawed away. Trails of fluid were drying upon his clothes.

Elgan stood up and headed back out into the hallway, trying to keep his stomach from churning.

"Are you all right?"

He looked up at Wynne's hopeful face, and tried not to shudder. "I'm sorry, but there's nothing we can do for him."

"He's gone then. How long do you… do you think it's been?"

"A couple of hours, maybe more. Don't go in there. It's not something you need to see."

She nodded sadly and turned to walk back down the stairs. "I'll have to tell Emyr once I've taken you to Catrin. Hopefully there's enough time left to save her."

They left the house in silence and Wynne led them to another that was in a similar state, save for candles burning in a few tarnished holders. She quickly ushered them into a room where a young woman lay upon a makeshift bed of straw, blankets and cushions. An array of small bowls filled with powders and herbs sat upon a well scrubbed table nearby, alongside some strips of clean cloth and a simple dagger, and a log smouldered in the hearth.

"How long has she been sick?" Aneira moved over to the woman's side and placed her hand upon her brow.

"A few weeks now. It wasn't that bad at first, she just had a bit of a headache and was feeling tired more often. But a lot of them started out that way and now... now she's..."

Seren's mood softened and she squeezed Wynne's hand gently. "They'll do everything they can. In the meantime, that fire needs to be stoked. Do you have any wood that we can use?"

"Not here. There should be some in one of the storerooms of the Great Hall, though."

"Well then, it looks like you and I are taking a little trip and leaving these two to work their magic. Perhaps we could pick up a few supplies whilst we're there? You look like you could do with a good meal."

The elf hesitated for a moment, her tearful gaze locked upon her daughter's face; finally she nodded.

Once they were alone, Aneira motioned Elgan to her side. He quickly studied the weeping sores upon the woman's arms, turning his attention to the dark green tint that crept across her fingernails. Her skin was tinged sky blue, deepening around her mouth to an inky cobalt that spidered out in tendrils across her jaw. Strands of her curly silver hair clung to the sweat that beaded her forehead and neck, and dark grey circles underlined her closed eyes.

"It looks like her mother has been keeping the wounds as clean as possible." Elgan glanced at the bowls. "And no doubt making poultices from those herbs."

"She may well have saved her life." The Minister took Catrin's hand and smoothed back her hair. "The Gods will guide us in what we need to do. Are you ready?"

"I think so."

Aneira closed her eyes and steadied her breathing; her thoughts calmed into a clear image of a meadow bathed in deep golden light. Birds chattered in nearby trees, and mountains climbed up the horizon; the air was heavy with the perfume of flowers and the songs of insects as they danced upon a light breeze. There was laughter somewhere in the distance, woven softly amongst a melody ancient and serene.

Figures stood some distance from her, their features lost beneath a haze of amethyst. She could feel them watching her, and after a few moments one of them reached out their hand, beckoning her to come towards them.

Her eyes shot open. Light filled the room as lilac smoke spiralled up from the floorboards and the air shimmered with tiny glowing beads.

Elgan raised his arms towards the ceiling, chanting quietly; his words tumbled into one another, echoing until they seemed to seep into the walls surrounding him. His fingers tingled for a moment before numbness began to set in and his arms burned; pain bristled along his spine and spread out across his back.

Aneira tilted her head, trying to concentrate as the muscles in her legs cramped and went into spasm; her jaw locked and she could feel energy surging within her chest, hammering against her ribs. Blood trickled from her nose, slithering down across her lips to drip onto the floor.

Power cascaded from them both and flared across the room, pushing back the residual gloom and chasing shadows out into the night, before settling above Catrin in a heavy mist.

Agony tore through Aneira, and she screamed.

*

Sunlight scattered across the dusty wooden boards, its pale glow sweeping silently through the quiet house.

Aneira sat quietly by the warm hearth, absentmindedly tracing patterns upon the floor; soft music drifted in from the courtyard outside, and she was momentarily lost in its lulling embrace. Seren slumbered nearby, her face pressed up against a threadbare cushion; she wrinkled her nose and murmured softly as dreams brushed across her thoughts.

Elgan watched them for a while, resting his chin upon his hands; he had woken with a heavy heart some time ago, drawn away from images of Saeth bathed in golden light. He blinked back the tears that had welled in his lilac eyes and finally got to his feet, walking over to check on Catrin as she slept. The woman's skin was still tinged a pale blue, but she was at peace; her chest rose and fell steadily, and no sweat beaded her brow. A small smile flickered over his lips; he smoothed a stray lock of hair back from her forehead and sighed.

The door creaked slowly open and the smell of freshly baked bread swam into the room; Wynne entered, carrying a tray of warm food and small cups of ale. Elgan glanced at her.

"I thought you might be hungry. The tavern isn't usually open this early, but once I told Eira everything that you have done to help us she was more than willing to whip up some breakfast. How's my girl?"

He bowed his head a little. "Faring much better this morning, it seems. Her fever broke late last night, but it is important that she still gets plenty of rest."

"I don't know how to thank you all." She set the tray down upon a table and wiped her hands on her apron. "You've done so much. I... I truly thought her lost when she started to show signs of having the blight. I had always hoped that my children would be blessed with magic like their father was, a sign from the Gods that our union was meant to be." She smiled. "It's such a help to have a mage around, especially on the farms."

"Are your other children well?"

"Oh..." She glanced away. "Catrin is the only one left. My son Arthur died last winter, and his brothers were killed years ago when our village was attacked."

"I'm sorry, I didn't mean –"

She wiped her eyes quickly and gestured for him to eat. "I have some more food bundled up that you can take with you, and a little gold stored away."

Aneira got to her feet and shivered. "You have done more than enough; we will not take your coin."

"As you wish."

"Is something wrong?"

"No, no, it's just that I'm not used to folks helping out for nothing. I didn't tell you before, but there were some other mages that passed by not too long ago. We begged them for help, but they wouldn't stop. I... I don't blame them, they probably had orders to stay away, but I keep thinking how Dyl might still be alive if they had thought us worthy of their time." She sighed heavily and shook her head. "They were well armoured and had an escort of people with weapons, so I suppose they were just busy, on their way to somewhere more important."

Aneira rubbed the back of her neck. "Do you remember anything about what they were wearing? A sigil perhaps, or a colour?"

Wynne shrugged. "Some of them were carrying shields that I think were dark green. No, wait… it was blue, not green."

"What about a crest? A moon maybe, with a dagger?"

"I'm not sure, I'm sorry. Oh! But before I forget, they left these." She pulled some small crystals out of her pocket. "Emyr watched them placing quite a few around the forest and some just outside of our gates, thinking no one could see."

Elgan took them and held them up to the light, squinting at them. "Locus crystals, meant for amplifying magic."

"Or a magical plague." Aneira struggled to keep the anger from her voice. "Are there any more of these?"

"No. Do you know who…? Those people, did they do this? But why? Why would anyone want to hurt my Catrin?"

"Have you heard of Queen Mylah of Amissa?"

"The new Eternal Monarch? The Gods granted some of us dreams and visions of her last summer." Wynne was silent for a moment as her thoughts raced. "I should have known that the Monarch was behind this. I had thought that with Dullahan dead we could live free of that fearful shadow."

Aneira put her hands on the elf's shoulders. "We are going to fix this, I promise. She razed my city to the ground and left my people to perish beneath the stones or in the maws of her monstrous allies. We know how to ensure that she cannot continue on this path of destruction, for just as your people were shown visions of her ascension, so have we been shown of her demise. She reigns with death and destruction at her heels, but we can defeat her. I cannot bring your kinsmen back, but I can prevent this from happening to anybody else."

A relieved smile flickered over Wynne's lips. "Then perhaps there is still some good left in this world. Thank you, for all that you have done. We will never forget it."

Seven

Moonlight cascaded down over the mountains and valleys like a soothing silver balm, snaking in and out of every meadow and forest until everything was quiet and serene. Slithers of smoke trailed up into the sky from villages and encampments, and lights twinkled in the distance as torches rose and fell.

Mylah paced back and forth, her hands clasped behind her back. She could sense hundreds of voices calling out to her, desperate and full of fragile hope, and thousands more swarmed with vengeance and hate.

She shivered and tilted her head back, her eyes closed against the glare of the heavens. Ancient melodies sang to her from a distant land, and for a moment she thought she could hear the clash of steel, but when she looked out at the world around her she was alone.

She flicked her wrist and a portal opened beside her, dispersing as soon as she walked through it.

Merfyd looked up from his place at the campfire and handed her a cup of sweetened tea. "How was your walk? Did you manage to clear your head?"

"No." She sipped the drink and wrinkled her nose. "There was no more peace there than here."

"When the war wages within, there can be no resolution without."

She sighed at him. "That sounds like temple rhetoric."

"Maybe it is." He shrugged. "Once you spend enough time listening to the devoted, you have a tendency to pick up certain phrases. Most of them are complete bullshit of course, but some occasionally ring with truth."

Mylah finished drinking the tea and stared for a while at the flames, listening to the wood crackle and watching sparks fly up towards the velveteen sky.

Merfyd looked over at Rhydian sleeping peacefully nearby, rolled up in several blankets. "I met a woman the other day with a young daughter named Mylah."

The queen glanced at him. "There have been many since my ascension, or at least so I am told. A tidal wave of children called Eris, Bowen, Mylah and Berne. It's going to make it rather confusing for their tutors, I imagine."

"No doubt." He grinned. "Perhaps they will all strive to be skilled warriors trained in the arts of battle, and seek honour and glory in your name. I'm sure our noble knight here could teach them a thing or two about that."

"Hmm. I would rather they become farmers or clerks or smiths, and live long and happy lives free from the horrors of war."

Sadness passed across the man's face. "We can but hope. Still, they do have names that beg to be lived up to."

"I suppose you would know."

"Yes, I suppose I would."

Silence descended then and squatted between them like a toad. Rodents scampered in the undergrowth nearby, and a flock of small birds rose in silhouette; a Jittern lounged atop a boulder, watching the campfire with passing interest.

Ancient songs whispered upon the breeze and wrapped themselves around Mylah's neck, tracing across her skin with ghostly fingers until she shivered; death and unrest stalked the nightly ground, leaving trails of blood and bone and calling out to any who would listen. The queen turned away.

Merfyd tapped his hand against the small log he sat upon as he contemplated their next move. Magic seemed to almost smoke from the woman's skin, leaking out into the atmosphere like a wounded vein. She glanced at him again and he wondered for a moment if she could read his thoughts; dangerous magic was not unknown to the Monarchs, and many before her had utilised it to eliminate those they considered enemies. She looked away and he followed her gaze to the small winged feline that appeared to be studying them even as it yawned and dropped down to the floor.

"We cannot stay here long." Her words were softer now.

"Do you wish to wait for sunrise?"

"It matters not to me, although I suspect Rhydian will snap if we interrupt his rest. But if we don't manage to reach this Aneira in time…"

He nodded grimly and sighed. "Then we're all fucked. She cannot know what it is she hopes to unleash."

Mylah snorted. "Don't be so naive. History is full of people who thought that they could handle power and cared little about the destructive way it was brought about. Erebus turned Luxnoctis into his hunting ground, even shaping the different landscapes through magic to make it an interesting game for him. The more I learn of that man, the more I worry about what I have taken upon myself."

"You do not think that you are alike, surely?"

She was quiet for a moment. "I know that I have lost a great part of myself somewhere along the way. Everything that I thought I understood about this world was turned upside down, and now there are shadows in every corner."

"There are ways to find that which has drifted from you."

"You assume that I wish to." She paused briefly. "Some things should be left where they fall. I have been thinking about how Erebus feared the Veiled Council more than anything, at least towards the end of his unnatural life, and there are moments when I wonder if he was right to do so."

"But they are just trying to protect Cadere."

"I know." A weak smile crossed her lips as she looked up at the stars. "Do you ever wonder about what is up there?"

"Should I?"

"What would you say if I told you that we are a part of something more than what is taught by priests and scholars? A great constellation of worlds named Sarheim, linked forever by tiny threads of magic?"

Merfyd cocked his head to one side and grinned. "Dullahan really did suppress knowledge in Luxnoctis. I do wonder if their food is better, or at the very least if they have good ale. That makes everything a little nicer for everyone."

She laughed then, and shook her head. She seemed about to say something more when the Occasus crystal at their feet glowed a vibrant purple and another portal burst into life nearby; a faint smell of burnt flesh lingered in the air as Bowen and Tarian stepped out into the cool night air.

"Your Grace." Bowen looked drained and his voice was hoarse. "We have done as you asked."

"Sit down and have some tea."

"I would prefer to rest, if you do not object ma'am."

She dismissed him with a wave and turned to Tarian, who sighed heavily and shook her head; Mylah got to her feet and walked away, leaving them to busy themselves with whatever they wished.

Tarian slumped down next to Merfyd and tilted her head back to look up at the night sky; a tinge of red still hovered over the horizon where the queen's magic had not yet been able to cleanse it, but here and for leagues behind them it was free of the smothering, bloodied shroud.

"Did you know that's a God's Blood stone?"

"What is?"

"The pendant around your neck. It's quite a rare crystal, I haven't seen one for years."

She took hold of it and closed her eyes; Bryn's face danced before her for a few moments before it faded away. A sigh upon her lips, she felt sleep drawing her in.

"Berne?"

"Boss?"

Mylah paced up and down, her footsteps ringing out through the small, empty tavern. A fire crackled in its blackened hearth, devouring the broken bones of a letter until they curled into ash.

The queen eyed the remaining pieces with a raised eyebrow. "Burning old love letters?"

He coughed. "Aye, something like that. What are you doing here, Fletching? I thought you were on the trail of that mage."

"I was. Am." She rubbed her brow. "I needed to come somewhere to think, and to speak with someone I know that I can trust."

"I'm flattered." He tossed another paper into the flames and grinned. "I might not even mention this to Bowen… unless he's given himself another title. So what is it that you can't talk to your

Seneschal about, but you can whisk yourself over the ocean to visit an old man in a deserted building?"

"This place is full of ghosts; you do know that, right?"

"Aye. It's comforting in a way, to think that Grim might still be hanging around somewhere. And don't evade the question, boss. What's wrong?"

Her shoulders sagged. "I don't know what to do. Strength has been returning to magic since I… since Erebus died, which means that every mage should find their spells naturally more potent and easier to cast. But this woman managed to conjure a spell wall that I didn't even detect. She wants me to follow her alone."

"Well that would be fucking stupid."

"But if I don't go after her, she could reach the Anghenfil."

"Why don't you just teleport somewhere and ambush her?" Berne scratched his bearded chin. "If she believes that you're following her, then she won't anticipate a frontal assault."

She smiled weakly. "An old strategy that worked well enough in Aranea. I had the same thought, but Bowen was concerned that she may have considered this already. After all, she's clearly well prepared and has evaded our attempts to hone in on her location before now. If she has already reached Mynydd and lies in wait…"

"Ah." Berne nodded gravely. "I see. Well we can't have that. We lost enough people to get rid of Dullahan, we're not losing you too."

Mylah was quiet for a time; she stared into the flames as tears welled in her eyes and her thoughts flowed out towards the past. She could hear the wails and screams of those banished to the void, their shrieking melodies nearly as familiar to her now as her own voice. A woman watched her from a shadowed corner; maggots dripped from her open mouth as a bloody stream gushed from the wounds where her eyes had once been. Her flaxen hair, half torn from her skull, was matted with dirt and gore.

The Monarch turned back to Berne. "I don't know what to do." She wiped the tears away and shivered. "Caeli has refused to aid us, and Sepelite is already buckling under fear. We cannot get through to enough people willing to understand that the old tales are more than what they seem, and that if Aneira reaches the Grave of the World then we will all perish. They think us children playing at politics and using empty threats to establish a foothold in lands long abandoned by my predecessor."

"We all suffered under Dullahan's rule, boss. They need to see you as a figure of hope and prosperity, and that takes time."

"We don't have time!" She clenched her jaw. "That idiotic mage is going to unleash a hellscape over my realm!"

Magic sparked in the air, jagged spikes of indigo and sapphire.

Berne glanced at them and cleared his throat. "Fletching –"

"Do you not understand? You sit here burning away relics of the past like it matters, when what we need to do is stop another catastrophe before it begins in earnest!"

The walls of the tavern began to shake; clouds of dust fell from the rafters.

"Ah, boss, listen…"

"Don't you dare address me in such a way!" She threw her hands outwards and snarled, sending a shock wave of magic through the air that caught the man in its grasp and hurled him against a table.

Darkness engulfed Berne as blood trickled from the back of his head.

Mylah vanished.

*

Scole walked up and down, her hands clasped behind her back; she sighed as she finally came to rest before the necromancer and shook her head. "Are you sure there's nothing more to be done?"

"My apologies High Priestess, but his spirit has already fled to Amara's side." He brightened a little. "I could still reanimate the corpse though, if you like."

She stared at him for a moment and then rolled her eyes. "It is grossly unfortunate that Master Thomas perished in the attack."

"Squashed like ripe fruit under a very large boulder." Cael sniffed loudly. "I like to think that it's how he would have wanted to go."

Mercer stifled a laugh behind them.

Scole fixed him with a look. "And when will his successor be named?"

"Oh not for a few months yet. We'll need to scrape every last piece of Thomas into a jar and leave it at the altar until the Goddess speaks to us about her plans for the future of the guild. But fear not, High Priestess. I've been given the honour of being ambassador to the temple in the meantime."

She tried to hide her disappointment by turning away.

Mercer watched her carefully and then glanced back at Cael. "I thought the souls of the Guild Masters were supposed to serve you after they die?"

"They are." He shrugged. "I guess Thomas was just as much of a piece of shit in death as he was in life. His bargain with Amara was struck decades ago, and it unsettles me that he should go against it. In fact, it unsettles me that she would *allow* him to go against it. There's no mention of such a thing in any of our records."

"And how far back do those go?"

"Oh, at least four hundred years." He waved his hand dismissively. "There were older ones of course, but they were lost in a fire. And more still were used as bedding by Guild Master Havoc last century.

It was decided that they weren't worth keeping after his death due to their... soiled nature."

"Yes well, that's hardly important now. If we can't get anything useful out of the scholar then there's no point in continuing with that line of thought. Mercer, take his body and dispose of it properly."

"At once, my lady."

"And I have a task for you, Necromancer."

"Ooh, how exciting. Do I get to wear a special sash?"

"What? No. I need you to find the envoy from Queen Mylah and keep an eye on them. We were unable to formally offer them any aid, but I want you to report back to me with any concerns or needs they have that we might assist with."

He smiled and nodded. "Very well."

"Talk to one of the mages in the medical encampment; I believe someone left a Solis crystal that you can use to teleport to their location. You may go."

"I'll need to pick up some supplies from the Guild Hall first."

"Yes fine, whatever, just leave."

The air over Delyth was heavy with the perfume of death. A large pyre had been built to deal with the remains of those who had been left by both monsters and magic; priests had conducted memorials each night for those who had not.

Rubble had been swept aside and repairs to the buildings that had suffered damage were already underway; the Sceleratis cadaver had been dragged into an empty alley to be divided up by a few of the more optimistic butchers.

Nelia wandered through the quietened streets, watching for any hints of unrest or mutters of vengeance that might seep out of the shadows. She thought back to the campaigns she had fought in Luxnoctis under the orders of a Monarch driven mad by time and jealousy and bitterness, and how it had been considered essential to identify and annihilate all signs of dissention and rebellion. She could still hear the cries of those who tried to resist the onslaught of Dullahan's forces, as though it would have made a difference. Bitterness had been rife in her homeland for the past few years now, and whispers of betrayal often drifted through the ranks. There were those who had lost all faith after Dullahan's fall, believing their lives to be nothing more than a hollow shell, and many had disappeared into the cold grasp of a winter's night.

She sighed and rolled her heavy shoulders as though the cloak she wore was made of stone. There could never truly have been victory, she knew that; her own kin lay long dead because of animosity dreamt up by people who rested in the blood soaked ground beside them. Mylah had been leading a mission of peace, of reparation, but even that had turned to thoughts of rent flesh and fragmented bone.

Nelia tapped her chin and shook her head; there was an undercurrent of pain in this world, and never could they seem to eradicate it.

Raised voices nearby snapped her back to reality. She frowned and headed over to the boundary of the medical encampment; one of the mages was shouting at a man dressed in black and silver robes.

"What's going on here? This is meant to be a place of peace and healing, not discord."

The mage whirled around at her words, his face flustered and sweaty. "This *necromancer* wants to use our Solis stone!"

She looked at Cael and raised her eyebrows. "Is there any particular reason you wish to ambush our friends?"

"Ambush? *Ambush?* Brig's balls, the very idea of it! I have been sent by the High Priestess to *help* them, and this idiot is preventing me from doing so. Look, I have a sash and everything." He pointed proudly to a scarf slung across his chest with a red and gold sun sewn onto the dark fabric.

A smile crossed Nelia's lips and she cleared her throat. "Help him activate the portal, Sam. He's no threat to them, believe me."

The mage threw his arms up in the air and scoffed. "Fine! But if he tries to kill them all and raise them up as an army of undead then it's on your head, not mine!"

"Uh huh. Just open the bloody portal."

Tarian looked up as the smell of burnt flesh blossomed around her and frowned at Cael stepping out of the hastily closed spell. He grinned and bowed at her.

"What the fuck are you doing here? I thought your guild would be overrun by requests to create a procession of shuffling corpses."

"What is with all the hatred against my artistry today? I've been sent by High Priestess Scole to help with your search for Aneira."

"But she refused us."

"No look, I've got this sash and everything."

Rhydian studied it and shrugged. "I've never seen that as an official emblem before, but who are we to go against the wishes of the temple?"

"But that's just a –"

"So..." Cael clapped his hands together. "What are we doing?"

"Travelling to Ynys Ysbryd." Mylah appeared behind him and smirked as his eyes widened at the name. "Unless you would rather run back to your priestess and cry?"

"That name is cursed... y-you shouldn't use it." He shuddered and whispered a quick prayer to the Goddess of Death. "Lady Amara will see us all before we leave its shores; why would you want to go there?"

"A name is a name, nothing more." She snarled at him and turned away. "Pack everything up, we leave immediately."

"Nothing more, unless it's an important reminder to you about men and monsters, apparently. Shouldn't we listen to him? He knows this place better than we do and –"

"I'd be quiet if I were you. Your friend is the reason we're in this mess in the first place." Mylah's eyes flashed with anger. "Perhaps I should just shatter her skull and melt all of its contents, and be done with this ridiculous endeavour."

Tarian stared at her. "I… I…"

"You – you – what? You're sorry for giving a powerful mystical tool to a moron who thinks that she can rid the world of its magical source? You want me to extend the kind of mercy to her that she has refused to give to others? Humans and their petty desire for power and control, and for what? So they can reign whilst death and destruction stalk their every step? Pah!"

"Your Grace I don't think that is –"

"Enough, Bowen! Your opinion is not needed on this matter, or on any other truthfully. Do you know how that spell wall was created? Hmm? Do you? Answer me!"

"No, Your Grace."

"Sacrifice." She hissed the word. "It screamed at me with the voices of a hundred rodents, birds, and beasts whose throats were slit and heads caved in just so she could reach her goal. Perhaps if you spent more time studying the world around you and less thinking about fucking your Conjury Guard here you would have noticed!"

"But I thought you didn't even detect it? Besides, the temples sacrifice animals on all the holy days." Rhydian shrugged. "I don't see what the problem is."

Mylah laughed bitterly at him. "Oh if only you knew the truth, you poor blinded fool. Perhaps I should let you see?"

Merfyd stepped forward and placed a hand upon her shoulder. "So to Ynys Ysbryd then, Your Grace?"

She studied him for a moment, and her anger calmed. "Yes. I need to speak the Meirwon."

The air shimmered around them and a smell like charred earth arose; the landscape vanished for a moment, replaced by an expanse of black and purple mist. It dispersed moments later, and they were standing upon the shore of a large island. The sand beneath their feet was grey and split in places where jagged leaves of dark green and yellow sprouted from the earth. A silhouette of mountains pierced the horizon behind them, flooding down into a valley of thick, impenetrable woodland.

A creature watched from nearby; her leathery skin was icy blue, though mottled with a darker shade in places around her neck and face, and her large red eyes blinked at them slowly. Four thick horns coiled out of the top of her head, a ring of cerulean curls at their base. She was dressed in ragged indigo robes strung together with golden chains, and her long bony fingers were wrapped around a carved staff.

"Why have you come here, Wretched Ones?" Her words were drawn out in rasping whispers. "Why do you sully these strands with your grease?"

"I am here to speak to the Meirwon."

"I spoke not to the Mortifera, you may go wherever your heart pleases and your poisoned feet see fit. But the humans," she spat at the word, "should not venture beyond the vines that wrap around the sacred trees."

"They will do no harm to your groves."

"So say you."

"I will cut off their heads and leave them as an offering upon the banks of Llyn Golau Lleuad should they offend you in any way."

The creature considered this for a moment. "Acceptable. Follow, and I shall lead you to where the Meirwon see fit to dwell."

The beach stretched its long arms out for miles, but to the north it slithered away into trees of black and dark green; thick trailing plants clung to the bark, their deep emerald hues interspersed with tiny explosions of lilac and amethyst petals.

The air was warm and scented with the heady musk of beast and bloom alike; serpents slid through the mossy undergrowth, and beady eyes watched from the shadows as the intruders trudged behind their guide. Birds called out from unseen perches within the rustling canopies and insects hummed as they danced upon a whistling breeze.

Cael shuddered and looked over at Bowen. "What the fuck kind of spell was that?"

"Her Grace doesn't need portals to travel anymore. Apparently."

"You weren't aware of this? We shouldn't be here. This is not a place meant for our kind."

"Of that the human speaks the truth." The creature turned to glare at him. "But with so many words does he pollute the quiet of the grove."

He dropped back a few paces to Tarian's side and waited for the intense cardinal gaze to return to the path ahead.

"I don't think she likes you."

He smiled ruefully. "I can't imagine why. *I'm* the one who said we shouldn't venture out here, and if I'd known your queen could just transport us with her fucking mind I might have told Scole to stick this idea of hers somewhere tender."

"But then you wouldn't have your sash."

"What a dark world that would have been."

Some leagues to the east a river gushed over a broken cliff face, the waterfall a raging force of glassy white; streams coursed away and disappeared into hidden pools.

The path stopped abruptly and gave way to stems of golden grass which shot up several feet from the deceptive earth; stones and pitfalls wound their way beneath unknowing feet and the creatures of the forest lay in wait nearby, mouths salivating and eyes widening.

The guide turned suddenly and without hesitation, taking them through a copse of trees whose trunks were covered in gossamer web and violet spiderlings. A river coursed alongside them for a way, sunlight skidding along the rippling water and vanishing into unknown depths.

Cael lost his footing and slipped, landing with a loud thud on the riverbank; one of his rings slid from his finger and disappeared beneath the surface. He cursed loudly and got to his knees, peering over the edge; Tarian rolled her eyes at him, a quick smile flickering across her lips.

"Brig's balls!" He fell back and tried to get away. "Brig's fucking balls, what the fuck is that?"

Tarian reached down and helped him to his feet; he stumbled towards the others, who had turned to see the cause of the commotion. She watched him for a moment, and then glanced back to see a humanoid creature staring up at her from its place beneath the clear water. Its pearlescent black eyes followed her every move as its thin, wide mouth opened into a snarling grin and revealed rows of sharp needle-like teeth; its pale face was devoid of other features, although edged by the obsidian scales that covered most of its body.

There were three long fingers on each hand, with a strange webbing stretched between them; the same silky mesh lashed across the tail fin and from the delicate ribs towards its arms. A crown of twisted white horns rose out of the top of its head.

"Syreni? I thought them to be nothing more than a tale told to scare children."

"Nay, call them not by the moniker of Erebus, whose legacy should but lie in ashes. The Draigmôr have dwelled here for countless winters beyond his boundaries."

"No matter the name you identify them by, they will tear you apart and feed on your flesh." Bowen ignored the angered glance of their escort.

"I thought there was an accord in place to stop that."

"Mortifera cannot bargain with every one of the Everlasting Princes. All creatures of this realm must feast upon something, and if reckless humans think to plunge into waters that belong not to them, their meat is surrendered."

They moved along in silence for a few minutes, the Draigmôr shadowing their movements; Tarian glanced back at it time and again, each curious look met with a spiny grimace in return. An icy chill coursed through her and she suppressed the desire to sneak back to take a closer look.

Cael took her hand and squeezed it gently. "Be wary of that thing. I've heard tales of Syreni, how they speak not a word and yet entice men and women alike to their domain in order to shred their skin and devour the sweet and tender tissue beneath. It is said that they can bury their thoughts inside your skull and drive you beyond the edges of reasoning, until your mind is no longer your own and insanity has you in its grip, and you just walk into their watery lair."

"I suppose you think you can protect me from it?"

"Gods no! If you go in there I'm not coming after you. Ah… no offense."

She chuckled. "None taken, hero. I have no intention of going for a swim, so you can let go of my hand now."

"I'll wager there are waterlogged caverns around here full of rotting limbs and skulls picked clean by ravenous hands and mouths; piles of bones cracked and splintered, never to be recovered and instead shrouded forevermore in the hidden depths."

"The deathly one speaks much of things he has little knowledge of. Perhaps he would like to visit the realm of the Draigmôr to see with his own little eyes what the Everlasting truly like to do to prey."

Cael clamped his mouth shut and glanced at Tarian, who just laughed at him and shook her head.

After a few miles the river curled away towards the horizon, and the long grasses receded back into mossy shrubs shielded by gnarled trees; deeper into the thicket they traipsed, not a word spoken amongst them, until the guide stopped outside the mouth of a large cave shrouded by a blanket of leaves and mist.

Mylah looked up at it with a satisfied nod.

The creature twitched a little as she pointed with her staff. "Here is where destiny parts us, Mortifera. Spirits and spells weave through eternity in this place; tread lightly and leave a gift of chattering heads if one more insult is breathed through fleshy mouths."

"I thank you for your assistance. Go in peace."

The guide shot one more glowering look at Cael before she disappeared into the trees.

Bowen walked up towards the cave and narrowed his eyes. "There are runes carved into the rock."

"Don't try to read them, you'll only give yourself a headache." The queen moved past him. "There are many things here that are not for the minds of mortals. You would all do well to remember that."

Merfyd followed her swiftly as she made her way inside. The air was colder here, and free of any perfumed scent; water trickled down the walls and dripped into pools hidden behind thick, glistening stalagmites. Insects nestled against the roof of the cavern, the dim purple light emanating from their tiny bodies barely enough to illuminate the jagged path that wound through the gloom.

Something stirred a little way ahead of them; Mylah slowed her pace and raised a hand. The others stopped behind her, glancing at one another as the seconds ticked by.

A voice purred suddenly through the darkness. "The Mylah Queen?"

"I am here."

"This one is Iolyn of the Meirwon." An orb of light appeared a few feet ahead of the Monarch and a figure over seven feet tall stepped into view.

"Brig's balls..." Cael's jaw dropped.

The creature tilted its head slightly to look at him before sweeping its gaze over the others, the large indigo eyes seeming to bore into each of them for a short while before moving on to the next. Its dark pink skin was tinged here and there with streaks of silver, which had also sunk into the fur upon its long legs, and its cloven hooves. Its features were sharp, and so heavy shadows fell across its face. "This one brings greetings to the Mylah Queen and her... otherlings. Come, this one has answers to bring forth."

Tarian grabbed hold of Bowen's arm. "What, by all the Gods, is that thing?"

"A being of pure magic, native to this part of Sepelite."

"The Mylah Queen's otherlings know much, but this one was born to live in Syrthio." Iolyn's voice drifted easily over to them.

"I don't understand."

"When the summers were still young, the Erebus came with words to brand and bind and constrict. Syrthio was twisted into Sepelite,

Eordaern into Inlustris and then later Luxnoctis. This one is unsure of other lands; much knowledge was given to the void."

"Are there more of you?"

Iolyn slowly blinked its large eyes at Tarian.

Mylah cleared her throat. "She means to ask if the Meirwon are numerous."

"*Much has been given to the void:* this one has seen many perish under the scarlet skies. The Mylah Queen was late, the Erebus held on and all were thought to be thrown to the nothingness. The Meirwon yet live, but this one has not seen many since the winters grew long. This one does not know how many endured the Withering."

Tarian shrugged lightly. "Like I said, I don't understand."

"I do. Forgive me, Iolyn. The Sundering came at a great cost, but my heart is lightened of a few of its burdens to see that at least some of your kin have managed to survive."

"The Mylah Queen means to repair what was damaged, but there is pain rendered deep in this place and in others. The Rival means to see all work undone, to rise to the peaks during unknown chaos, and to bring from death that which was thought lost. Choices, shadowed and yet burning bright, await those who would seek them. Beware, the Mylah Queen, for the path is yet treacherous."

Footsteps sounded from the darkness and within moments another Meirwon emerged into the pale glow. It glared at the gathering of humans that stood before it wide-eyed and silent; Iolyn blinked at it slowly.

"What is that one doing?" It hissed at Iolyn. "The Wretched Ones come before the Meirwon and beating hearts drum out echoes in blood! Think of when the time of the Luctus was done, and the swords came sharper than ever before! Think of those seeds of Syrthio who will never grow again."

"This one is not ignorant of the history that binds this land! The Mylah Queen is *not* the Erebus, and that otherling has no power in vein." Iolyn gestured at Tarian. "Questions spill forth like water and knowledge is given, but to no depths that Meirwon may drown. There must be understanding between Everlasting and Wretched Ones, and the Mylah Queen knows this. The world breath is a gift, not a curse, but the Wretched Ones' burdens grow evermore."

"That one cannot cast? The Sundering did this?"

"No. The Tarian has no power by vein of birth."

"How does it know my name?" She whispered quietly to Bowen, but Iolyn swivelled its eyes back to her before he could answer.

"This one knows much, the Tarian."

The other Meirwon watched her for a time and then turned back to Iolyn. "No power by vein of birth? Then these Wretched Ones may know that this one is named Idwal of the Meirwon, reborn in the Spring of the Luctus."

"It is an honour to meet you, Idwal."

The creature stared at the Monarch for a while. "The Mylah Queen is not Wretched."

"No, not anymore."

"The colour of the magic of Syrthio is in the Mylah Queen's veins. It was never in the Erebus, nor in the Luctus. The Mylah Queen is beyond what even the elf king could find. Why then travels the Mylah Queen to Syrthio? This one does not like the Wretched to step foot inside the sacred places."

"The Idwal should return to the quiet corners." Iolyn urged him away with a drawn out wave. "This one is here in times of darker shrouds."

Cael backed away a little and steadied himself against a large jutting rock; a soft mewling noise caught his attention, and a small Jittern leapt down onto the cold floor. It stared up at him for a few moments before scampering away. Tarian walked over to him and he sighed.

"Are those bloody things everywhere?"

"Probably." She put her hand on his shoulder. "Are you all right?"

"I just feel a little lightheaded. Never been one for venturing into caves in search of treasure and fair maidens, let alone to converse with magical entities who speak in a way that gives me a headache just trying to work out what they mean."

"And here I thought necromancers would like skulking around in the dark. If you wring your hands and cackle manically, would that help?"

"At least I would have something to do. Right now I don't even know why the fuck we're in this place." He tried to smile but fear was creeping through his veins. "I think perhaps I should have stayed outside with Rhydian where I could see the monsters trying to claw at me rather than jumping at every shadow that flickers in the darkness."

"Come on then, I'll go with you. I've had enough of riddles for one day."

Magic sparked at Mylah's fingertips, a swirl of blue and purple mist; Iolyn nodded at it approvingly and spread his arms wide.

"The Mylah Queen is not in the Withering, and so the breath of Syrthio whispers from her touch. The Erebus was in the Withering for many long winters and summers alike, and so the ancient melodies wailed and screeched and fell into despair."

"Magic is strengthening." Merfyd seemed to breathe a sigh of relief. "That's a good sign."

Iolyn studied him for a few moments. "The Merfyd speaks well, but loss haunts the Wretched Ones yet. The Aneira walks and casts and dreams, and the blood of the Mylah Queen is in sight."

"She will kill the queen?" Bowen's voice was suddenly fraught. "But… that would bring about another Sundering, surely? Weaken magic again, throw us all into chaos?"

"Power is not at the Bowen's heart this eventide. This one did not speak of death, but of blood. Blood is the key to unlock the gravest of spirits, and only then may untold destruction follow."

"She needs Mylah's blood to reach the Anghenfil?" Merfyd frowned. "But I thought…"

"The Merfyd has a mind filled with many words that should not be uttered in this sacred place. The Mylah Queen must not meet with the Aneira, for what flows through her veins will awaken what should never be roused from deepest slumber." Iolyn turned from them and began to venture back into the cavern. "This one is Iolyn of the Meirwon, reborn in the Winter of the Luctus. This one does not wish to be reborn in the Spring of the Mylah Queen. Stay far from those of gold and flesh. Take to paths hidden from mortal eyes, and see the fires rekindled between kin long lost amongst wilder stars. The Rival crushes spine and blossom and spell; if gateways are opened to newer breaths, then all will be withered beneath fiery gaze."

Rocks fell from above as thick branches burst out of the ground to catch them, closing the way behind the Meirwon; Mylah sighed heavily and turned to leave.

Bowen looked at her in despair. "Did you understand any of that?"

"I should not go after Aneira." She pushed past the men who watched her and made her way swiftly out into the dying sunlight.

Tarian looked at her. "So, did you get the answers you needed?"

Mylah closed her eyes and bit her bottom lip, but said nothing; Merfyd and Bowen walked out of the cave and scanned the landscape.

"It went well, then." Cael got to his feet and dusted himself off. "Perhaps we could get back to the mainland now? This place makes my skin crawl."

"That's probably the flesh eating spiders." Mylah glanced back at the Seneschal. "We should go."

"Your Grace, we need to discuss what we're going to do. If you cannot go after Aneira, then we need a new plan."

"What do you mean?" Tarian frowned. "Has something happened? What did that thing say to you?"

A cold breeze snaked its way through the undergrowth and wrapped around the legs of those who were gathered in front of the rune encrusted mouth. For a moment, all that could be heard was the singing of a distant waterfall.

"Your friend means to kill me, or at the very least harvest some of my blood. That will enable her to awaken the Anghenfil and slaughter it."

"But why is that such a problem? We've killed before, monsters and men alike. You two were in an army that swept across Luxnoctis and put anyone to the sword who would not bow before a cruel and vicious king."

Mylah hesitated. "The Anghenfil is no mere monster. There are legends far older than any we have hidden away in dusty temples, which tell of how its slaughter will bring about consequences to shake the very foundations of this world. There are torments locked within graves and tombs from a time so long past all of their names have been forgotten. If they are set free then we will all suffer."

Tarian scoffed. "That's bullshit – it's got to be. We're supposed to believe that if one creature is done away with, the rest of us will follow?"

Merfyd looked at her sadly. "It is no lie, Tarian. The Anghenfil and the Eternal Monarch are linked by magic so ancient it is rooted in Cadere's creation; the first breath of this realm gave birth to the wards and spells that would keep it alive. The Monarch is the lifeblood of magic, without which it would wither and die, and the Anghenfil is the anchor that keeps it stable. It also acts as a guardian against a gateway that, once opened, would see havoc rain down upon us until nothing was left but scorched oblivion."

"How do you know that?" Bowen peered at him, his icy purple eyes narrowed. "That's not in any book I've ever read."

Merfyd shrugged. "I have listened where others have not."

"Your Grace, do you believe all of this to be true?" Rhydian finally stood and rolled his shoulders. "Because it sounds to me just like a tale woven to keep people from seeking the truth."

Mylah rubbed her forehead and closed her eyes. There were voices upon the wind in this place, and they called out to her more and more with each moment that passed. Her thoughts trailed away and she forgot the questions that had been put before her, imagining instead a blazing campfire in front of two mountainous rocks and the smile of a woman whose soul danced within her dark eyes.

Cael swore loudly as the black and purple mist enveloped them once again; within moments they were standing back at their makeshift camp in Sepelite. Mylah was nowhere to be seen. Rhydian bent over to one side and vomited.

"Well that was… different." Tarian looked at Bowen and shook her head. "I don't understand what just happened."

"Neither do I, in truth. I miss studying Vessels." He tilted his head back to watch the stars for a few moments.

"What if Aneira is right?" The woman's words were quiet and tinged with fear. "This all seems like lie upon lie to keep a few privileged people in power. The Monarchs have ruled over us for millennia, and for what? What is it that they actually do?"

"Keep us safe from fiery oblivion, apparently. Personally, I don't mind the sound of that, I bet there would be plenty of willing spirits I could raise from the dead and set to dancing upon the front lines."

"Oh do be quiet, Necromancer. This is not the time for such jokes."

"I wasn't *joking*, Seneschal. Anyway, she's got a point; we were pulled into this march of yours because we were told it was the right thing to do, but I'm yet to see any evidence of that. Both of our cities were attacked by creatures that your queen supposedly has a peace treaty with, so either that agreement is pointless or she's lying. And this is far too much exercise for such futile reasons."

"Have you all forgotten what happened before Mylah came to power? Perhaps you would like to experience another plague, or be stalked in the night by Fallow?" Ice formed in the ground at Bowen's feet. "I am tired of people questioning her just because they're beginning to forget what came before! We all suffered, we all bled for this! She and I saw our friends being tortured, eaten alive, burnt and slaughtered whilst you sat in your comfortable homes getting fat upon the offerings to gods who should have been listening to *our* prayers! You stand there and judge her because some idiotic woman got an idea into her head based on what? Dreams? Bitterness? An inflated sense of self? You don't even know, do you?"

"She threatened to melt Aneira's head!"

"Well maybe she should!" Bowen's eyes blazed with anger. "I'm sick of traipsing around the countryside because your idiotic friend thinks she can mess with things well beyond her control!"

"She insults you just like she does us! You don't mean anything more to her than a stranger's spirit in the mist! Why can't you see that?"

He snarled and, turning on his heel, strode quickly away; Merfyd went after him.

Cael grinned at Tarian with a quick shrug. "Well that takes care of that, I suppose. So, now what? Would anyone like to play cards? I wouldn't mind a quick game of Priest in the Privy."

"I don't think we need to see you in your smallclothes." Rhydian sniffed repeatedly as he looked about for bowl to make some tea.

"Speak for yourself."

"Excellent! I left my deck in that bag there, that's right. So, sovereigns high?"

Daggers of ice shot up into the sky and exploded into glittering shards; Bowen threw his arms out to the side and a spiral of bright lightning arced between them before fading away into the shadows.

Merfyd watched the display with interest, and after a few moments he cautiously approached the other mage, flicking his wrist to dispel the ferocious magic. "May I speak to you?"

Bowen grunted and sent another bolt surging through the atmosphere. "I doubt I have any choice in the matter."

"You weren't surprised by the idea of the Anghenfil being a guardian."

"What's your point?" He clenched his hand into a fist and a ball of pale green fire shot across the sky. "Ignorance has never held any attraction for me."

"The Monarch told you about it all?"

"Why do you care?" He finally turned to face the man. "I know the truth, and those stubborn fools over there are going to see us all burn because they can't accept that their friend isn't who they thought she was."

The seconds ticked by in silence, before Bowen's shoulders sagged and he pinched the bridge of his nose.

Merfyd nodded slowly. "The more people who know about the Anghenfil's true purpose, the more likely it is that oblivion will swallow us whole. Tarian trusts you, even if she doesn't know what to make of the Queen. Talk to her, convince her to see things from our side."

"Our side? I know absolutely nothing about you, save for Berne picking you up in some tavern and the fact that your parents were pretentious enough to name you after a god. There is no reason for me to believe that you have good intentions."

"True. I could simply be tagging along with your merry band to get close enough to the ancient guardian to slit its throat myself, anger the divine pantheon, and suck up all of the power I can before the world explodes. Or I could genuinely want to help."

Bowen sighed sadly. "I never thought I'd miss sitting around in Corignis with Berne, with nothing better to do than patrol an imaginary boundary."

*

Aneira walked away from the warm, soft glow of the campfire into the cold gloom of the woodland. She closed her ears to the sounds of Elgan and Seren sleeping nearby, and opened her mind instead to the voice of Veteris forest. It was a sad, lowing call, like a lost calf in search of its mother, and her heart became heavy with the sorrow that whistled upon the breeze.

There was magic in this place older than any she had ever known before; it was bound by blood and bone, and she could feel the presence of sacrificial remains hidden far below the earth's surface.

The Gods had abandoned Sepelite and left it to rot; as the mage walked barefoot across the mournful expanse it called out to her with voices that should have fled long ago to Amara's side. Souls were trapped here, ancient and angry, and they pleaded with her to see the story to its end.

Power sparked upon her upturned palms, dancing along the skin like silver stars, and she felt a new strength coursing through her veins. A smile flickered across her lips and she reached out to those who followed her, needed her; she had failed to protect Mysta and its people, but she would not do so here.

Veteris was thought to be the easterly shadow of Vulnere, stretching across the shoreline and snaking out in all directions, but Aneira knew as she walked its paths that they had once been whole, blanketing the land of Sepelite and giving shelter to its inhabitants. In ages past the Monarchs had come and hollowed out the belly of the forest for farms and cities and temples; through the long winters it had cried out in pain, and even now it rang through the broken roots and branches.

She shivered and opened her eyes. "I remember you."

It would not be long now before Furatus rose up against the horizon and welcomed her home; fate was leading her, and she had felt at peace the moment they had stepped into this part of the world. Her heart, heavy with the deaths of her people, would lighten the moment she set everything back to its proper place; over time and with the Monarch dead, Cadere could recover, and balance would be restored.

She felt the air ripple behind her and sighed gently; it was time.

It only took her a few moments to get back to the makeshift camp, but the courier had already vanished. The smell of burnt flesh lingered upon the air. She picked up the ornate box that had been left by the fireside.

Seren blinked up at her sleepily. "What's that?"

She smiled. "The last piece of the puzzle."

Archaic melodies spiralled out into the bloodstained atmosphere, pushing against the corruption that had smothered the skyline for so many seasons. The Gods looked down from their celestial cradle, watching the echoes of destiny play out once more; their whispers, like thunder, rumbled throughout Sylvadeorum.

Magic stirred in the divine realm, gliding through its silhouette and kindling life where none should have been able to form.

Moonlight shone down upon the Eminent Minister as she closed the lid of the box and smiled, tears in her icy purple eyes. Seren and Elgan were silently packing up their things, and she could feel the fear that had crept upon them; it was of no consequence now. They would see as she did come the dawn.

Burdens would fall to the wayside and the breath of the world could be restored to its rightful place; she had seen in dreams and heard upon the wind the voices of the dead, who told her that the power in the veins of Cadere belonged to all. There should be no mages, no tutors, no mentors, for all should be able to wield magic naturally and without aid; visions came to her time and again of how the world was supposed to be, how the Gods had intended it before the Monarchs had torn it apart for their own gain.

The lies that had propelled the hierarchy were ancient and embedded in the minds of scholars and priests alike, but she was sure that once Mylah's grip had been eradicated, all would share in this knowledge and everything would finally be whole, back to the beautiful realm it was always meant to be.

"Are you ready?" Elgan touched her shoulder gently. "We won't get much rest from this point on."

"I have been ready since Mysta was reduced to ashes." A smile passed across her and she turned to face her companions. "We are going to save this world, and songs will be sung of us even when our bones have long turned to dust. I am glad you are with me. Come, let us go. Destiny awaits."

Eight

Shadows danced along the courtyard, draping over the herb garden and creeping up around the base of the marble statue of Elfriede in her slumbering flowerbed, as silver light shimmered across the bowl of sanctified water she held in her hands. A gentle hum drifted upon the warm air, echoes of chanted prayer from deep within the temple; the priestesses mourned those who would not tread upon the earth again, whilst the injured survivors of Delyth slept in chambers nearby.

Mercer strolled through the gardens and headed out across the courtyard, taking a moment to breathe in the sweet perfume of the night blooming flowers. He looked up into the sky and bowed his head, giving thanks to the Gods, and then moved slowly towards the nearest open doorway to the maze of corridors inside.

He had been in service to the temple since he was six years old, and so knew every winding path and shortcut hidden away behind tapestries and deceptive blocks of stone. His footsteps often rang out through the darkened hours as he patrolled here and there looking for evidence of wrongdoing and listening out for salacious gossip that might prove worthwhile later on.

A bleary eyed novice scuttled past him, sniffing loudly and wiping his nose on his sleeve; Mercer raised an eyebrow but said nothing, making a note to look into that once his duty was done.

Candles flickered in their sconces upon the walls, and in this shade of nightfall it almost seemed as though this place had been left untouched by the convulsions that had rocked its very foundations.

He turned a corner and swept down an empty hallway, ignoring every door except for the last; he rapped lightly against its intricately carved wood and waited for a reply. Seconds ticked by without any response, so he knocked once more and then slowly pushed it open.

The Inner Sanctum was draped in silks and velvets of deep garnet and gold; ornate candelabra rose up from the dark wood floor, the thick ivory candles in their grasp throwing out a delicate glow that sent shadows spiralling into concealed corners. Tapestries of Elfriede covered the walls, the largest and most elaborate hanging behind the grand altar.

Scole stood in front of the opulent shrine with her back to Mercer; her arms were spread out wide and her head was tilted back slightly, her eyes closed as quiet prayers murmured across her painted lips.

A few moments ticked by before she finally sighed and opened her eyes. "What news do you bring?"

"Apologies for the interruption my lady, but I have news about the theft from the library."

"Can it not wait?"

"I think you're going to want to hear this now, High Priestess."

"Very well." She lowered her head. "We'll finish this later."

A woman rose to her feet and pulled the hood of her robe over her head; Scole kissed her lightly on the cheek and whispered something to her before she walked quickly away.

Mercer bowed his head at her as she passed. "Meredith."

"Mercer."

Scole turned to face him, her hands swiftly buttoning her cassock. "Well?"

"You'll be pleased to know that the ritual you performed yesterday has already brought us the grace of the Gods. James and I finished the inventory of the library at midday, and took a few of the scholars to the study in order to question them in more private surroundings. We now know which items were stolen, when, and who is responsible for allowing the theft to take place."

Relief washed over Scole and she smiled. "Well of that I am glad. What was taken?"

"Ah. That, I think, will please you less my lady. Three scrolls and one book from the early reign of King Luctus, all on the topic of the Venerated King of Hallowed Ember and Carrion."

Her happiness died. "You're sure?"

"Unfortunately so. And they were not taken by anyone from the temple, we are certain of that; James easily got a confession from one of the scholars known as Pale Thomas. He was on duty when the theft occurred, and so has been kept aside ready for your orders as to his punishment."

"That seems to be an unlucky name." She tapped a finger against her chin and shuddered. "At least this one is still in a state to talk. I'll leave that task in your capable hands, Mercer."

"I know just the thing for it, High Priestess. Oh, before I go, should I have the meat from the sacrifice taken to the kitchens? It has been a while since we dined on mutton."

She nodded. "Yes, yes of course. We have more mouths to feed, so no doubt it will be a welcome addition. And make sure to remind them that the bones are to go to the altars to be blessed before the novices carve them into whatever tools are necessary. Oh, except for one of the leg bones, bring that to me. I need a certain item replaced. Have the tallow made into candles and fill a basket to be placed outside the Necromancers Guild."

He bowed his head again and turned to leave. "Should I send Meredith back in, my lady?"

"No... no, I have other things I need to attend to."

Whispers were upon the wind; malevolent and malnourished they span into a wider web, stretching out across an amaranthine expanse to snare any unsuspecting soul that dared to wander too far from the silver sun.

Ice formed beneath crepuscular eyes in long, jagged spikes that threatened to pierce the velveteen darkness; screams echoed in the distance. Archaic fire burst forth from ashes long since buried, and death stalked the weary realm.

Scole steadied herself against the altar and waited for the dizziness to abate. Her dreams had been troubled of late, and now even during her waking hours she was plagued by strange voices, thoughts, and visions of Seren's blood drenched corpse.

The ancient chorus quietened to a subdued hiss, and she breathed a little easier. The Gods seemed silent these days but something was calling out to her, though the priestess found no comfort in it. She looked up at the altar in all its splendour, and sorrow crept into her heart; she knew it was not enough. It had never been enough, and now the Goddess would punish her for it.

A door opened somewhere in the distance and muffled voices filled the corridor outside; the High Priestess pushed back her fears and shivered. This was no time for her faith to falter.

She walked briskly out of the Inner Sanctum and found the hallway filled with wide eyed novices and clerks, nervous chatter sweeping through them like morning song. Sunlight began to break over the horizon and a pale gloom filtered in through the large windows, doing nothing to comfort the gathering crowd.

Scole held up a hand and silence fell across them. "Would someone like to tell me what is going on here?"

The novices shifted uncomfortably, their eyes flickering away from her; she gritted her teeth and asked the question again.

A man moved to the front, his ruby robes stained and torn in places; his pale green eyes darted to hers, and a grin stretched across his thin mouth. "It is time, Lowly One. Those who were forgotten and buried deep within the sacraments have seen fit to rise."

She stared at him. "You dare to address me in such a manner?"

Hissing laughter rippled throughout the onlookers, and the man bowed; fury began to take hold of Scole's heart and she narrowed her eyes.

"There is room no longer for title or ceremony." He licked his bottom lip. "And there is no time for vengeance. At least, not for us, not for you, but for them, for them…"

The chant was taken up by those closest to him. "For them… for them… for them…"

"Go back to your rooms immediately. The temple will not stand for such nonsense!"

"The temple will not stand at all. Do you not hear us, Lowly One? Do you not hear the noble voices? There will be no ashes to drift down from crimson skies, no putrid essence coursing through the veins of glorious oblivion." A trickle of colourless liquid seeped from his nose. "The temples will fade into distant dust, and the bones of you and your people will be nothing more than a forgotten tune upon a dying breeze."

"Get out! Leave this place immediately, all of you! Get out!"

His grin widened and his eyes, now bloodshot, bored into hers. "There is nothing left to abandon, Lowly One. You feel it, do you not? The emptiness? It is a siren's call to your pitiful soul and even now the shadows clamber into your mind."

"Enough! Get out!"

"We go, Priestess. But remember this: all is lost. All that ever was, or ever could be, is now no more than damnation."

"For them... for them... for..." The mantra trailed away.

Scole looked at the silent group, and her anger deepened.

The light from outside dimmed.

"It is time." The novice's neck cracked loudly as he twisted to one side. "It is time." He glanced back at the High Priestess and a bout of laughter echoed down the hallway; his body began to tremble until it shook violently, and his shoulders started to spasm. He held up his arms, his fingers taut and pointing at the ceiling; blood trailed from beneath his nails, sliding down across his hands and wrists like darkened snakes.

Bells were tolling somewhere, their deep melancholic moans rippling out across the heavy atmosphere.

He reached out in front of him as if to touch Scole's face, his wounded fingers stopping just short of her skin. He traced a small circle in the air and peace settled across his face.

His head exploded.

Flesh and blood splattered Scole's neck and chest, a spray of gore reaching from her jaw to her brow.

Dawn finally broke over the horizon and the first spears of golden light returned to the temple.

Screams filled the hallway as the spell broke and the other novices scrambled to get away. Scole stared at the body, now slumped upon the flagstones, her mind blank. Someone was calling her name, but a fog clouded her thoughts and although the word echoed, she couldn't turn back.

Mercer finally pushed through the throng of people; pain throbbed behind his eyes and he could feel vomit rising in the back of his throat.

Meredith was gently shaking the High Priestess, but the woman seemed lost in a trance.

"Brig's breath." He looked down at the spatter from the headless corpse and wrinkled his nose. "What happened here?"

"I don't know. Help me wake her, will you? Scole! Darling one, please listen to my voice. Scole?"

Mercer's heart skipped a beat. The clerks and novices had dispersed and the place was finally quiet, but the High Priestess still didn't move. Her eyes were glassy and her breathing steady, and he suspected that her mind might be trapped somewhere dark.

"Scole! Please wake up? Please?"

"We need to get her away from here. Can she walk?"

"I don't – I don't know." Meredith tried to pull her forwards but she remained in place. "What should we do? What's wrong with her?"

Light splintered across the floor, pale saffron brushing over the dark vermilion; Scole inhaled sharply and blinked. A second or two passed by in silence as Mercer and Meredith stared at her.

She frowned at them. "What's going on?"

"My lady, are you feeling all right?" Mercer's concern only grew at her confusion. "Can we do anything to help?"

She waved him away and rubbed her forehead. "Get me some Rotroot for this headache would you? Ah, Meredith, is there something you need?"

The woman glanced at Mercer and then bit her lip. "I... Scole, is something wrong? You were... we couldn't..."

"Don't concern yourself, my love. If you don't need me for anything important then go back to your duties." She kissed her lightly on the cheek. "Mercer, the Rotroot? I'll be in my bedchamber. Ask someone to come and take this body away too, please."

"At once, my lady." He bowed his head and shrugged at Meredith's pleading look.

Scole walked quickly away, her heart pounding against her chest; she could feel the novice's blood clinging to her skin, and it turned her stomach. The maze of hallways and corridors were blissfully quiet, and she made it back to her room without seeing anyone else.

The door shut behind her and she closed her eyes for a moment; the air here was cool and free of incense and perfume, the only light coming from a thinly veiled window. A four poster bed was pushed up against one wall, the dark wood intricately carved to look like rose vines; its pillows, sheets and blankets of soft cream and gold were half buried beneath stacks of books, as well as various instruments and tools fashioned from bone. In front of the window sat a wash basin in a wooden stand, and a small cabinet nearby was filled with soaps, strips of clean cloth, and powders and pigments; a large mirror was propped up against the wall, its base surrounded by crystals and small carvings of mythical beasts. Wooden chests were strewn around, the lids pushed back to reveal crumpled cassocks, robes, cloaks and stockings; a few pairs of shoes rested against the side of one of them. More books littered the floorboards and were stacked upon dusty shelves; a tapestry of Elfriede rising out of a silver lake hung upon the back of the door.

Scole disrobed quickly and walked over to the basin, her bloodied hands plunging into the cold water; she took up a small bar of soap and a makeshift washcloth and scrubbed at her face, neck and hair until the linen clotted with gore. Another washcloth, another vicious cleanse, over and over until she looked down at the cardinal water, small chunks of flesh and bone bobbing along the surface, and vomited.

Once she had steeled herself and dried her skin, she slipped into a clean cassock and buttoned it quickly before dragging an ivory comb through her hair and pinning it back into a bun.

A knock sounded at the door. She glanced in the mirror and sighed quietly; Mercer entered the room a few moments later.

"Your tea, my lady." He held out a wooden cup and looked around the room. "I'll have someone come and take away all the soiled items."

"Thank you. I need to speak to that scout from the healer's camp."

"Nelia? I can have her brought here for you."

She sipped the drink and grimaced slightly. "There's no need, I'll head out there myself. I should check on the injured that they have holed up there anyway."

"Is that a good idea, High Priestess? Given the state of things right now, it would probably be best if you just stayed here where it's safe."

She rolled her eyes and downed the last of the tea. "Do not think to lecture me on what is wise, Mercer. You're a good man and invaluable to the temple, don't make me slit your throat."

He smiled and raised his eyebrows. "Feeling better I see?"

"If this damned headache would go I'd be fine. Have you seen Meredith today?"

"I…" He stared at her. "She was with you back there in the –"

"I know that, you babbling idiot! Go and get on with your duties, and leave me to mine." She tried to keep the concern from her face. "Go on, get out."

"Yes my lady." He bowed and turned away.

She waited until she was alone once more, and then fell to her knees; holding her head in her hands, she tried to fight back the sorrow that coursed through her veins.

*

A cold wind slithered through the streets of Delyth, wrapping around empty houses and tugging at torn guild banners that had been propped up against piles of dirty rags. Carrion birds sat atop fractured statues and pillars, watching the scenes below with beady eyes and sated bellies; stalls were slowly being set up for the day's market, the scent of spices and perfumes picked up by the breeze and carried out across the sea. Bundles of brightly coloured fabric were laden upon carts being pulled through the cobbled streets, passing by a butcher proudly filling his display with lumps of salted meat.

People came to the High Priestess as she passed through, their heads bowed and uncovered; she touched their brows and offered prayers and blessings to those in need, occasionally handing out simple supplies from the satchel she carried. Her own head ached and drowsiness pulled at her mind; strange words whispered through her thoughts, and every now and then she thought she could see shadows reaching out to her from dark alleyways.

She pulled her cloak tighter around her shoulders and glanced up at the unabashed heavens as if perhaps the Gods would look down and sweep away her worries.

"Can I help you with something?" A man with bushy eyebrows and a mop of unkempt white hair stood in her path. "Only if not, kindly move on. There are many in this place who don't want to be gawked at."

A smile flickered across her lips. "I suspect you are correct, but I am not here to stare at anybody."

"Hmm, I'm beginning to think interfering is considered an acceptable pastime here. What do you want anyway? I'm a busy man and I don't have time to idle, especially for no good reason."

Scole glanced around at the makeshift camp and sighed. "I am the High Priestess of the Temple of Elfriede. I need to speak to a woman who has been working here, and I thought I could offer help should you need anything."

"Aye, well, that's acceptable enough then I suppose. Do you have a certain woman in mind, or are you content to speak to any who has taken it upon herself to run around this particular area of town?" He grunted and looked away. "There's too many bloody mages these days and not enough properly trained physicians. Oh look, I can waggle my fingers and fix everything without even a thought to –"

"Rafael." Nelia walked up to him with a basket of clean bandages. "Are you bothering the High Priestess?"

"Pah! How can I bother someone who isn't meant to be here? This is a place for the sick and injured, not a secure building full of incense and silk cushions!"

"Do forgive him my lady, he's been grouchy ever since we pulled him through here to help out."

"Help out? You think what I do counts as *helping*, lass? I've saved more people from gangrene and death than you'll ever meet. Help out indeed!"

Scole stifled her amusement and bowed her head at the scout. "Delyth is eternally grateful for the assistance that Queen Mylah has provided. We would be at a loss without all those who have given of their skills, talents, and time. The temple is willing to offer any aid that will ease your burdens, both here and abroad, but I fear I must ask you for your help once more."

"Of course my lady." There was an underlying, well masked strain in her voice. "What do you need of us?"

"I must talk to your queen."

"Ah. Rafael, there's a mage beckoning for your help over there."

"Amara's tits." He rounded on his heel and walked away, grumbling to himself.

Nelia looked back at the older woman with a forced smile. "I… may not be able to grant your request, High Priestess. Her Grace is proving somewhat difficult to locate at the moment."

"Oh." Scole tried to keep panic from rising within her. "That is unfortunate. My matter is urgent, and I fear that without intervention it may get worse."

"Forgive me, I can only offer to have a portal opened between here and wherever it is that Tarian and Bowen are at present. It is possible of course that Her Grace has returned to them."

"Is something wrong, child?" Scole took Nelia's hand, their eyes locking for a moment. "You are worried about something. It carries in your words, well hidden though it is."

"I… I also need to speak to the queen. A message came from Luxnoctis late last night, and it needs to be relayed to her as soon as possible, but no one seems to know where she has gone."

The air grew colder between them.

"Perhaps we could travel to Sepelite together, then?"

"I would not want to leave my duties here my lady, not when so many are still in need of our care."

"Pah!" Rafael's voice carried from a few yards away. "Get away with that nonsense! Bugger off and leave us alone. What use is a bloody scout in a medical camp anyway? Go find the boss, and hold that woman's hand through the portal. She's terrified of them."

Scole blushed slightly and looked away, dropping her hands to her side.

Nelia shook her head and sighed. "I apologise *again* for the old goat my lady, but I would be more than happy to accompany you to Tarian's location. I have business to attend to there, even if Her Grace is still absent. Rafael! Send one of the mages over to activate the Solis, would you?"

He gestured rudely at her and stomped away to find someone suitable; Nelia rummaged around in a nearby wooden chest until she produced a dark red crystal. Scole studied it silently for a few moments, before she shuddered and turned away.

"Is something wrong, my lady?"

"Those things are not always what they seem, child. Do be careful if you intend to use them often."

Nelia frowned and was about to ask what she meant, when a short plump woman with bright purple eyes came bounding up to them; she grinned, running a hand through her silvery waves that knocked her golden circlet to one side. Scole smiled warmly.

"Aveline Ashdown reporting for duty, ma'am. Rafael said you needed my help."

"Can you activate a portal for us?"

The woman nodded, placing her beringed fingers over the crystal. "This isn't nearly as difficult as it used to be." Magic hummed around them, and the gemstone glowed. "Diis aeterna. Ego aperiam in via."

Pale light shot out of the woman's palm and sweat beaded her brow; the air began to smell slightly of burnt flesh as it split open in front of Nelia. The scout nodded at the mage, and then took hold of Scole's arm and led her through; the spell winked out behind them.

Tarian looked up in surprise.

"Is Queen Mylah here?" Scole glanced around. "I must speak with her as soon as possible."

"And here I thought you had come for tea and our glorious company, my lady." Cael grinned and bowed dramatically.

"Her Grace has not yet returned." Merfyd held out a bowl of vegetable stew. "Is something wrong, Priestess?"

"Are all mages finding it easier to cast spells now?" She took the wooden dish and a chunk of bread, eyeing Cael's sash for a moment. "Thank you."

"I believe that magic began returning to its full strength once the Eternal Monarchs restored the balance. Dullahan lingered for far too long, and it has taken some time for the world to heal. Why do you ask? Has something happened?"

The High Priestess waved her hand dismissively as she ate.

Tarian was quiet for a few moments and then she sighed heavily. "Aneira thought that the stronger magic had something to do with fewer hands draining the power of Cadere, due to the blight that killed so many mages."

"That's understandable, if she truly was unaware that Dullahan was dead. The restoration was well documented in older texts but a lot of those were lost during his early reign, and it seems as though much knowledge just faded away over time."

"And yet you seem to have regained a lot." Tarian narrowed her eyes. "Did they truly find you in a tavern?"

Merfyd grinned. "Can a man not like ale as well as books and stories? I have heard many tales by the fireside in such places."

Scole's neck twitched violently and she dropped her bowl.

The mage looked over at her, concerned. "Are you all right, High Priestess?"

"I lay her down in a meadow of wildflowers, the golden sunlight dancing upon her skin and catching within her raven hair. This was my heaven. The only redemption I sought was in her eyes, the only peace in her arms, the only divinity in her words."

Tarian frowned. "What the fuck is going on now?"

"That's from the Ballad of Mylah the Bloody."

"She has her own ballad?"

"No." Merfyd reached out to touch Scole's shoulder. "It's the story of a warrior who lived thousands of years ago. She was in the service of Queen Sidra, an elven Monarch who ruled briefly several centuries before the reign of King Luctus."

Tarian shrugged. "I've never heard of it."

"Sidra was feuding with a human noble, and eventually grew tired of the skirmishes that rang out along the borders of their lands, so dispatched her favoured and most trusted warrior, Mylah, to take care of the problem. But she fell in love with the noble, and they ran away together one night when the moon hid itself away and the shadows gave them shelter. They knew Sidra would consider Mylah's actions the utmost betrayal and the punishment would be as brutal as it was swift, so they hoped to find respite in some kingdom far from the queen's vicious gaze."

"I cradle the bones of her in gnarled and weary hands as we retreat under the moonlight to a meadow of balm and blossom. And it is here, under the shadow of the dawn, that I shall bury her. Let the blood of the guilty rain down upon her grave until she rises once again as wrath and fury. But for now, my love shall sleep beneath the earth's steady bosom and find her sweeter dreams."

Tarian raised an eyebrow at Merfyd. "More of the ballad? Care to explain what the fuck she's talking about?"

"Mylah returned to their home one evening to find her lover slain, her head atop a wooden stake and her body cut into pieces. It is said that she howled like a wolf, her voice carrying over mountains and rivers and lakes until it reached the ears of the displeased queen;

Sidra flew into a rage and ordered the immediate execution of the warrior."

"I hold the ghost of her in my outstretched hand, her broken heart bleeding between my fingers so freshly scarred. But I… I am the drums of war, I will echo through eternity, and if you seek to renew your ungodly reign I will tear you from your seat of grace and none but the hounds of the Otherworld will hear your screams."

"Hearing the tale of the wronged woman, people rallied to her cause and she led a revolt against Sidra. Her ragtag army crossed the land brandishing song and spear alike, until they were met on the battlefield by the Monarch's forces. Outnumbered ten to one, the people fell quickly beneath bloodstained blades, and Mylah was captured, paraded through the streets in a dirty cage, and then tortured in the town square for five days and nights. At dawn on the sixth day she was taken to be hanged. Sidra stood on the gallows and watched, open mouthed, as the wooden structure broke and the woman fell to the ground. Said to be a sign from the Gods, Mylah was pardoned and allowed to go free, soon returning to the gravesite of the noble where she lay down upon the grass and died of her wounds. Angered by such depravity and injustice, Amara's realm could not hold her beloved, who arose from the grave and crept to Sidra's side, whispering in her ear until she went mad. When the queen died several years later, her successor ensured that her decapitated head was set atop a spike and her bones were fashioned into weapons known as the Valiskar."

"That was one of my father's favourite stories, although he only ever knew of Sidra as a queen of some distant and foreign land. The truth of her power seems to have faded from the tale over time."

Tarian looked up at the Monarch and frowned. "I wish you wouldn't sneak up on us like that."

Mylah sighed and rolled her shoulders, her hands clasped behind her back. "A lot of people wish for a lot of things. Is Bowen here?"

"He went off with Rhydian to look around a nearby cave some time ago, Your Grace." Merfyd spoke without turning away from the High Priestess. "It shouldn't be much longer before they return, I doubt there was any worthwhile loot stashed in there."

"Ma'am, I must speak to you." Nelia bowed quickly, trying to keep her face free of concern. "There is a matter from Luxnoctis that cannot wait."

"I did wonder why you and the Priestess had wandered away from Delyth."

Scole shivered and blinked for a few seconds. "Ah, Your Imperial Highness. It is an honour to finally meet you."

The campfire crackled, sending sparks into the cold air; light danced upon the golden embroidery on the queen's black gown.

A slight smile crossed Mylah's lips and she inclined her head. "And you, High Priestess. You are a long way from home."

"I'm afraid that I too require your time and attention, Your Grace."

"Then you shall have it." Mylah threw the head of a Saprus on the floor between them. It landed with a squelch. "Come, we shall speak privately. I have many things to discuss with you, too."

"Is your peace treaty with the monsters worth anything at all?" Tarian wrinkled her nose at the smell that emanated from the gooey flesh.

"He was uncooperative when I asked for answers regarding the attack on Delyth. Nelia, go and find the Seneschal and inform him that he is needed back here."

"Yes ma'am." The woman hesitated for a moment, before she pulled up the hood of her cape and walked away from the group, disappearing quickly into the trees.

"Shall we?" Mylah took Scole's arm and led her swiftly away.

Music lifted upon the breeze, a gentle hum that coursed through shaded undergrowth and belighted canopy. Prying eyes looked down from the celestial cradle as hints of treachery murmured upon death bound lips.

"You have done much to heal this land," Scole glanced at the clear skies, "but I fear its people are far from recovered. I can only thank the Gods that Caeli did not suffer as much as Sepelite or Luxnoctis."

Mylah was quiet for a few moments. "You kept your focus on trying to appease the Divine."

"You may not approve of our methods Your Grace, but you cannot argue with the results. Ritual sacrifice has seen followers of Elfriede kept free of disease and hunger, and we use all that is given to us. Nothing is ever wasted."

"I honestly do not care, High Priestess. I have no desire to challenge deities or their acolytes, and I seek no quarrel with those who do what they must to keep their people from starvation. That is not always an easy task."

Scole's thoughts darkened for a moment and she closed her eyes against the breaching sunlight; something whispered to her from afar, clawing at her with jagged words. She shivered. A loud rumble echoed around her, and her heart began to throb against her chest; she could smell the temple, no longer safe and secure, and feel the ground tremble beneath her feet. People were screaming somewhere, calling out to her, and she could hear Mercer's ragged breathing suddenly cut out beneath a terrible crack.

Mylah watched her and for a moment her expression softened. She drew a symbol in the air in front of the priestess, and then looked away.

The thoughts vanished from Scole's mind and she opened her eyes with a quiet sigh of relief. The forest was calm, cool, and still.

"You said you had something you needed to discuss?"

"What? Oh, oh yes of course, my apologies Your Grace. Some items were stolen from our library a short while ago, all concerning the Venerated King of Hallowed Ember and Carrion, and I believe that I know who took them."

Mylah clenched her jaw. "Are all priests useless?"

"I am sorry for what you have suffered at the hands of those in the religious order, Your Grace. The deeds of Elisus were shown to us through dreams and visions not long after your ascension, and I was told about the recent raid on the Temple of Katarina. Had I known Seren was in the sway of such influential… had I known her intentions, I would have stopped her, I promise you that. We spoke in the library but I had no idea she even knew the books and scrolls existed, let alone where they were kept. She and Rhydian were told the stories of the Gilded Lord of course, when they were young, but it was not a topic I had even thought to mention for many years."

The queen rubbed her face and sighed. "Do you know if she's ever associated with a woman from western Sepelite known as Aneira Morgan?"

"Do you mean the Eminent Minister of Mysta?" Scole stared at her for a moment before regaining her composure. "I… I have not been shown anything to suggest that. But my Seren is a troubled woman and tends to be drawn to those who share such heartache. If the Minister has decided to make an enemy of you, Your Grace, we may be in more trouble than I had anticipated."

"And why is that?"

"She was always a determined and powerful creature, skilled in diplomacy as well as magic. I had some brief correspondence with her the year she took over Mysta's care, as well as the pleasure of speaking to a couple of brothers who knew of her personally. If she has a staunch belief stoking a fire in her belly, she will not let it go and those flames will never be put to rest. Do you believe that she is attempting to trace the path of the Gilded Lord? Many have tried before her, and all have failed. You look surprised at that, my dear."

Mylah allowed herself to smile. "I had not considered that mortals might have tried to knock Erebus from his throne in such a way, but I am glad to hear of it."

"There were countless tales that got swept away over the centuries, leaving only whispered traces in their wake. I know many stories of the Gilded Lord, but I suppose those are for another time." Scole's heart sank a little. "Are you going to kill them?"

The question hung between them for a moment.

"The Meirwon advised against my direct intervention."

Her eyes widened. "It is already at such a point?"

"I need to take down a barrier that is preventing us from travelling beyond it, and then I mean to escort the others somewhere near to Mynydd. So long as I do not encounter Aneira and her… friends on my own before we reach it, the Seneschal believes we will be able to stop them. I cannot guarantee the survival of any one of them, however. Aneira is more dangerous than many seem willing to understand."

"I suppose if they truly are responsible for the thefts, then the Minister may have knowledge at her disposable that those who railed against the dead king did not. But why would she throw herself against you in this way?"

"She believes me responsible for the attack that razed her city to the ground."

"And are you?"

Mylah studied the High Priestess for some time. "Would it matter if I was? The board has already been set, the tale is already being told. What is important now is finding a way to stop this sanctimonious fool before she ends it."

The drums of war echoed upon a distant horizon; storm clouds gathered far to the west, a spiral of magic and mysticism scored deep in the ashen clouds. Spectres who reached out with gnawing hunger fell away to the shadows as thunder rumbled once again.

Scole shuddered and tried to steady her thoughts. Fear was creeping through her like merciless poison, and she could feel the lull of slumber pulling at her mind. Voices were whispering to her, softly spoken and brimming with spite; she glanced at the foreign queen.

Mylah returned her look and cocked her head to one side. "Do you ever rail against your gods, High Priestess? Do you ever turn your eyes to the heavens and scream their names? You search for something within me that will still your fears, and yet I don't have anything to give you. There are times when I feel there is nothing left but emptiness, as though a piece of the abyss floats within me, and yet there are others when I think that all of this sorrow and anguish will overflow until I am nothing but vengeance and grief and blood." Her shoulders sagged. "I am so tired that I could not stop it, and in truth I have no wish to. I just want to rest."

The intruding thoughts vanished and Scole squeezed the Monarch's hand gently. "This may be a wound that never fully heals. Perhaps you will carry some of this pain with you for eternity, or maybe it will fade into naught but a whispered dream, vanishing with the first light of dawn. I do not know, and I would not implore Elfriede to impart such knowledge to me, for I think the agony of it would sweep me away like a roaring tide. Your beloved was taken from you, your daughter slain, and vengeance did not seem like justice, but they are free of the burdens of this world and they walk in the sunlit meadows and valleys in the shadows of the Gods. They were already proud of the woman you were, child, all that is left is to make them proud of the woman you will become."

A tremor passed through the ground beneath their feet. Mylah frowned and turned away from the priestess; a shadow danced across her face for a moment before it fled.

"Your Grace!" Nelia came running through the trees, her cheeks flushed and her breath unsteady. "Your Grace, I... I must speak with you. Please, it's urgent."

"Very well. Forgive me High Priestess, but I think we need to return to the others."

"As you wish." Scole hesitated for a moment. "Your Grace? Please don't hurt my girl. I do not know what she thinks to find in the journey she has chosen, but I am sure she is not lost to the darkness just yet."

Mylah said nothing, but turned back to the scout, her thoughts suddenly stilled; she frowned and looked to the horizon.

Everything was quiet for a moment, until a whisper caught upon the air.

The queen's eyes widened. "Get down!"

Magic crackled in the air and shook the world around them; a cascade of leaves fell to the floor as an icy wind swept through the canopies, howling and shrieking with the vengeful tones of ancient wraiths. Mounds of dirt exploded around the three women, shooting up into the air and sending out chunks of earth and stone in all directions.

Mylah threw up her hands and conjured a barrier against the arcane onslaught; she gritted her teeth and focused her mind, cutting through the desperate screams until her thoughts steadied and calmed, and she could hear the song of magic beneath it all.

The storm vanished as quickly as it had begun.

She opened her eyes and scanned the destruction before her. Some trees had been torn from the ground and thrown away whilst others lingered, scarred and blackened; the forest floor was scorched in places, and the air was heavy with the scent of burning flesh and wood. Scole was cowering on the floor, sobbing uncontrollably, but Nelia was nowhere to be seen. The queen knelt down and quietly took the priestess into her embrace.

"Tarian?" Cael got unsteadily to his feet. "Tarian, where… where are you?"

Clouds of ash and dust drifted back down towards the unsettled ground; remnants of the campfire were scattered about in soot stained piles. Rhydian lay face down some yards away with Merfyd at his side; Bowen was nearby, his hands over his ears, blood trickling through his fingers.

"Tarian? This isn't… this isn't funny, where are you? Tarian! Has… has anyone seen her?"

Merfyd glanced over and shook his head.

"Brig's bloody balls." Rhydian turned slowly to look at the mage. "What happened?"

"Just lie still for a moment, I need to tend to these wounds." He took a small linen cloth from his pocket and dabbed at the oozing gash on the man's brow.

"Couldn't you just use magic?"

"That would be unwise at the moment."

The necromancer looked from them to the Seneschal, and his frown deepened; his thoughts were hazy and scattered, and pain throbbed at the back of his head. Strange patterns flickered in front of his eyes as confusion settled into his mind. He staggered a little, trying to find his balance, before falling onto his knees with a loud crack.

Bowen finally lowered his hands; the horrifying noises had relented, and all he could focus on now was the emptiness that seemed to surround him. There was a slight ringing in his ears and his hands were trembling, but he managed to stand and make his way over to Cael. "Are you all right?"

"I… I can't quite… remember who… who you are?"

Bowen raised an eyebrow as a slight smirk crossed the man's lips.

"Tell me…" He coughed. "Do you have any… titles?"

"I ought to encase you in a prison of ice."

"Aha! So you *are* an elemental mage. And ice, you say? You old hoar! …No? Not even a smile? Oh come on, I've been waiting for ages to use that joke on somebody."

*

Soft music drifted from deep within Cadere's heart; the ancient melodies spiralled out into the firmament and caressed the celestial cradle, brushing against the unnerved heavens and falling away into the east.

Sunlight finally broke through the lingering clouds and washed over the ground with its rich golden hues; creatures scampered away into the safety of the trees and hid in the warm shadows.

Tarian stirred as a large spider crept over her face and skittered away into a pile of leaves. Her eyes opened slowly, painfully, and she murmured under her breath before turning away to fall into darkened dreams once more.

Aneira settled down next to her, her lips quivering slightly as she gently traced the scars that ran along the left side of the woman's jaw. Tiny swirls of magic escaped from the mage's fingertips and vanished into the ether.

"Is she alive?" Elgan approached them slowly, his hands clasped behind his back. "How can this be? She perished in Mysta… it must be some kind of elaborate trick."

Aneira shook her head and a weak smile flickered across her lips. "No, she's no illusion. This is our Tarian, our girl. See how the spells dissipate above her skin? They wouldn't do that if this was the work of an enchantment or glamour. The Gods have given her back to us." She looked up at him with tears in her pale purple eyes. "We can save her, Elgan."

He sighed quietly and nodded. "If you believe it to be so Minister, then I shall not speak against you."

"How is Seren?"

He winced and looked away. "She is sleeping now."

"And the courier?"

"The portals stabilised long enough to allow safe passage back, although everything had to happen so quickly that some gear was left behind. I do not think it would be sensible to call upon them again unless we are in dire need. I can ensure that it is all left in a safe place for us to summon later, in case we might have need of it. The weapon at least might prove useful."

She nodded and closed her eyes for a moment. "Are you afraid?"

"Yes."

"So am I." A gentle breeze caressed her face. "But our ancestors are with us… I can feel them guiding our every step. The tyranny will soon be over, and we will be able to go home. Mysta is gone, but perhaps we could rebuild somewhere else. Tarian survived, so it's possible there are others, and I will not let them down again. I will not fail them a second time, I promise you; I will do better."

Tarian groaned and pushed her head into Aneira's arm. The mage smiled.

The clearing they had taken refuge in was calm, and quiet; a hint of soft perfume arose from flowering vines that curled around the cliff face behind them and the trees that bordered a silvery stream. Rodents and critters scurried about in the mossy undergrowth whilst insects fluttered and danced in the cool air.

"I wouldn't mind coming back here." Elgan inhaled deeply, breathing in the scent of the flowers. "It's so peaceful."

"Soon everywhere will be like this. Once magic is allowed to return properly and there is no more threat of war, once the Monarch lies dead in the ground and knowledge is given back to the people, we will all be free to enjoy a life without hardship. The true Gods are with us."

"I hear them too."

Tarian shivered and awoke, instinctively shielding her face against the bright sunlight. She frowned as she sat up, rubbing her forehead and yawning loudly.

"Did you sleep well?"

Her hands dropped to her lap and she stared at the woman who sat beside her. "It… it can't be. Aneira?"

The woman grinned and grabbed hold of her. "Oh Tarian! You have no idea how happy we are to have found you!"

"What's going on?" She pulled away. "What the fuck are you doing here?"

"Don't be alarmed. We thought you were dead and yet here you are, safely delivered to us in our time of need. The Gods are good."

"What the *fuck* are you talking about?" Tarian glanced around and panic began to take hold of her. "Where am I?"

"Take it easy." Elgan crouched down and studied her intently. "You are safe now, nobody can harm you here. We brought you to this clearing because you had been badly injured during a magical attack, do you remember?"

She narrowed her eyes at him. "I feel fine."

"Our magic is growing stronger, look!" Aneira held out her hand and conjured a small ball of fire that bobbed upon her palm. "Our healing spells have improved beyond anything you could imagine, so we were able to make sure that you wouldn't have any injuries to worry about when you awoke. Oh my friend, you don't know what this means to us!"

Tarian shifted uncomfortably. Her head throbbed with sudden pain and the glare of the sunlight was almost too much to bear.

"Is something wrong?" There was an icy tinge to Elgan's words.

She tried to shake her head. "No… I just hadn't expected to see you again."

"We thought you had perished alongside everyone else."

"Alban cast a spell that prevented my death long enough for me to escape."

"That old goat survived?" Aneira's face lit up.

"I'm not sure, but I… I don't think so." Tarian tried to keep her expression calm. "I haven't seen him in quite some time. Where are we?"

Elgan tilted his head back and threw his arms out to the side. "Veteris forest, only a few leagues away from Furatus. Isn't it glorious?"

"I'm sure Saeth would have loved it."

His eyes snapped open and he glared at her, his face flushing dark red. She raised an eyebrow and waited for a few moments before looking away.

Aneira cleared her throat. "Are you thirsty? Elgan, make some tea would you? She has been gone from us for such a long time, I'm sure she hasn't been properly looked after."

Tarian resisted the urge to point out that she didn't need to be cared for, and so the man simply followed the Minister's orders. She watched him slink away into the trees, and noticed something glinting as it caught hold of the light not far from where she was sitting. After a few moments, Aneira moved away to a pile of bags stacked to one side and began rooting around in them; whilst she was distracted, Tarian took the opportunity to slide her hand through the tall grass. Her fingers wrapped around the hilt of a small blade that was lying on top of something soft. She quietly pulled it all towards her, slipping the weapon into her belt with her eyes trained on the busy mage, and only when she was sure that it was safe did she look down. Her heart skipped a beat. A hooded cape of dark blue sat innocently beneath her fingertips, sticky blood smeared across its sigil of a silver crescent moon pierced by an ornate dagger. Not knowing what else to do, she pushed it back towards a nearby tree stump and tried to suppress the panic that was rising within her.

"Aha!" Aneira stood up triumphantly and turned back to her friend. "I found it!" She held her hand aloft and sunlight caught upon the object in her hand, quickly sinking into its blackened depths.

Tarian's mouth went dry.

"Do you recognise it?" Aneira's words were filled with excitement. "It's the Solis crystal that you had with you back in Mysta!"

"It can't be… that stone was red."

"Oh Tarian, you truly were the key!"

"The key to what?"

"To all of this! It would have been impossible for us to get this far without the power contained within this little beauty. You should be so proud my friend. Sepelite is *saved* because of you!"

"I don't understand." Her head began to swim and she felt sick. "It's just a portal stone."

The Minister's tinkling laughter filled the clearing. "Oh, but it is so much more than that. Just as you were a key for us, so these precious gems are for the Grave of the World. Gateways and portals are not so different I suppose; I can see why the ancient, narrow minded mages would have utilised them in such a trivial way. Perhaps it was misguided translation?"

Tarian's stomach knotted. "Aneira? What are you trying to do?"

The woman didn't answer, mesmerised instead by the scorched crystal she held in her open hand; footsteps soon heralded Elgan's return. His face was crumpled into a deep frown, and he almost snarled at Tarian as he held out a small cup of hot tea. She looked at it with concern.

"Take it." There was no hint of tenderness in his voice. "Take it and drink it, and stop asking questions."

"Oh Elgan, don't be like that. She's bound to be curious, and only through answers can we show her how misguided she has been since leaving my side."

He shook his head. "She wears their clothes, she stinks of their magic. How can we possibly trust her when she has been in their company for so long?"

"No. No, don't say such things. Her own gear was probably ruined when Mysta fell to the traitor's corruption. Would you have had her traipse around the countryside naked?" Her gaze fluttered back to her confused friend. "Drink that tea; it will help to shake off any strange dreams that might linger in your mind. Don't you trust me?"

Tarian put the cup down and got to her feet. The pendant around her neck clung to her chest beneath her armour, biting down into her skin. She looked around at the serene landscape and for a moment everything was peaceful; sleep began to pull at her thoughts, luring her back into its shadowy realm. Something was amiss, but she knew not what. The two mages who stood nearby were watching her intently, and she began to sweat.

A moment ticked by in heavy silence.

"Aneira, listen to me, you've got it all wrong. Her Grace –"

Elgan snorted and turned away. "She even uses their titles for the bitch. I told you that this wasn't the real Tarian. Where is the fury that burned brighter than fire? Where is the woman who mourned the death of her closest friend?"

"No you don't understand! This isn't right; the queen isn't here to conquer us. She's the one who has been healing the land and…"

Aneira shook her head sadly. "She's in your head, Tarian. How long did it take for her lies to crawl under your skin? Don't you see what she's done? She is nothing but pain and anger lashed up in a ridiculous ritual that has siphoned energy from this world for century upon century."

"No…" The word trailed away, and Tarian fought against the doubt that was settling into her mind.

"We have known each other for such a long time, do you really think I would deceive you? Listen," Aneira took her hand, "I know that we didn't always see eye to eye on certain things, but I would never betray you. Sepelite is dying, Cadere is dying, and without our intervention there can be no cure. The Eternal Monarchs have ruled over us for such a long time that we just accept their presence, and for what? Dullahan was a cruel beast, and this Mylah is no different. She slaughtered our friends and destroyed our home. She is an ally of monsters, a murderer and a thief. She attacked you, or have you forgotten that?"

Tarian rubbed the back of her neck and glanced away. "No, I haven't forgotten."

"And yet you defend her. Why is that? Can you tell me one single thing she has done for you that wasn't designed to hurt you in some way? I know that you feel guilty over what happened in Mysta, guiding our people into the very place that became their tomb, but we can make sure that nothing like that ever happens again."

The wind wrapped around Tarian's shoulders and whistled away; her head pulsed with sudden pain, and she could hear something whispering to her.

Elgan clapped his hands together and sent a bolt of magic spiralling into the sky.

Aneira did the same and her lips widened into a grin. "We are going to save this place with or without your help. I hope that you see sense and come with us, because if that accursed queen finds you here she will surely tear your head from your shoulders. If you side with her, you will see to the annihilation of our entire world – she means to kill us all, whether that is with plague or spell or serrated blade."

Tarian shivered. Darkness was creeping in around her, fraying the edge of her vision, and a chill was settling into her bones.

"Come with us. Death stalks us even here, in this glorious courtyard where life should forever blossom and bloom. Come with us."

The wind blew colder.

Elgan shook his head. "She cannot, for her mind already belongs to them. She cannot help us, she is lost. We must press on ahead without her. Leave her to sleep now, here where legends roar."

A flock of carrion birds rose into the air, silhouetted against the sun. Tarian fell to the ground, engulfed in sudden shadow.

Nine

"I will give you everything I own if you just let me kill it."

"No."

"Just a bit of light torture then? At least let me cut out its tongue, I've never known such an irritating voice."

"Have you not listened to your own?"

"Gentleman." Mylah glanced back over her shoulder. "Focus, please."

"Hear the Undead One speak! Hear it and listen and then perish beneath the waves of the stars! They call me Sprig, I don't know why, it's not my name. Smoke and breath and poison, sweet poison, lift me higher into the grateful beyond!"

Cael narrowed his eyes at the squirming creature and lowered his voice. "I could just sew your mouth shut."

It hissed at him and swivelled its eyes. "They call me Sprig, I don't know why. The Undead One walks in the footsteps of those who went before; they call to me, they call to her, they call to you but you cannot hear, oh no! They call me Sprig. Where is the brighter star?"

"You have to let me shut it up."

Bowen chuckled. "I absolutely do not."

"How am I supposed to concentrate on annihilating a complicated wall of magic with this thing spouting nonsense every few seconds?"

"I can't possibly imagine."

"See now that's…wait, did you actually make a joke? I'll need to alert the guilds!"

Bowen put a finger to his lips; Cael frowned and was about to respond when the queen clapped him on the shoulder.

"Necromancer, Seneschal, I believe we have need of your particular talents now. Merfyd and I will begin the spell, and I need you both to call upon whatever you can to assist before joining us directly."

"Yes, Your Grace."

She turned to the High Priestess and her expression softened. "Take Rhydian to cover. I don't want either of you getting hurt if something should go awry."

"I will pray for you." Scole bowed her head. "Come my dear, we must not delay."

Rhydian glanced at the serpentine wall of blue and shuddered; he bowed to Mylah and turned to lock eyes with Cael. "Don't do anything stupid."

"Do I ever?"

"Well Tarian won't be there to save you if you fuck up this time, so just… don't."

He grinned. "I'll be as careful as I possibly can, you know, when mucking about with peculiar and ancient arcane threads that I have no prior knowledge of. Go on now, take that bulk of shiny armour, and this irritating little creature, to a nice shady spot away from all the action before you make me nervous."

Rhydian thumped his chest in salute before grabbing hold of the Oculi and moving over to the priestess. They headed for a large outcrop a short distance west of the barrier; a small winged feline lounged atop the mossy rocks, watching them carefully as they approached. It stretched and yawned before dropping down onto Scole's shoulder.

Mylah waited until they had disappeared from view and then turned back to the men who waited quietly for her instructions. "Is everyone ready?"

"Yes ma'am."

"All right. Be careful gentlemen, and do not put yourselves at unnecessary risk. Let me bear the brunt of whatever consequence comes of this."

Bowen tried to smile. "Fight well, Your Grace."

"Bleed little."

Cael walked along the perimeter and closed his eyes for a few moments as he calmed his breathing, his hands outstretched. Sepelite sang to him then, its mournful call echoing out through the darkened trees.

He sighed and glanced up at the heavens. "This place is built on bones upon bones. Still, that's just as well really."

Power flowed through his veins and he tilted his head back. A bitter wind wrapped around him, pulsating through the gloom, and finally silence came to his mind. He sank into it, embracing the lonely expanse until it engulfed his every thought and then spiralled away. Shapes formed and voices called out in strange tones, their words lost in the void; he focused and they turned slowly into silhouettes. He could see their eyes, blazing indigo flames against serrated ivory flesh, and the wind blew colder.

Lady Amara was listening.

Bowen whispered quietly to himself, the prayer upon his lips an old and rarely spoken one. Ice formed in the ground at his feet, the crystalline threads curling into intricate patterns as they spread out beneath the bracken.

Energy crackled in the cold air around him as his words clung to it; magic surged deep within him and his eyes shot open. He thrust out his hands and let his head fall back.

A whirlwind of snow and sparks swept up from the earth, engulfing the man in its arctic caress.

Mylah glanced at Merfyd; the wall of magic glittered before them, a swirling dance of blue and silver, and it howled at her with unholy desperation. Thunder rumbled overhead and lightning cracked in front of them, its golden spears so bright that Merfyd flinched and looked away.

The queen turned back to face the arcane web, and sighed in relief. A line of spirits stood between them and the barrier; the skeletal figures shimmered like stars as they bowed their heads at the Monarch. She fought back a sudden swell of sorrow and thumped her chest in a return salute, before lifting her arms up towards the sky. Merfyd waited for a moment before doing the same, gradually forming a shield of magic.

Mylah could feel the draw of ancient sorcery calling out to her and pain throbbed through her head; she frowned and hesitated, a strange buzzing in her ears. She could hear the screams of thousands drowning in forgotten blood and impaled upon antiquated blades, and mothers who cried out for their children whilst only dreaded silence came in answer. Cadere was angry, and it was brutalised; her touch was one of decay and darkness, death followed her like a sanguine shadow, and vengeance would have its day.

The air around her became cold and snapped her from such thoughts, and a hand clamped down gently upon her shoulder.

"It is time, Your Grace."

Bowen's voice drew her back to reality and she sighed quietly as she rolled her shoulders. The world could be angry at her if it wished, but she had to see her duty through.

"Ancient Gods of Death and Magic." Everything around them was lulled into an unnatural stillness as her mournful whispers drifted out into the ether. "Aelfylc upon your silver shores, leave now the beaches of gold and amber and behold the Monarch you have not yet forsaken."

The spectres took a step back towards the wall. Cael clenched his fists and gritted his teeth, focusing through the swarm of pain in his head.

Sweat trickled down Bowen's neck. Tension hung upon the air like a gory shroud, and it bore down ever harder upon him.

"In your great silence a mark of death has climbed beyond its bounds and seeks to send all who stand before it into a fiery pit."

The ground trembled beneath their feet. Merfyd furrowed his brow and tried to concentrate as a snow speckled wind began to howl around them.

"It reigns in this corrupted realm and now, beneath the force that guides it, the lands are all aflame, burning sweetly as their tallow drips from these withered bones. You stare back from the edge of the abyss, soft and saccharine Aelfylc, an old rhyme upon your conscience, but we are lost here in this hollow ashen dust. I beseech you to bring forth the softened deceit, and the ghosts of ages past who cling to our shadowed fortresses, and let this strange magic wane and vanish from this place. Be gone."

Cael fell to his knees, bellowing in agony; his hands smashed against the frozen earth and snapped off two of his fingernails as blood spewed from his nostrils.

Mylah slowly lifted her arms, her palms turned towards the hallowed cradle; threads of cerulean energy arose from the ground and entwined around each other, spiralling swiftly skyward. A chill breath wrapped around her legs, biting into her flesh until it sent small jolts of pain up through her thighs. She clenched her jaw and narrowed her eyes, focusing on the curse that seemed to taunt her, and then threw her head back.

The forest around them was aflame. Smoke billowed as magic coursed through the charred trees.

Mylah screamed. Power surged from her fingertips, clavicle, and mouth, and shot out in every direction, the world almost flattened by the shock wave. She convulsed as the spell intensified, her body contorting and writhing beneath its grip; tears and blood streamed from her eyes before being overwhelmed by a burnished blue glow. Icy light exploded before them, consuming everything in its path.

Darkness and silence fell like rain.

*

Flowers covered the inky meadow, their dark blooms swaying in the warm, gentle breeze that passed quietly by. Trees lined the outskirts, their soft foliage rustling to an ancient tune; gossamer veils were gathered upon some of the closest branches, the perfumed cloth fluttering as the wind danced and played within. There was laughter in the air, quiet and distant, and it called like an enchanted song to any who wished to listen; a brook babbled somewhere to the west, the silvery rindle ever flowing towards an ocean that lay beyond the starry horizon.

"Your Grace?"

Mylah slowly opened her eyes; she sighed and tried to turn away, the pain receding from her brow.

Merfyd knelt beside her, a look of concern etched upon his weary face. "Your Grace, are you all right?"

She groaned quietly as she sat up; dirt and ash were smeared upon her skin and there was a tangle of gore in her hair. Her crown had vanished and her dress was torn in places. She looked at her hands for a few moments, confused by the burns and blisters that covered them, and then reached up to touch her brow. Her fingers came away wet with blood.

"Let me help you." Merfyd had a strip of clean cloth and a small pot of balm.

She stared at him, her thoughts a tangled mess of fearful voices.

"I've never even heard of something like that. How are you feeling?"

"I…" Her throat was sore and the words melted away.

Bowen approached, limping. There were small wounds on his face and a cut along his right arm. "Your Grace I hope… Brig's balls, you're hurt! She's hurt!"

"How perceptive of you." Cael appeared behind him. "What obvious statement are you going to relay to us next? That the blight in this place seems to have wiped out most of its people? Or perhaps that hot bread and butter is a nice combination on a wintry morn?"

"She shouldn't be able to get hurt, you idiot!"

"Oh. Well, shit."

Merfyd waved them away and finished applying the salve to Mylah's brow. He cleaned away some of the dirt and got to his feet, carefully helping her to stand. She glanced at the devastation that lay around them and her heart grew heavy.

Fire had ravaged the surrounding woodland, burning away huge chunks of bracken and undergrowth, leaving trees blackened and bare; scorched bodies were scattered across the soot smothered floor, and the scent of cooked flesh and fur was ripe in the hazy air. Bones crunched underfoot as figures approached from the west; Mylah turned away and shivered.

Merfyd gestured to Bowen. "Can either of you two make a small natural fire? Don't use magic. I need to dispose of this cloth."

The Seneschal sighed heavily and nodded. "Of course. It might be a little difficult, but there are some sharp rocks around here we can use if there's anything left to serve as kindling."

"Couldn't you just throw it into that tree over there? It's still alight."

"Do you not understand the word *natural*, Necromancer?"

"Someone's grouchy."

"I'm exhausted, and from the looks of it so are you." Bowen knelt down and started to look for suitable stones. "Will we be able to rest before we move on?"

Merfyd rubbed the back of his neck. "I don't know. Time is working against us, and we clearly cannot allow Her Grace anywhere near Aneira."

"I don't suppose you have a bandage hidden away somewhere, do you?" Cael studied his bloodied fingertips. "It seems that I could use one. Ah, High Priestess. Do you, by any chance, carry healing supplies with you when you come on perilous quests?"

Rhydian raised an eyebrow. "I thought I told you not to do anything stupid."

"I'm afraid I can't lay claim to all of this." Cael held out his arms and grinned. "Magnificent work by the Monarch, though. I did manage to conjure a spirit barricade to absorb some of the damage, so you're welcome. Seriously, does someone have something I can wrap around my wounds?"

Scole handed him the leather satchel she was carrying. "There should be plenty of things in there to help you. What happened here? This… destruction carried on for what seemed miles beyond our shelter, and yet it does not appear to travel past this point."

"Are you hurt?"

"No. We pressed up against the rocks and were left unharmed, thanks be to the Goddess."

"This isn't like any magic I have ever seen." Bowen shifted uncomfortably as he watched Merfyd dispose of the bloodstained rag into a small fire. "And I was surprised that Her Grace did not use the ancient dialects for a more powerful spell."

"Perhaps that is just as well."

"Those translations are often incorrect, Seneschal." Mylah twisted around to look at him. "And so it matters very little what words you actually use, as long as your intent is clear."

His mouth dropped slightly. "You cannot be serious?"

"I am." A small smile crossed her lips. "But that is a discussion for another time. We must press on."

"Your Divine Grace, it seems that your mages are in no condition to travel further and… and you yourself appear to be injured." Rhydian's eyes widened a little.

"No one is truly invulnerable, even the Valiskar."

"I thought those were weapons?" Scole frowned at her. "Wasn't that in the story Merfyd told us?"

"Valiskar is just another name for the immortals of this place, and many weapons have been named after us over the years." Mylah looked at her carefully for a moment. "You had as prominent a role in recounting that tale as he did. Do you not remember?"

"I…" She cleared her throat. "It has been a long day, that's all."

"They call me Sprig!" The high pitched squeal made the priestess jump. "They call me Sprig! Let me go! See now the true colour of the Undead One and its vile sorcery! Untold and Undead and all are forsaken!"

Rhydian lifted the Oculi up to his face for a moment and peered at it before snarling and holding it away.

"Come, we must continue on." Mylah tried to keep her voice steady. "Tarian may be somewhere beyond this point. We cannot leave her in the clutches of that woman."

*

Shadows slithered across the forest floor only to vanish beneath upturned roots and veiled stones; carmine light drifted through the thick verdant foliage and scattered across the ground as a flock of carrion birds rose into silhouetted twilight. Waterfalls cascaded into glassy pools somewhere to the southeast, their echoes of divine torture carrying out across Sepelite's eventide woodland.

The celestial cradle was alight with whispers and glowing stares as the first wave of darkness began to push against the dusk.

Magic lifted into the air, ancient and steeped in hidden power; spectre and beast alike shied away from the clawing tendrils, fleeing instead to concealed crevices to shake and wail and fade.

Mylah held up a hand and the group stopped behind her. She listened for a moment, her eyes flicking from one tree to the next, the only sound that of the hissing Oculi struggling against its captor. The wind whistled through then, brushing against her skin and wrapping around her shoulders, and she lowered her trembling hand.

Bowen stepped quickly to her side. "Is everything all right, Your Grace?"

She narrowed her eyes against the gloom. "I don't know. Keep your wits about you Seneschal, we may have need of them again."

"Yes ma'am." He dropped back to walk beside Cael.

Mylah glanced up at the rising moon and sighed softly. Her skin tingled and there was a faint music upon the air, as though bells were ringing in some distant temple. A thin, faint mist swirled around her feet as she moved slowly into the shadows.

"They call me Sprig! They call me Sprig! Let gloom and gloaming fall to the wayside, Undead Ones! Undead Ones! Where is the light? Where are the voices? Call the Vessel! Call the Vessel, Undead One! They call to you, hear them and run, run, run! They call me Sprig! Unhand me, vile soulless mound!"

Rhydian squinted at the squirming creature. "Something's riled this thing and I wish it would stop. By the Gods, it's annoying."

"They call me Sprig! They call me Sprig! They call me Sprig!"

"Yes yes, we get it, they gave you a name. Do you have any useful information, or is that it?" Cael rolled his shoulders and shivered. "It's getting colder."

"They call me Sprig! Unhand me! Let me go! Shadows run and the venom sinks and all are to be lost! Let me go! They call me Sprig! Let me *go!*"

Rhydian hissed as the creature managed to bite into his arm; he stumbled and fell to his knees with a hoarse grunt and the Oculi squealed and bolted, disappearing into the trees without a trace.

"Well that takes care of that at least."

"We need to get it back." Bowen frowned and held out a trembling hand. "It is probably compelled to give away our position to others."

"What are you doing?"

The Seneschal sighed heavily and lowered his arm. "I cannot cast. I am... tired."

"So let one of the others do it. Cael?"

The necromancer shook his head. "It's not as easy as putting on and taking off that shiny armour of yours. I've never felt this exhausted before, so I dread to think how the old man feels."

The High Priestess helped Rhydian to his feet. "Perhaps we could find somewhere to rest soon, if only for a little while? I am getting a headache and my hips are beginning to ache; it's been a long time since I hiked through this much woodland."

Thunder rumbled overhead. The skies darkened, clouds pulling in an early tide of night beneath their bruising shroud as rain began to splinter through the trees; creatures skittered in the shadows, watching the group move slowly through their guarded territory. Lightning arced across the skyline and illuminated the murky thicket below.

Mylah held up her hand once more. They stood before a clearing, its grove eerily quiet and calm. A strange perfume emanated from flowering vines that wrapped around the trunks of the sentinel trees, and insects buzzed over a stagnant stream nearby.

The Monarch approached carefully, signalling for the others to wait. She glanced around at the remnants of a makeshift camp, and then cried out.

The body of a woman lay against a fallen log, her eyes closed and her skin ashen grey. Thick webs covered the gnarled tree trunks just behind her, their smoky white threads spinning across the floor and over part of her face, heading out towards the middle of the clearing.

Bowen and Cael came bounding up to Mylah's side.

The necromancer followed her gaze and his expression fell. "No... oh no, it can't be." Tears welled in his eyes as he walked over and dropped to his knees. "It can't be."

Mylah shrugged off Bowen's grip and made her way to the woman. She crouched down and smoothed some of the webbing away.

Thunder rolled once more.

"Is she... is she dead?"

The queen cupped her face and whispered something quietly. The woman's dark eyes fluttered open, although she didn't seem to focus on either of them.

Cael bit his lip. "Tarian?"

She murmured softly and her eyes swivelled over to him. Her brow wrinkled into a frown and she gasped for air.

Bowen watched Mylah with concern. Fear gripped him and he could feel his heart begin to race.

"Tarian?" The Monarch helped her to gradually sit up. "Well, at least this time you're not covered in your own blood, I suppose."

Lightning cascaded from the veiled cradle and lit up the clearing for a few moments. Large spiders encircled the border, watching the scene play out with beady copper eyes. Bowen took a step back, panic flooding his veins; he looked at Merfyd as sweat began beading his brow.

"Your Grace?" The man's voice cut out across the glade. "We have a problem."

She turned slightly and her eyes widened. She got to her feet and walked over to the nearest arachnid. "What is the meaning of this?"

It blinked at her and then hissed, sending out a splatter of venomous web that wrapped around her shin.

She sighed and shook her head, peeling off the sticky goo and tossing it aside. "I see."

The creature didn't move, although it tracked her face with its stony gaze. She waited for a few moments until another spider lurched towards Bowen; she flicked her wrist, and it screeched as its body burst into flame. The others withdrew immediately.

The High Priestess shuddered and looked away.

"Must you… kill everything?" Tarian's words were little more than a croak.

The queen turned back to her. "Should I have let them consume everyone here? These beasts are not your friends, you should remember that."

"I wonder if they… would say the same about you. What kind of a… rescue party is this? You must be the… most ragtag band of… idiots that I've ever… seen." She looked around at the people who stood before her, and a weak smile passed across her lips. "But I am glad… to see you."

Cael held onto her to keep her steady, his fears slowly ebbing away. The rain began to lash harder through the forest.

"It should be safe to linger here for a while, if anyone needs to." Mylah clicked her fingers and a small campfire alighted amidst the dirt. "I would like to move on as soon as possible. There are many things that dwell in this place that should not be disturbed, so tread lightly."

"That's great advice, except for the fact that you already incinerated a giant spider. Don't you have some kind of peace treaty with monsters like that?"

"Why do necromancers always try to be funny, and why does everyone seem so intent on asking if I remember the accord? It is true that I have one with the Everlasting, but not every species agreed to the terms."

"Had theirs?"

Mylah said nothing and simply walked away; Tarian leant against Cael's shoulder and he quietened his concern, concentrating instead on wiping away some of the sticky remnants from her clothes.

Bowen had already settled down next to the fire and was quickly falling into dreamless slumber, with Merfyd at his side; Rhydian busied himself trying to make some tea, muttering about spiders and their complicated threat levels. Scole looked at them all and then glanced over to see that the Monarch had vanished.

Mylah closed her eyes and reached out to Cadere's song, feeling the threads of magic that coursed through its earthen veins. There was a deep sorrow within its echo, as though centuries of grief had taken root and buried far into the dirt.

She tilted her head to one side and shivered. "You are not welcome here, Vatis."

A low, guttural snarl echoed out from the trees and within moments the creature appeared, its elongated limbs cracking as it moved. Its amber eyes narrowed as it looked at her and it bared its fangs. "Mortifera leaks out into shadow, tainting sacred ground with blood and bile and bone. Words slip down into chasm and memories turn to ash, like forsaken crowns. Skulls are upon your mantle; see how the hearts beat against the flayed skin!"

"This is not the place for you to vent your frustration. Go back to your island and rot."

"You spin such layers of storm! Peace hides beneath watery graves, tinged with sunset and betrayed! Mortifera thinks to tangle webs around Saprus, Jittern, Meirwon… endless names meant to fall into tainted grip of Valiskar. Death stalks your wake and upon your hands lies a stain beyond river's edge." The creature jolted suddenly, its expression changing from one of anger to confusion. "There… is not a song of moonlight in…" Its head burst.

Mylah looked briefly at the gore splattered body as it slumped to the ground, and closed her eyes once more.

Scole took the small wooden cup and sipped the tea, wrinkling her nose at its bitter taste. She pulled the hood of her cloak up over her hair and listened for a while to the sound of the rain falling through the trees. The scent of death and decay was heavy here, and it soaked into every pore. Mist swirled around the forest floor, brushing over her and dancing away from the nearby flames.

"I'm not sure that this setting is glamorous enough for you, High Priestess."

Scole awoke from her thoughts and looked over at Tarian. "I see that the tea has helped to heal your throat a little."

"I wish it would improve his." She looked down at Cael, who was snoring loudly, and sighed. "What is the point in magic if they all just fall asleep afterwards?"

"It is a gift from the Gods my dear, meant to be used sparingly as a tool. These people have been through quite the ordeal to get here."

"It's just a shame it wasn't a bit sooner."

"Why do you say that?"

A howl echoed from the darkness. Scole dropped her empty cup and Rhydian leapt to his feet.

"My lady, I should –"

"Hush. We need to stay here and make sure nothing happens to Tarian. Those mages won't be any use for a while."

"But what if there's…" His words trailed away as another wail came from the darkness. "Why does the queen always have to chase after danger?"

"Maybe she's trying to get away from you." Tarian grinned. "Are you really just going to stand around here and sweat, or are you going after her?"

"Don't you dare, my boy. That woman is perfectly capable of taking care of herself. She's in no danger."

"But –"

"No."

"But what?" Tarian grunted quietly as she shifted into a more comfortable position. "What's going on?"

"There was some kind of strange magic blocking us from getting to you."

"Rhydian." The word cut through the darkness like a dagger. "That's enough."

He was quiet for a moment. "Her Divine Grace was injured whilst casting against it."

Tarian frowned. "She can't have been. Do I need to get a scholar to explain to you all what *immortal* actually means? I thought it should have been obvious, but apparently not, unless… unless she isn't the Eternal Monarch at all."

Scole barked a laugh. "You cannot be serious."

"Her Divine Grace is what she seems, she must be. There's no other explanation for all of her power."

Tarian shivered and buried her face against Cael's arm for a moment; pain clawed through her mind and there was a faint hum in her ears, as though trapped fireflies danced all around her. It faded after a few seconds and she lifted her head to look at the priestess. "It was Aneira's magic that hurt her?"

Scole said nothing, choosing instead to study the woman's face, but Rhydian nodded.

"Then maybe she is correct after all. What if we have been deceived all this time, just so someone could hoard power and magic like it was gold? She suffered under Dullahan's rule and yet she took up the role herself without a second thought, only to bring death and destruction to our shores instead of her own."

"How can you say such a thing?" The priestess shook her head. "She *saved* you, more than once from what I hear."

"Did she? My city was annihilated by some mysterious force, only for her men to find me apparently moments from death. Yours was attacked with no warning, no reason, and was miraculously saved by the people in her service."

"Including you, if my memory serves me correctly."

"Yes." Tarian grimaced as her head throbbed with pain. "Yes, including me, and I am glad that I was able to help. But… Aneira and Elgan believe her to be the cause of these attacks, just as

Dullahan was the cause of the wars that ravaged Luxnoctis for centuries. After all, what use is a Monarch in peacetime? She holds onto ghosts and grief with such ferocity that it frightens me. She calls her predecessor by another name because she can't abide the fact that they're more similar than she wishes, and if he was just a man making mistakes then she can live with her own questionable decisions."

A veil of whispers coursed through the gloom, skittering into the heavy shadows to hide and watch the hesitant scene play out. Creatures lurked in the undergrowth, their ears open to ancient melodies full of sorrow and fury; solace crept away into unknown depths, leaving only wrath.

Scole shivered and looked away. "You speak from a place of pain child, not logic. If your friend walks a righteous path and it is we who have strayed, then perhaps we have been brought together to allow us to learn our lessons as one. If, however, it is she who has fallen from reverence and we do nothing to stop her, what will you tell yourself when the world is consumed by flames?"

Tarian didn't reply, instead becoming lost in the drowsiness that pulled at her. She pushed her face into Cael's arm again and for a moment everything seemed calm, peaceful. Dreams hovered at the edges of her mind, dancing upon the dying light and calling to her in lulling tones. Bryn's voice floated around her thoughts and his laughter was caught upon the breeze, reaching out for her and drawing her towards slumber.

  The High Priestess got to her feet and shivered as she stretched out her back; there was an unnatural chill lingering in this grove, and it was making her feel uneasy. She handed the empty cup to Rhydian and warmed her hands by the fire for a moment, her eyes darting from gnarled trunks to shadowed canopies until they settled upon a pearlescent mass stretched out between two low hanging branches. She glanced at Rhydian, who was busy searching in one of the leather packs, and then quietly walked over to investigate. The sticky webbing glistened, emitting a strange, sweet odour not unlike that of Rotroot flowers. She reached up to touch it lightly, and her hand came away damp; she stared at the milky crimson liquid upon her fingertips for a moment, her brow creased in a frown, and then realisation dawned. She thrust her hands into the cocoon and started to pull out viscid chunks, throwing them to the ground as panic flooded her veins. The branches shuddered and sagged, and the webbing began to stretch and split.

  Rhydian moved to her side. "What are you doing?"

  Scole stepped back, panting, her hands covered in a mix of red and white. They watched in horror as contorted fingers emerged from the ripped mesh, the skin tinted dark grey and the nails stained black.

  "By the Gods…"

"Mylah!" Fear gripped the priestess, but her voice managed to carry clearly through the trees. "Mylah! Come back!"

The cocoon squelched as it finally opened, and a twisted lump of flesh and bone fell onto the floor with a wet thud. Rhydian stared at the headless body for a moment before he turned and vomited.

Quickened footsteps echoed from behind, and within moments the queen was standing beside Scole.

An air of peace descended upon the grove, and the uneasiness that had crept around the shadows vanished.

"What's going on? Are you all…" Her gaze fell to the mutilated corpse and her words trailed away.

Silence hung between them as seconds slammed into one another. Mylah finally knelt down and gently took hold of the torso, clearing away remnant sludge until faint traces of a sigil could be seen. Tears filled her eyes and she whimpered softly.

Bowen stirred from his slumber. He groaned quietly as he got to his feet, his body aching and tender; in a few moments his vision and mind had cleared, and he looked for the source of the sobbing that had roused him from peaceful dreams. His heart sank and he moved quickly to the Monarch, his senses overwhelmed by the stench of corrupted magic and burnt flesh.

Rhydian glanced at him, his face pale. Bowen sank to his knees and carefully placed his hand on the queen's arm. She didn't look up at him.

"Your Grace?"

"She didn't deserve this."

He let his gaze drop down to the remains cradled in her arms and grief crept upon him.

"She didn't deserve this. I could have let her stay in Luxnoctis, ordered her to leave my service… not caused her family more grief because of my incompetence." She closed her eyes for a moment. "We should take her to be buried, not leave her here to rot in foreign soil."

"We do not have the time, Your Grace." His words were gentle.

"I can do it!" Anger wove through her voice. "I can take her there and see her back to her home, where she should be allowed to finally rest! I am no mere mage who crumples at the first draining thread of magic!"

"I know, but we cannot allow Aneira even the smallest fraction of time to get away from us now. I'm sorry, Mylah."

Scole tilted her head a little. "I can perform the death rites for her, if you wish?"

Bowen nodded at her. "Thank you, High Priestess."

"I can prepare the body too."

"There is no need." Mylah stood slowly, tears streaming down her cheeks. "Her heart is gone, as is her head. Say your words and I will ensure nothing more can be taken from her."

The mist thickened as it swirled around their feet, leaping back from the flickering flames of the campfire and curling up towards the boughs of the trees.

Scole raised her arms towards the sky and gradually brought them down in front of her face. "We call to Lady Amara, who looks upon us from her throne amongst the stars, and ask her to bless the spirit of this child taken from Cadere. May she guide Nelia Hale to her place amongst the honoured dead."

Mylah set her precious cargo upon the ground and, after a moment laden with sorrow, flicked her wrist. Fire shot up from the earth and engulfed the remains of her friend and trusted scout.

"Your Grace?" Bowen rubbed the back of his neck. "Before she… disappeared, did she manage to speak to you about the message she received from Luxnoctis?"

"No."

"Ah. She was concerned that she wouldn't be able to relay it to you, given the volatile nature of our current expedition."

"She was a wise woman."

"Yes, High Priestess, she… she was. Your Grace, it seems that yet another item has been stolen."

Mylah put her head in her hands. "Well?"

He cleared his throat. "It was… that is, I believe that it was one of the daggers that belonged to Eris."

Her cry echoed through the clearing, and the ground started to tremble beneath her. Cracks formed in the earth, sending out plumes of thick ivory smoke; the rain hardened to piercing hail that doused the campfire.

"Your Grace?"

Mylah spun around as a hand wrapped around her own; rage and sorrow seethed within her, and for a moment she couldn't see Merfyd standing in front of her.

"Your Grace?" He tried again, his voice tinged with fatigue. "I know this is difficult, but we need you to focus on the task at hand. If you could just tell me what –"

She snapped her hand away from his and snarled. "Do not presume to tell me what is needed of me! For three years I have known nothing else! I have seen those I care about fall into dust so that order can be maintained. Well fuck order. Fuck everything!"

He studied her for a moment, and then pulled her into a tight embrace. Bowen and Scole glanced at each other but said nothing.

The queen sobbed into the mage's chest for a while, before pushing him away. "I need to be alone. You may follow at your leisure, I will not go far without you."

They watched her walk away into the trees.

Scole rubbed her face wearily. "I'm beginning to wish I had stayed in Caeli."

Rhydian grunted in agreement.

"We are where we need to be." Merfyd rolled his shoulders. "We should not linger in this place for much longer."

"I will rouse Cael and Tarian. I still don't understand how she and Nelia managed to end up here?"

Bowen bent down and plucked a scorched crystal out of the mist. "I believe that this is the answer."

Scole inhaled sharply. "Tell me that's not what I think it is."

"That *was* an Occasus crystal." He frowned. "But I have never seen this kind of effect embedded inside one before."

"If you search for a while you will no doubt find a Solis in a similar state." Merfyd's voice was strained. "This is not good. She should not have been able to do this… no one should. See how the pattern there looks like a burn? The magical pathways that connected this crystal to its partner were redirected forcibly, to allow a portal to open between it and an unnatural recipient, and to then pull the latter through the gateway alongside the quarry. They obviously wanted both women and so somehow created a powerful but unstable vessel. This is disturbing indeed. The corrupted stones, and their original counterparts, are now barren and incapable of conjuring anything at all."

Bowen stared at him. "I've never even heard of such a thing."

"It should not be possible. It's likely that they used Locus crystals, or something similar, to amplify the magic, but if they are capable of manipulating it at this kind of level, then Her Grace is in serious danger. We need to go after her. Now."

The hail eased back into rain. Cael and Tarian were woken abruptly and pulled to their feet, and the makeshift camp was hastily abandoned. The mist thickened into a heavy fog that swamped the forest and oozed through the darkness, clinging to every upturned root and jagged stone, seeking to hinder and delay the weary travellers. Feral magic hissed through the cold air as thunder rumbled overhead, whipping across the tired landscape and plunging into the depths of the earth. Spirits screeched and wheeled in the sky, finally freed from ancient bonds that had held them captive underground; their cries ricocheted through the trees and out to the mountains beyond.

Scole stumbled and swore as she fell heavily upon her knees, an errant thorn cutting deep into her skin. The world swam before her and she closed her eyes, trying to block out the fear that threatened to creep up and settle in her mind.

"Are you all right, my lady?"

She grunted as she took Merfyd's outstretched hand, getting slowly to her feet. He gestured carefully and healed the fresh wound upon her leg.

"I am trying not to question the Gods' reasoning in bringing me here, but it is getting a little difficult." She dusted herself down and winced as new pain coursed through her brow. "And these headaches don't help."

"The temples try to teach us to blindly follow the divine paths laid out before us and to trust in the judgement of the creators, but I doubt that the Gods would be angered by your desire for rest. I am sorry that you are suffering, my lady. It seems that something has gone awry in this place and it is affecting us all, but I don't think I can prevent that in any way. If there is anything else I can do to help ease your burdens though, please just let me know."

She patted his hand and sighed. "You're a good lad. It seems that your parents knew what they were doing when they named you. And yet I hear there was a tavern brawl that helped to first bring you into the queen's service?"

He grinned. "Something like that."

"Well once we're done saving the world, perhaps we could take a trip to Cragen. There's a lovely inn near the Bay of Embers that serves the most wonderful honey wine. I always make sure to bring a bottle back for my Meredith when duty draws me there."

"Is she your wife?"

She glanced at him with a wry smile. *"Something like that."*

The Gilded Lord

"I shall look forward to it, High Priestess. We shouldn't be too far from Her Grace now, so if we just…" He stopped suddenly and frowned.

She followed his gaze and her stomach knotted. Milky eyes were watching them from the shadows, and golden arms, tainted copper near the gnarled hands, were stretching out to grab hold of hair and cloth alike.

A bolt of ice shot through the air and caught the nearest creature across the face, sending it scurrying back into the shadows. Bowen snarled as he watched it limp away, and with a long sweeping gesture sent out a cascade of frost and snow to chase after the others.

"There shouldn't be any Fallow here." Merfyd's words seemed childish in the darkness. "This isn't right."

"I thought they had all retreated after Dullahan's death, but perhaps that was a foolish notion."

"No no, you don't understand. They are a manifestation of dying magic; there is no logical reason for them to be here! Queen Mylah is strengthening Cadere, not draining it. They shouldn't… it's not the right time, I don't… I don't understand!"

"They weren't behaving like those we encountered in Luxnoctis." Bowen tapped his chin and shrugged. "Could they have been an illusion meant to throw us off course?"

Cael appeared through the mist, Tarian leaning heavily on his shoulder. "If only we had a resident expert on such matters. Ah well!"

"Did you have something to add, Necromancer?"

"Me, Seneschal? Not at all. I mean, I have studied the Fallow and their kind for over a decade, but what possible use could that be now that you scared them away with a little chill? Ah, see how my dear Tarian stares at me? She thinks me a madman."

"I think you're an idiot."

He winked and raised an eyebrow. "An idiot who knows that the Fallow can be summoned in any place where magic has become fetid or corrupted far beyond its original purpose. It is unusual for this to happen outside a cataclysmic event such as a Sundering, but there are records hidden in the bowels of the guild's library that tell of the odd occurrence."

"Well whilst you were *reading* about the fucking things, I spent several years actually fighting them. Next you'll be telling me you know how to wield a sword because you read a short passage about it once during a winter storm."

"Now that you mention it, there *was* a very interesting –"

"Not the time, Cael." Tarian shook her head. "If you're going to bicker like this, perhaps you could leave it until after we find Mylah and Aneira? We really should put an end to this mess before you tear chunks out of each other."

A bellowing cry echoed around them as Rhydian flew backwards and landed in a heap upon the floor. He swore loudly.

"It seems that getting to Her Grace might be easier said than done." Merfyd helped him up. "Another spell wall?"

"Another bloody spell wall."

"Shit."

Scole walked quickly to the point of the second barrier, watching the thickened fog swirl up against the slight resistance of an otherwise invisible barricade. She held out her hand and felt the air push back with force; pain prickled her fingers and numbness spread through her palm until she stepped back.

Merfyd sat on the ground, his head in his hands.

Tarian frowned at him. "That's not going to do any good. We need to think of a way to dismantle this… whatever it is, and move forward."

"We cannot do that without the queen's power."

"Perhaps if we called on the Veiled Council, they would help us?"

Tarian looked over at the High Priestess. "What the fuck is the Veiled Council?"

"You… you cannot be serious? They're responsible for helping to keep Cadere safe, and they're the ones who ensure that all magically inclined mortals have dreams and visions when a new Monarch ascends."

She shrugged. "No one in Mysta seemed to know that Dullahan was dead."

"Not one mage? That's impossible." Merfyd glanced up at her. "There's no way for an entire sect to block them. One or two could have missed out, but not everyone. They must have been lying to you."

A bitter wind passed through the trees and curled around Tarian's shoulders, whispering in her ear before spiralling away towards the west. A strange hum coursed through her mind for a moment, smothering out her thoughts and pulling her back towards slumber.

"Is something wrong?"

She blinked for a moment and then shivered. "No, I'm just… I'm just tired. Can you not portal us around this thing?"

"We cannot penetrate it."

Tarian silenced Cael with a look before he could make a remark. "So just wiggle your fingers and make it go away. That's the whole point of you lot, isn't it?"

"This is no ordinary magic. Nothing here should even be possible for the most powerful of mages. When we faced this kind of wall before, success was only feasible because of the protection and power Mylah managed to imbue us with. We wouldn't have survived without that. And the energy resonating from this one seems even stronger. If we try the same spell, we will not see another dawn."

Cael grunted. "Perhaps that is what the Gods truly wish for. We all die trying to stop a madwoman from ending the world."

"Aneira isn't mad."

"I never said she was."

*

Mylah wandered through the darkened state, her eyes closed against the murky gloom; hushed memories clung to this place, their jagged claws buried deep within the sorrowful earth, and they called out to her as she walked by. She became mesmerised for a short time by the gaunt and bloody faces of elves who, two centuries ago, had starved to death after their village was attacked by bandits, and others still who had survived and fled only to suffocate under the greasy clasp of a virulent plague. Prayers and ancient songs murmured out from hidden corners and unseen depths; pleas for mercy, love and freedom slithered through the undergrowth and clambered up towards an oblivious heaven.

The fog thickened until it swallowed all traces of the newly birthed moonlight, and settled upon her skin with an icy kiss. A cold breeze slithered through the miasmic copse, teasing through her hair and pulling at the skirts of her ornate black and gold gown; her fingertips brushed against a hanging vine, tracing over amethyst petals before they fell to the floor.

"Mommy?"

Her eyes shot open.

For a brief moment, everything was still. Nothing moved in the darkness, and the melancholic spirits were silenced. Rain dripped lightly through the leaves.

Mylah sighed and rubbed her brow; a bird called out from its shadowed perch somewhere high above. The queen cleared her throat as she straightened the bodice of her dress, and then started to move once more.

"Mommy?"

She stopped. Her heart began to throb against her ribs and adrenaline flooded her veins; she scoured the world around her, but could see nothing through the haze.

"Who goes there?"

There was only silence in response. Mylah waited for a second or two and frowned as she glanced up towards the shrouded celestial cradle.

"Mommy! Help me!"

"Kitten?" Her voice cracked and she spun on her heel, sudden desperation gripping her mind. "Kitten, is that you? Where are you?"

Birds broke away from their hiding places, fleeing into the night sky.

Mylah snapped around to watch, her chest rising and falling in rapid succession. She took a few steps forward and clenched her fists. "Katherine? Is it you? Answer me!"

"Mommy? Help me!"

"I'm here Kitten! Where are you? Tell me!" Fear and hope combined snaked through her, and magic sparked abruptly at her fingertips. "I'm here!"

"She's going to hurt us, Mommy! We need you!"

"I'm coming Kitten! Just hold on!" She thrust her hands out to the side and glowing orbs appeared in an arc before her. "Tell me how to find you!"

The sound of weeping drifted through the trees. Mylah stared in its direction for a moment and then took flight, running as swiftly as she could; a cascade of conjured light swept out in her wake. Twigs broke beneath her steps and leaves caught momentarily in her hair as they drifted down towards the fractured ground.

The sound of the crying child grew louder, and the queen sent out bolts of icy white to illuminate what she could.

Her heart was racing and her hands began to tremble; she passed three stone beacons, none of them lit, and a sharp pain spread out across her neck. The trees thinned out a little, and the fog began to lift slightly. There were figures up ahead, silhouetted through the mist.

"Kitten? Kitten, I'm coming! Mommy's here!"

A burning sensation took hold of her lower back and spidered up her spine; she snarled and pushed it from her thoughts, focusing all of her energy on the sight before her.

The clouds parted and the rain stopped; the fog around her dispersed just enough for her to see two people standing in a clearing.

Mylah slowed her pace and held up her hand; moonlight filtered down onto the scene, and the queen cried out.

Eris stood in the small clearing, their daughter Katherine at her side.

The child held out her arms. "Mommy!"

"I… I'm here sweetheart." She tried to step forwards, but her body felt suddenly numb.

"Help us!"

"I'm right here Kitten! I…"

"Mommy!" The girl's words were filled with dread. "Don't leave us like this!"

Something moved behind them; shadows stirred in the darkness, moving through the lingering smog.

Mylah's eyes widened and she tried frantically to move. "Eris! Eris, get her out of here! I'll find you, I promise, just go! It's not safe!"

Bitter laughter echoed out from the gloom. Kitten glanced over her shoulder and started to scream. Mylah's stomach knotted. She gritted her teeth and tried to focus her thoughts, but her magic wouldn't respond.

"Mommy! Save us! Mommy, don't just stand there, *please!*"

"Eris, get her out! Go! Get out of here!"

"Mommy! Mommy, *please help us!*"

A hooded figure stepped out into the clearing.

Tears were streaming down the young girl's face as she reached out for the Monarch once again. Mylah narrowed her eyes and clenched her fists, battling against ethereal restraints that seemed unwilling to break. She swore loudly, sweat running down the back of her neck, trying everything she could to get her legs to move.

The silhouetted figure grabbed hold of Kitten and pulled her up off the ground; her terrified cries echoed around the clearing. Mylah strained and struggled, gasping for breath, only to see yet another shadow appear behind Eris.

"Mommy! Help Mama! Save her!"

A dagger was in the stranger's hand. Mylah's eyes widened, full of tears; she cursed herself, desperate to find the smallest spark of magic.

"Mommy, you have to help Mama! Mommy!"

"Let them go! Please, I don't know who you are, just let them go! I'll give you whatever you want!"

Kitten's screams intensified. Mylah's heart lurched and she pushed herself harder, knowing that she had to get away from the binds that had coiled around her. Her thoughts scattered as a shrill buzzing coursed through her mind, and a crow of bitter laughter came from the creature who stood behind Eris.

Power finally kindled, and magic drew breath. She battled against the forces that held her back, tensing every muscle and pulling at unknown reserves of strength. Her face flushed dark red, and the skin around a deep scar upon her chest began to split. Her daughter's pleas echoed around the woodland, sinking like poisoned daggers into her heart.

"Mommy! Please!"

The figure who held onto Eris raised its weapon.

Mylah bellowed, her hands taut.

In a swift motion, the shadow drew the blade across Eris' throat. Blood spurted out into the cold dark, and the woman crumpled to the floor.

"*Mommy!*"

The creature who had seized Kitten held her out towards the Monarch, its grip intensifying as she writhed and struggled. Mylah didn't move, her body filling with terror; another wave of tears welled in her eyes and she redoubled her efforts, trying to block out the sight of her beloved lying upon the ground.

"*Mommy! Please!*"

The figure smashed Kitten against a jagged boulder; her head burst open, scattering brain and bone across the clearing.

Mylah stared in horror. For a moment, everything was still once more; the only sound was that of her own heartbeat. Sweat ran down the side of her face and her chest ached as rage and guilt and sorrow collided and seethed.

Energy swelled within her.

An arctic wind howled through the trees, whipping across the scene with spears of ice and snow. Boughs trembled and broke, flinging severed branches back into the darkness as flowers and leaves were ripped from their stems and cast aside. Thunder growled and clashed over the heavens, clawing at the uncaring Gods and challenging them to fall from their silvery cradle into the bloody pit they had so carelessly constructed.

She roared.

Magic erupted, an explosion of blinding light that surged in a turbulent column towards the sky, showering the land below in a cascade of sparks. A ring of crystals on the ground started to glow, reflecting and amplifying the vicious sorcery; lightning arced between them, lashing through the electrified air until it plunged into the spell. The ground shook and rumbled, breaches forming and stretching open until they started to spit out plumes of thick smoke.

Mylah threw her head back, magic emanating from every pore; her chest split open and a torrent of ancient power gushed forth.

A loud crack rang out through the hollow grove, and a shock wave of magic catapulted across the woodland. Trees collapsed in a succession of brawling clamour, their crooked arms stripped of all foliage; dead birds dropped to the ravaged floor, a flurry of feathers and flesh; debris flew through the air and skittered across the flattened undergrowth.

The Monarch fell to the ground, motionless.

Ten

Aneira shielded her face from the onslaught of dirt and ash that swept across the landscape like a vengeful wind. She glanced up at the ebony cliff face for a moment, watching as the stone caught the moonlight in its crevices and seemed to shimmer like the stars. Runes were carved into the rock and powerful wards glimmered like pearlescent veins, sealing the entrance. Vines had climbed some way up the fractured precipice, their small flowers peppering it with bursts of colour.

She closed her eyes and steeled herself; every fibre of her being was screaming at her to run and hide. Pain throbbed in her head, spidering down to her neck and jaw; she could hear bells ringing somewhere in the distance. Tears formed in her lilac eyes.

"Fate and destiny await. Should we fail, may we curl up beneath this mountain, sleeping for thousands of years and drifting into legend."

She clenched her fists to summon a protective barrier, and braced for the impact.

Magic rushed towards her, hissing and howling as it spiralled out of control; fuelled by wrath and fury, it screamed her name as it sank its teeth into the mountain and then continued on its way.

The skin on the back of her arms and neck blistered. There were cuts and bruises forming along her legs and scorch marks upon the ground beneath her, but she was alive.

After a few more moments a small smile danced across her lips. Mynydd was responding to the spell, the runic inscriptions shimmering like garnets in the sunset. Pieces of flint and small stones fell to the floor as the mountain seemed to groan and sigh, and after a few tentative minutes, a portion of rock imploded.

Aneira let her protection spell dissipate. She waited for the dust to clear, scanning the perilous area around her for any sign of movement. There was none.

Seconds passed, slamming down into one another like broken tombstones; a musty aroma emanated from the cavern, slinking out from the newly uncovered entrance and creeping into the world beyond. Soft blue light washed down through the darkness, illuminating the way deep into the heart of the mountain.

She glanced briefly at the bag she clutched so tightly in one hand, and then stepped inside.

Tarian awoke.

The world around her was a mess of ashen wreckage; the air was heavy with mournful song, and the scent of death and charred flesh entwined. Trees, once tall and proud, were nothing more than charcoal bracken upon the scorched floor; mounds of bloodied meat had been flung in every direction and now squatted upon serrated rocks, small flaps of skin lifting in the sleet speckled breeze. Vile fragrances hung in waves like ragged shrouds, leaving a greasy film upon everything they touched.

She got unsteadily to her feet. Pain had sunk into every part of her body, and there was a wet warmth running along one side of her chest.

"Tarian? Are you... are you okay?"

She turned her head slowly to one side; Merfyd was kneeling upon the floor, his features awash with dirt and gristle. Scole and Rhydian were lying face down nearby, whilst Cael was slumped against a fallen trunk, his body covered in burns. Bowen was slung over it a little further along, an errant branch sticking out of his back.

"What happened?"

"I... I'm not sure, but the barrier is gone. I think we might be too late."

Tarian's eyes widened and the haze cleared from her thoughts. "Mylah."

"I can take care of all of this." He glanced around. "I can help them, but it's going to take time that we don't have. Not if we're going to stop her."

"I'll go."

He closed his eyes for a moment, seemingly about to say something, when he changed his mind. "It is a dangerous path to walk alone. I will follow as soon as I am able."

She gazed at the carnage around her, lingering for a few moments upon the necromancer; with a heavy sigh, she took to her heels and ran.

Aneira looked up in wonder at the shadows that hung around the cavernous ceiling; thin threads of silver and gold were draped between thick chunks of quartz. Ebony stalagmites rose from the slick ground, a bed of sapphire moss at their feet; veins of dark amethyst ran through the rock, which glistened and glittered as light resonated from large crystals embedded in the jagged walls.

The whole place pulsed with magic ancient and unrefined; it crackled and murmured as it swept through the air and sent ripples across a pool of inky black. Aneira held out her hand and watched as tiny spheres of red and gold danced across her skin.

She carefully made her way deeper inside, heading towards what she believed to be the heart of the mountain; the coarse pathway split here and there into winding tracks, a few of them blocked by fallen rubble whilst others simply disappeared into the dense shadows. She tightened her grip on her bag and continued moving forwards, avoiding the call of the depths and focusing her thoughts on what she knew would lie ahead.

One moment dripped into the next, each filled with a sense of both amazement and dread; her footsteps echoed out through the beautiful den as wild sorcery seemed to follow and play in her wake. A whisper of warm breath caressed her throat and teased at strands of her hair; moments later, a peal of laughter rang out behind her. She shivered and continued on.

The path sloped down after a while, dropping into misshapen steps that were bordered by small stalactites dangling perilously above a sheer drop. She closed her eyes and inhaled deeply, the air suddenly crisp and cool. Power resonated within her; she could feel it reaching out to its feral kin as it coursed through her veins. A second or two passed, and she started the treacherous descent.

Her heartbeat grew louder, trying to fill the void that surrounded her on all sides; magic was being drawn from her fingertips, the skin splitting open and turning numb. Sweat beaded her forehead, and she struggled against the desire to open her eyes, remembering the passage in one of the books that her faithful courier had given to her:

Trust only in the path that lies ahead
Give heed to neither darkness nor light
But think upon the fires that ravaged sacred Brynewelm
City of gold and amber, once home of Aldhada
And whilst burning in the shadows of this gilded hollow
Forget the words of traitorous Aelfylc
And step after step we shall be your salvation.

Aneira opened her eyes. She was standing on the lower platform, a plateau of onyx and sapphire. Large braziers lined the walkway on either side as it led to a colossal archway, each one bursting into flames of palest green as she walked past, the scent of Rotroot flowers suddenly heavy in the air. Two titans carved from stone blocked her path, an ornate offering bowl held between them. She studied their faces for a few moments, the intricate details of those long dead kings etched into forgotten history, and then glanced at the gateway beyond. She reached into her bag and withdrew a severed head, placing the gory mess gently into the bowl.

"Sleep now, sweet sacrifice, in the bosom of those who walked in a time before light had breached the horizon." She smiled weakly, her fingertips delicately tracing the jagged remnants of skin. "It won't be long now."

Tarian gritted her teeth, ignoring the stab of pain in her right flank; the world flew past as she ran through the sea of dust and debris, her heels kicking up clouds of ashen grit. The small blue creature that clung to her howled as she dived suddenly to one side and smashed it against a beacon, the ivory and violet flames sputtering in response.

She pushed herself off the cracked stone and carried on past two more, her footsteps ringing out through the gloom until she finally skidded to a halt a few minutes later. The Oculi detached itself from her ribs and leapt to the ground with glee, dancing about a ring of scorched earth that smouldered and smoked. She watched it with disdain.

"They call me Sprig! I don't know why!" It hopped up and down, pulling at strands of its greasy hair. "See how they fall! See how they fall!"

Tarian thought for a moment about breaking the creature's neck, when her gaze caught upon something glinting in the moonlight. She walked over to the other side of the blackened halo and bent down, her fingers curling around a clay poppet, its headless body small enough to fit inside her palm. Another lay nearby with a thorny twig embedded in its throat.

"See how magic undoes magic!" Sprig cackled and hissed. "See how phantoms drift and lift and live again! And from life comes death… sweet, sweet death! Undead One has no more breath to draw, and as it drops into graceless pits we will rise again!"

Tarian let the broken doll fall back to the ground and closed her eyes for a moment. She inhaled deeply, letting her mind clear, and then took flight once more.

"I gift to you this crown… crown of… bone…" Aneira took a book from her bag and opened the weathered pages, the ancient script transforming in front of her eyes. "I gift to you this crown of bone, and my eternal heart. I give to you a broken throne, in this undying dark. In these caves of tarnished gold I offer you my hand, I welcome you, sweet Aldhada, into this savage land. May Aelfylc fall and fires rise, where shadows never cease, and see the ones that they despise from eternal bonds released."

An icy wind whipped around her, tearing at her clothes and clawing at her skin, and a heavy drum beat thundered from the depths below.

Magic thrummed in the air, encasing the Minister in its song as the rock beneath her feet began to tremble. Dust and grit cascaded from the statues, veins of dark red slowly emerging upon their stony skin; swirling silver light protected Aneira from it all as the titans groaned and creaked, finally wrenching apart to reveal a darkened path beyond. The offering bowl clattered to the ground and the severed head rolled away, tumbling over the edge of the path into the chasm below. More braziers burst into life, illuminating a walkway littered with bones.

The chanting in Aneira's mind died down, and a smile flickered across her lips as she inhaled deeply, taking in the scent of old death and older hope.

A trail of moonlit splatter led Tarian across the ashen wasteland until through the gathering mists she could see its end: a towering mountain of black, beautiful and terrifying in the darkness. A gaping wound had marred the surface, and now enticed all manner of shadow and spite inside.

She halted at the unnatural entrance, looking at the fractures and jagged edges that made up the serrated arch; she glanced back over her shoulder for a moment, and then headed inside.

There was a figure up ahead, leaning heavily against a fallen boulder; as Tarian got closer, she saw a woman holding her left side and gasping for breath, her hand covered in blood. She snarled as she tried to push herself away from the stone, but only fell back against it with a cry.

"Mylah?" Tarian moved swiftly, her footsteps echoing through the cavern. "By the Gods, what happened to you?"

The Monarch coughed, a frown creasing her brow. "T-Tarian? What are you... what are you doing here?"

Panic rose through her as she took in the extent of the queen's injuries. Mylah's torso was rent almost in two, her flesh and bones exposed beneath a torrent of gore; burn marks clawed at her neck and jaw, and the skin upon her face had split in places. Her left eye was stained milky white.

Laughter echoed somewhere deep within the bowels of the mountain, and the Monarch sighed heavily.

Tarian hesitated for a moment. "Merfyd is on his way, you should stay here. He might be able to help you."

"No." She winced. "I… I have to stop… her b-before she… kills us all. She has the… the dagger that… killed Erebus. She has his blood. There can b-be… no other choice now."

"You're in no condition to move."

Mylah smiled weakly, and pushed herself away from the rock once more. She raised a shaking hand and focused, allowing a swirl of indigo magic to drift from her palm and slowly encase her injuries in deep blue light. She held out her trembling hand to Tarian. "Come then. To the end."

"To the end."

Skulls layered in golden dust gazed up at Aneira as she moved past, their unseeing sockets filled with ochre shadow. Excitement coursed through her as power resonated archaic and unrefined, a glorious chorus of voices echoing around the incandescent hallway. Runes etched into the walls swirled and reformed into the modern common tongue; images clambered through the rock and reached out to the Minister's mind, filling her thoughts with warm shores and glittering seas.

For a moment she could hear the lamentations of those who had fallen in Mysta, their sorrow gently fading as she neared the final chamber.

Magic intensified and one of the voices called out to her enthusiastically; she smiled as she looked around and saw the remains of some ancient king, a tarnished crown lying upon the ground nearby. She knelt down carefully and took it into her hands, ignoring the outstretched skeletal fingers that had never been able to reclaim their prize. The metal was foul, but she could make out a pattern of suns and moons that had been worked into the thick band; she ran her bloodied fingertips over it for a moment, before placing it gently upon her head. She closed her eyes and waited, listening to the threnody of the past.

One final chamber lay beyond. Broken paths fell away into the darkness, twisted remnants of walkways belonging to a priesthood long lost to time; islands of rock rose up from the depths, their braziers and statues now little more than ruins and dirt.

Aneira looked up at the marble archway and her eyes shone; seconds dripped into minutes as she studied every little detail, each stroke of the inscriptions and the movement of the magic that coursed through the veins of the rock. She delved once more into the bag she carried and brought forth a human heart; her fingers curled around the grisly trinket and her mind filled with joyful song. She held it aloft, and tilted her head back.

The world was still for a moment.

"Let no gate bar the way of she who seeks most blessed redemption." She brought the bloodied bauble down to her lips and flicked her tongue over the surface before she bit down hard.

Magic exploded around her and she grinned, spitting cruor, and then smashed the heart against the stony door.

"Wait! Revered One, wait!"

The Minister stopped, turning slowly to glance over her shoulder at the small creature who had managed to intrude upon her sanctuary. Anger riled deep within and she gritted her teeth.

An Oculi hopped and bobbed before her, dancing from foot to foot as it pulled at strands of thin hair; its eyes swivelled for a moment as it grinned, showing its spiny teeth.

A shiver of magic brushed against Aneira's throat.

"They call me Sprig, I don't know why. It's not my name. Revered One comes late to the fires." Its words were almost lost in the cavernous expanse. "Knowledge is gone from shades and shadows, but Revered One breaks the chains that bind and hold and all magic will be free. They call me Sprig! Wait, oh wait, with dangerous words skittered upon lips of stone we may all yet fall into the icy grip."

Shrill laughter broke across her lips. "You think *you* can tell me that?"

"The path before the Revered One is fraught with deception shiny and bright." Sprig shook its head violently. "Knowledge is not bestowed, silly silly human, of what happens when the words are spoken and the deed is done."

"You do not get to talk to me in such a manner." Aneira's eyes narrowed. "You are a pitiful creature indeed, little Oculi. Your life is so near to its end, and yet you think to have influence over me?" She cackled bitterly. "I should flick you off that walkway and listen to your screams as you plummet into the dark."

"Revered One is cruel in her foolishness." Sprig cocked its head to one side. "There are whispers from deep, deep, deep down there. Mistress of Tempests cannot hear the cries that echo within the enchantments. Mistress of Storms and Exile of Mysta, where are the ones you wished to pull from the brink? Silly, silly, silly human! There are the dead, and the suffering, and the soulless, and they all cling to your skin!"

"Enough!" The Minister bared her teeth. "I will not listen to any more of this nonsense! Your kind is not welcome in this holy place. Be gone!"

Sprig screeched as it skipped about. "Promises made and promises broken! As you did to us, so they do to you! As you did to us, so they did to you! As you did to us!"

Aneira walked over to the creature and, taking hold of its hair, plucked it off the floor. It squealed and hissed, struggling against her grip; she brought it close to her face and studied it for a moment, before moving back towards the door. The Oculi squirmed, trying to free itself from her grip.

"How pathetic you truly are, trying to play with forces so far beyond your comprehension. You and your kin ignored the summons, and now you alone will bear the consequences for those actions."

"No no no, Revered One!" It threw up its hands and tried to claw at her arm. "Let Sprig go! The void holds nothing for me! Secrets and lies and spells and prayers are no more than –"

Aneira smashed it against the door. The Oculi exploded in a mess of flesh, bone and blood, some of which sank into the stone.

"Where are your gods now, pathetic little beast? I can hear mine, they speak to me with words of such divine grace as you could never have imagined. I feel them all around me, feeding me, blessing me. They show me secrets that even you, like an enslaved priest, would have kept from my mind."

The world shuddered beneath her feet as the ancient gateway drank of death and despair; spirits emerged from the murky core, rising higher and higher until they wheeled and screeched around the craggy ceiling. Crystals embedded in the rock glowed deep scarlet as bolts of lightning arced between them; drumbeats thudded from the depths, the foundations of the mountain shaking and fracturing.

Aneira's laughter burst out over the cacophony and she cast one last look behind her. "A champion hails from the humble dark, determined to light the way for those who were betrayed in the vilest manner. Tinniant de campanis, cnylle belltaoen, canu'r clychau."

A chanting chorus arose then, and as Aneira held out her hands the voices swept through her like fire; power surged within, electrifying every part of her body, awakening thoughts and memories that were not her own.

She tilted her head back and took a deep breath, then slammed her hands against the stone. A shock wave of magic rippled out in every direction, and the door crumbled to dust.

Mylah leant against a broken pillar, her eyes closed as she tried to catch her breath. Desperation clung to the air, the magic here a mess of obsolete chaos as it whirled and spiralled.

Tarian was a little way ahead, inspecting the strange carvings of an ancient brazier. "We need to get moving." Her voice seemed so small, dwarfed by the vast chasm all around them. "I really don't think you should try to follow her. It's dangerous."

A weak smile passed over the Monarch's lips. "My life has never been anything else. Tell me something, Tarian. Did you truly believe that I was here to invade Sepelite? A land that I already hold dominion over?"

She was about to answer, when she stopped and frowned. "Did you hear that?"

"What are you... oh, fuck! Get down!"

A swell of magic raced towards them; Tarian dropped to the floor and tried to flatten herself as much as possible, pushing up against the base of elaborate stonework. Mylah looked from the spell to her and back again, and thrust out her hands; a protective barrier formed around the woman moments before it swept over her. The Monarch tried to throw up another deflective shield but her energy was too weak, and the sorcery hit her full force in the chest. She was hurled backwards to the edge of the pathway, her skin blistering and her clothes aflame. Her eyes widened and she grabbed hold of the pillar, feeble swirls of magic sputtering into the darkness; the fire winked out, leaving the skirts of her gown singed, but her grip weakened and she slipped a little, her body dangling above the shadowed abyss.

Primordial spectres arose from shadowed graves, their howling ascent shattering the earthen mantle that had kept them safe from so many winter moons. Grief and vengeance echoed out across Cadere's fragile rind, scouring the bitter landscape for the broken and the resentful, and sweeping them up in a torrent of despair.

Tarian got unsteadily to her feet. Her arms and legs ached and there were fresh burns across her shoulders; her head buzzed with noise, her vision was disrupted by spheres of blue and black, and blood trickled from her nose.

Remnants of magic hissed through the air.

"Mylah?" She wiped her eyes with the back of her hand and shivered. "Mylah, where… where are you?"

The world shuddered violently and she fell to her knees, cursing her weakened state; a scream drew her gaze to the woman struggling to keep hold of the ruined column as another tremor rippled through Mynydd.

"I'm… I'm coming." Tarian pulled herself along the unstable floor as a shower of ashen grit fell from the ceiling high above. "Just… hold… hold on."

"Leave me! You have to go after her!"

"No! We… we need you." She reached the pillar and clasped her hands around Mylah's. "Tell me how to… how to help."

Another quake rippled through the mountain; Tarian cried out, feeling the woman slip through her fingers.

"Let me go, Tarian. You need to get out of here."

"Don't you dare give up on me now! I know that you're hurting, but we need to work together to stop her from making another mistake. You're powerful enough to get yourself back up here, don't let me down now!"

"The more frequently that I cast in this place, the more she can feed off my power. There are old wards here too, meant to dampen magic like mine. Tarian, I… I'm sorry for everything that I've put you through, but I can't… I can't do this anymore."

"Yes you can! Gods forsake this mountain, why won't it stop shaking? Don't... don't let go!" She clawed her nails into the queen's skin. "I won't let you go!"

Footsteps echoed through the cavern and relief washed over Tarian; her strength was already waning, and there was a strange dizziness trying to creep into her thoughts.

"Your Grace! Tarian!"

Tears welled in her eyes. Slumber was dragging through her mind and it took all of her focus to stay awake, but Bowen's voice had never been so welcome. Arms were around her then, as others grabbed hold of Mylah and pulled her to safety. She let herself be cradled for a moment, her mind a sea of hazy voices and her body awash with blood.

The queen steadied herself against the Seneschal. "We have to stop her. The consequences... she doesn't understand what she's doing."

"Brig's balls! What the fuck happened here?"

"Rafael?"

"Aye, it's me boss. That Merfyd fellow summoned me right out of Delyth like it was nothing, said he'd need of my talents. And looking at you, I'm bloody glad he did. I've never patched up an immortal before, do you have any special requirements? No? Good, then shut up and let me have a look at these wounds."

Aneira ran her hands through her hair, knocking the soiled crown onto the floor, and a serene smile returned to her lips as she finally stepped into the shadowed chamber. Lanterns and sconces burst into life, their antique candles ablaze with emerald flame. Thick veins of gold and silver rippled through the ebony walls, dropping down to hide behind richly embroidered tapestries. A carpet of bone led up to a dais, upon which stood a throne of jet and sapphire, its skeletal occupant staring vacantly into the abyss.

Aneira stopped in her tracks, and her confidence vanished. Tears welled in her eyes as fear grabbed hold, snaking its hands around her throat. She could see two more gaudy crowns amidst the throng of calcified carnage, but it was the one of dark red upon the skull of the seated king that caught her gaze. She pushed aside the despair that threatened to overwhelm her and waded through the remnants of forgotten heroes until she reached the throne of the Gilded Lord.

Her heart lurched in her chest and she sobbed, her hopes suddenly crushed beneath a long dead heel. In that moment, it was as if all those who had perished in Mysta's fires were bearing down upon her, their disappointment and grief entwined within her own.

She fell to her knees and wept, her dreams fading into oblivion, and remorse slithered into her soul. She had failed those who had put their faith in her, who had sacrificed everything so that she might journey beyond the limitations set by tyrants and despots. Mylah would be upon her soon, and there was nothing she could do to save herself.

She leant her head against the throne and slammed her hands into its ornately carved legs; the skull of the feeble king fell from its resting place and crashed onto the dais, shattering into debris and dust.

She let her fingers coil around the prongs of the metal crown. It bit into her skin with an icy kiss, and a jolt of power surged through her arm. She raised it slowly, watching it catch the light, and then placed it down upon her head.

Feral magic howled around the room,

Aneira got to her feet and opened her eyes. She looked around her, the faces of a thousand dead warriors ingrained in the very walls of the accursed room, and a grin broke out across her face. She glanced back at the desecrated throne and picked up an ebony sceptre that had fallen slightly to one side, lifting it above her head. She brought it crashing down into the remains, shattering what was left.

A hiss of sorcery slithered across the vaulted ceiling.

"Your legend lies in ashes at my feet."

A necklace of gold lay in the dust. She took hold of it, letting the links clatter against pieces of the king's ribcage; they rang out like tiny bells.

The floor beneath her gave way.

A cascade of bone, dust and dirt plummeted some thirty feet alongside her; a gust of magic broke her fall and although she landed with a loud crack, she survived largely unhurt.

Laughter slid free and echoed all around her.

She stood up once more, albeit somewhat shakily, and surveyed her surroundings; gone were the opulent tapestries and gilded walls, replaced instead with shadow and gloom.

"What brings you to me, Little One?"

She turned at the guttural sounds, scouring the darkness to find their source.

"This is not a place meant for adventure or fortune. You should not have sought to journey down this path that you have found. The surface gave you freedom and light – you will find neither here."

"Show yourself, demon! I am not afraid of you!"

"I did not mention fear." Sorrow flickered through the words. "I had hoped Beloved Erebus would keep to his dreamscape words and ensure that the tongue of his people was altered enough to prevent the misguided from seeking my presence."

Aneira hesitated. "I know not of what you speak. Show yourself!"

"Very well."

A sphere of pale blue light appeared upon a distant wall, growing slowly until it pushed back the darkness around it. Amidst the rubble and remains of ancient knights was yet another dais, this one much larger and plainer than that of the previous room; it held up a giant stone slab, upon which lounged a colossal humanoid creature, ancient but unmarred by time. Its skin was a marble of dark purple and palest gold, and was heavily scaled in places, the ebony plates glittering like stars; its three eyes, each a swirl of iridescent black, gazed upon Aneira without blinking. Black horns curled out of the top of its head, adorned with small silver charms and bells that chimed as it moved; ornate enchanted torcs curled around its elongated arms, linked to the heavy chains that kept it shackled to the dais. Its torso, densely patterned with indigo runes and seals, slunk down into a serpentine tail that ended in a large arrowhead spike. Chaotic magic radiated from it, intensifying as it opened its mouth and showed rows of serrated fangs.

She recoiled. "What are you?"

"You come here and yet know not what you sought?" It waited for a moment, the question heavy upon the air. "You cannot leave this place, Little One."

A loud hum overtook her thoughts for a moment, and her panic died. She smiled wryly and tilted her head to one side.

Sorcery sparked all around her.

"You are the Anghenfil."

It said nothing, waiting only for her to finish her thought before the breath of Mynydd sank into her flesh and dissolved her, as it had done to so many before.

"You were worshipped once, long ago. But the fools who prayed to you had no idea what you are capable of, did they?"

It watched her.

She moved closer, and the light spread out across the room, revealing a dilapidated ivory shrine nearby.

She barked a laugh that was free of all mirth. "What use is a god that cannot answer those who call to it? You and the Monarchs are remnants of a bygone age, and no longer serve a purpose. Cadere does not need you."

Doubt flickered across the creature's face. "Why do you say these things, Little One? You wear a crown not meant for your weary head, and you spout knowledge as a Sage of days long turned to dust. What burdens your heart enough to bring you here? What knowledge was it that you sought?"

She sighed and shook her head. "The true Gods tell me all that I need to know."

"Not all words ring true. Be not fool enough to listen to those who would turn you from the light and see you slink into a dreamscape of hollow horrors."

Aneira wiped her brow and turned, walking slowly towards the once grand altar. She ran her hands along it and sighed, letting her bag drop to the floor.

The Anghenfil watched her every move.

"You know, I never could have done this without my faithful courier. It's amazing what people are willing to do when they feel like they've been betrayed. Charms to call forth storms, spells to bind the weaker Everlasting to one's will, books and tomes thought to be safely sequestered in ancient vaults… it is truly wondrous what certain people can get their hands on." She gestured quickly and a small portal tore open beside her. "Elgan? The time of our ascension is nigh. Bring the courier's weapon with you, I wish to leave it here amongst these obsolete relics. Perhaps it can bring some semblance of honour back to this place."

"Of course." His voice wavered slightly, but within moments he and Seren walked through the gateway, the magic winking out behind them.

A mirthless grin danced across Aneira's face.

Elgan handed her a greataxe. "I told you I would keep it safe until it was needed."

She kissed it and placed it carefully upon the marble. Seren watched her with a shiver, being careful not to catch the woman's gaze.

Aneira clapped her hands together. "Are you ready to begin?"

Merfyd and Tarian led the way into the broken throne room, their conversation ending abruptly as soon as they stepped inside the ruined chamber.

Rafael whistled through his teeth. "What a fucking mess. No wonder nobody makes pilgrimages to places like this anymore, who wants to wander into a room and fall through the fucking floor?"

The queen rubbed her temples and sighed. "Do you have any more of that Rotroot infusion?"

"Your Divine Grace, you really should get somewhere safe. You need to rest, to allow yourself to recover properly." Scole watched her with concern. "I don't doubt your healer's –"

"*Physician.*"

"I don't doubt your physician's abilities, but something is clearly amiss in this place. I had always believed the Monarchs to be invulnerable."

"Not under certain circumstances." Tarian grinned at Bowen's look of surprise. "There's no need to look at me like that, we do listen to you sometimes."

"I appreciate your concern, but this is… this is not the…" Mylah's head lolled forward and she slumped into a pile of bones.

"Your Grace!"

"I… I'm fine, Seneschal. Don't… don't fuss. Listen for a moment… can you hear that music? It's coming from down there."

Merfyd peered at the gaping hole, his face ashen. "Shit. Shit, shit, shit."

Tarian glanced back at Bowen. "Can any of you conjure a way for us to get down? Is that possible?"

He frowned, his mind abuzz with strange thoughts and unfamiliar voices. He pressed his palm to his forehead, and a burst of magic swirled nearby, picking up pieces of rubble and debris and setting them into makeshift stairs.

Tarian stared at it. "Is this even safe?"

Merfyd leapt down onto the first step without a word.

"I'll take that as a yes." She sighed and shrugged. "At least it seems that death doesn't want us today."

"I'm not so sure about that." Rhydian grunted. "We were halfway to the realm of the dead when we got pulled back – and nobody seems to care enough to discuss it."

Cael raised an eyebrow. "Don't look at me. Lady Amara never agreed to release your spirits into my care, and besides, necromancy is a fine art. I can't just snap people back into their bodies haphazardly."

Mylah got to her feet and brushed away pieces of some ancient would-be hero. Scole helped to steady her for a moment until she regained her balance.

"High Priestess, I'm not sure that you should come with us. Aneira is an incredibly powerful mage, and there are still so many people in Delyth, and beyond, who will have need of your talents in the years to come. Rafael is heading back to the entrance, perhaps you should accompany him?"

"Nonsense, my dear." She squeezed her hand gently. "If my Seren decided to follow this woman then there must be something in her character we can appeal to, some sliver of humanity. And if not, I would rather face her with the Gods by my side and take my fate as it is meant to be…" She sighed. "May Meredith forgive me. Come, we will help each other descend and see what awaits us."

Aneira turned suddenly, her eyes narrowing. She barked a cruel laugh and beckoned Elgan to her side. He moved quickly, trying to avoid looking at her directly.

"Do you see, old friend? They have come to offer themselves as fodder for the ritual! How exciting."

They watched the group clamber down the makeshift staircase; Seren rubbed the back of her neck and then wrung her hands, trying to rid herself of the strange sensation that crept upon her skin and sank into her flesh.

"And look, the unholy queen herself walks into this pit of despair! What madness drove her thus, that she would abandon all reason and offer her blood to me?" Aneira bit her lip. "No… no she would not be so foolish, she thinks to lay a trap of some kind for me to fall into!"

"But if we just kill her, surely we can be done with all of this and go home?"

"Such optimism, little rogue, and such naivety. There are others who will need our help in breaking the unnatural bonds that have been wrapped around their necks. Besides, do you honestly believe that this tyrannical apostate would simply *allow* us to slit her throat and rid the world of both her and that disgusting abomination over there?"

"Maybe the poppet spell was enough to send her over the edge, and she's not thinking rationally?"

Aneira inhaled sharply as she slapped Seren across the face. "Be quiet! I cannot think with your incessant chattering in my ear."

Elgan stepped forward, his lilac eyes trained upon the group that had gathered in the far side of the room. "It… it cannot be. Tarian?"

"What?" The Minister craned her neck and sighed. "I cannot *see* with all of this damnable darkness!"

She lifted the sceptre above her head, and an explosion of blinding light shot out across the cavern; the intruders staggered a little, trying to protect their eyes from its icy brilliance as it revealed the rich golden hues of the cavern. Seren swore loudly, squinting and shying away.

Mylah stared at the creature that struggled against its eternal chains. Her heart raced, pulsating against her chest as though it would burst, and for a moment everything around her went still.

Its sorrowful eyes met hers, and it seemed to almost wilt before her. "You should not be here, Beloved Mylah."

She stepped closer, her hand lifting slowly; the Anghenfil returned the gesture, its manacles clanking against the ancient stone. An arc of indigo magic drifted between the two, dispersing quickly into the ether.

"I am so sorry." Her voice cracked and she fought back a sudden swell of tears.

The creature looked at her with pity. "Do not fear what is to come, Beloved." It switched its attention to Merfyd. "And you, Augur? Do you feel remorse for what is in the hearts of these Wretched Ones?"

Aneira snarled. "Why are they speaking to that thing? They conspire to trick us into failure! Just as your pathetic priestess fooled us with her book of lies! Perhaps you are actually working with her against us! Now that I think upon it, it was a little too convenient that we just happened upon you during your meandering travels."

Seren stared at her. "What are you talking about? I only ever did what you asked of me."

"The Gilded Lord was nothing more than a fable turned to dust." She spat at the woman's feet. "But do you see me now? I am legend reborn!"

Magic burgeoned around her, hissing and crackling as it spiralled through the ground.

Blood trickled down the woman's head as a grin curled across her lips. She strode forward, holding the former guard in her sights. "She means to kill me, Tarry! Is that you want?"

Tarian stared at her, aghast.

Bowen glanced over. "What's wrong?"

"Tarry is a nickname that Bryn had for me. She never used it, no one else did." Her hand darted to the pendant around her neck. "But... but that voice..."

Cael sniffed loudly. "It's a distinct one, I'll give her that."

"No, no you don't understand. I recognise it, but it is not *hers*. That's the one I heard in my head when Mylah and I first met."

Merfyd and Bowen exchanged a glance.

"Well... fuck."

Aneira cackled. "Did you see her face? Tarry, oh Tarry, sweetened wine drips from the heavens and seeps through your worthless tears! That pitiful sovereign is nothing more than a web of outdated chaos, just like those who came before her. I will see her to her inglorious end and only when —"

A bolt of ice caught her across the cheek. She turned slowly to see Bowen glaring at her from across the cavernous room.

"Shut the *fuck* up."

She touched her face, feeling the welt that was already forming upon her skin, and her eyes darkened. "So be it."

Flames erupted from the ground, a barricade of blazing white that pushed the group back towards the wall; it was quickly met with a shower of hail and snow that sent a hiss of steam and mist rolling across the gaping expanse.

Anger rose through Mylah; the drums of war sounded in her head, echoing down through the ages, and for a brief moment it seemed as though all of the Monarchs of Cadere stood by her side, a bastion of sorcery and strength sending a cascade of magic sweeping through the room. Old bones and scraps of tarnished armour clattered as they fell away into a distant chasm; spirits howled and hissed as they too were pulled clear.

The Queen gestured towards Aneira, radiating a surge of energy which hit the woman in the chest and flung her back upon the altar; her spine cracked and she cursed as she fell against the stone.

"Go back to the ruins of your once great city Minister, and weep for all that you have done."

Her embittered laughter came in response.

Elgan leapt back as a towering inferno erupted near his feet; he growled, thrust out his hands and sent a torrent of lightning in response. Cael shook his head and quickly drew a sigil in the air; the spell slammed into a spectral barrier and dispersed into the ground.

"You cannot win this." Mylah flicked her wrist and Aneira contorted, pushed up against the ivory structure. "Surrender now or suffer defeat at my hands."

"Poor, stupid, gullible creature." Aneira grinned, blood seeping through her teeth. "There is no victory for you here, no glory or redemption. I have been inside your head; I have seen the darkest secrets that slither through that pitiful soul of yours." She twitched slightly. *"Help me, Mommy. Save me! Mommy, please!* But you didn't, did you? You're the reason they're dead. *Save me Mommy! Help me!"*

Mylah snarled and clenched her fists. Magic shot out across the decrepit hall, twisting and writhing as it coiled around Aneira and engulfed her in scorching flame. The queen bellowed, and the world shook; chunks of crystal fell to the ground, shattering and splintering, their tiny daggers skittering into skin and rock alike. Her wounds reopened and she screamed, falling to her knees; the spell persisted, drawing strength and vitality from her until her hands warped and her fingers curled, suddenly taut and gnarled. Her head threw backwards and an onslaught of indigo light gushed forth, twisting through the gilded hollow like a wild serpent.

Merfyd tried desperately to reach her, but it was as though spectral vines had wrapped around his legs and pinned him down; his own power was draining quickly, and darkness overcame him.

A fissure ripped open beside Bowen; he watched in horror as a Vatis clambered through the tear, its elongated limbs wrapping around Rhydian and Cael, snatching them back through before the corrupted portal disintegrated. Scole stared at the empty space where they had been, tears forming in her eyes.

The Seneschal roared, the ground splitting suddenly in front of Elgan as a column of ice arose; the spell, amplified by that of the Monarch, surged towards the shadowed canopy of Mynydd and mutated into frozen quartz before it collapsed, falling on top of the quivering mage and crushing him beneath a mass of crystalline wrath.

Aneira stood, her burnt arms broken and hanging at odd angles; her neck seemed to have snapped, but her mouth was still curled into a grin. She hissed at Bowen and he collapsed, clutching his head as pain ripped through it; blood gushed from his nostrils and ears, and he slumped forwards.

The Minister turned her attention to the High Priestess.

Scole stared at her and raised her trembling hands, hesitating for a moment before closing her eyes. "Oh Glorious Ones who look down upon us…" Her whispers were almost lost amongst the cacophony of untamed magic. "See now your faithful children who stumble in the ungracious dark, and take them into your loving embrace. Lady Amara, guide us into your arms and see our souls to your silvery shores."

"Wait!" Seren grabbed hold of Aneira, sweat beading her brow. "Leave her be, I beg you!"

"And why would I do such a thing?" The woman hissed and narrowed her eyes. "She is nothing to me but a pathetic reminder of an age now past!"

"I'll do whatever you want! Just… just don't hurt her."

Aneira laughed as she snapped her broken bones back into place. "Very well. You belong to me now, you foolish little girl, but I will spare your… pet."

The High Priestess dropped to the ground, cowering in fear.

Seren pulled away from the Minister and ran to her side. "Scole? Scole!" She wrapped her arms around her. "I'm sorry, I'm so sorry! Gods forgive me."

"It's just you and me now, Tarry."

Tarian threw back her shoulders and marched out through the mess of debris and dust, her eyes ablaze with anger. She kept them trained on the woman she had once known as a friend, and pushed aside the fear that threatened to overwhelm her.

Aneira watched her, her eyes wild.

"Do you mean to murder me now too?"

"*Murder?* Oh my dear, dear Tarry, I have not murdered anyone! Vengeance and justice are all that you see in this hallowed hall. They deserved everything that has been done to them."

She shook her head. "And Elgan? Did he deserve to die for your cause?"

Aneira smiled. "He was willing, he knew the risks. As did we all. But look at us, Tarry – look at how far we have come! The Monarch is on her knees, and she bleeds for *us*."

"You say this is justice, but for what? For who? Mysta was not her doing, was it?"

The woman's face darkened. "Sacrifices had to be made! Change could not come without it. We were stuck, all of us, in a cycle of unending torment! When all others were snagged in dreams of her, the Aldhada… they came to me with whispers of release. I did not share in the visions of my peers; I was given *so much more* than that. They guided me to tomes and tombs thought lost, hidden and abandoned; all were full of knowledge sweetened by truth. And see how the people flocked to us, see how they revile her and revere us! We are more than their kings and queens could ever hope to be, we are their greatest saviour, and with war and pestilence have set them free."

Tarian's stomach churned. "You? You were responsible for the blight?"

"Ah my darling friend, do not be so childish. The Sundering of Luxnoctis was the cause of that, but see how it was a gateway – just as all of this, too, will be one! Come now, it is time for us to leave.

Go and pull Seren from that ridiculous fool she thinks she's defending, and we will be on our way."

"I cannot let you do this. I don't know what has happened to you, but this isn't right, Aneira." Tarian drew Nelia's dagger from her side. "I'm sorry."

The Minister watched her for a moment and sighed. "I see. We thought... well, no matter. It is clear that you spent too much time in that vile creature's company, and your mind has become warped to the truth."

Tarian charged. She thrust the blade towards the woman's chest, channelling all the strength and fury she could muster.

Aneira unclenched her fist and the weapon shattered, shards hurtling out in all directions. The mage cracked the guard across the jaw and sent her flying backwards. "You'll stay down Tarry, if you know what's good for you."

A bitter wind blew through the darkness then, curling around Aneira's shoulders and teasing out strands of her hair. A warm breath passed across her neck and disappeared.

She looked around for her leather bag, which had stayed faithfully by the shabby altar; she stooped down and plunged her hand inside, after a moment bringing forth its last offering: an ornate dagger. Her hands ran lovingly over the hilt as she bit her lip.

High above Mynydd, the heavens darkened.

"Do you know what this is?" She glanced up at the Anghenfil and grinned. "The Valiskar blade that took the life of King Dullahan, or so I'm told." She turned it over in her hand. "You wouldn't think such a small thing could have that kind of power, would you? But it sank into his skin and ripped out his entrails until there was nothing left. She truly is a vicious beast, this new queen of yours. Look at how much death stalks her wake. The Aldhada have told me a great many things, and I see them all now."

It hissed violently. "Speak not that name in my presence!"

She walked over to the dais and raised her eyebrows. "Is that fear I finally see upon your repulsive face?"

"This is not how it is meant to happen!" It struggled violently against its chains. "This is not meant to be!"

"Death awakens
And we are as dust
Settling upon these old bones
And when colder winds blow
We drift over necrotic seas
Filled with starlit carrion
And broken crowns
Kings lost, and betrayed
Are now the ashes of our pyre
They sing for us
The dust beneath the moon

We are Death enkindled

Aldhada, glorious and free."

"Speak not so! You are not the harbinger of a new age! They are lying to you!"

She barked another laugh. "Why is that *always* something people cling to, as if it has some kind of sacred meaning? They have shown me so much that you and your tyrannical Monarch would have kept from me. It is over, Anghenfil."

"No! No, wait! You cannot do this, Little One!"

"Oh, but I can." She ascended the steps slowly, savouring the look of terror that had engulfed the strange beast. "The echo of a Monarch's life still taints this blade, does it not? Some tiny speck of his memory is etched into it, a droplet dried and never removed. And now your pathetic queen bleeds her magic, her lifeblood, all over this room."

The Anghenfil strained and fought to break free of its shackles, but it was all in vain.

"Hush now. It will all be over soon."

Mylah screamed.

Blood spurted out of her chest and neck, a torrent of blue and dark garnet red. Her eyes bulged and her body convulsed. The light winked out.

The air filled suddenly with piercing cries and shrieking cackles. Bolts of magic arced through the shadows and spiralled away into the abyss. Ancient shackles exploded, and a hiss of feral sorcery arose from the depths.

In their celestial cradle, the Gods panicked.

Aneira withdrew the dagger from the Anghenfil's throat, power surging through her. She plunged the weapon once more into its torso and dragged it through the spiny flesh, scales flicking off into the darkness, and then discarded it onto the floor.

The beast roared and gurgled, a gush of violet and indigo gore pouring out across the stone. Its eyes burst and its face erupted, showering the Minister in chunks of dewy meat.

She thrust her hand into its collapsing chest and withdrew its enlarged sapphire heart, holding it high as her laughter rippled across the expanse. Blood dripped freely down her arm, and she drank of it, tasting the sweetened liquor without remorse.

Ancient spectres howled as they raced across the cavernous ceiling.

"See now the Heart of the Constellation! Sarheim will no longer be shackled beneath the heels of false gods and their tyrannical prophets! Rogue, to me!"

Scole looked up at Seren with reddened eyes. "Don't go! *Please* don't go with her. Stay here with me."

"I can't. I'm sorry."

"No... Seren, I-I need you. *Please* don't listen to her. Let her kill me if you must, just don't leave me here without you."

"I love you." She kissed the priestess quickly upon her brow and got to her feet, moving swiftly across the room without so much as a backward glance.

Aneira's eyes brightened. "Alweadan Aldhada ecnes. Cnylle belltaoen. Eorthen mettigness beginan."

A portal ripped open in front of them, larger and darker than any they had seen before.

Aneira glanced around at the ruins of the dead chamber, and smiled. "I will set them free. I will set them all free." She stepped into the magic, pulling Seren in behind her, and was gone.

Mylah staggered to her feet, her body a ragged mess; as she shook her head to disperse the wailing cries that had invaded her thoughts, she narrowed her eyes. The portal rippled before her, a taunting, heaving mass; with one hand clasped over the gaping hole in her chest and a snarl upon her lips, she charged.

The inky gateway glimmered and pulsated, but it would not let the Monarch pass through. She stumbled backwards and screamed, beating against it with her fists; wisps of magic surged out of her fingertips only to shatter against it like a blackened mirror. She dropped to her knees and roared.

*

"Brig's bloody balls. What the fuck happened here?" Rafael jumped down into the ruined pit. "It looks like the end of the world."

Bowen eyed him wearily, his face drawn. He beckoned him over and shivered.

"Are you going to tell me or should I just guess? We're fucked, right?"

"I don't know."

"Is the boss all right?"

They looked over to Mylah, who knelt upon the stone slab, sobbing.

Bowen shook his head. "No."

"And where does that bloody thing lead to? Smells like the back end of a corpse." The physician nodded at the swirling black portal. "Shouldn't someone collapse it?"

Tarian sat amidst the dust, her face bruised and awash with tears. Merfyd stood nearby, his head bowed in silent thought; fear crept amongst them like a prowling wolf, and only the High Priestess moved, pacing back and forth.

After a few minutes, the queen got to her feet. She turned slowly, her sorrowful sighs bringing Merfyd out of his trance. He inclined his head sadly and waited for her to approach.

"I failed." Her voice cracked. "She is gone from Cadere, free to spread her senseless poison across the worlds of Sarheim."

"Go after her." Tarian didn't look up at them. "Steel your heart, and find whatever hole she has taken refuge in. Stop her from hurting anyone else."

"I can't." Mylah put her head in her hands.

"Don't start with that shit now! We need you to break free of this melancholy and go after her!"

"Her Grace is tied to Cadere, and so cannot leave its borders. But you can."

"No!" The Monarch stared at him. "We cannot expect her to take that upon herself!"

"Aneira easily could have killed her many times since the fall of Mysta, and yet never did. She cares for her, even if she does not want to admit it. Tarian has the best chance out of all of us of hunting her down."

"What the *fuck* are you talking about? I'm not going through that… whatever it is. And I… I don't think I can kill her. Stop fucking around and just go!"

Mylah sat down next to her and gently took her hand. "I believe that the woman you once knew as your friend no longer exists; she is someone else... something else. I cannot say for certain that Merfyd is right in his theory that she still cares for you. I thought that with the Anghenfil dead I might be able to pursue her, but my binds to Cadere are too strong. Tarian, I said that there would be consequences if she carried out her plan. Do you feel the chill in the air?"

She was quiet for a moment, and then nodded. "What of it?"

"Do you know of Sarheim?"

Tarian shrugged. "My brothers would speak of it to others in the Conjury, but I had training to do. I didn't have time for myths and legends."

"It is the Constellation, of which Cadere is the heart. There are nine worlds, all connected by threads of magic. Each one has a Monarch and a Guardian to keep it balanced, and to ensure that its power remains harnessed and balanced. That portal will lead to one of them."

Her eyes widened. "What the *fuck?*"

"The cold breath that you can feel upon your skin, that numb tingling? That is the start of the shackles breaking for Cadere. Our magic is going to burgeon beyond the point that it can be controlled." She sighed and closed her eyes for a moment. "It will become too dangerous to use. And with the... the death of my anchor, I cannot stop this."

Merfyd crouched beside them. "You knew the woman that Aneira once was, and I believe that some shard of her yet remains that can be reasoned with. There is no natural magic within you, so she will not able to use that as a weapon. You are the only one here who stands any kind of chance at being able to track her down. The inhabitants of the other worlds may be sympathetic or they may prove hostile, but all will suffer if she is allowed to continue with this madness."

"What did she mean when she spoke of the Aldhada? Just how much trouble is she in?"

"I... I don't know. I've not heard that name before." Mylah locked eyes with her for a moment. "I don't know what kind of danger you would be walking into, but nothing good can come of her breaching the expanse like this. The worlds were closed off from one another millennia ago to prevent war. If she intends to do to them what she has done to us, only catastrophe and ruin can follow."

Tarian said nothing for a while, listening instead to the melancholic cries of the High Priestess. "I will find her, and I will stop this."

Tears rolled down Mylah's face. "I'm so sorry, Tarian."

"None of us can avoid fate."

Merfyd helped her stand and nodded at the pendant she wore around her neck. "I tried to tell you once that this stone was special. It will help to keep you safe whilst you traverse the Constellation.

The worlds should be inhabitable, but that does not mean they are harmless."

She touched it and fought against a swell of grief. "Then I guess I should thank Bryn once last time. And try to make sure I don't lose it somewhere, I suppose."

He held out his hand and a sharp light filtered out, pushing the crystal into her skin; the chain dropped to the floor.

She cried out in momentary pain.

"My apologies. But at least now you cannot leave it anywhere and forget it. Just remember that Seren and Aneira do not have such protection. They may need to rely on other methods, and that could prove to be hazardous." He tried to smile, and failed. "Go with the Gods, Tarian of Mysta."

Mylah walked with her to the portal. It shone and swirled, hissing and crackling with feral magic.

Tarian rubbed her clavicle and frowned. "You could have warned me he was going to do that."

"I didn't know."

"Well, I suppose there isn't much point in dragging this out. I kind of wish we had never met."

Mylah cupped her face and sighed. "I…"

"You're sorry, yes I know. Make sure that you find Cael, and Rhydian. Don't let them suffer. And don't do anything stupid." She nodded briskly and, without waiting for a reply, strode into the portal. It hissed and snarled, emitting a smell of rotten flesh.

The Monarch watched it sadly for a few moments before turning away.

Bowen walked over to pick up the Valiskar dagger, and then headed to Mylah's side; they approached the altar together. The queen placed her hands upon the greataxe, and tears fell freely down her face as her heart broke a little more. After a moment she looked up at him, and he shook his head in disbelief.

"I will ensure that he is apprehended, Your Grace. What would you have us do now?"

She sighed quietly. "It seems that in her folly, that woman means to kill us all. Come, Seneschal. We must prepare for war."

Epilogue

The temple gardens filled with a woman's bloodcurdling screams. The stench of burning flesh filled the air as the fire that shot from her palm blistered and burned her skin; a sulphurous breeze slithered through the darkness, coiling around the onlookers and slowly tightening its grip.

"Make it stop! Gods, *make it stop!*"

"Cut the spell, Ashdown! Cut the fucking spell!"

Mylah skidded into the courtyard and stared; with a quick flick of her wrist, the magic streaming from Aveline died and she collapsed to her knees. Her hand had all but melted; waxy mass oozed towards the ground as blackened bones pointed up towards the silent heavens.

The Queen muttered a quiet incantation and Aveline slipped into unconsciousness. Bowen knelt by her side, covering his mouth with a cloth as he glanced up at the Monarch in despair.

"I said there would be consequences." She turned away. "The bonds that kept magic controlled have finally broken. Don't let anyone else cast without the aid of a staff, and only then if it is absolutely necessary. Take her to the physicians, and see if they can do anything for her. Notify her family if not."

"Yes, Your Grace."

Mylah sighed heavily and tried to push away the grim images that danced in front of her eyes; she shivered and pulled her teal cloak tighter around her shoulders.

The Monarch lost herself in thought for a while, letting the whispers slide away, and then turned to head back inside the temple. There would be need of her before dawn broke over the horizon.

As the scent of death started to creep in over the walls, night began to fall once more.

The Gilded Lord

Character List

Eternal Monarchs:

Mylah

Erebus / Dullahan: deceased

Luctus: deceased

Sidra: deceased

Adain, Eira, and Terrwyn: deceased

Mages:

Bowen

Merfyd

Cael

Delia

Aveline

Aneira

Elgan

Saeth

Alban

Guards, Warriors, and Knights:

Tarian

Berne

Rhydian

Tusk

Mama: deceased

Rogues and Scouts

Nelia

Seren

Eris of the Winterborn, Chosen One of the Gods and former lover of Mylah: deceased

Sawbones

Rafael

Priesthood and Acolytes:

High Priestess Scole of the Temple of Elfriede

High Priest Henrik of the Temple of Katarina

Meredith

Mercer

Civilians

Katherine, known as Kitten, daughter of Eris and Mylah: deceased

Elves

Wynne

Catrin

Emyr

Eira

Dyl

Divine Pantheon

Brig

Katarina

Merfyd

Elfriede

Amara

Glossary

Cadere: the world

Sepelite: a continent

Ynys Ysbryd: an island south of Sepelite

Caeli: a continent to the east

Luxnoctis: a continent to the west

Amissa: a large island far to the west of Luxnoctis

Sarheim / The Constellation: nine worlds interlinked by threads of magic

The Conjury: a council of mages governing Mysta, now disbanded

Oculi: small carnivorous monsters

Venandi: predatory beasts

Saprus: a bloodthirsty creature

Jittern: a very small winged feline

Vorax: a monster

Vatis: an intelligent monster

Morsus: an intellectual creature

Meirwon: gifted beings of magic

Occasus and Solis crystals: gemstones that create portals

Locus crystals: gemstones that amplify magic

Tegau: an elven term of endearment

Gelyn / gelynion: an elven term for human / humans

Aelfylc: an archaic name for the Gods

Printed in Great Britain
by Amazon